JUDE THE OBSCURE

THE NEW WESSEX EDITION

General Editor P. N. Furbank

THE NEW WESSEX EDITION

Jude the Obscure

THOMAS HARDY

INTRODUCTION BY
Terry Eagleton

WITH NOTES BY
P. N. Furbank

'The letter killeth'

ISBN: 333 33495 7

First edition published 1896
New Wessex Edition first published 1974 by
MACMILLAN LONDON LTD
4 Little Essex Street London WC2R 3LF
and Basingstoke
Associated companies in Auckland, Dallas, Delhi, Dublin,
Hong Kong, Johannesburg, Lagos, Manzini, Melbourne,
Nairobi, New York, Singapore, Tokyo, Washington and Zaria
Seventh impression 1981
Reprinted 1982, 1984

CO-ORDINATING EDITORS
Caroline Hobhouse
Edward Leeson

First published in the United States 1977 by
ST MARTIN'S PRESS INC.
175 Fifth Avenue, New York, N.Y. 10010

Library of Congress catalog card no.: 77 70258

ISBN: 0–312–44661–6

Filmset in Photon Times 10 on 11 pt and
printed in Great Britain by
RICHARD CLAY (THE CHAUCER PRESS) LTD
Bungay, Suffolk

Contents

Acknowledgements

THE General Editor thanks the following for their kind assistance in answering queries: the Librarian of the English Folk Dance and Song Society; Mr John S. Creasey of the Museum of English Rural Life; and the Editor of *Notes and Queries*. He would also like to express a general indebtedness to R. L. Purdy's *Thomas Hardy: a bibliographical study* (Oxford University Press, 1954; reissued 1968); F. B. Pinion's *A Hardy Companion* (Macmillan, 1968); and Denys Kay-Robinson's *Hardy's Wessex Re-appraised* (David & Charles, 1972).

P. N. FURBANK

Biography

1840   Hardy born at Higher Bockhampton, near Dorchester. His father and grandfather were master-stonemasons, also keen performers in the band or 'quire' of the local parish church.

1848   Attended school established by his local patroness Julia Augusta Martin. About this time his mother gave him Dryden's *Virgil*, *Rasselas* and *Paul and Virginia*.

1849   Transferred to school in Dorchester. Played fiddle at local weddings and dances.

1856–61   Articled to Dorchester architect John Hicks. Studied Latin and Greek from five to eight in the morning. Began writing verse. Was introduced to modern thought by his friend Horace Moule, son of the Vicar of Fordington.

1862–7   In London, working for the architect Arthur Blomfield. Read widely; studied paintings in National Gallery; became an agnostic.

1867–70   Returned to Dorset for health reasons and was employed by Hicks, and his successor Crickmay, on church restoration.

1868   Completed draft of first novel, 'The Poor Man and the Lady' (later destroyed).

1870   Sent by Crickmay to St Juliot in Cornwall and met future wife Emma Lavinia Gifford. Writing *Desperate Remedies*, his first published novel.

1873   Invited by Leslie Stephen to contribute serial (*Far from the Madding Crowd*) to *Cornhill*.

1874   Married and took rooms in Surbiton.

1876–8   Living at Sturminster Newton; writing *The Return of the Native*.

1878–81   Living in London. Was becoming well known in literary circles. Had serious illness while writing *A Laodicean*.

1881   Took house at Wimborne Minster.

1883   Went to live in Dorchester.

1885   Moved into the house, Max Gate, in Dorchester, which he had built for himself. He and his wife continued to make long annual visits to London.

1888–91   Writing many short stories. Publication of *Tess of the d'Urbervilles* in 1891 created furore.

1892   His father died.

1892–4   Worsening relations with his wife, the trouble being exacerbated by the writing of *Jude the Obscure*. In 1893 they visited Dublin and met Mrs Henniker, with whom he collaborated on a short story and perhaps fell in love.

1895–6   Publication of *Jude* causes scandal. He resolved to give up novel-writing.

1897–8   Writing and revising poems for his first collection, *Wessex Poems.*

1902   Began *The Dynasts.*

1904   His mother died.

1910   Received the Order of Merit.

1912   Making final revision of the Wessex novels. His wife died in November.

1913   In March made penitential pilgrimage to St Juliot and later to his wife's
         birthplace, Plymouth. Wrote flood of poems 'in expiation'.

1914   Married Florence Dugdale. At outbreak of war joined group of writers
         pledged to write for the Allied Cause.

1914–28 Wrote and revised the material for several more collections of verse.

1928   Died. His ashes were buried in Westminster Abbey and his heart in his
         first wife's grave in Stinsford churchyard.

Hardy's Major Works
with year of book publication

1871 Desperate Remedies
1872 Under the Greenwood Tree
1873 A Pair of Blue Eyes
1874 Far from the Madding Crowd
1876 The Hand of Ethelberta
1878 The Return of the Native
1880 The Trumpet-Major
1881 A Laodicean
1882 Two on a Tower
1886 The Mayor of Casterbridge
1887 The Woodlanders
1888 Wessex Tales
1891 A Group of Noble Dames
1891 Tess of the d'Urbervilles
1894 Life's Little Ironies
1896 [1895] Jude the Obscure
1897 The Well-Beloved

1898 Wessex Poems
1902 Poems of the Past and the
     Present
1903 The Dynasts, pt 1
1905 The Dynasts, pt 2
1908 The Dynasts, pt 3
1909 Time's Laughingstocks
1913 A Changed Man and Other
     Tales
1914 Satires of Circumstance
1917 Moments of Vision
1922 Late Lyrics and Earlier
1923 The Famous Tragedy of the
     Queen of Cornwall
1925 Human Shows
1928 Winter Words
1952 Our Exploits at West Poley

Introduction

Jude the Obscure, Hardy's last novel, was first printed as a serial story in *Harper's New Monthly Magazine* from December 1894 to November 1895, and in November 1895 was published as a complete novel. In reply to a warning by Harper's that the novel should 'be in every respect suitable for a family magazine', Hardy had doggedly written 'that it would be a tale that could not offend the most fastidious maiden'; but Harper's ideal maiden was clearly more fastidious than Hardy's, and the serial version, like *Tess of the d'Urbervilles* before it, had to be heavily bowdlerised. When the novel was finally published as an unexpurgated whole, the critical comment it attracted was mean, bigoted and offensive. A bitter attack in the *New York World* led Hardy to urge Harper's to withdraw the book from circulation; Mrs Oliphant spearheaded the English onslaught with a review in *Blackwood's* entitled 'The Anti-Marriage League'; and the Bishop of Wakefield, disgusted with the novel's 'insolence and indecency', threw it into the fire. 'It is simply one of the most objectionable books that we have ever read in any language whatsoever,' commented the *New York Bookman*; and a reviewer in the *World*, betraying the characteristic Victorian middle-class opinion that gloom is somehow socially subversive, remarked that 'None but a writer of exceptional talent indeed could have produced so gruesome and gloomy a book.'

The effect of all this on Hardy was, in his own words, to cure him completely of further interest in novel-writing. But whether a major novelist really stops writing simply as a reaction to public opinion is surely doubtful. Hardy was certainly shaken by the mixture of panic, philistinism and hypocrisy his novel evoked, and saw exactly how that response ironically validated the book's case; but there were other reasons for his turning away from fiction. With *Tess of the d'Urbervilles* and *Jude the Obscure*, Hardy had brought his long exploration of the human condition of his society to a point of mature complexity; and, although it would be presumptuous to

argue that, after that point, there was nowhere else for him to go,
these two novels have a sense of imaginative resolution about them
which makes their status as last novels logical rather than fortuitous
— something more, anyway, than a submissive bowing to bad
reviews. If 'resolution' in a different sense wasn't possible —
resolution in the sense of providing formulated answers to the
conflicts with which these novels deal — this was a mark of Hardy's
realism about the limits of art rather than a symptom of despair.

Until quite recently, the story of Jude might have been sum-
marised in a conventional critical account as the tragedy of a
peasant boy who uproots himself from a settled and timeless rural
community in the pursuit of learning, fails to achieve that worthy
ideal through excessive sexual appetite, and in failing reveals the
inexorable destiny of man himself, doomed to perpetual unfulfilment
on a blighted planet. No part of that statement is in fact true, and to
ask why not provides a starting-point for a more accurate reading of
the novel. Jude is neither a peasant nor particularly over-sexed;
Marygreen, his childhood home, has nothing settled or timeless
about it; the Christminster culture which attracts him is shoddy
rather than worthy; and his failure to attain it has no 'cosmic'
significance whatsoever. The novel goes out of its way to emphasise
all these facts, and only a reading biased by ideological preconcep-
tions about Hardy's fiction could fail to recognise them.

Jude is not a peasant: that class had long since been destroyed by
changes in the social structure of the English countryside. He is the
ward of a struggling shopkeeper who has herself declined from
socially superior status, becomes a baker's delivery boy and later a
stonemason. His place in Marygreen society, in other words, is
with the semi-independent 'tradesman' class which, as Hardy points
out in his essay 'The Dorsetshire Labourer' (in *Longman's
Magazine*, July 1883), was being decimated by economic depression, increased social mobility and growing industrialisation. As a
class, they offered a peculiarly intense focus for the disruptive social
forces at work in the countryside, and so are almost always in the
centreground of Hardy's fiction; it was the class into which he
himself was born, as the son of a stonemason. As part of this class,
Jude isn't 'uprooted' from Marygreen because there is nothing to be
uprooted from. The fact that he doesn't belong to Marygreen in the

first place, but was dumped there one dark night (as his own son is later unloaded in Aldbrickham), is significant: Jude's own lack of roots is symptomatic of the generally deracinated condition of the place. Marygreen is not timeless but stagnant, not settled but inert; it is a depressed and ugly enclave by-passed by history, stripped of its thatched and dormered dwelling-houses as the tradesmen, craftsmen and lifeholders move from the land. Like the five bottles of sweets and three buns behind the oxidised panes of Drusilla Fawley's shop-window, Marygreen is a stale remnant, a plundered landscape denuded of its historical traditions. What has ousted those traditions is utility:

> The fresh harrow-lines seemed to stretch like the channellings in a piece of new corduroy, lending a meanly utilitarian air to the expanse, taking away its gradations, and depriving it of all history beyond that of the few recent months, though to every clod and stone there really attached associations enough and to spare – echoes of songs from ancient harvest-days, of spoken words, and of sturdy deeds. [pp. 33–4]

The abstract imperatives of profit and utility have flattened and levelled all qualitative distinctions and concrete associations in Marygreen, superimposing their directions on the place as rigidly as the harrow lines do on the fields.

The boy Jude is himself a tool of those imperatives: as the harrow-lines dominate the arable land, so he is compelled for sixpence a day to impose his authority on the birds in the fields by scaring them away with his clacker. Sorry for the birds, Jude rebels against his slavish role and takes a redistribution of resources into his hands: '"Poor little dears!" said Jude, aloud. "You *shall* have some dinner – you shall. There is enough for us all. Farmer Troutham can afford to let you have some"' (p. 34). This view isn't shared by Farmer Troutham, Jude's employer, who assaults him with his own clacker. The punitive, profit-based relations of Marygreen are in clear contradiction with the claims of cultured sensitivity: it is Phillotson, the local representative of 'culture', who tells Jude to be kind to animals. Yet, as always in the novel, the relation between ideals and harsh actuality is a dialectical one: the ideal criticises the reality but is in turn exposed by it as limited or utopian.[1] Jude's

[1] Thus the novel's original title, 'The Simpletons', is both an irony at the expense of the society and a comment on the nature of Jude and Sue's idealism.

tender gesture prefigures his later courageous affirmations of human
solidarity (in the adoption of Father Time, for example), but it is
also, of course, amusingly sentimental. When it comes to food, men
take priority over birds. Later in the novel Jude is sickened by
Arabella's pig-sticking, but her angry comment, 'Poor folks must
live', has a point, and Jude must learn it.

There is another important sense in which the relation between
ideal and reality in the novel is dialectical. The more starved and
barren actual life is, the more the ideals it generates will be twisted
into bodiless illusions; Jude's 'dreams were as gigantic as his surroundings were small' (p. 41). The most obvious instance of this is
Christminster. Christminster's phantasmal allure, glimpsed by Jude
from the top of his ladder, becomes after his arrival in the city the
sinister phantasm of feeling himself spectrally disembodied, stared
through by passers-by when he is working (again, with neat irony,
on a ladder). If Marygreen is stripped of history, Christminster is
buried under it, a repressive rubble of crumbling masonry and dead
creeds. The two spots are ominously connected early in the novel,
when the man who points out Christminster to Jude gestures in the
direction of the field where the boy was beaten by Troutham. Just as
Marygreen is swathed in deception and superstition — Vilbert's
quack medicine, Arabella's artificial hair, manufactured dimples,
false pregnancy and sexual trickery, the sham Gothic edifice which
has usurped the traditional church — so Christminster is a maze of
false consciousness and sham ceremony which imprisons Jude as
effectively as Arabella's wiles. His future turns out, precisely, to be
a past; in moving hopefully forward he is rapidly regressing.

The historical irony in which Jude is trapped is that personal
fulfilment can be achieved only by painfully appropriating the very
culture which denies and rejects him as a man. It is a contradiction
in his relation with Christminster which is focused most sharply in
the issue of work — a central interest of Hardy's, in this and other
novels. As a stonemason trained in the countryside, and so
relatively unscathed by an urban division of labour, Jude's work
expresses a productive creativity which contrasts strongly with the
sterility of the University. He works in direct, responsive relation to
the material world; and as such his craft is an image of that attempt
to subdue the 'insensate and stolid obstructiveness' of things to

significant human purpose which is of wider importance in the novel. Craftsmanship, like authentic sexual relationship, mediates between the ideal and the actual. It is in the labour of the Christminster working class that Hardy discovers an alternative to the decayed world of the dons: 'For a moment there fell on Jude a true illumination; that here in the stone yard was a centre of effort as worthy as that dignified by the name of scholarly study within the noblest of the colleges. . . . He began to see that the town life was a book of humanity infinitely more palpitating, varied, and compendious than the gown life. These struggling men and women before him were the reality of Christminster, though they knew little of Christ or Minster' (pp. 104, 137). In examining the mouldings of the colleges, Jude discovers true historical continuity — not with the élitist University culture, but with 'the dead handicraftsmen whose muscles had actually executed those forms', men with whom he feels comradeship. On the basis of this sense of historical continuity, the identity he is seeking could be genuinely established.

Yet the irony, once again, is that Jude's labour-power is exploited literally to prop up the structures which exclude him. His work is restorative of the old world rather than productive of the new, devalued to 'copying, patching and imitating'. The dead, phantasmal past of Christminster sucks nutriment from the labour of the living, reducing them too to husks and corpses, spectres of their former selves. The true relations between labour and culture, conceived as simple opposites by the deluded Jude of Marygreen, are starkly disclosed in the divided world of Christminster: the cultural ideal is parasitic on working energies it ignores and represses, on labourers without whom 'the hard readers could not read nor the high thinkers live'.

Sue Bridehead has seen through the cultural idea, and emancipated herself from the stagnant medievalism of Christminster; but her emancipation is partial and in some ways false. She sees the University as a place 'full of fetichists and ghost-seers', but by the end of the novel she herself is both. If Jude can finally extricate himself from false consciousness through the painful process of experiencing the harsh conditions in which such illusions are needed in the first place, Sue's reaction against orthodoxy is idealist: the substitution of one spiritual ideology for another. She is still under the influence of idols: it is merely that statues of Greek deities replace statues of Christian saints on her mantelpiece. If Jude regresses in trying to move forward, so does she: she is 'more ancient than medievalism'. Jude lives a contradictory relationship with Christminster, strengthening the very walls which exclude him, and finally breaks with ecclesiastical art-work. Sue, the pagan designer of pious texts, lives out a similar conflict, and breaks free to become a teacher; but the deeper contradiction she incarnates is left relatively untouched by this act. Sue is Hardy's most masterly exploration of the limits of liberation in Victorian society — more masterly by far than Angel Clare, who is an earlier experiment in the same mode. As both a chronically timid prisoner of convention and an impetuous rebel, Sue dramatises all the conflicts and evasions of what can best be termed a transitional form of consciousness, deadlocked between the old and the new. The psychological pattern to which that deadlock gives rise is one of masochism and self-torture — a continual process of acting impulsively and then punitively repressing herself for it.

This is most clear in her deep fear of sexuality. *Jude the Obscure* is a novel about passion — passion for human and sexual fulfilment, and its agonised frustration at the hands of a society which must everywhere deny it. Passion is a potentially liberating force in the novel, as Jude shows well enough. With 'a simple-minded man's ruling passion', Jude pursues his demand for recognition, refuses to back down from the question of his own identity, and is finally defeated and betrayed. But Jude is a genuinely tragic protagonist because the value released in that defeat, the insistence on a recognition of his total humanity, challenges, consciously or not, a society polarised between abstraction and appetite, labour and intellect. The problem is how to prevent that passion from being tamed and shackled by oppressive convention, and it is this which motivates Sue's rejection of marriage. But her rejection of marriage springs from the same source as her rejection of physical sexuality; in denying the false social embodiments of love, she denies the body itself. Her freedom, as a result, is in part negative and destructive — a self-possessive individualism which sees all permanent commitment as imprisoning, a fear of being possessed which involves a fear of giving. Her scorn for those whose 'philosophy only recognises relations based on animal desire' is genuinely progressive in its insistence on fully human relationship and conventionally Victorian in its belittling of physicality. Jude, fresh from the misery of a marriage with Arabella based 'on a temporary feeling which had no necessary connection with affinities that alone render a life-long comradeship tolerable' (p. 90), shares Sue's opinion; but, as that 'life-long' suggests, he is more inclined to welcome permanent and definitive commitments than she is, and less inclined to see sex as merely incidental to them.

There are other ways in which Jude and Sue differ. It isn't unimportant, for instance, that Sue's individualism springs in part from her reading of J. S. Mill, whose bourgeois notion of the autonomously developing self conflicts with Jude's own more communal and collectivist ethic. His membership of an Artizan's Mutual Improvement Society at Aldbrickham signifies his concern for the advancement of his class as a whole; and that concern for solidarity underlies his decision to adopt Father Time:

'What does it matter, when you come to think of it, whether a child is yours by blood or not? All the little ones of our time are collectively the children of us adults of the time, and entitled to our general care. That excessive regard of parents for their own children, and their dislike of other people's, is, like class-feeling, patriotism, save-your-own-soul-ism, and other virtues, a mean exclusiveness at bottom.' [p. 293]

Sue agrees that 'if [Father Time] isn't yours it makes it all the better', but for rather less altruistic reasons: she is reluctant to have his child by a previous marriage in the house. It is a difference between them which emerges again at the end of the book: Jude behaves 'honourably' towards Arabella because he is not 'a man who wants to save himself at the expense of the weaker among us' (pp. 401–2), whereas Sue, in her guilty return to Phillotson, is in the end such a woman. Even Jude can see this – can see that Sue has degenerated to a save-your-souler. 'I stuck to her, and she ought to have stuck to me. I'd have sold my soul for her sake, but she wouldn't risk hers a jot for me' (p. 394).

But this is to be too hard on Sue and not hard enough on Jude. Sue does, after all, give herself fully to Jude for a brief period of

happiness, and the events which drive her back to Phillotson are
horrific enough to make her betrayal understandable, if not excus-
able. And, if Sue is elusively unpossessable, Jude for his part is too
ready to be appropriated, too uncritically willing to be the adopted
son of the deathly lineage of Christminster. If Sue is finally enslaved
by ghosts and fantasies, Jude has been so all along. It is a choice
between that genuine disentanglement from delusion at which Jude
must laboriously arrive, by which time his energies are spent, and
the more rapid emancipation of Sue which, because it is ungrounded
from the outset in much more than a mental conversion, is unable to
withstand the buffetings of reality.

What is remarkable, in fact, is how Hardy retains some of our
sympathy for Sue against all the odds. For there isn't, when one
comes down to it, much to be said in her defence. Having speeded
on the death of her first lover, Sue captivates Jude to enjoy the thrill
of being loved, and then enters with dubious motives and curiously
mechanical detachment into marriage with Phillotson, treating Jude
with astounding callousness in the process. Having refused to sleep
with Phillotson she abandons him for Jude, temporarily wrecking
the schoolmaster's career, and refuses to sleep with Jude too. She
then agrees to marry him out of jealousy of Arabella, changes her
mind, and finally returns again to Phillotson, leaving Jude to die. It's
clear that such an external account of Sue's behaviour is inadequate
as a basis for total judgement, but it's also important not to slide too
quickly over the incriminating facts. The problem is how we come
to feel that Sue *is* more than just a perverse hussy, full of petty
stratagems and provocative pouts; for that this is at one level an
accurate description of her seems undeniable. One reason why we
feel that she is more than this is, of course, because she is so deeply
loved by Jude; but Jude's love of Sue, like his love of Christminster,
is an authentic desire refracted through a flawed medium, and he
himself comes at times as near as possible to seeing her in a much
less attractive light. The answer to the enigma of Sue seems to lie,
not in balancing her undoubtedly 'good' qualities against her more
unpleasant characteristics, but in reconsidering the question of the
'level' at which Sue is finally to be evaluated. After Jude has com-
plained that Sue wouldn't risk her soul for him, he adds that it
wasn't her fault; and it is important to see here that Jude is both

wrong (he is sentimentally idealising her, as he did before he had even met her), and in a different sense right. It isn't Sue's fault, not because she is morally innocent, but because Hardy, through his presentation of Sue, is evoking movements and forces which can't be exhaustively described or evaluated at a simply personal level. Sue, like Jude himself, is a 'representative' character, in the great tradition of nineteenth-century realism which Hardy inherited; and her elusive complexity stems in part from the fact that she points beyond herself, to a confused, ambiguous structure of feeling which belongs to the period in general. Her opaqueness and inconsistency as a character are thus neither merely personal attributes nor evidence of some failure of full realisation on Hardy's part; it is precisely in her opaqueness and inconsistency that she is at once most fully realised and most completely representative. If she were a 'fully rounded' character, as wholly knowable as, say, Eustacia Vye in *The Return of the Native*, it would be easier to treat her as an autonomous moral agent, meriting directly personal praise or blame; but she would be also to that extent narrowed, simplified, unrepresentative.

Hardy described the novel in his preface as dramatising 'a deadly war waged between flesh and spirit', and it seems worth trying to unpack some of the meanings of that phrase. It is tempting to think of it first of all in terms of a conflict between Arabella and Sue — or rather of those aspects of Jude which each woman is supposed to externalise. But to reduce the novel to an interior battle between appetite and ideal is surely to over-simplify. It isn't just that Sue can only in a very qualified sense be taken as some 'ideal'; it's also that Arabella is an equally unobvious candidate to fulfil the role of 'appetite'. The soft smack of the pig's pizzle which Arabella throws at Jude signifies, evidently enough, a materialist deflation of his priggish dreams of grandeur; but Arabella herself is far from symbolising the lure of some earthy sensuality which impedes Jude's striving for spiritual development. This is true at the level of plot — it isn't Arabella who prevents Jude from entering the University — and true also of the way she is characterised. What we remember about Arabella isn't her sensuality but her calculating acquisitiveness, her sharp, devious opportunism. She uses her sensual appeal twice to captivate Jude, but what she captivates him for is, in the end, economic security. Arabella is one of a financially insecure class who need to look sharp in a predatory society: 'Poor folks must live' is her watchword from beginning to end. The claim on Jude which she represents is less that of some symbolic abstraction like 'sensuality' or 'appetite' than the need for material provision in conditions of scarcity; she wants to utilise his labour to buy herself frocks and hats, as Christminster uses it to sustain its elaborate façades.

Whereas Jude and Sue struggle bravely against empty convention, Arabella recognises the artifice of those conventions but manipulates them pragmatically for her own advantage. 'Life with a man is more business-like after [marriage]', she tells Sue, 'and money matters work better' (p. 288). Fly and practical as she is in contrast with Sue, her investment in conventions which she basically scorns offers a parallel to Sue's position, and indeed the two women are alike in more than this. Both are individualists, and both exploit Jude: Arabella crudely and materially, Sue subtly and spiritually. (It is interesting that Jude's entry into relationship with Arabella is characterised less by the prodding of 'appetite' than by a sense of dreaming and drifting which resembles his first feelings about Sue.) Arabella, indeed, recognises the similarities between herself and Sue ('Bolted from your first, didn't you, like me?', p. 289), a parallel which Sue snobbishly refuses. In terms of the comparison, Arabella comes off in some ways rather better: there's a crude but candid authenticity about her desire for Jude ('I must have him. I can't do without him. He's the sort of man I long for', p. 69) which contrasts tellingly with the evasions of a woman who, as Jude complains, can never say directly whether she loves him or not. Arabella is able to throw over her false religious conversion and fatalistically acknowledge the thrust of her real feelings for Jude ('Feelings are feelings!'); Sue moves in precisely the opposite direction, disowning her true feelings for Jude for a fatalistic adherence to religious orthodoxy.

Sue's action in abandoning Jude for Phillotson is, in a precise, Sartrean sense of the term, one of bad faith. The attempt to live authentically in a false society collapses into guilty self-punishment, a flight from freedom into the consoling embrace of an impersonal system of authority which will relieve one of the burden of selfhood, and so of responsibility. Sue, the celebrator of a pagan joy in life, becomes the woman who is glad her children are dead, eager to flay her flesh and bring her body into corpse-like submission to a man she physically detests. There is no need for this society to crush those who make the break for freedom; the roots of its deathly ideology sink sufficiently deep in the mind for the self to act as its own censor, anxiously desiring its own extinction.

Jude fights hard against Sue's death-dealing fantasy. 'It is only [a fight] against man and senseless circumstance,' he argues, in response to her demands for conformity to 'the ancient wrath of the Power above us' (p. 362). His argument merely rehearses Sue's own earlier opinion that the roots of the tragedy are social — that 'the social moulds civilization fits us into have no more relation to our actual shapes than the conventional shapes of the constellations have to the real star-patterns' (p. 226). The deadly war between flesh and spirit is fundamentally a war between the spirit of man and the obstructive flesh of a recalcitrant society. Sue's attempt to absolutise a particular tragedy as an act of Providence is the most dangerous form of false consciousness, relieving of responsibility the true killer of her children — the society which turned the family from its lodging-houses. It is a mark of Jude's resilience and rationality that he refuses to make this error: absolute as the tragedy is for him, he sees it nonetheless as historically relative. 'When people of a later age look back upon the barbarous customs and superstitions of the times that we have the unhappiness to live in, what *will* they say!' (p. 236). He reflects that 'It takes two or three generations to do what I tried to do in one' (p. 345), and is interested to hear of schemes already afoot to help poor scholars into Christminster.

Two elements in the novel might seem to argue for Sue's fatalism. One is the emphasis on a hereditary curse in the Fawley family; the other is the role of Jude's son, Father Time. The factor of heredity certainly crops up from time to time, but in the end little is made of it, and it isn't an element in the final tragic catastrophe. It remains as an awkwardly unintegrated dimension of the novel, generating 'atmosphere' but not much else; and even if it is taken seriously it seems to amount to no more than Mrs Edlin's judgement that there is a temperamental instability in the family which unfits them for coping with difficulties ('But things happened to thwart 'em, and if everything wasn't vitty they were upset', p. 301). Then there is Father Time, who for so many critics has stood for an authentic authorial consciousness, gloomy, pessimistic and omniscient. But it isn't only that Father Time, for all the ponderous symbolism which surrounds him, has essentially the limited understanding of a child, killing himself and the other children on the basis of what is really a mistake — a breakdown of communication between himself and an adult. It's also that Father Time's pessimism springs from the weary passivity of a character who is outside history, unable to intervene constructively in it, condemned (like the naturalistic novelists of the period) to see things in a rounded, distanced, deterministic way. This is not, in fact, Hardy's way: Father Time is rather like the God in Hardy's poems who, precisely because of his transcendental, unhistorical status, is doomed to impotence and disillusion. Father Time can assume his omniscient, spectatorial stance only because his living will has been effectively destroyed; and in this he differs from his father, whose will does not consent to be beaten, and who continues to struggle almost until the end. *Jude the Obscure*, like all of Hardy's novels, proclaims no inexorable determinism, though anyone aware of the paltry percentage of working-class undergraduates now at Oxford might be forgiven for thinking differently.

TERRY EAGLETON

A star in the text indicates that an explanatory note is to be found at the end of the book, while superior numbers refer to footnotes. References to the quotations on the title-page and part-titles will be found at the appropriate place in the Notes.

JUDE THE OBSCURE

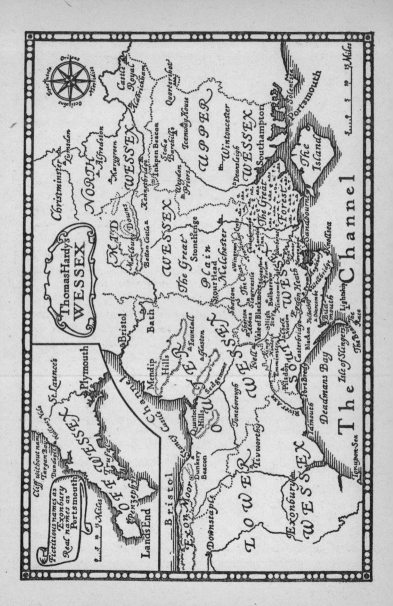

Preface to the First Edition

THE history of this novel (whose birth in its present shape has been much retarded by the necessities of periodical publication) is briefly as follows. The scheme was jotted down in 1890, from notes made in 1887 and onwards,* some of the circumstances being suggested by the death of a woman in the former year.* The scenes were revisited in October 1892; the narrative was written in outline in 1892 and the spring of 1893, and at full length, as it now appears, from August 1893 onwards into the next year; the whole, with the exception of a few chapters, being in the hands of the publisher by the end of 1894. It was begun as a serial story in *Harper's Magazine* at the end of November 1894, and was continued in monthly parts.

But, as in the case of *Tess of the d'Urbervilles*, the magazine version was for various reasons an abridged and modified one, the present edition being the first in which the whole appears as originally written. And in the difficulty of coming to an early decision in the matter of a title, the tale was issued under a provisional name, two such titles having, in fact, been successively adopted. The present and final title, deemed on the whole the best, was one of the earliest thought of.

For a novel addressed by a man to men and women of full age; which attempts to deal unaffectedly with the fret and fever, derision and disaster, that may press in the wake of the strongest passion known to humanity; to tell, without a mincing of words, of a deadly war waged between flesh and spirit; and to point the tragedy of unfulfilled aims, I am not aware that there is anything in the handling to which exception can be taken.

Like former productions of this pen, *Jude the Obscure* is simply an endeavour to give shape and coherence to a series of seemings, or personal impressions, the question of their consistency or their discordance, of their permanence or their transitoriness, being regarded as not of the first moment.

August 1895

Postscript

The issue of this book sixteen years ago, with the explanatory Preface given above, was followed by unexpected incidents, and one can now look back for a moment at what happened. Within a day or two of its publication the reviewers pronounced upon it in tones to which the reception of *Tess of the d'Urbervilles* bore no comparison, though there were two or three dissentients from the chorus. This salutation of the story in England was instantly cabled to America, and the music was reinforced on that side of the Atlantic in a shrill crescendo.

In my own eyes the sad feature of the attack was that the greater part of the story — that which presented the shattered ideals of the two chief characters, and had been more especially, and indeed almost exclusively, the part of interest to myself — was practically ignored by the adverse press of the two countries; the while that some twenty or thirty pages of sorry detail deemed necessary to complete the narrative, and show the antitheses in Jude's life, were almost the sole portions read and regarded. And curiously enough, a reprint the next year of a fantastic tale * that had been published in a family paper some time before, drew down upon my head a continuation of the same sort of invective from several quarters.

So much for the unhappy beginning of *Jude's* career as a book. After these verdicts from the press its next misfortune was to be burnt by a bishop * – probably in his despair at not being able to burn me – and his advertisement of his meritorious act in the papers.

Then somebody discovered that *Jude* was a moral work – austere in its treatment of a difficult subject — as if the writer had not all the time said in the Preface that it was meant to be so. Thereupon many uncursed me, and the matter ended, the only effect of it on human conduct that I could discover being its effect on myself – the experience completely curing me of further interest in novel-writing.

One incident among many arising from the storm of words was that an American man of letters, who did not whitewash his own morals, informed me that, having bought a copy of the book on the strength of the shocked criticisms, he read on and on, wondering when the harmfulness was going to begin, and at last flung it across the room with execrations at having been induced by the rascally reviewers to waste a dollar-and-half on what he was pleased to call 'a religious and ethical treatise.'

I sympathised with him, and assured him honestly that the mis-representations had been no collusive trick of mine to increase my circulation among the subscribers to the papers in question.

Then there was the case of the lady who having shuddered at the book * in an influential article bearing intermediate headlines of horror, and printed in a world-read journal, wrote to me shortly afterwards that it was her desire to make my acquaintance.

To return, however, to the book itself. The marriage laws being used in great part as the tragic machinery of the tale, and its general drift on the domestic side tending to show that, in Diderot's words, * the civil law should be only the enunciation of the law of nature (a statement that requires some qualification, by the way), I have been charged since 1895 with a large responsibility in this country for the present 'shop-soiled' condition of the marriage theme (as a learned writer characterized it the other day). I do not know. My opinion at that time, if I remember rightly, was what it is now, that a marriage should be dissolvable as soon as it becomes a cruelty to either of the parties — being then essentially and morally no mar-riage — and it seemed a good foundation for the fable of a tragedy, told for its own sake as a presentation of particulars containing a good deal that was universal, and not without a hope that certain cathartic, Aristotelian qualities might be found therein.

The difficulties down to twenty or thirty years back of acquiring knowledge in letters without pecuniary means were used in the same way; though I was informed that some readers thought these episodes an attack on venerable institutions, and that when Ruskin College was subsequently founded it should have been called the College of Jude the Obscure.

Artistic effort always pays heavily for finding its tragedies in the forced adaptation of human instincts to rusty and irksome moulds that do not fit them. To do Bludyer * and the conflagratory bishop justice, what they meant seems to have been only this: 'We Britons hate ideas, and we are going to live up to that privilege of our native country. Your picture may not show the untrue, or the uncommon, or even be contrary to the canons of art; but it is not the view of life that we who thrive on conventions can permit to be painted.'   .

But what did it matter. As for the matrimonial scenes, in spite of their 'touching the spot', and the screaming of a poor lady in *Blackwood** that there was an unholy anti-marriage league afoot, the famous contract – sacrament I mean – is doing fairly well still, and people marry and give in what may or may not be true marriage as light-heartedly as ever. The author has even been reproached by some earnest correspondents that he has left the question where he found it, and has not pointed the way to a much-needed reform.

After the issue of *Jude the Obscure* as a serial story in Germany, an experienced reviewer of that country informed the writer that Sue Bridehead, the heroine, was the first delineation in fiction of the woman who was coming into notice in her thousands every year – the woman of the feminist movement – the slight, pale 'bachelor' girl – the intellectualized, emancipated bundle of nerves that modern conditions were producing, mainly in cities as yet; who does not recognize the necessity for most of her sex to follow marriage as a profession, and boast themselves as superior people because they are licensed to be loved on the premises. The regret of this critic was that the portrait of the newcomer had been left to be drawn by a man, and was not done by one of her own sex, who would never have allowed her to break down at the end.

Whether this assurance is borne out by dates I cannot say. Nor am I able, across the gap of years since the production of the novel, to exercise more criticism upon it of a general kind than extends to a few verbal corrections, whatever, good or bad, it may contain. And no doubt there can be more in a book than the author consciously puts there, which will help either to its profit or to its disadvantage as the case may be.

April 1912   T.H.

PART FIRST

At Marygreen

'Yea, many there be that have run out of their wits for women, and become servants for their sakes. Many also have perished, have erred, and sinned, for women. . . . O ye men, how can it be but women should be strong, seeing they do thus?' — ESDRAS

THE schoolmaster was leaving the village, and everybody seemed sorry. The miller at Cresscombe lent him the small white tilted★ cart and horse to carry his goods to the city of his destination, about twenty miles off, such a vehicle proving of quite sufficient size for the departing teacher's effects. For the school-house had been partly furnished by the managers, and the only cumbersome article possessed by the master, in addition to the packing-case of books, was a cottage piano that he had bought at an auction during the year in which he thought of learning instrumental music. But the enthusiasm having waned he had never acquired any skill in playing, and the purchased article had been a perpetual trouble to him ever since in moving house.

The rector had gone away for the day, being a man who disliked the sight of changes. He did not mean to return till the evening, when the new school-teacher would have arrived and settled in, and everything would be smooth again.

The blacksmith, the farm bailiff, and the schoolmaster himself were standing in perplexed attitudes in the parlour before the instrument. The master had remarked that even if he got it into the cart he should not know what to do with it on his arrival at Christminster, the city he was bound for, since he was only going into temporary lodgings just at first.

A little boy of eleven, who had been thoughtfully assisting in the packing, joined the group of men, and as they rubbed their chins he spoke up, blushing at the sound of his own voice: 'Aunt have got a great fuel-house, and it could be put there, perhaps, till you've found a place to settle in, sir.'

'A proper good notion,' said the blacksmith.

It was decided that a deputation should wait on the boy's aunt — an old maiden resident — and ask her if she would house the piano till Mr Phillotson should send for it. The smith and the bailiff started to see the practicability of the suggested shelter, and the boy and the schoolmaster were left standing alone.

'Sorry I am going, Jude?' asked the latter kindly.

Tears rose into the boy's eyes, for he was not among the regular day scholars, who came unromantically close to the schoolmaster's life, but one who had attended the night school only during the present teacher's term of office. The regular scholars, if the truth must be told, stood at the present moment afar off, like certain historic disciples, indisposed to any enthusiastic volunteering of aid.

The boy awkwardly opened the book he held in his hand, which Mr Phillotson had bestowed on him as a parting gift, and admitted that he was sorry.

'So am I,' said Mr Phillotson.

'Why do you go, sir?' asked the boy.

'Ah – that would be a long story. You wouldn't understand my reasons, Jude. You will, perhaps, when you are older.'

'I think I should now, sir.'

'Well – don't speak of this everywhere. You know what a university is, and a university degree? It is the necessary hall-mark of a man who wants to do anything in teaching. My scheme, or dream, is to be a university graduate, and then to be ordained. By going to live at Christminster, or near it, I shall be at headquarters, so to speak, and if my scheme is practicable at all, I consider that being on the spot will afford me a better chance of carrying it out than I should have elsewhere.'

The smith and his companion returned. Old Miss Fawley's * fuel-house was dry, and eminently practicable; and she seemed willing to give the instrument standing-room there. It was accordingly left in the school till the evening, when more hands would be available for removing it; and the schoolmaster gave a final glance round.

The boy Jude assisted in loading some small articles, and at nine o'clock Mr Phillotson mounted beside his box of books and other *impedimenta*, and bade his friends good-bye.

'I shan't forget you, Jude,' he said, smiling, as the cart moved off. 'Be a good boy, remember; and be kind to animals and birds, and read all you can. And if ever you come to Christminster remember you hunt me out for old acquaintance' sake.'

The cart creaked across the green, and disappeared round the corner by the rectory-house. The boy returned to the draw-well at the edge of the greensward, where he had left his buckets when he went to help his patron and teacher in the loading. There was a quiver in his lip now, and after opening the well-cover to begin lowering the bucket he paused and leant with his forehead and arms against the frame-work, his face wearing the fixity of a thoughtful child's who has felt the pricks of life somewhat before his time. The well into which he was looking was as ancient as the village itself, and from his present position appeared as a long circular perspective ending in a shining disk of quivering water at a distance of a hundred feet down. There was a lining of green moss near the top, and nearer still the hart's-tongue fern.

He said to himself, in the melodramatic tones of a whimsical boy, that the schoolmaster had drawn at that well scores of times on a morning like this, and would never draw there any more. 'I've seen him look down into it, when he was tired with his drawing, just as I do now, and when he rested a bit before carrying the buckets home! But he was too clever to bide here any longer — a small sleepy place like this!'

A tear rolled from his eye into the depths of the well. The morning was a little foggy, and the boy's breathing unfurled itself as a thicker fog upon the still and heavy air. His thoughts were interrupted by a sudden outcry:

'Bring on that water, will ye, you idle young harlican!'*

It came from an old woman who had emerged from her door towards the garden gate of a green-thatched cottage not far off. The boy quickly waved a signal of assent, drew the water with what was a great effort for one of his stature, landed and emptied the big bucket into his own pair of smaller ones, and pausing a moment for breath, started with them across the patch of clammy greensward whereon the well stood — nearly in the centre of the little village, or rather hamlet of Marygreen.

It was as old-fashioned as it was small, and it rested in the lap of an undulating upland adjoining the North Wessex downs. Old as it was, however, the well-shaft was probably the only relic of the local history that remained absolutely unchanged. Many of the thatched and dormered dwelling-houses had been pulled down of late years, and many trees felled on the green. Above all, the original church, hump-backed, wood-turreted, and quaintly hipped, had been taken

down, and either cracked up into heaps of road-metal in the lane, or
utilized as pig-sty walls, garden seats, guard-stones to fences, and
rockeries in the flower-beds of the neighbourhood. In place of it a
tall new building of modern Gothic design, unfamiliar to English
eyes, had been erected on a new piece of ground by a certain
obliterator of historic records who had run down from London and
back in a day. The site whereon so long had stood the ancient
temple to the Christian divinities was not even recorded on the
green and level grass-plot that had immemorially been the churchyard, the obliterated graves being commemorated by eighteenpenny
cast-iron crosses warranted to last five years.

SLENDER as was Jude Fawley's frame he bore the two brimming house-buckets of water to the cottage without resting. Over the door was a little rectangular piece of blue board, on which was painted in yellow letters, 'Drusilla Fawley, Baker'. Within the little lead panes of the window – this being one of the few old houses left – were five bottles of sweets, and three buns on a plate of the willow pattern.*

While emptying the buckets at the back of the house he could hear an animated conversation in progress within-doors between his great-aunt, the Drusilla of the signboard, and some other villagers. Having seen the schoolmaster depart, they were summing up particulars of the event, and indulging in predictions of his future.

'And who's he?' asked one, comparatively a stranger, when the boy entered.

'Well ye med* ask it, Mrs Williams. He's my great-nephew – come since you was last this way.' The old inhabitant who answered was a tall, gaunt woman, who spoke tragically on the most trivial subject, and gave a phrase of her conversation to each auditor in turn. 'He come from Mellstock, down in South Wessex, about a year ago – worse luck for 'n, Belinda' (turning to the right) 'where his father was living, and was took wi' the shakings for death, and died in two days, as you know, Caroline' (turning to the left). 'It would ha' been a blessing if Goddy-mighty had took thee too, wi' thy mother and father, poor useless boy! But I've got him here to stay with me till I can see what's to be done with un, though I am obliged to let him earn any penny he can. Just now he's a-scaring of birds for Farmer Troutham. It keeps him out of mischty. Why do ye turn away, Jude?' she continued, as the boy, feeling the impact of their glances like slaps upon his face, moved aside.

The local washerwoman replied that it was perhaps a very good plan of Miss or Mrs Fawley's (as they called her indifferently) to have him with her – 'to kip 'ee company in your loneliness, fetch

water, shet the winder-shetters o' nights, and help in the bit o'
baking'.

Miss Fawley doubted it. .... 'Why didn't ye get the schoolmaster
to take 'ee to Christminster wi' un, and make a scholar of 'ee,' she
continued, in frowning pleasantry. 'I'm sure he couldn't ha' took a
better one. The boy is crazy for books, that he is. It runs in our
family rather. His cousin Sue is just the same — so I've heard; but I
have not seen the child for years, though she was born in this place,
within these four walls, as it happened. My niece and her husband,
after they were married, didn' get a house of their own for some
year or more; and then they only had one till — Well, I won't go into
that. Jude, my child, don't *you* ever marry. 'Tisn't for the Fawleys to
take that step any more. She, their only one, was like a child o' my
own, Belinda, till the split come! Ah, that a little maid should know
such changes!'

Jude, finding the general attention again centering on himself,
went out to the bakehouse, where he ate the cake provided for his
breakfast. The end of his spare time had now arrived, and emerging
from the garden by getting over the hedge at the back he pursued a
path northward, till he came to a wide and lonely depression in the
general level of the upland, which was sown as a corn-field. This
vast concave was the scene of his labours for Mr Troutham the
farmer, and he descended into the midst of it.

The brown surface of the field went right up towards the sky all
round, where it was lost by degrees in the mist that shut out the
actual verge and accentuated the solitude. The only marks on the
uniformity of the scene were a rick of last year's produce standing
in the midst of the arable, the rooks that rose at his approach, and
the path athwart the fallow by which he had come, trodden now by
he hardly knew whom, though once by many of his own dead
family.

'How ugly it is here!' he murmured.

The fresh harrow-lines seemed to stretch like the channellings in
a piece of new corduroy, lending a meanly utilitarian air to the
expanse, taking away its gradations, and depriving it of all history
beyond that of the few recent months, though to every clod and
stone there really attached associations enough and to spare —

echoes of songs from ancient harvest-days, of spoken words, and of
sturdy deeds. Every inch of ground had been the site, first or last, of
energy, gaiety, horse-play, bickering, weariness. Groups of gleaners
had squatted in the sun on every square yard. Love-matches that
had populated the adjoining hamlet had been made up there between
reaping and carrying. Under the hedge which divided the field from
a distant plantation girls had given themselves to lovers who would
not turn their heads to look at them by the next harvest; and in that
ancient cornfield many a man had made love-promises to a woman
at whose voice he had trembled by the next seed-time after fulfill-
ing them in the church adjoining. But this neither Jude nor the
rooks around him considered. For them it was a lonely place,
possessing, in the one view, only the quality of a work-ground, and
in the other that of a granary good to feed in.

The boy stood under the rick before mentioned, and every few
seconds used his clacker or rattle briskly. At each clack the rooks
left off pecking, and rose and went away on their leisurely wings,
burnished like tassets * of mail, afterwards wheeling back and
regarding him warily, and descending to feed at a more respectful
distance.

He sounded the clacker till his arm ached, and at length his heart
grew sympathetic with the birds' thwarted desires. They seemed,
like himself, to be living in a world which did not want them. Why
should he frighten them away? They took upon them more and
more the aspect of gentle friends and pensioners – the only friends
he could claim as being in the least degree interested in him, for his
aunt had often told him that she was not. He ceased his rattling, and
they alighted anew.

'Poor little dears!' said Jude, aloud. 'You *shall* have some dinner
– you shall. There is enough for us all. Farmer Troutham can afford
to let you have some. Eat, then, my dear little birdies, and make a
good meal!'

They stayed and ate, inky spots on the nut-brown soil, and Jude
enjoyed their appetite. A magic thread of fellow-feeling united his
own life with theirs. Puny and sorry as those lives were, they much
resembled his own.

His clacker he had by this thrown away from him, as being a
mean and sordid instrument, offensive both to the birds and to

himself as their friend. All at once he became conscious of a smart blow upon his buttocks, followed by a loud clack, which announced to his surprised senses that the clacker had been the instrument of offence used. The birds and Jude started up simultaneously, and the dazed eyes of the latter beheld the farmer in person, the great Troutham himself, his red face glaring down upon Jude's cowering frame, the clacker swinging in his hand.

'So it's "Eat, my dear birdies," is it, young man? "Eat, dear birdies," indeed! I'll tickle your breeches, and see if you say, "Eat, dear birdies," again in a hurry! And you've been idling at the schoolmaster's too, instead of coming here, ha'n't ye, hey? That's how you earn your sixpence a day for keeping the rooks off my corn!'

Whilst saluting Jude's ears with this impassioned rhetoric, Troutham had seized his left hand with his own left, and swinging his slim frame round him at arm's-length, again struck Jude on the hind parts with the flat side of Jude's own rattle, till the field echoed with the blows, which were delivered once or twice at each revolution.

'Don't 'ee, sir — please don't 'ee!' cried the whirling child, as helpless under the centrifugal tendency of his person as a hooked fish swinging to land, and beholding the hill, the rick, the plantation, the path, and the rocks going round and round him in an amazing circular race. 'I — I — sir — only meant that — there was a good crop in the ground — I saw 'em sow it — and the rooks could have a little bit for dinner — and you wouldn't miss it, sir — and Mr Phillotson said I was to be kind to 'em — O, O, O!'

This truthful explanation seemed to exasperate the farmer even more than if Jude had stoutly denied saying anything at all; and he still smacked the whirling urchin, the clacks of the instrument continuing to resound all across the field and as far as the ears of distant workers — who gathered thereupon that Jude was pursuing his business of clacking with great assiduity — and echoing from the brand-new church tower just behind the mist, towards the building of which structure the farmer had largely subscribed to testify his love for God and man.

Presently Troutham grew tired of his punitive task, and depositing the quivering boy on his legs, took a sixpence from his pocket and gave it him in payment for his day's work, telling him to go home and never let him see him in one of those fields again.

Jude leaped out of arm's reach, and walked along the trackway weeping — not from the pain, though that was keen enough; not from the perception of the flaw in the terrestrial scheme, by which what was good for God's birds was bad for God's gardener; but with the awful sense that he had wholly disgraced himself before he had been a year in the parish, and hence might be a burden to his great-aunt for life.

With this shadow on his mind he did not care to show himself in the village, and went homeward by a roundabout track behind a high hedge and across a pasture. Here he beheld scores of coupled earth-worms lying half their length on the surface of the damp ground, as they always did in such weather at that time of the year. It was impossible to advance in regular steps without crushing some of them at each tread.

Though Farmer Troutham had just hurt him, he was a boy who could not himself bear to hurt anything. He had never brought home a nest of young birds without lying awake in misery half the night after, and often reinstating them and the nest in their original place the next morning. He could scarcely bear to see trees cut down or lopped, from a fancy that it hurt them; and late pruning, when the sap was up and the tree bled profusely, had been a positive grief to him in his infancy. This weakness of character, as it may be called, suggested that he was the sort of man who was born to ache a good deal before the fall of the curtain upon his unnecessary life should signify that all was well with him again. He carefully picked his way on tiptoe among the earthworms, without killing a single one.

On entering the cottage he found his aunt selling a penny loaf to a little girl, and when the customer was gone she said, 'Well, how do you come to be back here in the middle of the morning like this?'

'I'm turned away.'

'What?'

'Mr Troutham have turned me away because I let the rooks have a few peckings of corn. And there's my wages — the last I shall ever hae!'

He threw the sixpence tragically on the table.

'Ah!' said his aunt, suspending her breath. And she opened upon

him a lecture on how she would now have him all the spring upon
her hands doing nothing. 'If you can't skeer birds, what can ye do?
There! don't ye look so deedy! ★ Farmer Troutham is not so much
better than myself, come to that. But 'tis as Job said, "Now they that
are younger than I have me in derision, whose fathers I would have
disdained to have set with the dogs of my flock." ★ His father was
my father's journeyman,★ anyhow, and I must have been a fool to
let 'ee go to work for 'n, which I shouldn't ha' done but to keep 'ee
out of mischty.'

More angry with Jude for demeaning her by coming there than
for dereliction of duty, she rated him primarily from that point of
view, and only secondarily from a moral one.

'Not that you should have let the birds eat what Farmer
Troutham planted. Of course you was wrong in that. Jude, Jude,
why didstn't go off with that schoolmaster of thine to Christminster
or somewhere? But, O no — poor or'nary ★ child — there never was
any sprawl★ on thy side of the family, and never will be!'

'Where is this beautiful city, aunt — this place where Mr
Phillotson is gone to?' asked the boy, after meditating in silence.

'Lord! you ought to know where the city of Christminster is:
Near a score of miles from here. It is a place much too good for you
ever to have much to do with, poor boy, I'm a-thinking.'

'And will Mr Phillotson always be there?'

'How can I tell?'

'Couldn't I go to see him?'

'Lord, no! You didn't grow up hereabout, or you wouldn't ask
such as that. We've never had anything to do with folk in
Christminster, nor folk in Christminster with we.'

Jude went out, and, feeling more than ever his existence to be an
undemanded one, he lay down upon his back on a heap of litter near
the pig-sty. The fog had by this time become more translucent, and
the position of the sun could be seen through it. He pulled his straw
hat over his face, and peered through the interstices of the plaiting
at the white brightness, vaguely reflecting. Growing up brought
responsibilities, he found. Events did not rhyme quite as he had
thought. Nature's logic was too horrid for him to care for. That
mercy towards one set of creatures was cruelty towards another
sickened his sense of harmony. As you got older, and felt yourself to

be at the centre of your time, and not at a point in its circumference, as you had felt when you were little, you were seized with a sort of shuddering, he perceived. All around you there seemed to be something glaring, garish, rattling, and the noises and glares hit upon the little cell called your life, and shook it, and warped it.

If he could only prevent himself growing up! He did not want to be a man.

Then, like the natural boy, he forgot his despondency, and sprang up. During the remainder of the morning he helped his aunt, and in the afternoon, when there was nothing more to be done, he went into the village. Here he asked a man whereabouts Christminster lay.

'Christminster? O, well, out by there yonder; though I've never bin there — not I. I've never had any business at such a place.'

The man pointed north-eastward, in the very direction where lay that field in which Jude had so disgraced himself. There was something unpleasant about the coincidence for the moment, but the fearsomeness of this fact rather increased his curiosity about the city. The farmer had said he was never to be seen in that field again; yet Christminster lay across it, and the path was a public one. So, stealing out of the hamlet he descended into the same hollow which had witnessed his punishment in the morning, never swerving an inch from the path, and climbing up the long and tedious ascent on the other side, till the track joined the highway by a little clump of trees. Here the ploughed land ended, and all before him was bleak open down.

NOT a soul was visible on the hedgeless highway, or on either side of it, and the white road seemed to ascend and diminish till it joined the sky. At the very top it was crossed at right angles by a green 'ridge-way' – the Icknield Street and original Roman road through the district. This ancient track ran east and west for many miles, and down almost to within living memory had been used for driving flocks and herds to fairs and markets. But it was now neglected and overgrown.

The boy had never before strayed so far north as this from the nestling hamlet in which he had been deposited by the carrier from a railway station southward, one dark evening some few months earlier, and till now he had had no suspicion that such a wide, flat, low-lying country lay so near at hand, under the very verge of his upland world. The whole northern semicircle between east and west, to a distance of forty or fifty miles, spread itself before him; a bluer, moister atmosphere, evidently, than that he breathed up here.

Not far from the road stood a weather-beaten old barn of reddish-gray brick and tile. It was known as the Brown House * by the people of the locality. He was about to pass it when he perceived a ladder against the eaves; and the reflection that the higher he got, the further he could see, led Jude to stand and regard it. On the slope of the roof two men were repairing the tiling. He turned into the ridgeway and drew towards the barn.

When he had wistfully watched the workmen for some time he took courage, and ascended the ladder till he stood beside them.

'Well, my lad, and what may you want up here?'

'I wanted to know where the city of Christminster is, if you please.'

'Christminster is out across there, by that clump. You can see it – at least you can on a clear day. Ah, no, you can't now.'

The other tiler, glad of any kind of diversion from the monotony of his labour, had also turned to look towards the quarter desig-

nated. 'You can't often see it in weather like this,' he said. 'The time
I've noticed it is when the sun is going down in a blaze of flame, and
it looks like — I don't know what.'

'The heavenly Jerusalem,' suggested the serious urchin.

'Ay — though I should never ha' thought of it myself. . . . But I
can't see no Christminster to-day.'

The boy strained his eyes also; yet neither could he see the far-off
city. He descended from the barn, and abandoning Christminster
with the versatility of his age he walked along the ridge-track,
looking for any natural objects of interest that might lie in the banks
thereabout. When he repassed the barn to go back to Marygreen he
observed that the ladder was still in its place, but that the men had
finished their day's work and gone away.

It was waning towards evening; there was still a faint mist, but it
had cleared a little except in the damper tracts of subjacent country
and along the river-courses. He thought again of Christminster, and
wished, since he had come two or three miles from his aunt's house
on purpose, that he could have seen for once this attractive city of
which he had been told. But even if he waited here it was hardly
likely that the air would clear before night. Yet he was loth to leave
the spot, for the northern expanse became lost to view on retreating
towards the village only a few hundred yards.

He ascended the ladder to have one more look at the point the
men had designated, and perched himself on the highest rung,
overlying the tiles. He might not be able to come so far as this for
many days. Perhaps if he prayed, the wish to see Christminster
might be forwarded. People said that, if you prayed, things
sometimes came to you, even though they sometimes did not. He
had read in a tract that a man who had begun to build a church, and
had no money to finish it, knelt down and prayed, and the money
came in by the next post. Another man tried the same experiment,
and the money did not come; but he found afterwards that the
breeches he knelt in were made by a wicked Jew. This was not
discouraging, and turning on the ladder Jude knelt on the third
rung, where, resting against those above it, he prayed that the mist
might rise.

He then seated himself again, and waited. In the course of ten or
fifteen minutes the thinning mist dissolved altogether from the

northern horizon, as it had already done elsewhere, and about a quarter of an hour before the time of sunset the westward clouds parted, the sun's position being partially uncovered, and the beams streaming out in visible lines between two bars of slaty cloud. The boy immediately looked back in the old direction.

Some way within the limits of the stretch of landscape, points of light like the topaz gleamed. The air increased in transparency with the lapse of minutes, till the topaz points showed themselves to be the vanes, windows, wet roof slates, and other shining spots upon the spires, domes, freestone-work, and varied outlines that were faintly revealed. It was Christminster, unquestionably; either directly seen, or miraged in the peculiar atmosphere.

The spectator gazed on and on till the windows and vanes lost their shine, going out almost suddenly like extinguished candles. The vague city became veiled in mist. Turning to the west, he saw that the sun had disappeared. The foreground of the scene had grown funereally dark, and near objects put on the hues and shapes of chimæras.

He anxiously descended the ladder, and started homewards at a run, trying not to think of giants, Herne the Hunter,* Apollyon* lying in wait for Christian, or of the captain with the bleeding hole in his forehead* and the corpses round him that remutinied every night on board the bewitched ship. He knew that he had grown out of belief in these horrors, yet he was glad when he saw the church tower and the lights in the cottage windows, even though this was not the home of his birth, and his great-aunt did not care much about him.

Inside and round about that old woman's 'shop' window, with its twenty-four little panes set in lead-work, the glass of some of them oxidized with age, so that you could hardly see the poor penny articles exhibited within, and forming part of a stock which a strong man could have carried, Jude had his outer being for some long tideless time. But his dreams were as gigantic as his surroundings were small.

Through the solid barrier of cold cretaceous upland to the northward he was always beholding a gorgeous city — the fancied place he had likened to the new Jerusalem, though there was perhaps more of the painter's imagination and less of the diamond merchant's in his dreams thereof than in those of the Apocalyptic writer. And the city acquired a tangibility, a permanence, a hold on his life, mainly from the one nucleus of fact that the man for whose knowledge and purpose he had so much reverence was actually living there; not only so, but living among the more thoughtful and mentally shining ones therein.

In sad wet seasons, though he knew it must rain at Christminster too, he could hardly believe that it rained so drearily there. Whenever he could get away from the confines of the hamlet for an hour or two, which was not often, he would steal off to the Brown House on the hill and strain his eyes persistently; sometimes to be rewarded by the sight of a dome or spire, at other times by a little smoke, which in his estimate had some of the mysticism of incense.

Then the day came when it suddenly occurred to him that if he ascended to the point of view after dark, or possibly went a mile or two further, he would see the night lights of the city. It would be necessary to come back alone, but even that consideration did not deter him, for he could throw a little manliness into his mood, no doubt.

The project was duly executed. It was not late when he arrived at the place of outlook, only just after dusk; but a black north-east sky, accompanied by a wind from the same quarter, made the occasion dark enough. He was rewarded; but what he saw was not the lamps in rows, as he had half expected. No individual light was visible, only a halo or glow-fog over-arching the place against the black heavens behind it, making the light and the city seem distant but a mile or so.

He set himself to wonder on the exact point in the glow where the schoolmaster might be – he who never communicated with anybody at Marygreen now; who was as if dead to them here. In the glow he seemed to see Phillotson promenading at ease, like one of the forms in Nebuchadnezzar's furnace.*

He had heard that breezes travelled at the rate of ten miles an hour, and the fact now came into his mind. He parted his lips as he faced the north-east, and drew in the wind as if it were a sweet liquor.

'You,' he said, addressing the breeze caressingly, 'were in

Christminster city between one and two hours ago, floating along the streets, pulling round the weather-cocks, touching Mr Phillotson's face, being breathed by him; and now you are here, breathed by me – you, the very same.'

Suddenly there came along this wind something towards him – a message from the place – from some soul residing there, it seemed. Surely it was the sound of bells, the voice of the city, faint and musical, calling to him, 'We are happy here!'

He had become entirely lost to his bodily situation during this mental leap, and only got back to it by a rough recalling. A few yards below the brow of the hill on which he paused a team of horses made its appearance, having reached the place by dint of half an hour's serpentine progress from the bottom of the immense declivity. They had a load of coals behind them – a fuel that could only be got into the upland by this particular route. They were accompanied by a carter, a second man, and a boy, who now kicked a large stone behind one of the wheels, and allowed the panting animals to have a long rest, while those in charge took a flagon off the load and indulged in a drink round.

They were elderly men, and had genial voices. Jude addressed them, inquiring if they had come from Christminster.

'Heaven forbid, with this load!' said they.

'The place I mean is that one yonder.' He was getting so romantically attached to Christminster that, like a young lover alluding to his mistress, he felt bashful at mentioning its name again. He pointed to the light in the sky – hardly perceptible to their older eyes.

'Yes. There do seem a spot a bit brighter in the nor'-east than elsewhere, though I shouldn't ha' noticed it myself, and no doubt it med be Christminster.'

Here a little book of tales which Jude had tucked up under his arm, having brought them to read on his way hither before it grew dark, slipped and fell into the road. The carter eyed him while he picked it up and straightened the leaves.

'Ah, young man,' he observed, 'you'd have to get your head screwed on t'other way before you could read what they read there.'

'Why?' asked the boy.

'O, they never look at anything that folks like we can understand,'

the carter continued, by way of passing the time. 'On'y foreign
tongues used in the days of the Tower of Babel,★ when no two
families spoke alike. They read that sort of thing as fast as a night-
hawk★ will whir. 'Tis all learning there — nothing but learning,
except religion. And that's learning too, for I never could understand it. Yes, 'tis a serious-minded place. Not but there's wenches in
the streets o' nights. . . . You know, I suppose, that they raise
pa'sons there like radishes in a bed? And though it do take — how
many years, Bob? — five years to turn a lirruping★ hobble-de-hoy
chap into a solemn preaching man with no corrupt passions, they'll
do it, if it can be done, and polish un off like the workmen they be,
and turn un out wi' a long face, and a long black coat and waistcoat,
and a religious collar and hat, same as they used to wear in the
Scriptures, so that his own mother wouldn't know un sometimes. . . .
There, 'tis their business, like anybody else's.'

'But how should you know—'

'Now don't you interrupt, my boy. Never interrupt your senyers.
Move the fore hoss aside, Bobby; here's som'at coming. . . . You
must mind that I be a-talking of the college life. 'Em lives on a lofty
level; there's no gainsaying it, though I myself med not think much
of 'em. As we be here in our bodies on this high ground, so be they in
their minds — noble-minded men enough, no doubt — some on 'em —
able to earn hundreds by thinking out loud. And some on 'em be
strong young fellows that can earn a'most as much in silver cups.
As for music, there's beautiful music everywhere in Christminster.
You med be religious, or you med not, but you can't help striking in
your homely note with the rest. And there's a street in the place —
the main street — that ha'n't another like it in the world. I should
think I did know a little about Christminster!'

By this time the horses had recovered breath and bent to their
collars again. Jude, throwing a last adoring look at the distant halo,
turned and walked beside his remarkably well-informed friend, who
had no objection to tell him as they moved on more yet of the city —
its towers and halls and churches. The waggon turned into a cross-
road, whereupon Jude thanked the carter warmly for his information, and said he only wished he could talk half as well about
Christminster as he.

'Well, 'tis oonly what has come in my way,' said the carter

unboastfully. 'I've never been there, no more than you; but I've picked up the knowledge here and there, and you be welcome to it. A-getting about the world as I do, and mixing with all classes of society, one can't help hearing of things. A friend o' mine, that used to clane the boots at the Crozier Hotel★ in Christminster when he was in his prime, why, I knowed un as well as my own brother in his later years.'

Jude continued his walk homeward alone, pondering so deeply that he forgot to feel timid. He suddenly grew older. It had been the yearning of his heart to find something to anchor on, to cling to — for some place which he could call admirable. Should he find that place in this city if he could get there? Would it be a spot in which, without fear of farmers, or hindrance, or ridicule, he could watch and wait, and set himself to some mighty undertaking like the men of old of whom he had heard? As the halo had been to his eyes when gazing at it a quarter of an hour earlier, so was the spot mentally to him as he pursued his dark way.

'It is a city of light,' he said to himself.

'The tree of knowledge grows there,' he added a few steps further on.

'It is a place that teachers of men spring from and go to.'

'It is what you may call a castle, manned by scholarship and religion.'

After this figure he was silent a long while, till he added:

'It would just suit me.'

WALKING somewhat slowly by reason of his concentration, the boy — an ancient man in some phases of thought, much younger than his years in others — was overtaken by a light-footed pedestrian, whom, notwithstanding the gloom, he could perceive to be wearing an extraordinarily tall hat, a swallow-tailed coat, and a watch-chain that danced madly and threw around scintillations of sky-light as its owner swung along upon a pair of thin legs and noiseless boots. Jude, beginning to feel lonely, endeavoured to keep up with him.

'Well, my man! I'm in a hurry, so you'll have to walk pretty fast if you keep alongside of me. Do you know who I am?'

'Yes, I think. Physician Vilbert?'

'Ah — I'm known everywhere, I see! That comes of being a public benefactor.'

Vilbert was an itinerant quack-doctor, well known to the rustic population, and absolutely unknown to anybody else, as he, indeed, took care to be, to avoid inconvenient investigations. Cottagers formed his only patients, and his Wessex-wide repute was among them alone. His position was humbler and his field more obscure than those of the quacks with capital and an organized system of advertising. He was, in fact, a survival. The distances he traversed on foot were enormous, and extended nearly the whole length and breadth of Wessex. Jude had one day seen him selling a pot of coloured lard to an old woman as a certain cure for a bad leg, the woman arranging to pay a guinea, in instalments of a shilling a fortnight, for the precious salve, which, according to the physician, could only be obtained from a particular animal which grazed on Mount Sinai, and was to be captured only at great risk to life and limb. Jude, though he already had his doubts about this gentleman's medicines, felt him to be unquestionably a travelled personage, and one who might be a trustworthy source of information on matters not strictly professional.

'I s'pose you've been to Christminster, Physician?'

'I have — many times,' replied the long thin man. 'That's one of my centres.'

'It's a wonderful city for scholarship and religion?'

'You'd say so, my boy, if you'd seen it. Why, the very sons of the old women who do the washing of the colleges can talk in Latin — not good Latin, that I admit, as a critic: dog-Latin — cat-Latin, as we used to call it in my undergraduate days.'

'And Greek?'

'Well — that's more for the men who are in training for bishops, that they may be able to read the New Testament in the original.'

'I want to learn Latin and Greek myself.'

'A lofty desire. You must get a grammar of each tongue.'

'I mean to go to Christminster some day.'

'Whenever you do, you say that Physician Vilbert is the only proprietor of those celebrated pills that infallibly cure all disorders of the alimentary system, as well as asthma and shortness of breath. Two and threepence a box — specially licensed by the government stamp.'

'Can you get me the grammars if I promise to say it hereabout?'

'I'll sell you mine with pleasure — those I used as a student.'

'O, thank you, sir!' said Jude gratefully, but in gasps, for the amazing speed of the physician's walk kept him in a dog-trot which was giving him a stitch in the side.

'I think you'd better drop behind, my young man. Now I'll tell you what I'll do. I'll get you the grammars, and give a first lesson, if you'll remember, at every house in the village, to recommend Physician Vilbert's golden ointment, life-drops, and female pills.'

'Where will you be with the grammars?'

'I shall be passing here this day fortnight at precisely this hour of five-and-twenty minutes past seven. My movements are as truly timed as those of the planets in their courses.'

'Here I'll be to meet you,' said Jude.

'With orders for my medicines?'

'Yes, Physician.'

Jude then dropped behind, waited a few minutes to recover breath, and went home with a consciousness of having struck a blow for Christminster.

Through the intervening fortnight he ran about and smiled outwardly at his inward thoughts, as if they were people meeting and nodding to him — smiled with that singularly beautiful irradiation which is seen to spread on young faces at the inception of some glorious idea, as if a supernatural lamp were held inside their transparent natures, giving rise to the flattering fancy that heaven lies about them * then.

He honestly performed his promise to the man of many cures, in whom he now sincerely believed, walking miles hither and thither among the surrounding hamlets as the physician's agent in advance. On the evening appointed he stood motionless on the plateau, at the place where he had parted from Vilbert, and there awaited his approach. The road-physician was fairly up to time; but, to the surprise of Jude on striking into his pace, which the pedestrian did not diminish by a single unit of force, the latter seemed hardly to recognize his young companion, though with the lapse of the fortnight the evenings had grown light. Jude thought it might perhaps be owing to his wearing another hat, and he saluted the physician with dignity.

'Well, my boy?' said the latter abstractedly.

'I've come,' said Jude.

'You? who are you? O yes — to be sure! Got any orders, lad?'

'Yes.' And Jude told him the names and addresses of the cottagers who were willing to test the virtues of the world-renowned pills and salve. The quack mentally registered these with great care.

'And the Latin and Greek grammars?' Jude's voice trembled with anxiety.

'What about them?'

'You were to bring me yours, that you used before you took your degree.'

'Ah, yes, yes! Forgot all about it — all! So many lives depending on my attention, you see, my man, that I can't give so much thought as I would like to other things.'

Jude controlled himself sufficiently long to make sure of the truth; and he repeated, in a voice of dry misery, 'You haven't brought 'em!'

'No. But you must get me some more orders from sick people, and I'll bring the grammars next time.'

Jude dropped behind. He was an unsophisticated boy, but the gift of sudden insight which is sometimes vouchsafed to children showed him all at once what shoddy humanity the quack was made of. There was to be no intellectual light from this source. The leaves dropped from his imaginary crown of laurel; he turned to a gate, leant against it, and cried bitterly.

The disappointment was followed by an interval of blankness. He might, perhaps, have obtained grammars from Alfredston, but to do that required money, and a knowledge of what books to order; and though physically comfortable, he was in such absolute dependence as to be without a farthing of his own.

At this date Mr Phillotson sent for his pianoforte, and it gave Jude a lead. Why should he not write to the schoolmaster, and ask him to be so kind as to get him the grammars in Christminster? He might slip a letter inside the case of the instrument, and it would be sure to reach the desired eyes. Why not ask him to send any old second-hand copies, which would have the charm of being mellowed by the university atmosphere?

To tell his aunt of his intention would be to defeat it. It was necessary to act alone.

After a further consideration of a few days he did act, and on the day of the piano's departure, which happened to be his next birthday, clandestinely placed the letter inside the packing-case, directed to his much-admired friend; being afraid to reveal the operation to his aunt Drusilla, lest she should discover his motive, and compel him to abandon his scheme.

The piano was despatched, and Jude waited days and weeks, calling every morning at the cottage post-office before his great-aunt was stirring. At last a packet did indeed arrive at the village, and he saw from the ends of it that it contained two thin books. He took it away into a lonely place, and sat down on a felled elm to open it.

Ever since his first ecstasy or vision of Christminster and its possibilities, Jude had meditated much and curiously on the probable sort of process that was involved in turning the expressions of one language into those of another. He concluded that a grammar of the required tongue would contain, primarily, a rule, prescription, or clue of the nature of a secret cipher, which, once known, would enable him, by merely applying it, to change at will all words of his own speech into those of the foreign one. His childish idea was, in fact, a pushing to the extremity of mathematical precision what is everywhere known as Grimm's Law * — an aggrandizement of rough rules to ideal completeness. Thus he assumed that the words of the required language were always to be found somewhere latent in the words of the given language by those who had the art to uncover them, such art being furnished by the books aforesaid.

When, therefore, having noted that the packet bore the postmark of Christminster, he cut the string, opened the volumes, and turned to the Latin grammar, which chanced to come uppermost, he could scarcely believe his eyes.

The book was an old one — thirty years old, soiled, scribbled wantonly over with a strange name in every variety of enmity to the letterpress, and marked at random with dates twenty years earlier than his own day. But this was not the cause of Jude's amazement. He learnt for the first time that there was no law of transmutation, as in his innocence he had supposed (there was, in some degree, but the grammarian did not recognize it), but that every word in both Latin and Greek was to be individually committed to memory at the cost of years of plodding.

Jude flung down the books, lay backward along the broad trunk of the elm, and was an utterly miserable boy for the space of a quarter of an hour. As he had often done before, he pulled his hat over his face and watched the sun peering insidiously at him through the interstices of the straw. This was Latin and Greek, then, was it, this grand delusion! The charm he had supposed in store for him was really a labour like that of Israel in Egypt.

What brains they must have in Christminster and the great schools, he presently thought, to learn words one by one up to tens of thousands! There were no brains in his head equal to this business; and as the little sun-rays continued to stream in through his hat at him, he wished he had never seen a book, that he might never see another, that he had never been born.

Somebody might have come along that way who would have asked him his trouble, and might have cheered him by saying that his notions were further advanced than those of his grammarian. But nobody did come, because nobody does; and under the crushing recognition of his gigantic error Jude continued to wish himself out of the world.

DURING the three or four succeeding years a quaint and singular vehicle might have been discerned moving along the lanes and by-roads near Marygreen, driven in a quaint and singular way.

In the course of a month or two after the receipt of the books Jude had grown callous to the shabby trick played him by the dead languages. In fact, his disappointment at the nature of those tongues had, after a while, been the means of still further glorifying the erudition of Christminster. To acquire languages, departed or living, in spite of such obstinacles as he now knew them inherently to possess, was a herculean performance which gradually led him on to a greater interest in it than in the presupposed patent process. The mountain-weight of material under which the ideas lay in those dusty volumes called the classics piqued him into a dogged, mouse-like subtlety of attempt to move it piecemeal.

He had endeavoured to make his presence tolerable to his crusty maiden aunt by assisting her to the best of his ability, and the business of the little cottage bakery had grown in consequence. An aged horse with a hanging head had been purchased for eight pounds at a sale, a creaking cart with a whity-brown tilt obtained for a few pounds more, and in this turn-out it became Jude's business thrice a week to carry loaves of bread to the villagers and solitary cotters * immediately around Marygreen.

The singularity aforesaid lay, after all, less in the conveyance itself than in Jude's manner of conducting it along its route. Its interior was the scene of most of Jude's education by 'private study'. As soon as the horse had learnt the road and the houses at which he was to pause awhile, the boy, seated in front, would slip the reins over his arm, ingeniously fix open, by means of a strap attached to the tilt, the volume he was reading, spread the dictionary on his knees, and plunge into the simpler passages from Cæsar, Virgil, or Horace, as the case might be, in his purblind stumbling way, and with an expenditure of labour that would have made a tender-hearted pedagogue shed tears; yet somehow getting at the meaning of what he read, and divining rather than beholding the spirit of the original, which often to his mind was something else than that which he was taught to look for.

The only copies he had been able to lay hands on were old Delphin editions,* because they were superseded, and therefore cheap. But, bad for idle schoolboys, it did so happen that they were passably good for him. The hampered and lonely itinerant conscientiously covered up the marginal readings, and used them merely on points of construction, as he would have used a comrade or tutor who should have happened to be passing by. And though Jude may have had little chance of becoming a scholar by these rough and ready means, he was in the way of getting into the groove he wished to follow.

While he was busied with these ancient pages, which had already been thumbed by hands possibly in the grave, digging out the thoughts of these minds so remote yet so near, the bony old horse pursued his rounds, and Jude would be aroused from the woes of Dido* by the stoppage of his cart and the voice of some old woman crying, 'Two to-day, baker, and I return this stale one.'

He was frequently met in the lanes by pedestrians and others without his seeing them, and by degrees the people of the neighbourhood began to talk about his method of combining work and play (such they considered his reading to be), which, though probably convenient enough to himself, was not altogether a safe proceeding for other travellers along the same roads. There were murmurs. Then a private resident of an adjoining place informed the local policeman that the baker's boy should not be allowed to read while driving, and insisted that it was the constable's duty to catch him in the act, and take him to the police court at Alfredston, and get him fined for dangerous practices on the highway. The policeman thereupon lay in wait for Jude, and one day accosted him and cautioned him.

As Jude had to get up at three o'clock in the morning to heat the oven, and mix and set in the bread that he distributed later in the day, he was obliged to go to bed at night immediately after laying the sponge;* so that if he could not read his classics on the highways he could hardly study at all. The only thing to be done was, therefore, to keep a sharp eye ahead and around him as well as he could in the circumstances, and slip away his books as soon as anybody loomed in the distance, the policeman in particular. To do that official justice, he did not put himself much in the way of Jude's bread-cart, considering that in such a lonely district the chief danger was to Jude himself, and often on seeing the white tilt over the hedges he would move in another direction.

On a day when Fawley was getting quite advanced, being now about sixteen, and had been stumbling through the 'Carmen Sæculare',* on his way home, he found himself to be passing over the high edge of the plateau by the Brown House. The light had changed, and it was the sense of this which had caused him to look up. The sun was going down, and the full moon was rising simultaneously behind the woods in the opposite quarter. His mind had become so impregnated with the poem that, in a moment of the same impulsive emotion which years before had caused him to kneel on the ladder, he stopped the horse, alighted, and glancing round to see that nobody was in sight, knelt down on the roadside bank with open book. He turned first to the shiny goddess, who seemed to look so softly and critically at his doings, then to the disappearing luminary on the other hand, as he began:

'Phœbe silvarumque potens Diana!'*

The horse stood still till he had finished the hymn, which Jude repeated under the sway of a polytheistic fancy that he would never have thought of humouring in broad daylight.

Reaching home, he mused over his curious superstition, innate or acquired, in doing this, and the strange forgetfulness which had led to such a lapse from common-sense and custom in one who wished, next to being a scholar, to be a Christian divine. It had all come of reading heathen works exclusively. The more he thought of it the more convinced he was of his inconsistency. He began to wonder whether he could be reading quite the right books for his object in life. Certainly there seemed little harmony between this pagan literature and the mediæval colleges at Christminster, that ecclesiastical romance in stone.

Ultimately he decided that in his sheer love of reading he had taken up a wrong emotion for a Christian young man. He had

dabbled in Clarke's Homer,* but had never yet worked much at the
New Testament in the Greek, though he possessed a copy, obtained
by post from a second-hand bookseller. He abandoned the now
familiar Ionic for a new dialect, and for a long time onward limited
his reading almost entirely to the Gospels and Epistles in
Griesbach's text.* Moreover, on going into Alfredston one day, he
was introduced to patristic literature by finding at the bookseller's
some volumes of the Fathers which had been left behind by an
insolvent clergyman of the neighbourhood.

As another outcome of this change of groove he visited on
Sundays all the churches within a walk, and deciphered the Latin
inscriptions on fifteenth-century brasses and tombs. On one of these
pilgrimages he met with a hunchbacked old woman of great intelligence, who read everything she could lay her hands on, and she
told him more yet of the romantic charms of the city of light and
lore. Thither he resolved as firmly as ever to go.

But how live in that city? At present he had no income at all. He
had no trade or calling of any dignity or stability whatever on which
he could subsist while carrying out an intellectual labour which
might spread over many years.

What was most required by citizens? Food, clothing, and shelter.
An income from any work in preparing the first would be too
meagre; for making the second he felt a distaste; the preparation of
the third requisite he inclined to. They built in a city; therefore he
would learn to build. He thought of his unknown uncle, his cousin
Susanna's father, an ecclesiastical worker in metal, and somehow
mediæval art in any material was a trade for which he had rather a
fancy. He could not go far wrong in following his uncle's footsteps,
and engaging himself awhile with the carcases that contained the
scholar souls.

As a preliminary he obtained some small blocks of freestone,
metal not being available, and suspending his studies awhile, occupied his spare half-hours in copying the heads and capitals in his
parish church.

There was a stone-mason of a humble kind in Alfredston, and as
soon as he had found a substitute for himself in his aunt's little
business, he offered his services to this man for a trifling wage. Here
Jude had the opportunity of learning at least the rudiments of

freestone-working. Some time later he went to a church-builder in the same place, and under the architect's direction became handy at restoring the dilapidated masonries of several village churches round about.

Not forgetting that he was only following up this handicraft as a prop to lean on while he prepared those greater engines which he flattered himself would be better fitted for him, he yet was interested in his pursuit on its own account. He now had lodgings during the week in the little town, whence he returned to Marygreen village every Saturday evening. And thus he reached and passed his nineteenth year.

AT this memorable date of his life he was, one Saturday, returning from Alfredston to Marygreen about three o'clock in the afternoon. It was fine, warm, and soft summer weather, and he walked with his tools at his back, his little chisels clinking faintly against the larger ones in his basket. It being the end of the week he had left work early, and had come out of the town by a roundabout route which he did not usually frequent, having promised to call at a flour-mill near Cresscombe to execute a commission for his aunt.

He was in an enthusiastic mood. He seemed to see his way to living comfortably in Christminster in the course of a year or two, and knocking at the doors of one of those strongholds of learning of which he had dreamed so much. He might, of course, have gone there now, in some capacity or other, but he preferred to enter the city with a little more assurance as to means than he could be said to feel at present. A warm self-content suffused him when he considered what he had already done. Now and then as he went along he turned to face the peeps of country on either side of him. But he hardly saw them; the act was an automatic repetition of what he had been accustomed to do when less occupied; and the one matter which really engaged him was the mental estimate of his progress thus far.

'I have acquired quite an average student's power to read the common ancient classics, Latin in particular.' This was true, Jude possessing a facility in that language which enabled him with great ease to himself to beguile his lonely walks by imaginary conversations therein.

'I have read two books of the Iliad, besides being pretty familiar with passages such as the speech of Phœnix in the ninth book, the fight of Hector and Ajax in the fourteenth, the appearance of Achilles unarmed and his heavenly armour in the eighteenth, and the funeral games in the twenty-third. I have also done some Hesiod, a little scrap of Thucydides, and a lot of the Greek Testament. . . . I wish there was only one dialect, all the same.

'I have done some mathematics, including the first six and the eleventh and twelfth books of Euclid; and algebra as far as simple equations.

'I know something of the Fathers, and something of Roman and English history.

'These things are only a beginning. But I shall not make much further advance here, from the difficulty of getting books. Hence I must next concentrate all my energies on settling in Christminster. Once there I shall so advance, with the assistance I shall there get, that my present knowledge will appear to me but as childish ignorance. I must save money, and I will; and one of those colleges shall open its doors to me – shall welcome whom now it would spurn, if I wait twenty years for the welcome.

'I'll be D.D. before I have done!'

And then he continued to dream, and thought he might become even a bishop by leading a pure, energetic, wise, Christian life. And what an example he would set! If his income were £5000 a year, he would give away £4500 in one form and another, and live sumptuously (for him) on the remainder. Well, on second thoughts, a bishop was absurd. He would draw the line at an archdeacon. Perhaps a man could be as good and as learned and as useful in the capacity of archdeacon as in that of bishop. Yet he thought of the bishop again.

'Meanwhile I will read, as soon as I am settled in Christminster, the books I have not been able to get hold of here: Livy, Tacitus, Herodotus, Æschylus, Sophocles, Aristophanes –'

'Ha, ha, ha! Hoity-toity!' The sounds were expressed in light voices on the other side of the hedge, but he did not notice them. His thoughts went on:

'– Euripides, Plato, Aristotle, Lucretius, Epictetus, Seneca, Antoninus. Then I must master other things: the Fathers thoroughly; Bede and ecclesiastical history generally; a smattering of Hebrew – I only know the letters as yet –'

'Hoity-toity!'

'– but I can work hard. I have staying power in abundance, thank

God! and it is that which tells. . . . Yes, Christminster shall be my
Alma Mater; and I'll be her beloved son,* in whom she shall be well
pleased.'

In his deep concentration on these transactions of the future
Jude's walk had slackened, and he was now standing quite still,
looking at the ground as though the future were thrown thereon by a
magic lantern. On a sudden something smacked him sharply in the
ear, and he became aware that a soft cold substance had been flung
at him, and had fallen at his feet.

A glance told him what it was – a piece of flesh, the characteristic
part of a barrow-pig,* which the countrymen used for greasing their
boots, as it was useless for any other purpose. Pigs were rather
plentiful hereabout, being bred and fattened in large numbers in
certain parts of North Wessex.

On the other side of the hedge was a stream, whence, as he now
for the first time realized, had come the slight sounds of voices and
laughter that had mingled with his dreams. He mounted the bank
and looked over the fence. On the further side of the stream stood a
small homestead, having a garden and pig-sties attached; in front of
it, beside the brook, three young women were kneeling, with buckets
and platters beside them containing heaps of pigs' chitterlings,*
which they were washing in the running water. One or two pairs of
eyes slyly glanced up, and perceiving that his attention had at last
been attracted, and that he was watching them, they braced themselves for inspection by putting their mouths demurely into shape
and recommencing their rinsing operations with assiduity.

'Thank you!' said Jude severely.

'I *didn't* throw it, I tell you!' asserted one girl to her neighbour,
as if unconscious of the young man's presence.

'Nor I,' the second answered.

'O, Anny, how can you!' said the third.

'If I had thrown anything at all, it shouldn't have been *that*!'

'Pooh! I don't care for him!' And they laughed and continued
their work, without looking up, still ostentatiously accusing each
other.

Jude grew sarcastic as he wiped his face, and caught their
remarks.

'*You* didn't do it — O no!' he said to the up-stream one of the three.

She whom he addressed was a fine dark-eyed girl, not exactly handsome, but capable of passing as such at a little distance, despite some coarseness of skin and fibre. She had a round and prominent bosom, full lips, perfect teeth, and the rich complexion of a Cochin hen's egg. She was a complete and substantial female animal — no more, no less; and Jude was almost certain that to her was attributable the enterprise of attracting his attention from dreams of the humaner letters to what was simmering in the minds around him.

'That you'll never be told,' said she deedily.*

'Whoever did it was wasteful of other people's property.'

'O, that's nothing.'

'But you want to speak to me, I suppose?'

'O yes; if you like to.'

'Shall I clamber across, or will you come to the plank above here?'

Perhaps she foresaw an opportunity; for somehow or other the eyes of the brown girl rested in his own when he had said the words, and there was a momentary flash of intelligence, a dumb announcement of affinity *in posse*,* between herself and him, which, so far as Jude Fawley was concerned, had no sort of premeditation in it. She saw that he had singled her out from the three, as a woman is singled out in such cases, for no reasoned purpose of further acquaintance, but in commonplace obedience to conjunctive orders* from headquarters, unconsciously received by unfortunate men when the last intention of their lives is to be occupied with the feminine.

Springing to her feet, she said: 'Bring back what is lying there.'

Jude was now aware that no message on any matter connected with her father's business had prompted her signal to him. He set down his basket of tools, picked up the scrap of offal, beat a pathway for himself with his stick, and got over the hedge. They walked in parallel lines, one on each bank of the stream, towards the small plank bridge. As the girl drew nearer to it, she gave, without Jude perceiving it, an adroit little suck to the interior of each of her cheeks in succession, by which curious and original manœuvre she brought as by magic upon its smooth and rotund surface a perfect dimple, which she was able to retain there as long as she continued to smile. This production of dimples at will was a not unknown operation, which many attempted, but only a few succeeded in accomplishing.

They met in the middle of the plank, and Jude, tossing back her missile, seemed to expect her to explain why she had audaciously stopped him by this novel artillery instead of by hailing him.

But she, slyly looking in another direction, swayed herself backwards and forwards on her hand as it clutched the rail of the bridge; till, moved by amatory curiosity, she turned her eyes critically upon him.

'You don't think *I* would shy things at you?'

'O no.'

'We are doing this for my father, who naturally doesn't want anything thrown away. He makes that into dubbin.' She nodded towards the fragment on the grass.

'What made either of the others throw it, I wonder?' Jude asked, politely accepting her assertion, though he had very large doubts as to its truth.

'Impudence. Don't tell folk it was I, mind!'

'How can I? I don't know your name.'

'Ah no. Shall I tell it to you?'

'Do!'

'Arabella Donn. I'm living here.'

'I must have known it if I had often come this way. But I mostly go straight along the high-road.'

'My father is a pig-breeder, and these girls are helping me wash the innerds for black-puddings and such like.'

They talked a little more and a little more, as they stood regarding each other and leaning against the hand-rail of the bridge. The unvoiced call of woman to man, which was uttered very distinctly by Arabella's personality, held Jude to the spot against his intention — almost against his will, and in a way new to his experience. It is scarcely an exaggeration to say that till this moment Jude had never looked at a woman to consider her as such, but had vaguely regarded the sex as beings outside his life and purposes. He gazed from her eyes to her mouth, thence to her bosom, and to her full round naked arms, wet, mottled with the chill of the water, and firm as marble.

'What a nice-looking girl you are!' he murmured, though the words had not been necessary to express his sense of her magnetism.

'Ah, you should see me Sundays!' she said piquantly.

'I don't suppose I could?' he answered.

'That's for you to think on. There's nobody after me just now, though there med be in a week or two.' She had spoken this without a smile, and the dimples disappeared.

Jude felt himself drifting strangely, but could not help it. 'Will you let me?'

'I don't mind.'

By this time she had managed to get back one dimple by turning her face aside for a moment and repeating the odd little sucking operation before mentioned, Jude being still unconscious of more than a general impression of her appearance. 'Next Sunday?' he hazarded. 'To-morrow, that is?'

'Yes.'

'Shall I call?'

'Yes.'

She brightened with a little glow of triumph, swept him almost tenderly with her eyes in turning, and retracing her steps down the brookside grass rejoined her companions.

Jude Fawley shouldered his tool-basket and resumed his lonely way, filled with an ardour at which he mentally stood at gaze. He had just inhaled a single breath from a new atmosphere, which had evidently been hanging round him everywhere he went, for he knew not how long, but had somehow been divided from his actual breathing as by a sheet of glass. The intentions as to reading, working, and learning, which he had so precisely formulated only a few minutes earlier, were suffering a curious collapse into a corner, he knew not how.

'Well, it's only a bit of fun,' he said to himself, faintly conscious that to common-sense there was something lacking, and still more obviously something redundant, in the nature of this girl who had drawn him to her, which made it necessary that he should assert mere sportiveness on his part as his reason in seeking her — something in her quite antipathetic to that side of him which had been occupied with literary study and the magnificent Christminster dream. It had been no vestal who chose *that* missile for opening her attack on him. He saw this with his intellectual eye, just for a short fleeting while, as by the light of a falling lamp one might momentarily see an inscription on a wall before being enshrouded in darkness. And then this passing discriminative power was withdrawn, and Jude was lost to all conditions of things in the advent of a fresh and wild pleasure, that of having found a new channel for emotional interest hitherto unsuspected, though it had lain close beside him. He was to meet this enkindling one of the other sex on the following Sunday.

Meanwhile the girl had joined her companions, and she silently resumed her flicking and sousing of the chitterlings in the pellucid stream.

'Catched un, my dear?' laconically asked the girl called Anny.

'I don't know. I wish I had thrown something else than that!' regretfully murmured Arabella.

'Lord! he's nobody, though you med think so. He used to drive old Drusilla Fawley's bread-cart out at Marygreen, till he 'prenticed himself at Alfredston. Since then he's been very stuck up, and always reading. He wants to be a scholar, they say.'

'O, I don't care what he is, or anything about 'n. Don't you think it, my child!'

'O, don't ye! You needn't try to deceive us! What did you stay talking to him for, if you didn't want un? Whether you do or whether you don't, he's as simple as a child. I could see it as you courted on the bridge, when he looked at 'ee as if he had never seen a woman before in his born days. Well, he's to be had by any woman who can get him to care for her a bit, if she likes to set herself to catch him the right way.'

THE next day Jude Fawley was pausing in his bedroom with the sloping ceiling, looking at the books on the table, and then at the black mark on the plaster above them, made by the smoke of his lamp in past months.

It was Sunday afternoon, four-and-twenty hours after his meeting with Arabella Donn. During the whole bygone week he had been resolving to set this afternoon apart for a special purpose, — the re-reading of his Greek Testament — his new one, with better type than his old copy, following Griesbach's text as amended by numerous correctors, and with variorum readings in the margin. He was proud of the book, having obtained it by boldly writing to its London publisher, a thing he had never done before.

He had anticipated much pleasure in this afternoon's reading, under the quiet roof of his great-aunt's house as formerly, where he now slept only two nights a week. But a new thing, a great hitch, had happened yesterday in the gliding and noiseless current of his life, and he felt as a snake must feel who has sloughed off its winter skin, and cannot understand the brightness and sensitiveness of its new one.

He would not go out to meet her, after all. He sat down, opened the book, and with his elbows firmly planted on the table, and his hands to his temples, began at the beginning:

Η ΚΑΙΝΗ ΔΙΑΘΗΚΗ *

Had he promised to call for her? Surely he had! She would wait indoors, poor girl, and waste all her afternoon on account of him. There was a something in her, too, which was very winning, apart from promises. He ought not to break faith with her. Even though he had only Sundays and week-day evenings for reading he could afford one afternoon, seeing that other young men afforded so many. After to-day he would never probably see her again. Indeed, it would be impossible, considering what his plans were.

In short, as if materially, a compelling arm of extraordinary muscular power seized hold of him – something which had nothing in common with the spirits and influence that had moved him hitherto. This seemed to care little for his reason and his will, nothing for his so-called elevated intentions, and moved him along, as a violent schoolmaster a schoolboy he has seized by the collar, in a direction which tended towards the embrace of a woman for whom he had no respect, and whose life had nothing in common with his own except locality.

H KAINH ΔIAΘHKH was no more heeded, and the predestinate Jude sprang up and across the room. Foreseeing such an event he had already arrayed himself in his best clothes. In three minutes he was out of the house and descending by the path across the wide vacant hollow of corn-ground which lay between the village and the isolated house of Arabella in the dip beyond the upland.

As he walked he looked at his watch. He could be back in two hours, easily, and a good long time would still remain to him for reading after tea.

Passing the few unhealthy fir-trees and cottage where the path joined the highway he hastened along, and struck away to the left, descending the steep side of the country to the west of the Brown House. Here at the base of the chalk formation he neared the brook that oozed from it, and followed the stream till he reached her dwelling. A smell of piggeries came from the back, and the grunting of the originators of that smell. He entered the garden, and knocked at the door with the knob of his stick.

Somebody had seen him through the window, for a male voice on the inside said:

'Arabella! Here's your young man come coorting! Mizzle,* my girl!'

Jude winced at the words. Courting in such a business-like aspect as it evidently wore to the speaker was the last thing he was thinking of. He was going to walk with her, perhaps kiss her; but 'courting' was too coolly purposeful to be anything but repugnant to his ideas. The door was opened and he entered, just as Arabella came downstairs in radiant walking attire.

'Take a chair, Mr What's-your-name?' said her father, an energetic, black-whiskered man, in the same business-like tones Jude had heard from outside.

'I'd rather go out at once, wouldn't you?' she whispered to Jude.

'Yes,' said he. 'We'll walk up to the Brown House and back, we can do it in half-an-hour.'

Arabella looked so handsome amid her untidy surroundings that he felt glad he had come, and all the misgivings vanished that had hitherto haunted him.

First they clambered to the top of the great down, during which ascent he had occasionally to take her hand to assist her. Then they bore off to the left along the crest into the ridgeway, which they followed till it intersected the high-road at the Brown House afore-said, the spot of his former fervid desires to behold Christminster. But he forgot them now. He talked the commonest local twaddle to Arabella with greater zest than he would have felt in discussing all the philosophies with all the Dons in the recently adored University, and passed the spot where he had knelt to Diana and Phœbus without remembering that there were any such people in the mythology, or that the Sun was anything else than a useful lamp for illuminating Arabella's face. An indescribable lightness of heel served to lift him along; and Jude, the incipient scholar, prospective D.D., Professor, Bishop, or what not, felt himself honoured and glorified by the condescension of this handsome country wench in agreeing to take a walk with him in her Sunday frock and ribbons.

They reached the Brown House barn — the point at which he had planned to turn back. While looking over the vast northern land-scape from this spot they were struck by the rising of a dense volume of smoke from the neighbourhood of the little town which lay beneath them at a distance of a couple of miles.

'It is a fire,' said Arabella. 'Let's run and see it — do! It is not far!'

The tenderness which had grown up in Jude's bosom left him no will to thwart her inclination now — which pleased him in affording him excuse for a longer time with her. They started off down the hill almost at a trot; but on gaining level ground at the bottom, and walking a mile, they found that the spot of the fire was much farther off than it had seemed.

Having begun their journey, however, they pushed on; but it was not till five o'clock that they found themselves on the scene, — the distance being altogether about half-a-dozen miles from Marygreen, and three from Arabella's. The conflagration had been got under by the time they reached it, and after a short inspection of the melancholy ruins they retraced their steps — their course lying through the town of Alfredston.

Arabella said she would like some tea, and they entered an inn of an inferior class, and gave their order. As it was not for beer they had a long time to wait. The maid-servant recognized Jude, and whispered her surprise to her mistress in the background, that he, the student, 'who kept hisself up so particular,' should have suddenly descended so low as to keep company with Arabella. The latter guessed what was being said, and laughed as she met the serious and tender gaze of her lover — the low and triumphant laugh of a careless woman who sees she is winning her game.

They sat and looked round the room, and at the picture of Samson and Delilah which hung on the wall, and at the circular beer-stains on the table, and at the spittoons underfoot filled with sawdust. The whole aspect of the scene had that depressing effect on Jude which few places can produce like a tap-room on a Sunday evening when the setting sun is slanting in, overnight smells linger, and no liquor is going, and the unfortunate wayfarer finds himself with no other haven of rest.

It began to grow dusk. They could not wait longer, really, for the tea, they said. 'Yet what else can we do?' asked Jude. 'It is a three-mile walk for you.'

'I suppose we can have some beer,' said Arabella.

'Beer, O yes. I had forgotten that. Somehow it seems odd to come to a public-house for beer on a Sunday evening.'

'But we didn't.'

'No, we didn't.' Jude by this time wished he was out of such an uncongenial atmosphere; but he ordered the beer, which was promptly brought.

Arabella tasted it. 'Ugh!' she said.

Jude tasted. 'What's the matter with it?' he asked. 'I don't understand beer very much now, it is true. I like it well enough, but it is bad to read on, and I find coffee better. But this seems all right.'

'Adulterated — I can't touch it!' She mentioned three or four ingredients that she detected in the liquor beyond malt and hops, much to Jude's surprise.

'How much you know!' he said good-humouredly.

Nevertheless she returned to the beer and drank her share, and they went on their way. It was now nearly dark, and as soon as they had withdrawn from the lights of the town they walked closer together, till they touched each other. She wondered why he did not put his arm round her waist, but he did not; he merely said what to himself seemed a quite bold enough thing: 'Take my arm.'

She took it, thoroughly, up to the shoulder. He felt the warmth of her body against his, and putting his stick under his other arm held with his right hand her right as it rested in its place.

'Now we are well together, dear, aren't we?' he observed.

'Yes,' said she; adding to herself: 'Rather mild!'

'How fast I have become!' he was thinking.

Thus they walked till they reached the foot of the upland, where they could see the white highway ascending before them in the gloom. From this point the only way of getting to Arabella's was by going up the incline, and dipping again into her valley on the right. Before they had climbed far they were nearly run into by two men who had been walking on the grass unseen.

'These lovers — you find 'em out o' doors in all seasons and weathers — lovers and homeless dogs only,' said one of the men as they vanished down the hill.

Arabella tittered lightly.

'Are we lovers?' asked Jude.

'You know best.'

'But you can tell me?'

For answer she inclined her head upon his shoulder. Jude took the hint, and encircling her waist with his arm, pulled her to him and kissed her.

They walked now no longer arm in arm but, as she had desired, clasped together. After all, what did it matter since it was dark, said Jude to himself. When they were half way up the long hill they paused as by arrangement, and he kissed her again. They reached the top, and he kissed her once more.

'You can keep your arm there, if you would like to,' she said gently.

He did so, thinking how trusting she was.

Thus they slowly went towards her home. He had left his cottage at half-past three, intending to be sitting down again to the New Testament by half-past five. It was nine o'clock when, with another embrace, he stood to deliver her up at her father's door.

She asked him to come in, if only for a minute, as it would seem so odd otherwise, and as if she had been out alone in the dark. He gave way, and followed her in. Immediately that the door was opened he found, in addition to her parents, several neighbours sitting round. They all spoke in a congratulatory manner, and took him seriously as Arabella's intended partner.

They did not belong to his set or circle, and he felt out of place and embarrassed. He had not meant this: a mere afternoon of pleasant walking with Arabella, that was all he had meant. He did not stay longer than to speak to her stepmother, a simple, quiet woman without features or character; and bidding them all good night plunged with a sense of relief into the track over the down.

But that sense was only temporary: Arabella soon reasserted her sway in his soul. He walked as if he felt himself to be another man from the Jude of yesterday. What were his books to him? what were his intentions, hitherto adhered to so strictly, as to not wasting a single minute of time day by day? 'Wasting!' It depended on your point of view to define that: he was just living for the first time: not wasting life. It was better to love a woman than to be a graduate, or a parson; ay, or a pope!

When he got back to the house his aunt had gone to bed, and a general consciousness of his neglect seemed written on the face of all things confronting him. He went upstairs without a light, and the dim interior of his room accosted him with sad inquiry. There lay his book open, just as he had left it, and the capital letters on the title-page regarded him with fixed reproach in the grey starlight, like the unclosed eyes of a dead man:

Η ΚΑΙΝΗ ΔΙΑΘΗΚΗΚ

Jude had to leave early next morning for his usual week of absence at lodgings; and it was with a sense of futility that he threw into his basket upon his tools and other necessaries the unread book he had brought with him.

He kept his impassioned doings a secret almost from himself. Arabella, on the contrary, made them public among all her friends and acquaintance.

Retracing by the light of dawn the road he had followed a few hours earlier under cover of darkness, with his sweetheart by his side, he reached the bottom of the hill, where he walked slowly, and stood still. He was on the spot where he had given her the first kiss. As the sun had only just risen it was possible that nobody had passed there since. Jude looked on the ground and sighed. He looked closely, and could just discern in the damp dust the imprints of their feet as they had stood locked in each other's arms. She was not there now, and 'the embroidery of imagination upon the stuff of nature' so depicted her past presence that a void was in his heart which nothing could fill. A pollard willow stood close to the place, and that willow was different from all other willows in the world. Utter annihilation of the six days which must elapse before he could see her again as he had promised would have been his intensest wish if he had had only the week to live.

An hour and half later Arabella came along the same way with her two companions of the Saturday. She passed unheedingly the scene of the kiss, and the willow that marked it, though chattering freely on the subject to the other two.

'And what did he tell 'ee next?'

'Then he said—' And she related almost word for word some of his tenderest speeches. If Jude had been behind the fence he would have felt not a little surprised at learning how very few of his sayings and doings on the previous evening were private.

'You've got him to care for 'ee a bit, 'nation if you han't!' murmured Anny judicially. 'It's well to be you!'

In a few moments Arabella replied in a curiously low, hungry tone of latent sensuousness: 'I've got him to care for me: yes! But I want him to more than care for me; I want him to have me – to marry me! I must have him. I can't do without him. He's the sort of man I long for. I shall go mad if I can't give myself to him altogether! I felt I should when I first saw him!'

'As he is a romancing, straightfor'ard, honest chap, he's to be had, and as a husband, if you set about catching him in the right way.'

Arabella remained thinking awhile. 'What med be the right way?' she asked.

'O you don't know — you don't!' said Sarah, the third girl.

'On my word I don't! — No further, that is, than by plain courting, and taking care he don't go too far!'

The third girl looked at the second. 'She *don't* know!'

''Tis clear she don't!' said Anny.

'And having lived in a town, too, as one may say! Well, we can teach 'ee som'at then, as well as you us.'

'Yes. And how do you mean — a sure way to gain a man? Take me for an innocent, and have done wi' it!'

'As a husband.'

'As a husband.'

'A countryman that's honourable and serious-minded such as he; God forbid that I should say a sojer, or sailor, or commercial gent from the towns, or any of them that be slippery with poor women! I'd do no friend that harm!'

'Well, such as he, of course!'

Arabella's companions looked at each other, and turning up their eyes in drollery began smirking. Then one went up close to Arabella, and, although nobody was near, imparted some information in a low tone, the other observing curiously the effect upon Arabella.

'Ah!' said the last-named slowly. 'I own I didn't think of that way! ... But suppose he *isn't* honourable? A woman had better not have tried it!'

'Nothing venture nothing have! Besides, you make sure that he's honourable before you begin. You'd be safe enough with yours. I wish I had the chance! Lots of girls do it; or do you think they'd get married at all?'

Arabella pursued her way in silent thought. 'I'll try it!' she whispered; but not to them.

ONE week's end Jude was as usual walking out to his aunt's at Marygreen from his lodging in Alfredston, a walk which now had large attractions for him quite other than his desire to see his aged and morose relative. He diverged to the right before ascending the hill with the single purpose of gaining, on his way, a glimpse of Arabella that should not come into the reckoning of regular appointments. Before quite reaching the homestead his alert eye perceived the top of her head moving quickly hither and thither over the garden hedge. Entering the gate he found that three young unfattened pigs had escaped from their sty by leaping clean over the top, and that she was endeavouring unassisted to drive them in through the door which she had set open. The lines of her countenance changed from the rigidity of business to the softness of love when she saw Jude, and she bent her eyes languishing upon him. The animals took advantage of the pause by doubling and bolting out of the way.

'They were only put in this morning!' she cried, stimulated to pursue in spite of her lover's presence. 'They were drove from Spaddleholt Farm only yesterday, where father bought 'em at a stiff price enough. They are wanting to get home again, the stupid toads! Will you shut the garden gate, dear, and help me to get 'em in? There are no men folk at home, only mother, and they'll be lost if we don't mind.'

He set himself to assist, and dodged this way and that over the potato rows and the cabbages. Every now and then they ran together, when he caught her for a moment and kissed her. The first pig was got back promptly; the second with some difficulty; the third, a long-legged creature, was more obstinate and agile. He plunged through a hole in the garden hedge, and into the lane.

'He'll be lost if I don't follow 'n!' said she. 'Come along with me!'

She rushed in full pursuit out of the garden, Jude alongside her, barely contriving to keep the fugitive in sight. Occasionally they would shout to some boy to stop the animal, but he always wriggled past and ran on as before.

'Let me take your hand, darling,' said Jude. 'You are getting out of breath.' She gave him her now hot hand with apparent willingness, and they trotted along together.

'This comes of driving 'em home,' she remarked. 'They always know the way back if you do that. They ought to have been carted over.'

By this time the pig had reached an unfastened gate admitting to the open down, across which he sped with all the agility his little legs afforded. As soon as the pursuers had entered and ascended to the top of the high ground it became apparent that they would have to run all the way to the farmer's if they wished to get at him. From this summit he could be seen as a minute speck, following an unerring line towards his old home.

'It is no good!' cried Arabella. 'He'll be there long before we get there. It don't matter now we know he's not lost or stolen on the way. They'll see it is ours, and send un back. O dear, how hot I be!'

Without relinquishing her hold of Jude's hand she swerved aside and flung herself down on the sod under a stunted thorn, precipitately pulling Jude on to his knees at the same time.

'O, I ask pardon — I nearly threw you down, didn't I! But I am so tired!'

She lay supine, and straight as an arrow, on the sloping sod of this hill-top, gazing up into the blue miles of sky, and still retaining her warm hold of Jude's hand. He reclined on his elbow near her.

'We've run all this way for nothing,' she went on, her form heaving and falling in quick pants, her face flushed, her full red lips parted, and a fine dew of perspiration on her skin. 'Well — why don't you speak, deary?'

'I'm blown too. It was all up hill.'

They were in absolute solitude — the most apparent of all solitudes, that of empty surrounding space. Nobody could be nearer than a mile to them without their seeing him. They were, in fact, on one of the summits of the county, and the distant landscape around Christminster could be discerned from where they lay. But Jude did not think of that then.

'O, I can see such a pretty thing up this tree,' said Arabella. 'A

sort of a — caterpillar, of the most loveliest green and yellow you
ever came across!'

'Where?' said Jude, sitting up.

'You can't see him there — you must come here,' said she.

He bent nearer and put his head in front of hers. 'No — I can't see
it,' he said.

'Why, on the limb there where it branches off — close to the
moving leaf — there!' She gently pulled him down beside her.

'I don't see it,' he repeated, the back of his head against her cheek.
'But I can, perhaps, standing up.' He stood accordingly, placing
himself in the direct line of her gaze.

'How stupid you are!' she said crossly, turning away her face.

'I don't care to see it, dear: why should I?' he replied, looking
down upon her. 'Get up, Abby.'

'Why?'

'I want you to let me kiss you. I've been waiting to ever so long!'

She rolled round her face, remained a moment looking deedily
aslant at him; then with a slight curl of the lip sprang to her feet, and
exclaiming abruptly 'I must mizzle!' walked off quickly homeward.
Jude followed and rejoined her.

'Just one!' he coaxed.

'Shan't!' she said.

He, surprised: 'What's the matter?'

She kept her two lips resentfully together, and Jude followed her
like a pet lamb till she slackened her pace and walked beside him,
talking calmly on indifferent subjects, and always checking him if he
tried to take her hand or clasp her waist. Thus they descended to the
precincts of her father's homestead, and Arabella went in, nodding
good-bye to him with a supercilious, affronted air.

'I expect I took too much liberty with her, somehow,' Jude said to
himself, as he withdrew with a sigh and went on to Marygreen.

On Sunday morning the interior of Arabella's home was, as
usual, the scene of a grand weekly cooking, the preparation of the
special Sunday dinner. Her father was shaving before a little glass
hung on the mullion of the window, and her mother and Arabella
herself were shelling beans hard by. A neighbour passed on her way
home from morning service at the nearest church, and seeing Donn
engaged at the window with the razor, nodded and came in.

She at once spoke playfully to Arabella: 'I zeed 'ee running with 'un – hee-hee! I hope 'tis coming to something?'

Arabella merely threw a look of consciousness into her face without raising her eyes.

'He's for Christminster, I hear, as soon as he can get there.'

'Have you heard that lately – quite lately?' asked Arabella with a jealous, tigerish indrawing of breath.

'O no! But it has been known a long time that it is his plan. He's on'y waiting here for an opening. Ah well: he must walk about with somebody I s'pose. Young men don't mean much now-a-days. 'Tis a sip here and a sip there with 'em. 'Twas different in my time.'

When the gossip had departed Arabella said suddenly to her mother: 'I want you and father to go and inquire how the Edlins be, this evening after tea. Or no – there's evening service at Fensworth – you can walk to that.'

'Oh? What's up to-night, then?'

'Nothing. Only I want the house to myself. He's shy; and I can't get un to come in when you are here. I shall let him slip through my fingers if I don't mind, much as I care for 'n!'

'If it is fine we med as well go, since you wish.'

In the afternoon Arabella met and walked with Jude, who had now for weeks ceased to look into a book of Greek, Latin, or any other tongue. They wandered up the slopes till they reached the green track along the ridge, which they followed to the circular British earth-bank adjoining, Jude thinking of the great age of the trackway, and of the drovers who had frequented it, probably before the Romans knew the country. Up from the level lands below them floated the chime of church bells. Presently they were reduced to one note, which quickened, and stopped.

'Now we'll go back,' said Arabella, who had attended to the sounds.

Jude assented. So long as he was near her he minded little where he was. When they arrived at her house he said lingeringly: 'I won't come in. Why are you in such a hurry to go in to-night? It is not near dark.'

'Wait a moment,' said she. She tried the handle of the door and found it locked.

'Ah – they are gone to church,' she added. And searching behind the scraper she found the key and unlocked the door. 'Now, you'll come in a moment?' she asked lightly. 'We shall be all alone.'

'Certainly,' said Jude with alacrity, the case being unexpectedly altered.

Indoors they went. Did he want any tea? No, it was too late: he would rather sit and talk to her. She took off her jacket and hat, and they sat down – naturally enough close together.

'Don't touch me, please,' she said softly. 'I am part egg-shell. Or perhaps I had better put it in a safe place.' She began unfastening the collar of her gown.

'What is it?' said her lover.

'An egg – a cochin's egg. I am hatching a very rare sort. I carry it about everywhere with me, and it will get hatched in less than three weeks.'

'Where do you carry it?'

'Just here.' She put her hand into her bosom and drew out the egg, which was wrapped in wool, outside it being a piece of pig's bladder, in case of accidents. Having exhibited it to him she put it back, 'Now mind you don't come near me. I don't want to get it broke, and have to begin another.'

'Why do you do such a strange thing?'

'It's an old custom. I suppose it is natural for a woman to want to bring live things into the world.'

'It is very awkward for me just now,' he said, laughing.

'It serves you right. There – that's all you can have of me.'

She had turned round her chair, and, reaching over the back of it, presented her cheek to him gingerly.

'That's very shabby of you!'

'You should have catched me a minute ago when I had put the egg down! There!' she said defiantly, 'I am without it now!' She had quickly withdrawn the egg a second time; but before he could quite reach her she had put it back as quickly, laughing with the excitement of her strategy. Then there was a little struggle, Jude making a plunge for it and capturing it triumphantly. Her face flushed; and becoming suddenly conscious he flushed also.

They looked at each other, panting; till he rose and said: 'One kiss, now I can do it without damage to property; and I'll go!'

But she had jumped up too. 'You must find me first!' she cried.

Her lover followed her as she withdrew. It was now dark inside the room, and the window being small he could not discover for a long time what had become of her, till a laugh revealed her to have rushed up the stairs, whither Jude rushed at her heels.

IT was some two months later in the year, and the pair had met constantly during the interval. Arabella seemed dissatisfied; she was always imagining, and waiting, and wondering.

One day she met the itinerant Vilbert. She, like all the cottagers thereabout, knew the quack well, and she began telling him of her experiences. Arabella had been gloomy, but before he left her she had grown brighter. That evening she kept an appointment with Jude, who seemed sad.

'I am going away,' he said to her. 'I think I ought to go. I think it will be better both for you and for me. I wish some things had never begun! I was much to blame, I know. But it is never too late to mend.'

Arabella began to cry. 'How do you know it is not too late?' she said. 'That's all very well to say! I haven't told you yet!' and she looked into his face with streaming eyes.

'What?' he asked, turning pale. 'Not . . . ?'

'Yes! And what shall I do if you desert me?'

'O Arabella — how can you say that, my dear! You *know* I wouldn't desert you!'

'Well then—'

'I have next to no wages as yet, you know; or perhaps I should have thought of this before. . . . But, of course, if that's the case, we must marry! What other thing do you think I could dream of doing?'

'I thought — I thought, deary, perhaps you would go away all the more for that, and leave me to face it alone!'

'You knew better! Of course I never dreamt six months ago, or even three, of marrying. It is a complete smashing up of my plans — I mean my plans before I knew you, my dear. But what are they, after all! Dreams about books, and degrees, and impossible fellowships, and all that. Certainly we'll marry: we must!'

That night he went out alone, and walked in the dark, self-

communing. He knew well, too well, in the secret centre of his
brain, that Arabella was not worth a great deal as a specimen of
womankind. Yet, such being the custom of the rural districts among
honourable young men who had drifted so far into intimacy with a
woman as he unfortunately had done, he was ready to abide by what
he had said, and take the consequences. For his own soothing he
kept up a factitious belief in her. His idea of her was the thing of
most consequence, not Arabella herself, he sometimes said laconically.

The banns were put in and published the very next Sunday. The
people of the parish all said what a simple fool young Fawley
was. All his reading had only come to this, that he would have to
sell his books to buy saucepans. Those who guessed the probable
state of affairs, Arabella's parents being among them, declared that
it was the sort of conduct they would have expected of such an
honest young man as Jude in reparation of the wrong he had done
his innocent sweetheart. The parson who married them seemed to
think it satisfactory too.

And so, standing before the aforesaid officiator, the two swore
that at every other time of their lives till death took them, they
would assuredly believe, feel, and desire precisely as they had
believed, felt, and desired during the few preceding weeks. What was
as remarkable as the undertaking itself was the fact that nobody
seemed at all surprised at what they swore.

Fawley's aunt being a baker she made him a bride-cake, saying
bitterly that it was the last thing she could do for him, poor silly
fellow; and that it would have been far better if, instead of his living
to trouble her, he had gone underground years before with his father
and mother. Of this cake Arabella took some slices, wrapped them
up in white note-paper, and sent them to her companions in the
pork-dressing business, Anny and Sarah, labelling each packet '*In
remembrance of good advice.*'

The prospects of the newly married couple were certainly not
very brilliant even to the most sanguine mind. He, a stone-mason's
apprentice, nineteen years of age, was working for half wages till he
should be out of his time. His wife was absolutely useless in a town-
lodging, where he at first had considered it would be necessary for
them to live. But the urgent need of adding to income in ever so little

a degree caused him to take a lonely roadside cottage between the Brown House and Marygreen, that he might have the profits of a vegetable garden, and utilize her past experiences by letting her keep a pig. But it was not the sort of life he had bargained for, and it was a long way to walk to and from Alfredston every day. Arabella, however, felt that all these makeshifts were temporary; she had gained a husband; that was the thing — a husband with a lot of earning power in him for buying her frocks and hats when he should begin to get frightened a bit, and stick to his trade, and throw aside those stupid books for practical undertakings.

So to the cottage he took her on the evening of the marriage, giving up his old room at his aunt's — where so much of the hard labour at Greek and Latin had been carried on.

A little chill overspread him at her first unrobing. A long tail of hair, which Arabella wore twisted up in an enormous knob at the back of her head, was deliberately unfastened, stroked out, and hung upon the looking-glass which he had bought her.

'What — it wasn't your own?' he said, with a sudden distaste for her.

'O no — it never is nowadays with the better class.'

'Nonsense! Perhaps not in towns. But in the country it is supposed to be different. Besides, you've enough of your own, surely?'

'Yes, enough as country notions go. But in towns the men expect more, and when I was barmaid at Aldbrickham—'

'Barmaid at Aldbrickham?'

'Well, not exactly barmaid — I used to draw the drink at a public-house there — just for a little time; that was all. Some people put me up to getting this, and I bought it just for a fancy. The more you have the better in Aldbrickham, which is a finer town than all your Christminsters. Every lady of position wears false hair — the barber's assistant told me so.'

Jude thought with a feeling of sickness that though this might be true to some extent, for all that he knew, many unsophisticated girls would and did go to towns and remain there for years without losing their simplicity of life and embellishments. Others, alas, had an instinct towards artificiality in their very blood, and became adepts in counterfeiting at the first glimpse of it. However, perhaps there was no great sin in a woman adding to her hair, and he resolved to think no more of it.

A new-made wife can usually manage to excite interest for a few weeks, even though the prospects of the household ways and means are cloudy. There is a certain piquancy about her situation, and her manner to her acquaintance at the sense of it, which carries off the gloom of facts, and renders even the humblest bride independent awhile of the real. Mrs Jude Fawley was walking in the streets of Alfredston one market-day with this quality in her carriage when she met Anny her former friend, whom she had not seen since the wedding.

As usual they laughed before talking; the world seemed funny to them without saying it.

'So it turned out a good plan you see!' remarked the girl to the wife. 'I knew it would with such as him. He's a dear good fellow, and you ought to be proud of un.'

'I am,' said Mrs Fawley quietly.

'And when do you expect——?'

'Ssh! Not at all.'

'What!'

'I was mistaken.'

'O Arabella, Arabella; you be a deep one! Mistaken! well, that's clever – it's a real stroke of genius! It is a thing I never thought o', wi' all my experience! I never thought beyond bringing about the real thing – not that one could sham it!'

'Don't you be too quick to cry sham! 'Twasn't sham. I didn't know.'

'My word – won't he be in a taking! He'll give it to 'ee o' Saturday nights! Whatever it was, he'll say it was a trick – a double one, by the Lord!'

'I'll own to the first, but not to the second. . . . Pooh – he won't care! He'll be glad I was wrong in what I said. He'll shake down, bless 'ee – men always do. What can 'em do otherwise? Married is married.'

Nevertheless it was with a little uneasiness that Arabella approached the time when in the natural course of things she would have to reveal that the alarm she had raised had been without foundation. The occasion was one evening at bed-time, and they were in their chamber in the lonely cottage by the wayside to which

Jude walked home from his work every day. He had worked hard the whole twelve hours, and had retired to rest before his wife. When she came into the room he was between sleeping and waking, and was barely conscious of her undressing before the little looking-glass as he lay.

One action of hers, however, brought him to full cognition. Her face being reflected towards him as she sat, he could perceive that she was amusing herself by artificially producing in each cheek the dimple before alluded to, a curious accomplishment of which she was mistress, effecting it by a momentary suction. It seemed to him for the first time that the dimples were far oftener absent from her face during his intercourse with her nowadays than they had been in the earlier weeks of their acquaintance.

'Don't do that, Arabella!' he said suddenly. 'There is no harm in it, but — I don't like to see you.'

She turned and laughed. 'Lord, I didn't know you were awake!' she said. 'How countrified you are! That's nothing.'

'Where did you learn it?'

'Nowhere that I know of. They used to stay without any trouble when I was at the public-house; but now they won't. My face was fatter then.'

'I don't care about dimples. I don't think they improve a woman — particularly a married woman, and of full-sized figure like you.'

'Most men think otherwise.'

'I don't care what most men think, if they do. How do you know?'

'I used to be told so when I was serving in the tap-room.'

'Ah — that public-house experience accounts for your knowing about the adulteration of the ale when we went and had some that Sunday evening. I thought when I married you that you had always lived in your father's house.'

'You ought to have known better than that, and seen I was a little more finished than I could have been by staying where I was born. There was not much to do at home, and I was eating my head off, so I went away for three months.'

'You'll soon have plenty to do now, dear, won't you?'

'How do you mean?'

'Why, of course — little things to make.'

'Oh.'

'When will it be? Can't you tell me exactly, instead of in such general terms as you have used?'

'Tell you?'

'Yes — the date.'

'There's nothing to tell. I made a mistake.'

'What?'

'It was a mistake.'

He sat bolt upright in bed and looked at her. 'How can that be?'

'Women fancy wrong things sometimes.'

'But—! Why, of course, so unprepared as I was, without a stick of furniture, and hardly a shilling, I shouldn't have hurried on our affair, and brought you to a half-furnished hut before I was ready, if it had not been for the news you gave me, which made it necessary to save you, ready or no. . . . Good God!'

'Don't take on, dear. What's done can't be undone.'

'I have no more to say!'

He gave the answer simply, and lay down; and there was silence between them.

When Jude awoke the next morning he seemed to see the world with a different eye. As to the point in question he was compelled to accept her word; in the circumstances he could not have acted otherwise while ordinary notions prevailed. But how came they to prevail?

There seemed to him, vaguely and dimly, something wrong in a social ritual which made necessary a cancelling of well-formed schemes involving years of thought and labour, of foregoing a man's one opportunity of showing himself superior to the lower animals, and of contributing his units of work to the general progress of his generation, because of a momentary surprise by a new and transitory instinct which had nothing in it of the nature of vice, and could be only at the most called weakness. He was inclined to inquire what he had done, or she lost, for that matter, that he deserved to be caught in a gin which would cripple him, if not her also, for the rest of a lifetime? There was perhaps something fortunate in the fact that the immediate reason of his marriage had proved to be non-existent. But the marriage remained.

THE time arrived for killing the pig which Jude and his wife had fattened in their sty during the autumn months, and the butchering was timed to take place as soon as it was light in the morning, so that Jude might get to Alfredston without losing more than a quarter of a day.

The night had seemed strangely silent. Jude looked out of the window long before dawn, and perceived that the ground was covered with snow — snow rather deep for the season, it seemed, a few flakes still falling.

'I'm afraid the pig-killer won't be able to come,' he said to Arabella.

'O, he'll come. You must get up and make the water hot, if you want Challow to scald him. Though I like singeing best.'

'I'll get up,' said Jude. 'I like the way of my own county.'

He went downstairs, lit the fire under the copper, and began feeding it with bean stalks, all the time without a candle, the blaze flinging a cheerful shine into the room; though for him the sense of cheerfulness was lessened by thoughts on the reason of that blaze — to heat water to scald the bristles from the body of an animal that as yet lived, and whose voice could be continually heard from a corner of the garden. At half-past six, the time of appointment with the butcher, the water boiled, and Jude's wife came downstairs.

'Is Challow come?' she asked.

'No.'

They waited, and it grew lighter, with the dreary light of a snowy dawn. She went out, gazed along the road, and returning said, 'He's not coming. Drunk last night, I expect. The snow is not enough to hinder him, surely!'

'Then we must put it off. It is only the water boiled for nothing. The snow may be deep in the valley.'

'Can't be put off. There's no more victuals for the pig. He ate the last mixing o' barleymeal yesterday morning.'

'Yesterday morning? What has he lived on since?'

'Nothing.'

'What — he has been starving?'

.'Yes. We always do it the last day or two, to save bother with the innerds. What ignorance, not to know that!'

'That accounts for his crying so. Poor creature!'

'Well — you must do the sticking — there's no help for it. I'll show you how. Or I'll do it myself — I think I could. Though as it is such a big pig I had rather Challow had done it. However, his basket o' knives and things have been already sent on here, and we can use 'em.'

'Of course you shan't do it,' said Jude. 'I'll do it, since it must be done.'

He went out to the sty, shovelled away the snow for the space of a couple of yards or more, and placed the stool in front, with the knives and ropes at hand. A robin peered down at the preparations from the nearest tree, and, not liking the sinister look of the scene, flew away, though hungry. By this time Arabella had joined her husband, and Jude, rope in hand, got into the sty, and noosed the affrighted animal, who, beginning with a squeak of surprise, rose to repeated cries of rage. Arabella opened the sty-door, and together they hoisted the victim on to the stool, legs upward, and while Jude held him Arabella bound him down, looping the cord over his legs to keep him from struggling.

The animal's note changed its quality. It was not now rage, but the cry of despair; long-drawn, slow and hopeless.

'Upon my soul I would sooner have gone without the pig than have had this to do!' said Jude. 'A creature I have fed with my own hands.'

'Don't be such a tender-hearted fool! There's the sticking-knife — the one with the point. Now whatever you do, don't stick un too deep.'

'I'll stick him effectually, so as to make short work of it. That's the chief thing.'

'You must not!' she cried. 'The meat must be well bled, and to do that he must die slow. We shall lose a shilling a score if the meat is red and bloody! Just touch the vein, that's all. I was brought up to it, and I know. Every good butcher keeps un bleeding long. He ought to be eight or ten minutes dying, at least.'

'He shall not be half a minute if I can help it, however the meat may look,' said Jude determinedly. Scraping the bristles from the pig's upturned throat, as he had seen the butchers do, he slit the fat; then plunged in the knife with all his might.

''Od damn it all!' she cried, 'that ever I should say it! You've over-stuck un! And I telling you all the time—'

'Do be quiet, Arabella, and have a little pity on the creature!'

'Hold up the pail to catch the blood, and don't talk!'

However unworkmanlike the deed, it had been mercifully done. The blood flowed out in a torrent instead of in the trickling stream she had desired. The dying animal's cry assumed its third and final tone, the shriek of agony; his glazing eyes riveting themselves on Arabella with the eloquently keen reproach of a creature recognizing at last the treachery of those who had seemed his only friends.

'Make un stop that!' said Arabella. 'Such a noise will bring somebody or other up here, and I don't want people to know we are doing it ourselves.' Picking up the knife from the ground whereon Jude had flung it, she slipped it into the gash, and slit the wind-pipe. The pig was instantly silent, his dying breath coming through the hole.

'That's better,' she said.

'It is a hateful business!' said he.

'Pigs must be killed.'

The animal heaved in a final convulsion, and, despite the rope, kicked out with all his last strength. A tablespoonful of black clot came forth, the trickling of red blood having ceased for some seconds.

'That's it; now he'll go,' said she. 'Artful creatures — they always keep back a drop like that as long as they can!'

The last plunge had come so unexpectedly as to make Jude stagger, and in recovering himself he kicked over the vessel in which the blood had been caught.

'There!' she cried, thoroughly in a passion. 'Now I can't make any blackpot.* There's a waste, all through you!'

Jude put the pail upright, but only about a third of the whole steaming liquid was left in it, the main part being splashed over the snow, and forming a dismal, sordid, ugly spectacle — to those who saw it as other than an ordinary obtaining of meat. The lips and nostrils of the animal turned livid, then white, and the muscles of his limbs relaxed.

'Thank God!' Jude said. 'He's dead.'

'What's God got to do with such a messy job as a pig-killing, I should like to know!' she said scornfully. 'Poor folks must live.'

'I know, I know,' said he. 'I don't scold you.'

Suddenly they became aware of a voice at hand.

'Well done, young married volk! I couldn't have carried it out much better myself, cuss me if I could!' The voice, which was husky, came from the garden-gate, and looking up from the scene of slaughter they saw the burly form of Mr Challow leaning over the gate, critically surveying their performance.

''Tis well for 'ee to stand there and glane!'* said Arabella. 'Owing to your being late the meat is blooded and half spoiled! 'Twon't fetch so much by a shilling a score!'

Challow expressed his contrition. 'You should have waited a bit,' he said, shaking his head, 'and not have done this – in the delicate state, too, that you be in at present, ma'am. 'Tis risking yourself too much.'

'You needn't be concerned about that,' said Arabella, laughing. Jude too laughed, but there was a strong flavour of bitterness in his amusement.

Challow made up for his neglect of the killing by zeal in the scalding and scraping. Jude felt dissatisfied with himself as a man at what he had done, though aware of his lack of common sense, and that the deed would have amounted to the same thing if carried out by deputy. The white snow, stained with the blood of his fellow-mortal, wore an illogical look to him as a lover of justice, not to say a Christian; but he could not see how the matter was to be mended. No doubt he was, as his wife had called him, a tender-hearted fool.

He did not like the road to Alfredston now. It stared him cynically in the face. The wayside objects reminded him so much of his courtship of his wife that, to keep them out of his eyes, he read whenever he could as he walked to and from his work. Yet he sometimes felt that by caring for books he was not escaping commonplace nor gaining rare ideas, every working-man being of that taste now. When passing near the spot by the stream on which he had first made her acquaintance he one day heard voices just as he had done at that earlier time. One of the girls who had been Arabella's companions was talking to a friend in a shed, himself being the subject of discourse, possibly because they had seen him in the distance. They were quite unaware that the shed-walls were so thin that he could hear their words as he passed.

'Howsomever, 'twas I put her up to it! "Nothing venture nothing have," I said. If I hadn't she'd no more have been his mis'ess than I.'

''Tis my belief she knew there was nothing the matter when she told him she was....'

What had Arabella been put up to by this woman, so that he should make her his 'mis'ess', otherwise wife? The suggestion was horridly unpleasant, and it rankled in his mind so much that instead of entering his own cottage when he reached it he flung his basket inside the garden-gate and passed on, determined to go and see his old aunt and get some supper there.

This made his arrival home rather late. Arabella, however, was busy melting down lard from fat of the deceased pig, for she had been out on a jaunt all day, and so delayed her work. Dreading lest what he had heard should lead him to say something regrettable to her he spoke little. But Arabella was very talkative, and said among other things that she wanted some money. Seeing the book sticking out of his pocket she added that he ought to earn more.

'An apprentice's wages are not meant to be enough to keep a wife on, as a rule, my dear.'

'Then you shouldn't have had one.'

'Come, Arabella! That's too bad, when you know how it came about.'

'I'll declare afore Heaven that I thought what I told you was true. Doctor Vilbert thought so. It was a good job for you that it wasn't so!'

'I don't mean that,' he said hastily. 'I mean before that time. I know it was not your fault; but those women friends of yours gave you bad advice. If they hadn't, or you hadn't taken it, we should at this moment have been free from a bond which, not to mince matters, galls both of us devilishly. It may be very sad, but it is true.'

'Who's been telling you about my friends? What advice? I insist upon your telling me.'

'Pooh — I'd rather not.'

'But you shall — you ought to. It is mean of 'ee not to!'

'Very well.' And he hinted gently what had been revealed to him. 'But I don't wish to dwell upon it. Let us say no more about it.'

Her defensive manner collapsed. 'That was nothing,' she said, laughing coldly. 'Every woman has a right to do such as that. The risk is hers.'

'I quite deny it, Bella. She might if no life-long penalty attached to it for the man, or, in his default, for herself; if the weakness of the moment could end with the moment, or even with the year. But when effects stretch so far she should not go and do that which entraps a man if he is honest, or herself if he is otherwise.'

'What ought I to have done?'

'Given me time. . . . Why do you fuss yourself about melting down that pig's fat to-night? Please put it away!'

'Then I must do it to-morrow morning. It won't keep.'

'Very well — do.'

NEXT morning, which was Sunday, she resumed operations about ten o'clock; and the renewed work recalled the conversation which had accompanied it the night before, and put her back into the same intractable temper.

'That's the story about me in Marygreen, is it – that I entrapped 'ee? Much of a catch you were, Lord send!' As she warmed she saw some of Jude's dear ancient classics on a table where they ought not to have been laid. 'I won't have them books here in the way!' she cried petulantly; and seizing them one by one she began throwing them upon the floor.

'Leave my books alone!' he said. 'You might have thrown them aside if you had liked, but as to soiling them like that, it is disgusting!' In the operation of making lard Arabella's hands had become smeared with the hot grease, and her fingers consequently left very perceptible imprints on the book-covers. She continued deliberately to toss the books severally upon the floor, till Jude, incensed beyond bearing, caught her by the arms to make her leave off. Somehow, in doing so, he loosened the fastening of her hair, and it rolled about her ears.

'Let me go!' she said.

'Promise to leave the books alone.'

She hesitated. 'Let me go!' she repeated.

'Promise!'

After a pause: 'I do.'

Jude relinquished his hold, and she crossed the room to the door, out of which she went with a set face, and into the highway. Here she began to saunter up and down, perversely pulling her hair into a worse disorder than he had caused, and unfastening several buttons of her gown. It was a fine Sunday morning, dry, clear and frosty, and the bells of Alfredston Church could be heard on the breeze from the north. People were going along the road, dressed in their holiday clothes; they were mainly lovers – such pairs as Jude and Arabella had been when they sported along the same track some

months earlier. These pedestrians turned to stare at the extraordinary spectacle she now presented, bonnetless, her dishevelled hair
blowing in the wind, her bodice apart, her sleeves rolled above her
elbows for her work, and her hands reeking with melted fat. One of
the passers said in mock terror: 'Good Lord deliver us!'

'See how he's served me!' she cried. 'Making me work Sunday
mornings when I ought to be going to my church, and tearing my
hair off my head, and my gown off my back!'

Jude was exasperated, and went out to drag her in by main force.
Then he suddenly lost his heat. Illuminated with the sense that all
was over between them, and that it mattered not what she did, or he,
her husband stood still, regarding her. Their lives were ruined, he
thought; ruined by the fundamental error of their matrimonial
union: that of having based a permanent contract on a temporary
feeling which had no necessary connection with affinities that alone
render a life-long comradeship tolerable.

'Going to ill-use me on principle, as your father ill-used your
mother, and your father's sister ill-used her husband?' she asked.
'All you be a queer lot as husbands and wives!'

Jude fixed an arrested, surprised look on her. But she said no
more, and continued her saunter till she was tired. He left the spot,
and, after wandering vaguely a little while, walked in the direction of
Marygreen. Here he called upon his great-aunt, whose infirmities
daily increased.

'Aunt – did my father ill-use my mother, and my aunt her
husband?' said Jude abruptly, sitting down by the fire.

She raised her ancient eyes under the rim of the bygone bonnet
that she always wore. 'Who's been telling you that?' she said.

'I have heard it spoken of, and want to know all.'

'You med so well, I s'pose; though your wife – I reckon 'twas she
– must have been a fool to open up that! There isn't much to know
after all. Your father and mother couldn't get on together, and they
parted. It was coming home from Alfredston market, when you
were a baby – on the hill by the Brown House barn – that they had
their last difference, and took leave of one another for the last time.
Your mother soon afterwards died – she drowned herself, in short,
and your father went away with you to South Wessex, and never
came here any more.'

Jude recalled his father's silence about North Wessex and Jude's mother, never speaking of either till his dying day.

'It was the same with your father's sister. Her husband offended her, and she so disliked living with him afterwards that she went away to London with her little maid. The Fawleys were not made for wedlock: it never seemed to sit well upon us. There's sommat in our blood that won't take kindly to the notion of being bound to do what we do readily enough if not bound. That's why you ought to have hearkened to me, and not ha' married.'

'Where did father and mother part – by the Brown House, did you say?'

'A little further on – where the road to Fensworth branches off, and the handpost stands. A gibbet once stood there not onconnected with our history. But let that be.'

In the dusk of that evening Jude walked away from his old aunt's as if to go home. But as soon as he reached the open down he struck out upon it till he came to a large round pond. The frost continued, though it was not particularly sharp, and the larger stars overhead came out slow and flickering. Jude put one foot on the edge of the ice, and then the other: it cracked under his weight; but this did not deter him. He ploughed his way inward to the centre, the ice making sharp noises as he went. When just about the middle he looked around him and gave a jump. The cracking repeated itself; but he did not go down. He jumped again, but the cracking had ceased. Jude went back to the edge, and stepped upon the ground.

It was curious, he thought. What was he reserved for? He supposed he was not a sufficiently dignified person for suicide. Peaceful death abhorred him as a subject, and would not take him.

What could he do of a lower kind than self-extermination; what was there less noble, more in keeping with his present degraded position? He could get drunk. Of course that was it; he had forgotten. Drinking was the regular, stereotyped resource of the despairing worthless. He began to see now why some men boozed at inns. He struck down the hill northwards and came to an obscure public-house. On entering and sitting down the sight of the picture of Samson and Delilah on the wall caused him to recognize the place as that he had visited with Arabella on that first Sunday evening of their courtship. He called for liquor and drank briskly for an hour or more.

Staggering homeward late that night, with all his sense of depression gone, and his head fairly clear still, he began to laugh boisterously, and to wonder how Arabella would receive him in his new aspect. The house was in darkness when he entered, and in his stumbling state it was some time before he could get a light. Then he found that, though the marks of pig-dressing, of fats and scallops,★ were visible, the materials themselves had been taken away. A line written by his wife on the inside of an old envelope was pinned to the cotton blower ★ of the fireplace:

'*Have gone to my friends. Shall not return.*'

All the next day he remained at home, and sent off the carcase of the pig to Alfredston. He then cleaned up the premises, locked the door, put the key in a place she would know if she came back, and returned to his masonry at Alfredston.

At night when he again plodded home he found she had not visited the house. The next day went in the same way, and the next. Then there came a letter from her.

That she had grown tired of him she frankly admitted. He was such a slow old coach, and she did not care for the sort of life he led. There was no prospect of his ever bettering himself or her. She further went on to say that her parents had, as he knew, for some time considered the question of emigrating to Australia, the pig-jobbing★ business being a poor one nowadays. They had at last decided to go, and she proposed to go with them, if he had no objection. A woman of her sort would have more chance over there than in this stupid country.

Jude replied that he had not the least objection to her going. He thought it a wise course, since she wished to go, and one that might be to the advantage of both. He enclosed in the packet containing the letter the money that had been realized by the sale of the pig, with all he had besides, which was not much.

From that day he heard no more of her except indirectly, though her father and his household did not immediately leave, but waited till his goods and other effects had been sold off. When Jude learnt that there was to be an auction at the house of the Donns he packed his own household goods into a waggon, and sent them to her at the aforesaid homestead, that she might sell them with the rest, or as many of them as she should choose.

He then went into lodgings at Alfredston, and saw in a shop-window the little handbill announcing the sale of his father-in-law's furniture. He noted its date, which came and passed without Jude's going near the place, or perceiving that the traffic out of Alfredston by the southern road was materially increased by the auction. A few days later he entered a dingy broker's shop in the main street of the town, and amid a heterogeneous collection of saucepans, a clothes-horse, rolling pin, brass candlestick, swing looking-glass, and other things at the back of the shop, evidently just brought in from a sale, he perceived a framed photograph, which turned out to be his own portrait.

It was one which he had had specially taken and framed by a local man in bird's-eye maple, as a present for Arabella, and had duly given her on their wedding-day. On the back was still to be read, '*Jude to Arabella*', with the date. She must have thrown it in with the rest of her property at the auction.

'Oh,' said the broker, seeing him look at this and the other articles in the heap, and not perceiving that the portrait was of himself: 'It is a small lot of stuff that was knocked down to me at a cottage sale out on the road to Marygreen. The frame is a very useful one, if you take out the likeness. You shall have it for a shilling.'

The utter death of every tender sentiment in his wife, as brought home to him by this mute and undesigned evidence of her sale of his portrait and gift, was the conclusive little stroke required to demolish all sentiment in him. He paid the shilling, took the photograph away with him, and burnt it, frame and all, when he reached his lodging.

Two or three days later he heard that Arabella and her parents had departed. He had sent a message offering to see her for a formal leave-taking, but she had said that it would be better otherwise, since she was bent on going, which perhaps was true. On the evening following their emigration, when his day's work was done, he came out of doors after supper, and strolled in the starlight along the too familiar road towards the upland whereon had been experienced the chief emotions of his life. It seemed to be his own again.

He could not realize himself. On the old track he seemed to be a boy still, hardly a day older than when he had stood dreaming at the top of that hill, inwardly fired for the first time with ardours for Christminster and scholarship. 'Yet I am a man, he said. 'I have a wife. More, I have arrived at the still riper stage of having disagreed with her, disliked her, had a scuffle with her, and parted from her.'

He remembered then that he was standing not far from the spot at which the parting between his father and his mother was said to have occurred.

A little further on was the summit whence Christminster, or what · he had taken for that city, had seemed to be visible. A milestone, now as always, stood at the roadside hard by. Jude drew near it, and felt rather than read the mileage to the city. He remembered that once on his way home he had proudly cut with his keen new chisel an inscription on the back of that milestone, embodying his aspirations. It had been done in the first week of his apprenticeship, before he had been diverted from his purposes by an unsuitable woman. He wondered if the inscription were legible still, and going to the back of the milestone brushed away the nettles. By the light of a match he could still discern what he had cut so enthusiastically so long ago:

THITHER ☞
J. F.

The sight of it, unimpaired, within its screen of grass and nettles, lit in his soul a spark of the old fire. Surely his plan should be to move onward through good and ill — to avoid morbid sorrow even though he did see uglinesses in the world? *Bene agere et lætari* — to do good cheerfully — which he had heard to be the philosophy of one Spinoza, might be his own even now.

He might battle with his evil star, and follow out his original intention. ·

By moving to a spot a little way off he uncovered the horizon in a north-easterly direction. There actually rose the faint halo, a small dim nebulousness, hardly recognizable save by the eye of faith. It was enough for him. He would go to Christminster as soon as the term of his apprenticeship expired.

He returned to his lodgings in a better mood, and said his prayers.

PART SECOND

At Christminster

'*Save his own soul he hath no star.*' — SWINBURNE

'*Notitiam primosque gradus vicinia fecit;*
Tempore crevit amor.' — OVID

THE next noteworthy move in Jude's life was that in which he appeared gliding steadily onward through a dusky landscape of some three years' later leafage than had graced his courtship of Arabella, and the disruption of his coarse conjugal life with her. He was walking towards Christminster City, at a point a mile or two to the south-west of it.

He had at last found himself clear of Marygreen and Alfredston: he was out of his apprenticeship, and with his tools at his back seemed to be in the way of making a new start – the start to which, barring the interruption involved in his intimacy and married experience with Arabella, he had been looking forward for about ten years.

Jude would now have been described as a young man with a forcible, meditative, and earnest rather than handsome cast of countenance. He was of dark complexion, with dark harmonizing eyes, and he wore a closely trimmed black beard of more advanced growth than is usual at his age; this, with his great mass of black curly hair, was some trouble to him in combing and washing out the stone-dust that settled on it in the pursuit of his trade. His capabilities in the latter, having been acquired in the country, were of an all-round sort, including monumental stone-cutting, gothic free-stone work for the restoration of churches, and carving of a general kind. In London he would probably have become specialized and have made himself a 'moulding mason', a 'foliage sculptor' – perhaps a 'statuary'.

He had that afternoon driven in a cart from Alfredston to the village nearest the city in this direction, and was now walking the remaining four miles rather from choice than from necessity, having always fancied himself arriving thus.

The ultimate impulse to come had had a curious origin – one more nearly related to the emotional side of him than to the intellectual, as is often the case with young men. One day while in lodgings at Alfredston he had gone to Marygreen to see his old aunt, and had observed between the brass candlesticks on her mantelpiece the photograph of a pretty girlish face, in a broad hat with radiating folds under the brim like the rays of a halo. He had asked who she was. His grand-aunt had gruffly replied that she was his cousin Sue Bridehead, of the inimical branch of the family; and on further questioning the old woman had replied that the girl lived in Christminster, though she did not know where, or what she was doing.

His aunt would not give him the photograph. But it haunted him; and ultimately formed a quickening ingredient in his latent intent of following his friend the schoolmaster thither.

He now paused at the top of a crooked and gentle declivity, and obtained his first near view of the city. Grey stoned and dun-roofed, it stood within hail of the Wessex border, and almost with the tip of one small toe within it, at the northernmost point of the crinkled line along which the leisurely Thames strokes the fields of that ancient kingdom. The buildings now lay quiet in the sunset, a vane here and there on their many spires and domes giving sparkle to a picture of sober secondary and tertiary hues.

Reaching the bottom he moved along the level way between pollard willows growing indistinct in the twilight, and soon confronted the outmost lamps of the town — some of those lamps which had sent into the sky the gleam and glory that caught his strained gaze in his days of dreaming, so many years ago. They winked their yellow eyes at him dubiously, and as if, though they had been awaiting him all these years in disappointment at his tarrying, they did not much want him now.

He was a species of Dick Whittington * whose spirit was touched to finer issues than a mere material gain. He went along the outlying streets with the cautious tread of an explorer. He saw nothing of the real city in the suburbs on this side. His first want being a lodging he scrutinized carefully such localities as seemed to offer on inexpensive terms the modest type of accommodation he demanded; and after inquiry took a room in a suburb nick-named 'Beersheba',* though he did not know this at the time. Here he installed himself, and having had some tea sallied forth.

It was a windy, whispering, moonless night. To guide himself he opened under a lamp a map he had brought. The breeze ruffled and fluttered it, but he could see enough to decide on the direction he should take to reach the heart of the place.

After many turnings he came up to the first ancient mediæval pile that he had encountered. It was a college, as he could see by the gateway. He entered it, walked round, and penetrated to dark corners which no lamplight reached. Close to this college was another; and a little further on another; and then he began to be encircled as it were with the breath and sentiment of the venerable city. When he passed objects out of harmony with its general expression he allowed his eyes to slip over them as if he did not see them.

A bell began clanging,* and he listened till a hundred-and-one strokes had sounded. He must have made a mistake, he thought: it was meant for a hundred.

When the gates were shut, and he could no longer get into the quadrangles, he rambled under the walls and doorways, feeling with his fingers the contours of their mouldings and carving. The minutes passed, fewer and fewer people were visible, and still he serpentined among the shadows, for had he not imagined these scenes through ten bygone years, and what mattered a night's rest for once? High against the black sky the flash of a lamp would show crocketed pinnacles and indented battlements. Down obscure alleys, apparently never trodden now by the foot of man, and whose very existence seemed to be forgotten, there would jut into the path porticoes, oriels, doorways of enriched and florid middle-age design, their extinct air being accentuated by the rottenness of the stones. It seemed impossible that modern thought could house itself in such decrepit and superseded chambers.

Knowing not a human being here, Jude began to be impressed with the isolation of his own personality, as with a self-spectre, the sensation being that of one who walked but could not make himself seen or heard. He drew his breath pensively, and, seeming thus almost his own ghost, gave his thoughts to the other ghostly presences with which the nooks were haunted.

During the interval of preparation for this venture, since his wife and furniture's uncompromising disappearance into space, he had read and learnt almost all that could be read and learnt by one in his position, of the worthies who had spent their youth within these reverend walls, and whose souls had haunted them in their maturer age. Some of them, by the accidents of his reading, loomed out in his fancy disproportionately large by comparison with the rest. The brushings of the wind against the angles, buttresses, and door-jambs were as the passing of these only other inhabitants, the tappings of each ivy leaf on its neighbour were as the mutterings of their mournful souls, the shadows as their thin shapes in nervous movement, making him comrades in his solitude. In the gloom it was as if he ran against them without feeling their bodily frames.

The streets were now deserted, but on account of these things he could not go in. There were poets abroad, of early date and of late, from the friend and eulogist of Shakespeare * down to him who has recently passed into silence,* and that musical one * of the tribe who is still among us. Speculative philosophers drew along, not always with wrinkled foreheads and hoary hair as in framed portraits, but pink-faced, slim, and active as in youth; modern divines sheeted in their surplices, among whom the most real to Jude Fawley were the founders of the religious school called Tractarian; the well-known three,* the enthusiast, the poet, and the formularist, the echoes of whose teachings had influenced him even in his obscure home. A start of aversion appeared in his fancy to move them at sight of those other sons of the place, the form in the full-bottomed wig,* statesman, rake, reasoner, and sceptic; the smoothly shaven historian * so ironically civil to Christianity; with others of the same incredulous temper, who knew each quad as well as the faithful, and took equal freedom in haunting its cloisters.

He regarded the statesmen in their various types, men of firmer movement and less dreamy air; the scholar, the speaker, the plodder; the man whose mind grew with his growth in years, and the man whose mind contracted with the same.

The scientists and philologists followed on in his mind-sight in an odd impossible combination, men of meditative faces, strained foreheads, and weak-eyed as bats with constant research; then official characters – such men as Governor-Generals and Lord-Lieutenants, in whom he took little interest; Chief-Justices and Lord Chancellors, silent thin-lipped figures of whom he knew barely the names. A keener regard attached to the prelates, by reason of his own former hopes. Of them he had an ample band – some men of heart, others rather men of head; he who apologized for the Church in Latin;* the saintly author of the Evening Hymn;* and near them the great itinerant preacher,* hymn-writer, and zealot, shadowed like Jude by his matrimonial difficulties.

Jude found himself speaking out loud, holding conversations with them as it were, like an actor in a melodrama who apostrophizes the audience on the other side of the footlights; till he suddenly ceased with a start at his absurdity. Perhaps those incoherent words of the wanderer were heard within the walls by some student or thinker over his lamp; and he may have raised his head, and wondered what voice it was, and what it betokened. Jude now perceived that, so far as solid flesh went, he had the whole aged city to himself with the exception of a belated townsman here and there, and that he seemed to be catching a cold.

A voice reached him out of the shade; a real and local voice:

'You've been a-settin' a long time on that plinth-stone, young man. What med you be up to?'

It came from a policeman who had been observing Jude without the latter observing him.

Jude went home and to bed, after reading up a little about these men and their several messages to the world from a book or two that he had brought with him concerning the sons of the University. As he drew towards sleep various memorable words of theirs that he had just been conning seemed spoken by them in muttering utterances; some audible, some unintelligible to him. One of the spectres* (who afterwards mourned Christminster as 'the home of lost causes', though Jude did not remember this) was now apostrophizing her thus:

'Beautiful city! so venerable, so lovely, so unravaged by the fierce intellectual life of our century, so serene! . . . Her ineffable charm keeps ever calling us to the true goal of all of us, to the ideal, to perfection.'

Another voice was that of the Corn Law convert,* whose phantom he had just seen in the quadrangle with a great bell. Jude thought his soul might have been shaping the historic words of his master-speech:

'Sir, I may be wrong, but my impression is that my duty towards a country threatened with famine requires that that which has been the ordinary remedy under all similar circumstances should be resorted to now, namely, that there should be free access to the food of man from whatever quarter it may come. . . . Deprive me of office to-morrow, you can never deprive me of the consciousness that I have exercised the powers committed to me from no corrupt or interested motives, from no desire to gratify ambition, for no personal gain.'

Then the sly author＊ of the immortal Chapter on Christianity: 'How shall we excuse the supine inattention of the Pagan and philosophic world, to those evidences [miracles] which were presented by Omnipotence? . . . The sages of Greece and Rome turned aside from the awful spectacle, and appeared unconscious of any alterations in the moral or physical government of the world.'

Then the shade of the poet, the last of the optimists:＊

> 'How the world is made for each of us!
>
> . . .
>
> And each of the Many helps to recruit
> The life of the race by a general plan.'

Then one of the three enthusiasts he had seen just now, the author of the *Apologia*:＊

'My argument was . . . that absolute certitude as to the truths of natural theology was the result of an assemblage of concurring and converging probabilities . . . that probabilities which did not reach to logical certainty might create a mental certitude.'

The second of them, no polemic, murmured quieter things:

> 'Why should we faint, and fear to live alone,
> Since all alone, so Heaven has will'd, we die?'＊

He likewise heard some phrases spoken by the phantom with the short face, the genial Spectator:＊

'When I look upon the tombs of the great, every motion of envy dies in me; when I read the epitaphs of the beautiful, every inordinate desire goes out; when I meet with the grief of parents upon a tombstone, my heart melts with compassion; when I see the tombs of the parents themselves, I consider the vanity of grieving for those whom we must quickly follow.'

And lastly a gentle-voiced prelate spoke, during whose meek,

familiar rhyme, endeared to him from earliest childhood, Jude fell
asleep:

> 'Teach me to live, that I may dread
> The grave as little as my bed.
> Teach me to die....'*

He did not wake till morning. The ghostly past seemed to have
gone, and everything spoke of to-day. He started up in bed, thinking
he had overslept himself, and then said:

'By Jove — I had quite forgotten my sweet-faced cousin, and that
she's here all the time! ... and my old schoolmaster, too.' His words
about his school-master had, perhaps, less zest in them than his
words concerning his cousin.

NECESSARY meditations on the actual, including the mean bread-and-cheese question; dissipated the phantasmal for a while, and compelled Jude to smother high thinkings under immediate needs. He had to get up, and seek for work, manual work; the only kind deemed by many of its professors to be work at all.

Passing out into the streets on this errand he found that the colleges had treacherously changed their sympathetic countenances: some were pompous; some had put on the look of family vaults above ground; something barbaric loomed in the masonries of all. The spirits of the great men had disappeared.

The numberless architectural pages around him he read, naturally, less as an artist-critic of their forms than as an artizan and comrade of the dead handicraftsmen whose muscles had actually executed those forms. He examined the mouldings, stroked them as one who knew their beginning, said they were difficult or easy in the working, had taken little or much time, were trying to the arm, or convenient to the tool.

What at night had been perfect and ideal was by day the more or less defective real. Cruelties, insults, had, he perceived, been inflicted on the aged erections. The condition of several moved him as he would have been moved by maimed sentient beings. They were wounded, broken, sloughing off their outer shape in the deadly struggle against years, weather, and man.

The rottenness of these historical documents reminded him that he was not, after all, hastening on to begin the morning practically as he had intended. He had come to work, and to live by work, and the morning had nearly gone. It was, in one sense, encouraging to think that in a place of crumbling stones there must be plenty for one of his trade to do in the business of renovation. He asked his way to the workyard of the stone-mason whose name had been given him at Alfredston; and soon heard the familiar sound of the rubbers and chisels.

The yard was a little centre of regeneration. Here, with keen edges and smooth curves, were forms in the exact likeness of those he had seen abraded and time-eaten on the walls. These were the ideas in modern prose which the lichened colleges presented in old poetry. Even some of those antiques might have been called prose when they were new. They had done nothing but wait, and had become poetical. How easy to the smallest building; how impossible to most men.

He asked for the foreman, and looked round among the new traceries, mullions, transoms, shafts, pinnacles, and battlements standing on the bankers * half worked, or waiting to be removed. They were marked by precision, mathematical straightness, smoothness, exactitude: there in the old walls were the broken lines of the original idea; jagged curves, disdain of precision, irregularity, disarray.

For a moment there fell on Jude a true illumination; that here in the stone yard was a centre of effort as worthy as that dignified by the name of scholarly study within the noblest of the colleges. But he lost it under stress of his old idea. He would accept any employment which might be offered him on the strength of his late employer's recommendation; but he would accept it as a provisional thing only. This was his form of the modern vice of unrest.

Moreover he perceived that at best only copying, patching and imitating went on here; which he fancied to be owing to some temporary and local cause. He did not at that time see that mediæ-valism was as dead as a fern-leaf in a lump of coal; that other developments were shaping in the world around him, in which Gothic architecture and its associations had no place. The deadly animosity of contemporary logic and vision towards so much of what he held in reverence was not yet revealed to him.

Having failed to obtain work here as yet he went away, and thought again of his cousin, whose presence somewhere at hand he seemed to feel in wavelets of interest, if not of emotion. How he wished he had that pretty portrait of her! At last he wrote to his aunt to send it. She did so, with a request, however, that he was not to bring disturbance into the family by going to see the girl or her relations. Jude, a ridiculously affectionate fellow, promised nothing, put the photograph on the mantelpiece, kissed it — he did not know why — and felt more at home. She seemed to look down and preside over his tea. It was cheering — the one thing uniting him to the emotions of the living city.

There remained the schoolmaster — probably now a reverend parson. But he could not possibly hunt up such a respectable man just yet; so raw and unpolished was his condition, so precarious were his fortunes. Thus he still remained in loneliness. Although people moved round him he virtually saw none. Not as yet having mingled with the active life of the place it was largely non-existent to him. But the saints and prophets in the window-tracery, the paintings in the galleries, the statues, the busts, the gurgoyles, the corbel-heads — these seemed to breathe his atmosphere. Like all new comers to a spot on which the past is deeply graven he heard that past announcing itself with an emphasis altogether unsuspected by, and even incredible to, the habitual residents.

For many days he haunted the cloisters and quadrangles of the colleges at odd minutes in passing them, surprised by impish echoes of his own footsteps, smart as the blows of a mallet. The Christminster 'sentiment', as it had been called, ate further and further into him; till he probably knew more about those buildings materially, artistically, and historically, than any one of their inmates.

It was not till now, when he found himself actually on the spot of his enthusiasm, that Jude perceived how far away from the object of that enthusiasm he really was. Only a wall divided him from those happy young contemporaries of his with whom he shared a common mental life; men who had nothing to do from morning till night but to read, mark, learn, and inwardly digest.* Only a wall — but what a wall!

Every day, every hour, as he went in search of labour, he saw them going and coming also, rubbed shoulders with them, heard their voices, marked their movements. The conversation of some of the more thoughtful among them seemed oftentimes, owing to his long and persistent preparation for this place, to be peculiarly akin to his own thoughts. Yet he was as far from them as if he had been at the antipodes. Of course he was. He was a young workman in a white blouse, and with stone-dust in the creases of his clothes; and in passing him they did not even see him, or hear him, rather saw

through him as through a pane of glass at their familiars beyond.
Whatever they were to him, he to them was not on the spot at all;
and yet he had fancied he would be close to their lives by coming
there.

But the future lay ahead after all; and if he could only be so
fortunate as to get into good employment he would put up with the
inevitable. So he thanked God for his health and strength, and took
courage. For the present he was outside the gates of everything,
colleges included: perhaps some day he would be inside. Those
palaces of light and leading; he might some day look down on the
world through their panes.

At length he did receive a message from the stonemason's yard —
that a job was waiting for him. It was his first encouragement, and
he closed with the offer promptly.

He was young and strong, or he never could have executed with
such zest the undertakings to which he now applied himself, since
they involved reading most of the night after working all the day.
First he bought a shaded lamp for four and sixpence, and obtained a
good light. Then he got pens, paper, and such other necessary books
as he had been unable to obtain elsewhere. Then, to the consternation of his landlady, he shifted all the furniture of his room — a
single one for living and sleeping — rigged up a curtain on a rope
across the middle, to make a double chamber out of one, hung up a
thick blind that nobody should know how he was curtailing the
hours of sleep, laid out his books, and sat down.

Having been deeply encumbered by marrying, getting a cottage,
and buying the furniture which had disappeared in the wake of his
wife, he had never been able to save any money since the time of
those disastrous ventures, and till his wages began to come in he was
obliged to live in the narrowest way. After buying a book or two he
could not even afford himself a fire; and when the nights reeked with
the raw and cold air from the Meadows he sat over his lamp in a
great-coat, hat, and woollen gloves.

From his window he could perceive the spire of the Cathedral,
and the ogee dome* under which resounded the great bell of the
city. The tall tower, tall belfry windows, and tall pinnacles of the
college by the bridge he could also get a glimpse of by going to the
staircase. These objects he used as stimulants when his faith in the

future was dim.

Like enthusiasts in general he made no inquiries into details of procedure. Picking up general notions from casual acquaintance, he never dwelt upon them. For the present, he said to himself, the one thing necessary was to get ready by accumulating money and knowledge, and await whatever chances were afforded to such an one of becoming a son of the University. 'For wisdom is a defence, and money is a defence; but the excellency of knowledge is, that wisdom giveth life to them that have it.' * His desire absorbed him, and left no part of him to weigh its practicability.

At this time he received a nervously anxious letter from his poor old aunt, on the subject which had previously distressed her – a fear that Jude would not be strong-minded enough to keep away from his cousin Sue Bridehead and her relations. Sue's father, his aunt believed, had gone back to London, but the girl remained at Christminster. To make her still more objectionable she was an artist or designer of some sort in what was called an ecclesiastical warehouse, which was a perfect seed-bed of idolatry, and she was no doubt abandoned to mummeries on that account – if not quite a Papist. (Miss Drusilla Fawley was of her date, Evangelical.*)

As Jude was rather on an intellectual track than a theological, this news of Sue's probable opinions did not much influence him one way or the other, but the clue to her whereabouts was decidedly interesting. With an altogether singular pleasure he walked at his earliest spare minutes past the shops answering to his great-aunt's description; and beheld in one of them a young girl sitting behind a desk, who was suspiciously like the original of the portrait. He ventured to enter on a trivial errand, and having made his purchase lingered on the scene. The shop seemed to be kept entirely by women. It contained Anglican books, stationery, texts, and fancy goods: little plaster angels on brackets, Gothic-framed pictures of saints, ebony crosses that were almost crucifixes, prayer-books that were almost missals. He felt very shy of looking at the girl in the desk; she was so pretty that he could not believe it possible that she should belong to him. Then she spoke to one of the two older women behind the counter; and he recognized in the accents certain qualities of his own voice; softened and sweetened, but his own. What was she doing? He stole a glance round. Before her lay a piece of zinc, cut to the shape of a scroll three or four feet long, and coated with a dead-surface paint on one side. Hereon she was designing or illuminating, in characters of Church text, the single word

𝔄𝔩𝔩𝔢𝔩𝔲𝔧𝔞

'A sweet, saintly, Christian business, hers!' thought he.

Her presence here was now fairly enough explained, her skill in work of this sort having no doubt been acquired from her father's occupation as an ecclesiastical worker in metal. The lettering on which she was engaged was clearly intended to be fixed up in some chancel to assist devotion.

He came out. It would have been easy to speak to her there and then, but it seemed scarcely honourable towards his aunt to disregard her request so incontinently. She had used him roughly, but she had brought him up: and the fact of her being powerless to control him lent a pathetic force to a wish that would have been inoperative as an argument.

So Jude gave no sign. He would not call upon Sue just yet. He had other reasons against doing so when he had walked away. She seemed so dainty beside himself in his rough working-jacket and dusty trousers that he felt he was as yet unready to encounter her, as he had felt about Mr Phillotson. And how possible it was that she had inherited the antipathies of her family, and would scorn him, as far as a Christian could, particularly when he had told her that unpleasant part of his history which had resulted in his becoming enchained to one of her own sex whom she would certainly not admire.

Thus he kept watch over her, and liked to feel she was there. The consciousness of her living presence stimulated him. But she remained more or less an ideal character, about whose form he began to weave curious and fantastic day-dreams.

Between two and three weeks afterwards Jude was engaged with some more men, outside Crozier College in Old-time Street,* in getting a block of worked freestone from a waggon across the pavement, before hoisting it to the parapet which they were repairing. Standing in position the head man said, 'Spaik when ye heave! He-ho!' And they heaved.

All of a sudden, as he lifted, his cousin stood close to his elbow, pausing a moment on the bend of her foot till the obstructing object should have been removed. She looked right into his face with liquid, untranslatable eyes, that combined, or seemed to him to combine, keenness with tenderness, and mystery with both, their expression, as well as that of her lips, taking its life from some words just spoken to a companion, and being carried on into his face quite unconsciously. She no more observed his presence than that of the dust-motes which his manipulations raised into the sunbeams.

His closeness to her was so suggestive that he trembled, and turned his face away with a shy instinct to prevent her recognizing him, though as she had never once seen him she could not possibly do so; and might very well never have heard even his name. He could perceive that though she was a country-girl at bottom, a latter girlhood of some years in London, and a womanhood here, had taken all rawness out of her.

When she was gone he continued his work, reflecting on her. He had been so caught by her influence that he had taken no count of her general mould and build. He remembered now that she was not a large figure, that she was light and slight, of the type dubbed elegant. That was about all he had seen. There was nothing statuesque in her; all was nervous motion. She was mobile, living, yet a painter might not have called her handsome or beautiful. But the much that she was surprised him. She was quite a long way removed from the rusticity that was his. How could one of his cross-grained, unfortunate, almost accursed stock, have contrived to reach this pitch of niceness? London had done it, he supposed.

From this moment the emotion which had been accumulating in his breast as the bottled-up effect of solitude and the poetized locality he dwelt in, insensibly began to precipitate itself on this half-visionary form; and he perceived that, whatever his obedient wish in a contrary direction, he would soon be unable to resist the desire to make himself known to her.

He affected to think of her quite in a family way, since there were crushing reasons why he should not and could not think of her in any other.

The first reason was that he was married, and it would be wrong.

The second was that they were cousins. It was not well for cousins to fall in love even when circumstances seemed to favour the passion. The third: even were he free, in a family like his own where marriage usually meant a tragic sadness, marriage with a blood-relation would duplicate the adverse conditions, and a tragic sadness might be intensified to a tragic horror.

Therefore, again, he would have to think of Sue with only a relation's mutual interest in one belonging to him; regard her in a practical way as some one to be proud of; to talk and nod to; later on, to be invited to tea by, the emotion spent on her being rigorously that of a kinsman and well-wisher. So would she be to him a kindly star, an elevating power, a companion in Anglican worship, a tender friend.

BUT under the various deterrent influences Jude's instinct was to approach her timidly, and the next Sunday he went to the morning service in the Cathedral-church of Cardinal College* to gain a further view of her, for he had found that she frequently attended there.

She did not come, and he awaited her in the afternoon, which was finer. He knew that if she came at all she would approach the building along the eastern side of the great green quadrangle from which it was accessible, and he stood in a corner while the bell was going. A few minutes before the hour for service she appeared as one of the figures walking along under the College walls, and at sight of her he advanced up the side opposite, and followed her into the building, more than ever glad that he had not as yet revealed himself. To see her, and to be himself unseen and unknown, was enough for him at present.

He lingered awhile in the vestibule, and the service was some way advanced when he was put into a seat. It was a louring, mournful, still afternoon, when a religion of some sort seems a necessity to ordinary practical men, and not only a luxury of the emotional and leisured classes. In the dim light and the baffling glare of the clerestory windows he could discern the opposite worshippers indistinctly only, but he saw that Sue was among them. He had not long discovered the exact seat that she occupied when the chanting of the 119th Psalm in which the choir was engaged reached its second part, *In quo corriget*,* the organ changing to a pathetic Gregorian tune as the singers gave forth:

'Wherewithal shall a young man cleanse his way?'

It was the very question that was engaging Jude's attention at this moment. What a wicked worthless fellow he had been to give vent as he had done to an animal passion for a woman, and allow it to lead to such disastrous consequences; then to think of putting an end to

himself; then to go recklessly and get drunk. The great waves of
pedal music tumbled round the choir, and, nursed on the supernatural as he had been it is not wonderful that he could hardly
believe that the psalm was not specially set by some regardful
Providence for this moment of his first entry into the solemn
building. And yet it was the ordinary psalm for the twenty-fourth
evening of the month.

The girl for whom he was beginning to nourish an extraordinary
tenderness, was at this time ensphered by the same harmonies as
those which floated into his ears; and the thought was a delight to
him. She was probably a frequenter of this place, and, steeped body
and soul in church sentiment as she must be by occupation and
habit, had, no doubt, much in common with him. To an impression-
able and lonely young man the consciousness of having at last found
anchorage for his thoughts, which promised to supply both social
and spiritual possibilities, was like the dew of Hermon,* and he remained throughout the service in a sustaining atmosphere of ecstasy.

Though he was loth to suspect it, some people might have said to
him that the atmosphere blew as distinctly from Cyprus * as from
Galilee.

Jude waited till she had left her seat and passed under the screen
before he himself moved. She did not look towards him, and by the
time he reached the door she was half way down the broad path.
Being dressed up in his Sunday suit he was inclined to follow her
and reveal himself. But he was not quite ready; and, alas, ought he
to do so with the kind of feeling that was awakening in him?

For though it had seemed to have an ecclesiastical basis during
the service, and he had persuaded himself that such was the case, he
could not altogether be blind to the real nature of the magnetism.
She was such a stranger that the kinship was affectation, and he
said, 'It can't be! I, a man with a wife, must not know her!' Still Sue
was his own kin, and the fact of his having a wife, even though she
was not in evidence in this hemisphere, might be a help in one sense.
It would put all thought of a tender wish on his part out of Sue's
mind, and make her intercourse with him free and fearless. It was
with some heartache that he saw how little he cared for the freedom
and fearlessness that would result in her from such knowledge.

*

Some little time before the date of this service in the cathedral the
pretty, liquid-eyed, light-footed young woman Sue Bridehead had an
afternoon's holiday, and leaving the ecclesiastical establishment in
which she not only assisted but lodged, took a walk into the country
with a book in her hand. It was one of those cloudless days which
sometimes occur in Wessex and elsewhere between days of cold and
wet, as if intercalated by caprice of the weather-god. She went along
for a mile or two until she came to much higher ground than that of
the city she had left behind her. The road passed between green
fields, and coming to a stile Sue paused there, to finish the page she
was reading, and then looked back at the towers and domes and
pinnacles new and old.

On the other side of the stile, in the footpath, she beheld a
foreigner with black hair and a sallow face, sitting on the grass
beside a large square board whereon were fixed, as closely as they
could stand, a number of plaster statuettes, some of them bronzed,
which he was re-arranging before proceeding with them on his way.
They were in the main reduced copies of ancient marbles, and
comprised divinities of a very different character from those the girl
was accustomed to see portrayed, among them being a Venus of
standard pattern, a Diana, and, of the other sex, Apollo, Bacchus,
and Mars. Though the figures were many yards away from her the
south-west sun brought them out so brilliantly against the green
herbage that she could discern their contours with luminous dis-
tinctness; and being almost in a line between herself and the church
towers of the city they awoke in her an oddly foreign and contrasting set of ideas by comparison. The man rose, and, seeing her,
politely took off his cap, and cried 'I i-i-mages!' in an accent that
agreed with his appearance. In a moment he dexterously lifted upon
his knee the great board with its assembled notabilities divine and
human, and raised it to the top of his head, bringing them on to her
and resting the board on the stile. First he offered her his smaller
wares — the busts of kings and queens, then a minstrel, then a
winged Cupid. She shook her head.

'How much are these two?' she said, touching with her finger the
Venus and the Apollo — the largest figures on the tray.

He said she should have them for ten shillings.

'I cannot afford that,' said Sue. She offered considerably less, and to her surprise the image-man drew them from their wire stay and handed them over the stile. She clasped them as treasures.

When they were paid for, and the man had gone, she began to be concerned as to what she should do with them. They seemed so very large now that they were in her possession, and so very naked. Being of a nervous temperament she trembled at her enterprise. When she handled them the white pipeclay came off on her gloves and jacket. After carrying them along a little way openly an idea came to her, and, pulling some huge burdock leaves, parsley, and other rank growths from the hedge, she wrapped up her burden as well as she could in these, so that what she carried appeared to be an enormous armful of green stuff gathered by a zealous lover of nature.

'Well, anything is better than those everlasting church fal-lals!' she said. But she was still in a trembling state, and seemed almost to wish she had not bought the figures.

Occasionally peeping inside the leaves to see that Venus's arm was not broken, she entered with her heathen load into the most Christian city in the country by an obscure street running parallel to the main one, and round a corner to the side door of the establishment to which she was attached. Her purchases were taken straight up to her own chamber, and she at once attempted to lock them in a box that was her very own property; but finding them too cumbersome she wrapped them in large sheets of brown paper, and stood them on the floor in a corner.

The mistress of the house, Miss Fontover, was an elderly lady in spectacles, dressed almost like an abbess; a dab at Ritual, as became one of her business, and a worshipper at the ceremonial church of St Silas,* in the suburb of Beersheba before-mentioned, which Jude also had begun to attend. She was the daughter of a clergyman in reduced circumstances, and at his death, which had occurred several years before this date, she boldly avoided penury by taking over a little shop of church requisites and developing it to its present creditable proportions. She wore a cross and beads round her neck as her only ornament, and knew the Christian Year * by heart.

She now came to call Sue to tea, and, finding that the girl did not respond for a moment, entered the room just as the other was hastily putting a string round each parcel.

'Something you have been buying, Miss Bridehead?' she asked, regarding the enwrapped objects.

'Yes – just something to ornament my room,' said Sue.

'Well, I should have thought I had put enough here already,' said Miss Fontover, looking round at the Gothic-framed prints of saints, the Church-text scrolls, and other articles which, having become too stale to sell, had been used to furnish this obscure chamber. 'What is it? How bulky!' She tore a little hole, about as big as a wafer, in the brown paper, and tried to peep in. 'Why, statuary? Two figures? Where did you get them?'

'O – I bought them of a travelling man who sells casts—'

'Two saints?'

'Yes.'

'What ones?'

'St Peter and St – St Mary Magdalen.'

'Well – now come down to tea, and go and finish that organ-text, if there's light enough afterwards.'

These little obstacles to the indulgence of what had been the merest passing fancy, created in Sue a great zest for unpacking her objects and looking at them; and at bedtime, when she was sure of being undisturbed, she unrobed the divinities in comfort. Placing the pair of figures on the chest of drawers, a candle on each side of them, she withdrew to the bed, flung herself down thereon, and began reading a book she had taken from her box, which Miss Fontover knew nothing of. It was a volume of Gibbon, and she read the chapter dealing with the reign of Julian the Apostate.* Occasionally she looked up at the statuettes, which appeared strange and out of place, there happening to be a Calvary print hanging between them, and, as if the scene suggested the action, she at length jumped up and withdrew another book from her box – a volume of verse – and turned to the familiar poem –

'Thou hast conquered, O pale Galilean:
The world has grown grey from thy breath!'*

which she read to the end. Presently she put out the candles, undressed, and finally extinguished her own light.

She was of an age which usually sleeps soundly, yet to-night she kept waking up, and every time she opened her eyes there was

enough diffused light from the street to show her the white plaster
figures standing on the chest of drawers in odd contrast to their
environment of text and martyr, and the Gothic-framed Crucifix-
picture that was only discernible now as a Latin cross,* the figure
thereon being obscured by the shades.

On one of these occasions the church clocks struck some small
hour. It fell upon the ears of another person who sat bending over
his books at a not very distant spot in the same city. Being Saturday
night the morrow was one on which Jude had not set his alarm-
clock to call him at his usually early time, and hence he had stayed
up, as was his custom, two or three hours later than he could afford
to do on any other day of the week. Just then he was earnestly
reading from his Griesbach's text. At the very time that Sue was
tossing and staring at her figures, the policeman and belated citizens
passing along under his window might have heard, if they had stood
still, strange syllables mumbled with fervour within — words that
had for Jude an indescribable enchantment: inexplicable sounds
something like these: —

'All hemin heis Theos ho Pater, cx hou ta panta, kai hemeis eis
auton:'*

Till the sounds rolled with reverent loudness, as a book was
heard to close: —

'Kai heis Kurios Iesous Christos, di hou ta panta kai hemeis di
autou!'*

CHAPTER FOUR

HE was a handy man at his trade, an all-round man, as artizans in country-towns are apt to be. In London the man who carves the boss or knob of leafage declines to cut the fragment of moulding which merges in that leafage, as if it were a degradation to do the second half of one whole. When there was not much Gothic moulding for Jude to run, or much window-tracery on the bankers, he would go out lettering monuments or tombstones, and take a pleasure in the change of handiwork.

The next time that he saw her was when he was on a ladder executing a job of this sort inside one of the churches. There was a short morning service, and when the parson entered Jude came down from his ladder, and sat with the half-dozen people forming the congregation, till the prayers should be ended, and he could resume his tapping. He did not observe till the service was half over that one of the women was Sue, who had perforce accompanied the elderly Miss Fontover thither.

Jude sat watching her pretty shoulders, her easy, curiously nonchalant risings and sittings, and her perfunctory genuflexions, and thought what a help such an Anglican would have been to him in happier circumstances. It was not so much his anxiety to get on with his work that made him go up to it immediately the worshippers began to take their leave: it was that he dared not, in this holy spot, confront the woman who was beginning to influence him in such an indescribable manner. Those three enormous reasons why he must not attempt intimate acquaintance with Sue Bridehead now that his interest in her had shown itself to be unmistakably of a sexual kind, loomed as stubbornly as ever. But it was also obvious that man could not live by work alone; that the particular man Jude, at any rate, wanted something to love. Some men would have rushed incontinently to her, snatched the pleasure of easy friendship which she could hardly refuse, and have left the rest to chance. Not so Jude — at first.

But as the days, and still more particularly the lonely evenings, dragged along, he found himself, to his moral consternation, to be thinking more of her instead of thinking less of her, and experiencing a fearful bliss in doing what was erratic, informal, and unexpected. Surrounded by her influence all day, walking past the spots she frequented, he was always thinking of her, and was obliged to own to himself that his conscience was likely to be the loser in this battle.

To be sure she was almost an ideality to him still. Perhaps to know her would be to cure himself of this unexpected and unauthorized passion. A voice whispered that, though he desired to know her, he did not desire to be cured.

There was not the least doubt that from his own orthodox point of view the situation was growing immoral. For Sue to be the loved one of a man who was licensed by the laws of his country to love Arabella and none other unto his life's end, was a pretty bad second beginning when the man was bent on such a course as Jude purposed. This conviction was so real with him that one day when, as was frequent, he was at work in a neighbouring village church alone, he felt it to be his duty to pray against his weakness. But much as he wished to be an exemplar in these things he could not get on. It was quite impossible, he found, to ask to be delivered from temptation when your heart's desire was to be tempted unto seventy times seven. So he excused himself. 'After all,' he said, 'it is not altogether an *erotolepsy* * that is the matter with me, as at that first time. I can see that she is exceptionally bright; and it is partly a wish for intellectual sympathy, and a craving for loving-kindness in my solitude.' Thus he went on adoring her, fearing to realize that it was human perversity. For whatever Sue's virtues, talents, or ecclesiastical saturation, it was certain that those items were not at all the cause of his affection for her.

On an afternoon at this time a young girl entered the stonemason's yard with some hesitation, and, lifting her skirts to avoid draggling them in the white dust, crossed towards the office.

'That's a nice girl,' said one of the men known as Uncle Joe.

'Who is she?' asked another.

'I don't know — I've seen her about here and there. Why, yes, she's the daughter of that clever chap Bridehead who did all the

wrought ironwork at St Silas' ten years ago, and went away to
London afterwards. I don't know what he's doing now — not much I
fancy — as she's come back here.'

Meanwhile the young woman had knocked at the office door and
asked if Mr Jude Fawley was at work in the yard. It so happened
that Jude had gone out somewhere or other that afternoon, which
information she received with a look of disappointment, and went
away immediately. When Jude returned they told him, and described her, whereupon he exclaimed, 'Why — that's my cousin Sue!'

He looked along the street after her, but she was out of sight. He
had no longer any thought of a conscientious avoidance of her, and
resolved to call upon her that very evening. And when he reached
his lodging he found a note from her — a first note — one of those
documents which, simple and commonplace in themselves, are seen
retrospectively to have been pregnant with impassioned consequences. The very unconsciousness of a looming drama which is
shown in such innocent first epistles from women to men, or *vice
versa*, makes them, when such a drama follows, and they are read
over by the purple or lurid light of it, all the more impressive,
solemn, and in cases, terrible.

Sue's was of the most artless and natural kind. She addressed him
as her dear cousin Jude; said she had only just learnt by the merest
accident that he was living in Christminster, and reproached him
with not letting her know. They might have had such nice times
together, she said, for she was thrown much upon herself, and had
hardly any congenial friend. But now there was every probability of
her soon going away, so that the chance of companionship would be
lost perhaps for ever.

A cold sweat overspread Jude at the news that she was going
away. That was a contingency he had never thought of, and it
spurred him to write all the more quickly to her. He would meet her
that very evening, he said, one hour from the time of writing, at the
cross in the pavement * which marked the spot of the Martyrdoms.

When he had despatched the note by a boy he regretted that in his
hurry he should have suggested to her to meet him out of doors,
when he might have said he would call upon her. It was, in fact, the
country custom to meet thus, and nothing else had occurred to him.
Arabella had been met in the same way, unfortunately, and it might

not seem respectable to a dear girl like Sue. However, it could not be helped now, and he moved towards the point a few minutes before the hour, under the glimmer of the newly lighted lamps.

The broad street was silent, and almost deserted, although it was not late. He saw a figure on the other side, which turned out to be hers, and they both converged towards the cross-mark at the same moment. Before either had reached it she called out to him:

'I am not going to meet you just there, for the first time in my life! Come further on.'

The voice, though positive and silvery, had been tremulous. They walked on in parallel lines, and, waiting her pleasure, Jude watched till she showed signs of closing in, when he did likewise, the place being where the carriers' carts stood in the daytime, though there was none on the spot then.

'I am sorry that I asked you to meet me, and didn't call,' began Jude with the bashfulness of a lover. 'But I thought it would save time if we were going to walk.'

'O – I don't mind that,' she said with the freedom of a friend. 'I have really no place to ask anybody in to. What I meant was that the place you chose was so horrid – I suppose I ought not to say horrid, – I mean gloomy and inauspicious in its associations. . . . But isn't it funny to begin like this, when I don't know you yet?' She looked him up and down curiously, though Jude did not look much at her.

'You seem to know me more than I know you,' she added.

'Yes – I have seen you now and then.'

'And you knew who I was, and didn't speak? And now I am going away!'

'Yes. That's unfortunate. I have hardly any other friend. I have, indeed, one very old friend here somewhere, but I don't quite like to call on him just yet. I wonder if you know anything of him – Mr Phillotson? A parson somewhere about the county I think he is.'

'No – I only know of one Mr Phillotson. He lives a little way out in the country, at Lumsdon. He's a village schoolmaster.'

'Ah! I wonder if he's the same. Surely it is impossible! Only a schoolmaster still! Do you know his Christian name – is it Richard?'

'Yes – it is; I've directed books to him, though I've never seen him.'

'Then he couldn't do it!'

Jude's countenance fell, for how could he succeed in an enterprise wherein the great Phillotson had failed? He would have had a day of despair if the news had not arrived during his sweet Sue's presence, but even at this moment he had visions of how Phillotson's failure in the grand University scheme would depress him when she had gone.

'As we are going to take a walk, suppose we go and call upon him?' said Jude suddenly. 'It is not late.'

She agreed, and they went along up a hill, and through some prettily wooded country. Presently the embattled tower and square turret of the church rose into the sky, and then the schoolhouse. They inquired of a person in the street if Mr Phillotson was likely to be at home, and were informed that he was always at home. A knock brought him to the schoolhouse door, with a candle in his hand and a look of inquiry on his face, which had grown thin and careworn since Jude last set eyes on him.

That after all these years the meeting with Mr Phillotson should be of this homely complexion destroyed at one stroke the halo which had surrounded the schoolmaster's figure in Jude's imagination ever since their parting. It created in him at the same time a sympathy with Phillotson as an obviously much chastened and disappointed man. Jude told him his name, and said he had come to see him as an old friend who had been kind to him in his youthful days.

'I don't remember you in the least,' said the school-master thoughtfully. 'You were one of my pupils you say? Yes, no doubt; but they number so many thousands by this time of my life, and have naturally changed so much, that I remember very few except the quite recent ones.'

'It was out at Marygreen,' said Jude, wishing he had not come.

'Yes. I was there a short time. And is this an old pupil, too?'

'No – that's my cousin. . . . I wrote to you for some grammars, if you recollect, and you sent them?'

'Ah – yes! – I do dimly recall that incident.'

'It was very kind of you to do it. And it was you who first started me on that course. On the morning you left Marygreen, when your goods were on the waggon, you wished me good-bye, and said your scheme was to be a University man and enter the church – that a degree was the necessary hall-mark of one who wanted to do anything as a theologian or teacher.'

'I remember I thought all that privately; but I wonder I did not keep my own counsel. The idea was given up years ago.'

'I have never forgotten it. It was that which brought me to this part of the country, and out here to see you to-night.'

'Come in,' said Phillotson. 'And your cousin, too.'

They entered the parlour of the schoolhouse, where there was a lamp with a paper shade, which threw the light down on three or four books. Phillotson took it off, so that they could see each other better, and the rays fell on the nervous little face and vivacious dark eyes and hair of Sue, on the earnest features of her cousin, and on the schoolmaster's own maturer face and figure, showing him to be a spare and thoughtful personage of five-and-forty, with a thin-lipped, somewhat refined mouth, a slightly stooping habit, and a black frock coat, which from continued frictions shone a little at the shoulder-blades, the middle of the back, and the elbows.

The old friendship was imperceptibly renewed, the schoolmaster speaking of his experiences, and the cousins of theirs. He told them that he still thought of the church sometimes, and that though he could not enter it as he had intended to do in former years he might enter it as a licentiate. Meanwhile, he said, he was comfortable in his present position, though he was in want of a pupil-teacher.

They did not stay to supper, Sue having to be indoors before it grew late, and the road was retraced to Christminster. Though they had talked of nothing more than general subjects Jude was surprised to find what a revelation of woman his cousin was to him. She was so vibrant that everything she did seemed to have its source in feeling. An exciting thought would make her walk ahead so fast that he could hardly keep up with her; and her sensitiveness on some points was such that it might have been misread as vanity. It was with heart-sickness he perceived that, while her sentiments towards him were those of the frankest friendliness only, he loved her more than before becoming acquainted with her; and the gloom of the walk home lay not in the night overhead, but in the thought of her departure.

'Why must you leave Christminster?' he said regretfully. 'How can you do otherwise than cling to a city in whose history such men as Newman, Pusey, Ward, Keble, loom so large!'

'Yes — they do. Though how large do they loom in the history of the world? . . . What a funny reason for caring to stay! I should never have thought of it!' She laughed.

'Well — I must go,' she continued. 'Miss Fontover, one of the partners whom I serve, is offended with me, and I with her; and it is best to go.'

'How did that happen?'

'She broke some statuary of mine.'

'Oh? Wilfully?'

'Yes. She found it in my room, and though it was my property she threw it on the floor and stamped on it, because it was not according to her taste, and ground the arms and the head of one of the figures all to bits with her heel — a horrid thing!'

'Too Catholic-Apostolic for her, I suppose? No doubt she called them Popish images and talked of the invocation of saints.'

'No. . . . No, she didn't do that. She saw the matter quite differently.'

'Ah! Then I am surprised!'

'Yes. It was for quite some other reason that she didn't like my patron-saints. So I was led to retort upon her; and the end of it was that I resolved not to stay, but to get into an occupation in which I shall be more independent.'

'Why don't you try teaching again? You once did, I heard.'

'I never thought of resuming it; for I was getting on as an art-designer.'

'*Do* let me ask Mr Phillotson to let you try your hand in his school? If you like it, and go to a Training College, and become a first-class certificated mistress, you get twice as large an income as any designer or church artist, and twice as much freedom.'

'Well — ask him. Now I must go in. Good-bye, dear Jude! I am so glad we have met at last. We needn't quarrel because our parents did, need we?'

Jude did not like to let her see quite how much he agreed with her, and went his way to the remote street in which he had his lodging.

To keep Sue Bridehead near him was now a desire which operated without regard of consequences, and the next evening he again set out for Lumsdon, fearing to trust to the persuasive effects of a note only. The schoolmaster was unprepared for such a proposal.

'What I rather wanted was a second year's transfer, as it is called,' he said. 'Of course your cousin would do, personally; but she has had no experience. O — she has, has she? Does she really think of adopting teaching as a profession?'

Jude said she was disposed to do so, he thought, and his ingenious arguments on her natural fitness for assisting Mr Phillotson, of which Jude knew nothing whatever, so influenced the schoolmaster that he said he would engage her, assuring Jude as a friend that unless his cousin really meant to follow on in the same course, and regarded this step as the first stage of an apprenticeship, of which her training in a normal school would be the second stage, her time would be wasted quite, the salary being merely nominal.

The day after this visit Phillotson received a letter from Jude, containing the information that he had again consulted his cousin, who took more and more warmly to the idea of tuition; and that she had agreed to come. It did not occur for a moment to the schoolmaster and recluse that Jude's ardour in promoting the arrangement arose from any other feelings towards Sue than the instinct of co-operation common among members of the same family.

CHAPTER FIVE

THE schoolmaster sat in his homely dwelling attached to the school, both being modern erections; and he looked across the way at the old house in which his teacher Sue had a lodging. The arrangement had been concluded very quickly. A pupil-teacher who was to have been transferred to Mr Phillotson's school had failed him, and Sue had been taken as stop-gap. All such provisional arrangements as these could only last till the next annual visit of H.M. Inspector, whose approval was necessary to make them permanent. Having taught for some two years in London, though she had abandoned that vocation of late, Miss Bridehead was not exactly a novice, and Phillotson thought there would be no difficulty in retaining her services, which he already wished to do, though she had only been with him three or four weeks. He had found her quite as bright as Jude had described her; and what master-tradesman does not wish to keep an apprentice who saves him half his labour?

It was a little over half-past eight o'clock in the morning, and he was waiting to see her cross the road to the school, when he would follow. At twenty minutes to nine she did cross, a light hat tossed on her head; and he watched her as a curiosity. A new emanation, which had nothing to do with her skill as a teacher, seemed to surround her this morning. He went to the school also, and Sue remained governing her class at the other end of the room, all day under his eye. She certainly was an excellent teacher.

It was part of his duty to give her private lessons in the evening, and some article in the Code made it necessary that a respectable, elderly woman should be present at these lessons when the teacher and the taught were of different sexes. Richard Phillotson thought of the absurdity of the regulation in this case, when he was old enough to be the girl's father; but he faithfully acted up to it; and sat down with her in a room where Mrs Hawes, the widow at whose house Sue lodged, occupied herself with sewing. The regulation was, indeed, not easy to evade, for there was no other sitting-room in the dwelling.

Sometimes as she figured — it was arithmetic that they were working at — she would involuntarily glance up with a little inquiring smile at him, as if she assumed that, being the master, he must perceive all that was passing in her brain, as right or wrong. Phillotson was not really thinking of the arithmetic at all, but of her, in a novel way which somehow seemed strange to him as preceptor. Perhaps she knew that he was thinking of her thus.

For a few weeks their work had gone on with a monotony which in itself was a delight to him. Then it happened that the children were to be taken to Christminster to see an itinerant exhibition, in the shape of a model of Jerusalem, to which schools were admitted at a penny a head in the interests of education. They marched along the road two and two, she beside her class with her simple cotton sunshade, her little thumb cocked up against its stem; and Phillotson behind in his long dangling coat, handling his walking-stick genteelly, in the musing mood which had come over him since her arrival. The afternoon was one of sun and dust, and when they entered the exhibition room few people were present but themselves.

The model of the ancient city stood in the middle of the apartment, and the proprietor, with a fine religious philanthropy written on his features, walked round it with a pointer in his hand, showing the young people the various quarters and places known to them by name from reading their Bibles; Mount Moriah, the Valley of Jehoshaphat, the City of Zion, the walls and the gates, outside one of which there was a large mound like a tumulus, and on the mound a little white cross. The spot, he said, was Calvary.

'I think,' said Sue to the schoolmaster, as she stood with him a little in the background, 'that this model, elaborate as it is, is a very imaginary production. How does anybody know that Jerusalem was like this in the time of Christ? I am sure this man doesn't.'

'It is made after the best conjectural maps, based on actual visits to the city as it now exists.'

'I fancy we have had enough of Jerusalem,' she said, 'considering we are not descended from the Jews. There was nothing first-rate about the place, or people, after all — as there was about Athens, Rome, Alexandria, and other old cities.'

'But my dear girl, consider what it is to us!'

She was silent, for she was easily repressed; and then perceived behind the group of children clustered round the model a young man in a white flannel jacket, his form being bent so low in his intent inspection of the Valley of Jehoshaphat that his face was almost hidden from view by the Mount of Olives. 'Look at your cousin Jude,' continued the schoolmaster. 'He doesn't think we have had enough of Jerusalem!'

'Ah – I didn't see him!' she cried in her quick light voice. 'Jude – how seriously you are going into it!'

Jude started up from his reverie, and saw her. 'O – Sue!' he said, with a glad flush of embarrassment. 'These are your school-children, of course! I saw that schools were admitted in the afternoons, and thought you might come; but I got so deeply interested that I didn't remember where I was. How it carries one back, doesn't it! I could examine it for hours, but I have only a few minutes, unfortunately; for I am in the middle of a job out here.'

'Your cousin is so terribly clever that she criticizes it unmerci-fully,' said Phillotson, with good-humoured satire. 'She is quite sceptical as to its correctness.'

'No, Mr Phillotson, I am not – altogether! I hate to be what is called a clever girl – there are too many of that sort now!' answered Sue sensitively. 'I only meant – I don't know what I meant – except that it was what you don't understand!'

'I know your meaning,' said Jude ardently (although he did not). 'And I think you are quite right.'

'That's a good Jude – I know you believe in me!' She impulsively seized his hand, and leaving a reproachful look on the schoolmaster turned away to Jude, her voice revealing a tremor which she herself felt to be absurdly uncalled for by sarcasm so gentle. She had not the least conception how the hearts of the twain went out to her at this momentary revelation of feeling, and what a complication she was building up thereby in the futures of both.

The model wore too much of an educational aspect for the children not to tire of it soon, and a little later in the afternoon they were all marched back to Lumsdon, Jude returning to his work. He watched the juvenile flock in their clean frocks and pinafores, filing down the street towards the country beside Phillotson and Sue, and a sad, dissatisfied sense of being out of the scheme of the latters' lives had possession of him. Phillotson had invited him to walk out

and see them on Friday evening, when there would be no lessons to
give to Sue, and Jude had eagerly promised to avail himself of the
opportunity.

Meanwhile the scholars and teachers moved homewards, and the
next day, on looking on the black-board in Sue's class, Phillotson
was surprised to find upon it, skilfully drawn in chalk, a perspective
view of Jerusalem, with every building shown in its place.

'I thought you took no interest in the model, and hardly looked at
it?' he said.

'I hardly did,' said she, 'but I remembered that much of it.'

'It is more than I had remembered myself.'

Her Majesty's school-inspector was at that time paying 'surprise-
visits' in this neighbourhood to test the teaching unawares; and two
days later, in the middle of the morning lessons, the latch of the
door was softly lifted, and in walked my gentleman, the king of
terrors – to pupil-teachers.

To Mr Phillotson the surprise was not great; like the lady in the
story he had been played that trick too many times to be
unprepared. But Sue's class was at the further end of the room, and
her back was towards the entrance; the inspector therefore came
and stood behind her and watched her teaching some half-minute
before she became aware of his presence. She turned, and realized
that an oft-dreaded moment had come. The effect upon her timidity
was such that she uttered a cry of fright. Phillotson, with a strange
instinct of solicitude quite beyond his control, was at her side just in
time to prevent her falling from faintness. She soon recovered
herself, and laughed; but when the inspector had gone there was a
reaction, and she was so white that Phillotson took her into his
room, and gave her some brandy to bring her round. She found him
holding her hand.

'You ought to have told me,' she gasped petulantly, 'that one of
the Inspector's surprise-visits was imminent! O what shall I do!
Now he'll write and tell the managers that I am no good, and I shall
be disgraced for ever!'

'He won't do that, my dear little girl. You are the best teacher
ever I had!'

He looked so gently at her that she was moved, and regretted that she had upbraided him. When she was better she went home.

Jude in the meantime had been waiting impatiently for Friday. On both Wednesday and Thursday he had been so much under the influence of his desire to see her that he walked after dark some distance along the road in the direction of the village, and, on returning to his room to read, found himself quite unable to concentrate his mind on the page. On Friday, as soon as he had got himself up as he thought Sue would like to see him, and made a hasty tea, he set out, notwithstanding that the evening was wet. The trees overhead deepened the gloom of the hour, and they dripped sadly upon him, impressing him with forebodings — illogical forebodings; for though he knew that he loved her he also knew that he could not be more to her than he was.

On turning the corner and entering the village the first sight that greeted his eyes was that of two figures under one umbrella coming out of the vicarage gate. He was too far back for them to notice him, but he knew in a moment that they were Sue and Phillotson. The latter was holding the umbrella over her head, and they had evidently been paying a visit to the vicar — probably on some business connected with the school work. And as they walked along the wet and deserted lane Jude saw Phillotson place his arm round the girl's waist; whereupon she gently removed it; but he replaced it; and she let it remain, looking quickly round her with an air of misgiving. She did not look absolutely behind her, and therefore did not see Jude, who sank into the hedge like one struck with a blight. There he remained hidden till they had reached Sue's cottage and she had passed in, Phillotson going on to the school hard by.

'O, he's too old for her — too old!' cried Jude in all the terrible sickness of hopeless, handicapped love.

He could not interfere. Was he not Arabella's? He was unable to go on further, and retraced his steps towards Christminster. Every tread of his feet seemed to say to him that he must on no account stand in the schoolmaster's way with Sue. Phillotson was perhaps twenty years her senior, but many a happy marriage had been made in such conditions of age. The ironical clinch to his sorrow was given by the thought that the intimacy between his cousin and the schoolmaster had been brought about entirely by himself.

JUDE'S old and embittered aunt lay unwell at Marygreen, and on the following Sunday he went to see her — a visit which was the result of a victorious struggle against his inclination to turn aside to the village of Lumsdon and obtain a miserable interview with his cousin, in which the word nearest his heart could not be spoken, and the sight which had tortured him could not be revealed.

His aunt was now unable to leave her bed, and a great part of Jude's short day was occupied in making arrangements for her comfort. The little bakery business had been sold to a neighbour, and with the proceeds of this and her savings she was comfortably supplied with necessaries and more, a widow of the same village living with her and ministering to her wants. It was not till the time had nearly come for him to leave that he obtained a quiet talk with her, and his words tended insensibly towards his cousin.

'Was Sue born here?'

'She was — in this room. They were living here at that time. What made 'ee ask that?'

'O — I wanted to know.'

'Now you've been seeing her!' said the harsh old woman. 'And what did I tell 'ee?'

'Well — that I was not to see her.'

'Have you gossiped with her?'

'Yes.'

'Then don't keep it up. She was brought up by her father to hate her mother's family; and she'll look with no favour upon a working chap like you — a townish girl as she's become by now. I never cared much about her. A pert little thing, that's what she was too often, with her tight-strained nerves. Many's the time I've smacked her for her impertinence. Why, one day when she was walking into the pond with her shoes and stockings off, and her petticoats pulled above her knees, afore I could cry out for shame, she said: "Move on, aunty! This is no sight for modest eyes!"'

'She was a little child then.'

'She was twelve if a day.'

'Well — of course. But now she's older she's of a thoughtful, quivering, tender nature, and as sensitive as—'

'Jude!' cried his aunt, springing up in bed. 'Don't you be a fool about her!'

'No, no, of course not.'

'Your marrying that woman Arabella was about as bad a thing as a man could possibly do for himself by trying hard. But she's gone to the other side of the world, and med never trouble you again. And there'll be a worse thing if you, tied and bound as you be, should have a fancy for Sue. If your cousin is civil to you, take her civility for what it is worth. But anything more than a relation's good wishes it is stark madness for 'ee to give her. If she's townish and wanton it med bring 'ee to ruin.'

'Don't say anything against her, aunt! Don't, please!'

A relief was afforded to him by the entry of the companion and nurse of his aunt, who must have been listening to the conversation, for she began a commentary on past years, introducing Sue Bridehead as a character in her recollections. She described what an odd little maid Sue had been when a pupil at the village school across the green opposite, before her father went to London — how, when the vicar arranged readings and recitations, she appeared on the platform, the smallest of them all, 'in her little white frock, and shoes, and pink sash'; how she recited 'Excelsior',* 'There was a sound of revelry by night',* and 'The Raven'; how during the delivery she would knit her little brows and glare round tragically, and say to the empty air, as if some real creature stood there —

'Ghastly, grim, and ancient Raven, wandering from the Nightly shore,
Tell me what thy lordly name is on the Night's Plutonian shore!'*

'She'd bring up the nasty carrion bird that clear,' corroborated the sick woman reluctantly, 'as she stood there in her little sash and things, that you could see un a'most before your very eyes. You too, Jude, had the same trick as a child of seeming to see things in the air.'

The neighbour told also of Sue's accomplishments in other kinds: 'She was not exactly a tomboy, you know; but she could do things that only boys do, as a rule. I've seen her hit in and steer down the long slide on yonder pond, with her little curls blowing, one of a file of twenty moving along against the sky like shapes painted on glass, and up the back slide without stopping. All boys except herself; and then they'd cheer her, and then she'd say, "Don't be saucy, boys," and suddenly run indoors. They'd try to coax her out again. But 'a wouldn't come.'

These retrospective visions of Sue only made Jude the more miserable that he was unable to woo her, and he left the cottage of his aunt that day with a heavy heart. He would fain have glanced into the school to see the room in which Sue's little figure had so glorified itself; but he checked his desire and went on.

It being Sunday evening some villagers who had known him during his residence here were standing in a group in their best clothes. Jude was startled by a salute from one of them:

'Ye've got there right enough, then!'

Jude showed that he did not understand.

'Why, to the seat of l'arning – the "City of Light" you used to talk to us about as a little boy! Is it all you expected of it?'

'Yes; more!' cried Jude.

'When I was there once for an hour I didn't see much in it for my part; auld crumbling buildings, half church, half almshouse, and not much going on at that.'

'You are wrong, John; there is more going on than meets the eye of a man walking through the streets. It is a unique centre of thought and religion – the intellectual and spiritual granary of this country. All that silence and absence of goings-on is the stillness of infinite motion – the sleep of the spinning-top, to borrow the simile of a well-known writer.'*

'O, well, it med be all that, or it med not. As I say, I didn't see nothing of it the hour or two I was there; so I went in and had a pot o' beer, and a penny loaf, and a ha'porth o' cheese, and waited till it was time to come along home. You've j'ined a College by this time, I suppose?'

'Ah, no!' said Jude. 'I am almost as far off that as ever.'

'How so?'

Jude slapped his pocket.

'Just what we thought! Such places be not for such as you – only for them with plenty o' money.'

'There you are wrong,' said Jude, with some bitterness. 'They are for such ones!'

Still, the remark was sufficient to withdraw Jude's attention from the imaginative world he had lately inhabited, in which an abstract figure, more or less himself, was steeping his mind in a sublimation of the arts and sciences, and making his calling and election sure to a seat in the paradise of the learned. He was set regarding his prospects in a cold northern light. He had lately felt that he could not quite satisfy himself in his Greek — in the Greek of the dramatists particularly. So fatigued was he sometimes after his day's work that he could not maintain the critical attention necessary for thorough application. He felt that he wanted a coach — a friend at his elbow to tell him in a moment what sometimes would occupy him a weary month in extracting from unanticipative, clumsy books.

It was decidedly necessary to consider facts a little more closely than he had done of late. What was the good, after all, of using up his spare hours in a vague labour called 'private study' without giving an outlook on practicabilities?

'I ought to have thought of this before,' he said, as he journeyed back. 'It would have been better never to have embarked in the scheme at all than to do it without seeing clearly where I am going, or what I am aiming at. . . . This hovering outside the walls of the colleges, as if expecting some arm to be stretched out from them to lift me inside, won't do! I must get special information.'

The next week accordingly he sought it. What at first seemed an opportunity occurred one afternoon when he saw an elderly gentleman, who had been pointed out as the Head of a particular College, walking in the public path of a parklike enclosure near the spot at which Jude chanced to be sitting. The gentleman came nearer, and Jude looked anxiously at his face. It seemed benign, considerate, yet rather reserved. On second thoughts Jude felt that he could not go up and address him; but he was sufficiently influenced by the incident to think what a wise thing it would be for him to state his difficulties by letter to some of the best and most judicious of these old masters, and obtain their advice.

During the next week or two he accordingly placed himself in such positions about the city as would afford him glimpses of several of the most distinguished among the Provosts, Wardens, and other Heads of Houses; and from those he ultimately selected five whose physiognomies seemed to say to him that they were appreciative and far-seeing men. To these five he addressed letters, briefly stating his difficulties, and asking their opinion on his stranded situation.

When the letters were posted Jude mentally began to criticize them; he wished they had not been sent. 'It is just one of those intrusive, vulgar, pushing, applications which are so common in these days,' he thought. 'Why couldn't I know better than address utter strangers in such a way? I may be an impostor, an idle scamp, a man with a bad character, for all that they know to the contrary. ... Perhaps that's what I am!'

Nevertheless, he found himself clinging to the hope of some reply as to his one last chance of redemption. He waited day after day, saying that it was perfectly absurd to expect, yet expecting. While he waited he was suddenly stirred by news about Phillotson. Phillotson was giving up the school near Christminster, for a larger one further south, in Mid-Wessex. What this meant; how it would affect his cousin; whether, as seemed possible, it was a practical move of the schoolmaster's towards a larger income, in view of a provision for two instead of one, he would not allow himself to say. And the tender relations between Phillotson and the young girl of whom Jude was passionately enamoured effectually made it repugnant to Jude's tastes to apply to Phillotson for advice on his own scheme.

Meanwhile the academic dignitaries to whom Jude had written vouchsafed no answer, and the young man was thus thrown back entirely on himself, as formerly, with the added gloom of a weakened hope. By indirect inquiries he soon perceived clearly, what he had long uneasily suspected, that to qualify himself for certain open scholarships and exhibitions was the only brilliant course. But to do this a good deal of coaching would be necessary, and much natural ability. It was next to impossible that a man reading on his own system, however widely and thoroughly, even over the prolonged period of ten years, should be able to compete with those who had passed their lives under trained teachers and had worked to ordained lines.

The other course, that of buying himself in, so to speak, seemed the only one really open to men like him, the difficulty being simply of a material kind. With the help of his information he began to reckon the extent of this material obstacle, and ascertained, to his dismay, that, at the rate at which, with the best of fortune, he would be able to save money, fifteen years must elapse before he could be in a position to forward testimonials to the Head of a College and advance to a matriculation examination. The undertaking was hopeless.

He saw what a curious and cunning glamour the neighbourhood of the place had exercised over him. To get there and live there, to move among the churches and halls and become imbued with the *genius loci*,* had seemed to his dreaming youth, as the spot shaped its charms to him from its halo on the horizon, the obvious and ideal thing to do. 'Let me only get there,' he had said with the fatuousness of Crusoe * over his big boat, 'and the rest is but a matter of time and energy.' It would have been far better for him in every way if he had never come within sight and sound of the delusive precincts, had gone to some busy commercial town with the sole object of making money by his wits, and thence surveyed his plan in true perspective. Well, all that was clear to him amounted to this, that the whole scheme had burst up, like an iridescent soap-bubble, under the touch of a reasoned inquiry. He looked back at himself along the vista of his past years, and his thought was akin to Heine's:

> 'Above the youth's inspired and flashing eyes
> I see the motley mocking fool's-cap rise!' *

Fortunately he had not been allowed to bring his disappointment into his dear Sue's life by involving her in this collapse. And the painful details of his awakening to a sense of his limitations should now be spared her as far as possible. After all, she had only known a little part of the miserable struggle in which he had been engaged thus unequipped, poor, and unforeseeing.

He always remembered the appearance of the afternoon on which he awoke from his dream. Not quite knowing what to do with himself, he went up to an octagonal chamber in the lantern of a singularly built theatre * that was set amidst this quaint and singular city. It had windows all round, from which an outlook over the whole town and its edifices could be gained. Jude's eyes swept all the views in succession, meditatively, mournfully, yet sturdily. Those buildings and their associations and privileges were not for him. From the looming roof of the great library,* into which he hardly ever had time to enter, his gaze travelled on to the varied spires, halls, gables, streets, chapels, gardens, quadrangles, which composed the *ensemble* of this unrivalled panorama. He saw that his destiny lay not with these, but among the manual toilers in the shabby purlieu which he himself occupied, unrecognized as part of the city at all by its visitors and panegyrists, yet without whose denizens the hard readers could not read nor the high thinkers live.

He looked over the town into the country beyond, to the trees which screened her whose presence had at first been the support of his heart, and whose loss was now a maddening torture. But for this blow he might have borne with his fate. With Sue as companion he could have renounced his ambitions with a smile. Without her it was inevitable that the reaction from the long strain to which he had subjected himself should affect him disastrously. Phillotson had no doubt passed through a similar intellectual disappointment to that which now enveloped him. But the schoolmaster had been since blest with the consolation of sweet Sue, while for him there was no consoler.

Descending to the streets, he went listlessly along till he arrived at an inn, and entered it. Here he drank several glasses of beer in rapid succession, and when he came out it was night. By the light of the flickering lamps he rambled home to supper, and had not long been sitting at table when his landlady brought up a letter that had just arrived for him. She laid it down as if impressed with a sense of its possible importance, and on looking at it Jude perceived that it bore the embossed stamp of one of the Colleges whose heads he had addressed. '*One* – at last!' cried Jude.

The communication was brief, and not exactly what he had expected; though it really was from the Master in person. It ran thus:

'BIBLIOLL COLLEGE

'SIR, – I have read your letter with interest; and, judging from your description of yourself as a working-man, I venture to think that you will have a much better chance of success in life by remaining in your own sphere and sticking to your trade than by adopting any other course. That, therefore, is what I advise you to do. Yours faithfully,

'T. TETUPHENAY*

'To Mr J. FAWLEY, Stone-mason.'

This terribly sensible advice exasperated Jude. He had known all that before. He knew it was true. Yet it seemed a hard slap after ten years of labour, and its effect upon him just now was to make him rise recklessly from the table, and, instead of reading as usual, to go downstairs and into the street. He stood at a bar and tossed off two or three glasses, then unconsciously sauntered along till he came to a spot called The Fourways* in the middle of the city, gazing abstractedly at the groups of people like one in a trance, till, coming to himself, he began talking to the policeman fixed there.

That officer yawned, stretched out his elbows, elevated himself an inch and a half on the balls of his toes, smiled, and looking humorously at Jude, said, 'You've had a wet, young man.'

'No; I've only begun,' he replied cynically.

Whatever his wetness, his brains were dry enough. He only heard in part the policeman's further remarks, having fallen into thought on what struggling people like himself had stood at that Crossway, whom nobody ever thought of now. It had more history than the oldest college in the city. It was literally teeming, stratified, with the shades of human groups, who had met there for tragedy, comedy, farce; real enactments of the intensest kind. At Fourways men had stood and talked of Napoleon, the loss of America, the execution of King Charles, the burning of the Martyrs, the Crusades, the Norman Conquest, possibly of the arrival of Caesar. Here the two sexes had met for loving, hating, coupling, parting; had waited, had suffered, for each other; had triumphed over each other; cursed each other in jealousy, blessed each other in forgiveness.

He began to see that the town life was a book of humanity infinitely more palpitating, varied, and compendious than the gown life. These struggling men and women before him were the reality of Christminster, though they knew little of Christ or Minster. That was one of the humours of things. The floating population of students and teachers, who did know both in a way, were not Christminster in a local sense at all.

He looked at his watch, and, in pursuit of this idea, he went on till he came to a public hall, where a promenade concert was in progress. Jude entered, and found the room full of shop youths and girls, soldiers, apprentices, boys of eleven smoking cigarettes, and light women of the more respectable and amateur class. He had tapped the real Christminster life. A band was playing, and the crowd walked about and jostled each other, and every now and then a man got upon a platform and sang a comic song.

The spirit of Sue seemed to hover round him and prevent his flirting and drinking with the frolicsome girls who made advances — wistful to gain a little joy. At ten o'clock he came away, choosing a circuitous route homeward to pass the gates of the College whose Head had just sent him the note.

The gates were shut, and, by an impulse, he took from his pocket the lump of chalk which as a workman he usually carried there, and wrote along the wall:

'I have understanding as well as you; I am not inferior to you: yea, who knoweth not such things as these?' — Job, XII 3.

THE stroke of scorn relieved his mind, and the next morning he laughed at his self-conceit. But the laugh was not a healthy one. He re-read the letter from the Master, and the wisdom in its lines, which had at first exasperated him, chilled and depressed him now. He saw himself as a fool indeed.

Deprived of the objects of both intellect and emotion, he could not proceed to his work. Whenever he felt reconciled to his fate as a student, there came to disturb his calm his hopeless relations with Sue. That the one affined soul he had ever met was lost to him through his marriage returned upon him with cruel persistency, till, unable to bear it longer, he again rushed for distraction to the real Christminster life. He now sought it out in an obscure and low-ceiled tavern up a court which was well known to certain worthies of the place, and in brighter times would have interested him simply by its quaintness. Here he sat more or less all the day, convinced that he was at bottom a vicious character, of whom it was hopeless to expect anything.

In the evening the frequenters of the house dropped in one by one, Jude still retaining his seat in the corner, though his money was all spent, and he had not eaten anything the whole day except a biscuit. He surveyed his gathering companions with all the equanimity and philosophy of a man who was been drinking long and slowly, and made friends with several: to wit, Tinker Taylor,* a decayed church-ironmonger who appeared to have been of a religious turn in earlier years, but was somewhat blasphemous now; also a red-nosed auctioneer; also two Gothic masons like himself, called Uncle Jim and Uncle Joe. There were present, too, some clerks, and a gown- and surplice-maker's assistant; two ladies who sported moral characters of various depths of shade, according to their company, nicknamed 'Bower o' Bliss' and 'Freckles'; some horsey men 'in the know' of betting circles; a travelling actor from the theatre, and two devil-may-care young men who proved to be gownless undergraduates; they had slipped in by stealth to meet a man about bull-pups, and stayed to drink and smoke short pipes with the racing gents aforesaid, looking at their watches every now and then.

The conversation waxed general. Christminster society was criticized, the Dons, magistrates, and other people in authority being sincerely pitied for their shortcomings, while opinions on how they ought to conduct themselves and their affairs to be properly respected, were exchanged in a large-minded and disinterested manner.

Jude Fawley, with the self-conceit, effrontery, and *aplomb* of a strong-brained fellow in liquor, threw in his remarks somewhat peremptorily; and his aims having been what they were for so many years, everything the others said turned upon his tongue, by a sort of mechanical craze, to the subject of scholarship and study, the extent of his own learning being dwelt upon with an insistence that would have appeared pitiable to himself in his sane hours.

'I don't care a damn,' he was saying, 'for any Provost, Warden, Principal, Fellow, or cursed Master of Arts in the University! What I know is that I'd lick 'em on their own ground if they'd give me a chance, and show 'em a few things they are not up to yet!'

'Hear, hear!' said the undergraduates from the corner, where they were talking privately about the pups.

'You always was fond o' books, I've heard,' said Tinker Taylor, 'and I don't doubt what you state. Now with me 'twas different. I always saw there was more to be learnt outside a book than in; and I took my steps accordingly, or I shouldn't have been the man I am.'

'You aim at the Church, I believe?' said Uncle Joe. 'If you are such a scholar as to pitch yer hopes so high as that, why not give us a specimen of your scholarship? Canst say the Creed in Latin, man? That was how they once put it to a chap down in my country.'

'I should think so!' said Jude haughtily.

'Not he! Like his conceit!' screamed one of the ladies.

'Just you shut up, Bower o' Bliss!' said one of the undergraduates. 'Silence!' He drank off the spirits in his tumbler, rapped with it on the counter, and announced, 'The gentleman in the corner is going to rehearse the Articles of his Belief, in the Latin tongue, for the edification of the company.'

'I won't!' said Jude.

'Yes – have a try!' said the surplice-maker.

'You can't!' said Uncle Joe.

'Yes, he can!' said Tinker Taylor.

'I'll swear I can!' said Jude. 'Well, come now, stand me a small Scotch cold, and I'll do it straight off.'

'That's a fair offer,' said the undergraduate, throwing down the money for the whisky.

The barmaid concocted the mixture with the bearing of a person compelled to live amongst animals of an inferior species, and the glass was handed across to Jude, who, having drunk the contents, stood up and began rhetorically, without hesitation:

'Credo in unum Deum, Patrem omnipotentem, Factorem coeli et terrae, visibilium omnium et invisibilium.'

'Good! Excellent Latin!' cried one of the undergraduates, who, however, had not the slightest conception of a single word.

A silence reigned among the rest in the bar, and the maid stood still, Jude's voice echoing sonorously into the inner parlour, where the landlord was dozing, and bringing him out to see what was going on. Jude had declaimed steadily ahead, and was continuing:

'Crucifixus etiam pro nobis: sub Pontio Pilato passus, et sepultus est. Et resurrexit tertia die, secundum Scripturas.'

'That's the Nicene,'* sneered the second undergraduate. 'And we wanted the Apostles'!'

'You didn't say so! And every fool knows, except you, that the Nicene is the most historic creed!'

'Let un go on, let un go on!' said the auctioneer.

But Jude's mind seemed to grow confused soon, and he could not get on. He put his hand to his forehead, and his face assumed an expression of pain.

'Give him another glass – then he'll fetch up and get through it,' said Tinker Taylor.

Somebody threw down threepence, the glass was handed, Jude stretched out his arm for it without looking, and having swallowed the liquor, went on in a moment in a revived voice, raising it as he neared the end with the manner of a priest leading a congregation:

'Et in Spiritum Sanctum, Dominum et vivificantem, qui ex Patre Filioque procedit. Qui cum Patre et Filio simul adoratur et conglorificatur. Qui locutus est per prophetas.

'Et unam Catholicam et Apostolicam Ecclesiam. Confiteor unum Baptisma in remissionem peccatorum. Et exspecto Resurrectionem mortuorum. Et vitam venturi saeculi. Amen.'

'Well done!' said several, enjoying the last word, as being the first and only one they had recognized.

Then Jude seemed to shake the fumes from his brain, as he stared round upon them.

'You pack of fools!' he cried. 'Which one of you knows whether I have said it or no? It might have been the Ratcatcher's Daughter* in double Dutch for all that your besotted heads can tell! See what I have brought myself to – the crew I have come among!'

The landlord, who had already had his license endorsed for harbouring queer characters, feared a riot, and came outside the counter; but Jude, in his sudden flash of reason, had turned in disgust and left the scene, the door slamming with a dull thud behind him.

He hastened down the lane and round into the straight broad street, which he followed till it merged in the highway, and all sound of his late companions had been left behind. Onward he still went, under the influence of a childlike yearning for the one being in the world to whom it seemed possible to fly – an unreasoning desire, whose ill judgment was not apparent to him now. In the course of an hour, when it was between ten and eleven o'clock, he entered the village of Lumsdon, and reaching the cottage, saw that a light was burning in a downstairs room, which he assumed, rightly as it happened, to be hers.

Jude stepped close to the wall, and tapped with his finger on the pane, saying impatiently, 'Sue, Sue!'

She must have recognized his voice, for the light disappeared from the apartment, and in a second or two the door was unlocked and opened, and Sue appeared with a candle in her hand.

'Is it Jude? Yes, it is! My dear, dear cousin, what's the matter?'

'O, I am – I couldn't help coming, Sue!' said he, sinking down upon the doorstep. 'I am so wicked, Sue – my heart is nearly broken, and I could not bear my life as it was! So I have been drinking, and blaspheming, or next door to it, and saying holy things in disreputable quarters – repeating in idle bravado words which ought never to be uttered but reverently! O, do anything with me, Sue – kill me – I don't care! Only don't hate me and despise me like all the rest of the world!'

'You are ill, poor dear! No, I won't despise you; of course I won't! Come in and rest, and let me see what I can do for you. Now lean on me, and don't mind.' With one hand holding the candle and the other supporting him, she led him indoors, and placed him in the only easy-chair the meagrely furnished house afforded, stretching his feet upon another, and pulling off his boots. Jude, now getting towards his sober senses, could only say, 'Dear, dear Sue!' in a voice broken by grief and contrition.

She asked him if he wanted anything to eat, but he shook his head. Then telling him to go to sleep, and that she would come down early in the morning and get him some breakfast, she bade him good-night and ascended the stairs. .

Almost immediately he fell into a heavy slumber, and did not wake till dawn. At first he did not know where he was, but by degrees his situation cleared to him, and he beheld it in all the ghastliness of a right mind. She knew the worst of him – the very worst. How could he face her now? She would soon be coming down to see about breakfast, as she had said, and there would he be in all his shame confronting her. He could not bear the thought, and softly drawing on his boots, and taking his hat from the nail on which she had hung it, he slipped noiselessly out of the house.

His fixed idea was to get away to some obscure spot and hide, and perhaps pray; and the only spot which occurred to him was Marygreen. He called at his lodging in Christminster, where he found awaiting him a note of dismissal from his employer; and having packed up he turned his back upon the city that had been such a thorn in his side, and struck southward into Wessex. He had no money left in his pocket, his small savings, deposited at one of the banks in Christminster, having fortunately been left untouched. To get to Marygreen, therefore, his only course was walking; and the distance being nearly twenty miles, he had ample time to complete on the way the sobering process begun in him.

At some hour of the evening he reached Alfredston. Here he pawned his waistcoat, and having gone out of the town a mile or two, slept under a rick that night. At dawn he rose, shook off the hayseeds and stems from his clothes, and started again, breasting

the long white road up the hill to the downs, which had been visible
to him a long way off, and passing the milestone at the top, whereon
he had carved his hopes years ago.

He reached the ancient hamlet while the people were at breakfast.
Weary and mud-bespattered, but quite possessed of his ordinary
clearness of brain, he sat down by the well, thinking as he did so
what a poor Christ he made. Seeing a trough of water near he
bathed his face, and went on to the cottage of his great-aunt, whom
he found breakfasting in bed, attended by the woman who lived with
her.

'What — out o' work?' asked his relative, regarding him through
eyes sunken deep, under lids heavy as pot-covers, no other cause for
his tumbled appearance suggesting itself to one whose whole life had
been a struggle with material things.

'Yes,' said Jude heavily. 'I think I must have a little rest.'

Refreshed by some breakfast, he went up to his old room and lay
down in his shirt-sleeves, after the manner of the artizan. He fell
asleep for a short while, and when he awoke it was as if he had
awakened in hell. It *was* hell — 'the hell of conscious failure', both
in ambition and in love. He thought of that previous abyss into
which he had fallen before leaving this part of the country; the
deepest deep he had supposed it then; but it was not so deep as this.
That had been the breaking in of the outer bulwarks of his hope: this
was of his second line.

If he had been a woman he must have screamed under the
nervous tension which he was now undergoing. But that relief being
denied to his virility, he clenched his teeth in misery, bringing lines
about his mouth like those in the Laocoön,* and corrugations
between his brows.

A mournful wind blew through the trees, and sounded in the
chimney like the pedal notes of an organ. Each ivy leaf overgrowing
the wall of the churchless churchyard hard by, now abandoned,
pecked its neighbour smartly, and the vane on the new Victorian-
Gothic church in the new spot had already begun to creak. Yet
apparently it was not always the outdoor wind that made the deep
murmurs; it was a voice. He guessed its origin in a moment or two;
the curate was praying with his aunt in the adjoining room. He
remembered her speaking of him. Presently the sounds ceased, and

a step seemed to cross the landing. Jude sat up, and shouted 'Hoi!'

The step made for his door, which was open, and a man looked in. It was a young clergyman.

'I think you are Mr Highridge,' said Jude. 'My aunt has mentioned you more than once. Well, here I am, just come home; a fellow gone to the bad; though I had the best intentions in the world at one time. Now I am melancholy mad, what with drinking and one thing and another.'

Slowly Jude unfolded to the curate his late plans and movements, by an unconscious bias dwelling less upon the intellectual and ambitious side of his dream, and more upon the theological, though this had, up till now, been merely a portion of the general plan of advancement.

'Now I know I have been a fool, and that folly is with me,' added Jude in conclusion. 'And I don't regret the collapse of my University hopes one jot. I wouldn't begin again if I were sure to succeed. I don't care for social success any more at all. But I do feel I should like to do some good thing; and I bitterly regret the Church, and the loss of my chance of being her ordained minister.'

The curate, who was a new man to this neighbourhood, had grown deeply interested, and at last he said: 'If you feel a real call to the ministry, and I won't say from your conversation that you do not, for it is that of a thoughtful and educated man, you might enter the Church as a licentiate. Only you must make up your mind to avoid strong drink.'

'I could avoid that easily enough, if I had any kind of hope to support me!'

PART THIRD

At Melchester

'For there was no other girl, O bridegroom, like her!'
— SAPPHO (H. T. Wharton)

IT was a new idea — the ecclesiastical and altruistic life as distinct from the intellectual and emulative life. A man could preach and do good to his fellow-creatures without taking double-firsts in the schools of Christminster, or having anything but ordinary knowledge. The old fancy which had led on to the culminating vision of the bishopric had not been an ethical or theological enthusiasm at all, but a mundane ambition masquerading in a surplice. He feared that his whole scheme had degenerated to, even though it might not have originated in, a social unrest which had no foundation in the nobler instincts; which was purely an artificial product of civilization. There were thousands of young men on the same self-seeking track at the present moment. The sensual hind who ate, drank, and lived carelessly with his wife through the days of his vanity * was a more likable being than he.

But to enter the Church in such an unscholarly way that he could not in any probability rise to a higher grade through all his career than that of the humble curate wearing his life out in an obscure village or city slum — that might have a touch of goodness and greatness in it; that might be true religion, and a purgatorial course worthy of being followed by a remorseful man.

The favourable light in which this new thought showed itself by contrast with his foregone intentions cheered Jude, as he sat there, shabby and lonely; and it may be said to have given, during the next few days, the *coup de grâce* to his intellectual career — a career which had extended over the greater part of a dozen years. He did nothing, however, for some long stagnant time to advance his new desire, occupying himself with little local jobs in putting up and lettering headstones about the neighbouring villages, and submitting to be regarded as a social failure, a returned purchase, by the half-dozen or so of farmers and other country-people who condescended to nod to him.

The human interest of the new intention — and a human interest is indispensable to the most spiritual and self-sacrificing – was created by a letter from Sue, bearing a fresh postmark. She evidently wrote with anxiety, and told very little about her own doings, more than that she had passed some sort of examination for a Queen's Scholarship, and was going to enter a Training College at Melchester to complete herself for the vocation she had chosen, partly by his influence. There was a Theological College at Melchester; Melchester was a quiet and soothing place, almost entirely ecclesiastical in its tone; a spot where worldly learning and intellectual smartness had no establishment; where the altruistic feeling that he did possess would perhaps be more highly estimated than a brilliancy which he did not.

As it would be necessary that he should continue for a time to work at his trade while reading up Divinity, which he had neglected at Christminster for the ordinary classical grind, what better course for him than to get employment at the further city, and pursue this plan of reading? That his excessive human interest in the new place was entirely of Sue's making, while at the same time Sue was to be regarded even less than formerly as proper to create it, had an ethical contradictoriness to which he was not blind. But that much he conceded to human frailty, and hoped to learn to love her only as a friend and kinswoman.

He considered that he might so mark out his coming years as to begin his ministry at the age of thirty – an age which much attracted him as being that of his exemplar when he first began to teach in Galilee. This would allow him plenty of time for deliberate study, and for acquiring capital by his trade to help his aftercourse of keeping the necessary terms at a Theological College.

Christmas had come and passed, and Sue had gone to the Melchester Normal School. The time was just the worst in the year for Jude to get into new employment, and he had written suggesting to her that he should postpone his arrival for a month or so, till the days had lengthened. She had acquiesced so readily that he wished he had not proposed it – she evidently did not much care about him, though she had never once reproached him for his strange conduct in coming to her that night, and his silent disappearance. Neither had she ever said a word about her relations with Mr Phillotson.

Suddenly, however, quite a passionate letter arrived from Sue. She was quite lonely and miserable, she told him. She hated the place she was in; it was worse than the ecclesiastical designer's; worse than anywhere. She felt utterly friendless; could he come immediately? – though when he did come she would only be able to see him at limited times, the rules of the establishment she found herself in being strict to a degree. It was Mr Phillotson who had advised her to come there, and she wished she had never listened to him.

Phillotson's suit was not exactly prospering, evidently; and Jude felt unreasonably glad. He packed up his things and went to Melchester with a lighter heart than he had known for months.

This being the turning over a new leaf he duly looked about for a temperance hotel, and found a little establishment of that description in the street leading from the station. When he had had something to eat he walked out into the dull winter light over the town bridge, and turned the corner towards the Close. The day was foggy, and standing under the walls of the most graceful architectural pile in England he paused and looked up. The lofty building was visible as far as the roof-ridge; above, the dwindling spire rose more and more remotely, till its apex was quite lost in the mist drifting across it.

The lamps now began to be lighted, and turning to the west front he walked round. He took it as a good omen that numerous blocks of stone were lying about, which signified that the cathedral was undergoing restoration or repair to a considerable extent. It seemed to him, full of the superstitions of his beliefs, that this was an exercise of forethought on the part of a ruling Power, that he might find plenty to do in the art he practised while waiting for a call to higher labours.

Then a wave of warmth came over him as he thought how near he now stood to the bright-eyed vivacious girl with the broad forehead and pile of dark hair above it; the girl with the kindling glance, daringly soft at times – something like that of the girls he had seen in engravings from paintings of the Spanish school. She was here – actually in this Close – in one of the houses confronting this very west façade.

He went down the broad gravel path towards the building. It was

an ancient edifice of the fifteenth century, once a palace, now a
training-school, with mullioned and transomed windows, and a
courtyard in front shut in from the road by a wall. Jude opened the
gate and went up to the door through which, on inquiring for his
cousin, he was gingerly admitted to a waiting-room, and in a few
minutes she came.

Though she had been here such a short while, she was not as he
had seen her last. All her bounding manner was gone; her curves of
motion had become subdued lines. The screens and subtleties of
convention had likewise disappeared. Yet neither was she quite the
woman who had written the letter that summoned him. That had
plainly been dashed off in an impulse which second thoughts had
somewhat regretted; thoughts that were possibly of his recent self-
disgrace. Jude was quite overcome with emotion.

'You don't — think me a demoralized wretch — for coming to you
as I was — and going so shamefully, Sue?'

'O, I have tried not to! You said enough to let me know what had
caused it. I hope I shall never have any doubt of your worthiness,
my poor Jude! And I am glad you have come!'

She wore a murrey-coloured ∗ gown with a little lace collar. It
was made quite plain, and hung about her slight figure with clinging
gracefulness. Her hair, which formerly she had worn according to
the custom of the day, was now twisted up tightly, and she had
altogether the air of a woman clipped and pruned by severe discipline, an under-brightness shining through from the depths which
that discipline had not yet been able to reach.

She had come forward prettily; but Jude felt that she had hardly
expected him to kiss her, as he was burning to do, under other
colours than those of cousinship. He could not perceive the least
sign that Sue regarded him as a lover, or ever would do so, now that
she knew the worst of him, even if he had the right to behave as one;
and this helped on his growing resolve to tell her of his matrimonial
entanglement, which he had put off doing from time to time in sheer
dread of losing the bliss of her company.

Sue came out into the town with him, and they walked and talked
with tongues centred only on the passing moments. Jude said he
would like to buy her a little present of some sort, and then she
confessed, with something of shame, that she was dreadfully hungry.

They were kept on very short allowances in the College, and a dinner, tea, and supper all in one was the present she most desired in the world. Jude thereupon took her to an inn and ordered whatever the house afforded, which was not much. The place, however, gave them a delightful opportunity for a *tête-à-tête*, nobody else being in the room, and they talked freely.

She told him about the school as it was at that date, and the rough living, and the mixed character of her fellow-students, gathered together from all parts of the diocese, and how she had to get up and work by gas-light in the early morning, with all the bitterness of a young person to whom restraint was new. To all this he listened; but it was not what he wanted especially to know – her relations with Phillotson. That was what she did not tell. When they had sat and eaten, Jude impulsively placed his hand upon hers; she looked up and smiled, and took his quite freely into her own little soft one, dividing his fingers and coolly examining them, as if they were the fingers of a glove she was purchasing.

'Your hands are rather rough, Jude, aren't they?' she said.

'Yes. So would yours be if they held a mallet and chisel all day.'

'I don't dislike it, you know. I think it is noble to see a man's hands subdued to what he works in. . . . Well, I'm rather glad I came to this Training School, after all. See how independent I shall be after the two years' training! I shall pass pretty high, I expect, and Mr Phillotson will use his influence to get me a big school.'

She had touched the subject at last. 'I had a suspicion, a fear,' said Jude, 'that he – cared about you rather warmly, and perhaps wanted to marry you.'

'Now don't be such a silly boy!'

'He has said something about it, I expect.'

'If he had, what would it matter? An old man like him!'

'O, come, Sue; he's not so very old. And I know what I saw him doing—'

'Not kissing me – that I'm certain!'

'No. But putting his arm round your waist.'

'Ah – I remember. But I didn't know he was going to.'

'You are wriggling out of it, Sue, and it isn't quite kind!'

Her ever-sensitive lip began to quiver, and her eye to blink, at something this reproof was deciding her to say.

'I know you'll be angry if I tell you everything, and that's why I don't want to!'

'Very well, then, dear,' he said soothingly. 'I have no real right to ask you, and I don't wish to know.'

'I shall tell you!' said she, with the perverseness that was part of her. 'This is what I have done: I have promised — I have promised — that I will marry him when I come out of the Training-School two years hence, and have got my Certificate; his plan being that we shall then take a large double school in a great town — he the boys' and I the girls' — as married school-teachers often do, and make a good income between us.'

'O, Sue! . . . But of course it is right — you couldn't have done better!'

He glanced at her and their eyes met, the reproach in his own belying his words. Then he drew his hand quite away from hers, and turned his face in estrangement from her to the window. Sue regarded him passively without moving.

'I knew you would be angry!' she said with an air of no emotion whatever. 'Very well — I am wrong, I suppose! I ought not to have let you come to see me! We had better not meet again; and we'll only correspond at long intervals, on purely business matters!'

This was just the one thing he would not be able to bear, as she probably knew, and it brought him round at once. 'O yes, we will,' he said quickly. 'Your being engaged can make no difference to me whatever. I have a perfect right to see you when I want to; and I shall!'

'Then don't let us talk of it any more. It is quite spoiling our evening together. What does it matter about what one is going to do two years hence!'

She was something of a riddle to him, and he let the subject drift away. 'Shall we go and sit in the Cathedral?' he asked, when their meal was finished.

'Cathedral? Yes. Though I think I'd rather sit in the railway station,' she answered, a remnant of vexation still in her voice. 'That's the centre of the town life now. The Cathedral has had its day!'

'How modern you are!'

'So would you be if you had lived so much in the Middle Ages as

I have done these last few years! The Cathedral was a very good
place four or five centuries ago; but it is played out now. . . . I am
not modern, either. I am more ancient than mediævalism, if you
only knew.'

Jude looked distressed.

'There — I won't say any more of that!' she cried. 'Only you don't
know how bad I am, from your point of view, or you wouldn't think
so much of me, or care whether I was engaged or not. Now there's
just time for us to walk round the Close, then I must go in, or I shall
be locked out for the night.'

He took her to the gate and they parted. Jude had a conviction
that his unhappy visit to her on that sad night had precipitated this
marriage engagement, and it did anything but add to his happiness.
Her reproach had taken that shape, then, and not the shape of
words. However, next day he set about seeking employment, which
it was not so easy to get as at Christminster, there being, as a rule,
less stone-cutting in progress in this quiet city, and hands being
mostly permanent. But he edged himself in by degrees. His first
work was some carving at the cemetery on the hill; and ultimately
he became engaged on the labour he most desired — the Cathedral
repairs, which were very extensive, the whole interior stonework
having been overhauled, to be largely replaced by new.

It might be a labour of years to get it all done, and he had
confidence enough in his own skill with the mallet and chisel to feel
that it would be a matter of choice with himself how long he would
stay.

The lodgings he took near the Close Gate would not have
disgraced a curate, the rent representing a higher percentage on his
wages than mechanics of any sort usually care to pay. His combined
bed and sitting room was furnished with framed photographs of the
rectories and deaneries at which his landlady had lived as trusted
servant in her time, and the parlour downstairs bore a clock on the
mantelpiece inscribed to the effect that it was presented to the same
serious-minded woman by her fellow-servants on the occasion of
her marriage. Jude added to the furniture of his room by unpacking
photographs of the ecclesiastical carvings and monuments that he
had executed with his own hands; and he was deemed a satisfactory
acquisition as tenant of the vacant apartment.

He found an ample supply of theological books in the city book-shops, and with these his studies were recommenced in a different spirit and direction from his former course. As a relaxation from the Fathers, and such stock works as Paley and Butler,* he read Newman, Pusey, and many other modern lights. He hired a har-monium, set it up in his lodging, and practised chants thereon, single and double.

CHAPTER TWO

'TO-MORROW is our grand day, you know. Where shall we go?'

'I have leave from three till nine. Wherever we can get to and come back from in that time. Not ruins, Jude — I don't care for them.'

'Well — Wardour Castle.* And then we can do Fonthill if we like — all in the same afternoon.'

'Wardour is Gothic ruins — and I hate Gothic!'

'No. Quite otherwise. It is a classic building — Corinthian, I think; with a lot of pictures.'

'Ah — that will do. I like the sound of Corinthian. We'll go.'

Their conversation had run thus some few weeks later, and next morning they prepared to start. Every detail of the outing was a facet reflecting a sparkle to Jude, and he did not venture to meditate on the life of inconsistency he was leading. His Sue's conduct was one lovely conundrum to him; he could say no more.

There duly came the charm of calling at the College door for her; her emergence in a nunlike simplicity of costume that was rather enforced than desired; the traipsing along to the station, the porters' 'B'your leave!' the screaming of the trains — everything formed the basis of a beautiful crystallization. Nobody stared at Sue, because she was so plainly dressed, which comforted Jude in the thought that only himself knew the charms those habiliments subdued. A matter of ten pounds spent in a drapery-shop, which had no connection with her real life or her real self, would have set all Melchester staring. The guard of the train thought they were lovers, and put them into a compartment all by themselves.

'That's a good intention wasted!' said she.

Jude did not respond. He thought the remark unnecessarily cruel, and partly untrue.

They reached the Park and Castle and wandered through the picture-galleries, Jude stopping by preference in front of the devotional pictures by Del Sarto, Guido Reni, Spagnoletto, Sassoferrato, Carlo Dolci, and others. Sue paused patiently beside him, and stole critical looks into his face as, regarding the Virgins, Holy Families, and Saints, it grew reverent and abstracted. When she had thoroughly estimated him at this, she would move on and wait for him before a Lely or Reynolds. It was evident that her cousin deeply interested her, as one might be interested in a man puzzling out his way along a labyrinth from which one had one's self escaped.

When they came out a long time still remained to them, and Jude proposed that as soon as they had had something to eat they should walk across the high country to the north of their present position, and intercept the train of another railway leading back to Melchester, at a station about seven miles off. Sue, who was inclined for any adventure that would intensify the sense of her day's freedom, readily agreed; and away they went, leaving the adjoining station behind them.

It was indeed open country, wide and high. They talked and bounded on, Jude cutting from a little covert a long walking-stick for Sue as tall as herself, with a great crook, which made her look like a shepherdess. About half-way on their journey they crossed a main road running due east and west — the old road from London to Land's End. They paused, and looked up and down it for a moment, and remarked upon the desolation which had come over this once lively thoroughfare, while the wind dipped to earth and scooped straws and hay-stems from the ground.

They crossed the road and passed on, but during the next half-mile Sue seemed to grow tired, and Jude began to be distressed for her. They had walked a good distance altogether, and if they could not reach the other station it would be rather awkward. For a long time there was no cottage visible on the wide expanse of down and turnip-land; but presently they came to a sheepfold, and next to the shepherd, pitching hurdles. He told them that the only house near was his mother's and his, pointing to a little dip ahead from which a faint blue smoke arose, and recommended them to go on and rest there.

This they did, and entered the house, admitted by an old woman

without a single tooth, to whom they were as civil as strangers can
be when their only chance of rest and shelter lies in the favour of the
householder.

'A nice little cottage,' said Jude.

'O, I don't know about the niceness. I shall have to thatch it soon,
and where the thatch is to come from I can't tell, for straw do get
that dear, that 'twill soon be cheaper to cover your house wi'
chainey * plates than thatch.'

They sat resting, and the shepherd came in. 'Don't 'ee mind I,' he
said with a deprecating wave of the hand; 'bide here as long as ye
will. But mid you be thinking o' getting back to Melchester to-night
by train? Because you'll never do it in this world, since you don't
know the lie of the country. I don't mind going with ye some o' the
ways, but even then the train mid be gone.'

They started up.

'You can bide here, you know, over the night — can't 'em,
mother? The place is welcome to ye. 'Tis hard lying, rather, but
volk may do worse.' He turned to Jude and asked privately: 'Be you
a married couple?'

'Hsh — no!' said Jude.

'O — I meant nothing ba'dy — not I! Well then, she can go into
mother's room, and you and I can lie in the outer chimmer * after
they've gone through. I can call ye soon enough to catch the first
train back. You've lost this one now.'

On consideration they decided to close with this offer, and drew
up and shared with the shepherd and his mother the boiled bacon
and greens for supper.

'I rather like this,' said Sue, while their entertainers were clearing
away the dishes. 'Outside all laws except gravitation and germina-
tion.'

'You only think you like it; you don't: you are quite a product of
civilization,' said Jude, a recollection of her engagement reviving his
soreness a little.

'Indeed I am not, Jude. I like reading and all that, but I crave to
get back to the life of my infancy and its freedom.'

'Do you remember it so well? You seem to me to have nothing
unconventional at all about you.'

'O, haven't I! You don't know what's inside me.'

'What?'

'The Ishmaelite.'*

'An urban miss is what you are.'

She looked severe disagreement, and turned away.

The shepherd aroused them the next morning, as he had said. It was bright and clear, and the four miles to the train were accomplished pleasantly. When they had reached Melchester, and walked to the Close, and the gables of the old building in which she was again to be immured rose before Sue's eyes, she looked a little scared. 'I expect I shall catch it!' she murmured.

They rang the great bell and waited.

'O, I bought something for you, which I had nearly forgotten,' she said quickly, searching her pocket. 'It is a new little photograph of me. Would you like it?'

'*Would* I!' He took it gladly, and the porter came. There seemed to be an ominous glance on his face when he opened the gate. She passed in, looking back at Jude, and waving her hand.

THE seventy young women, of ages varying in the main from nineteen to one-and-twenty, though several were older, who at this date filled the species of nunnery known as the Training-School at Melchester, formed a very mixed community, which included the daughters of mechanics, curates, surgeons, shop-keepers, farmers, dairymen, soldiers, sailors, and villagers. They sat in the large school-room of the establishment on the evening previously described, and word was passed round that Sue Bridehead had not come in at closing-time.

'She went out with her young man,' said a second-year's student, who knew about young men. 'And Miss Traceley saw her at the station with him. She'll have it hot when she does come.'

'She said he was her cousin,' observed a youthful new girl.

'That excuse has been made a little too often in this school to be effectual in saving our souls,' said the head girl of the year, drily.

The fact was that, only twelve months before, there had occurred a lamentable seduction of one of the pupils, who had made the same statement in order to gain meetings with her lover. The affair had created a scandal, and the management had consequently been rough on cousins ever since.

At nine o'clock the names were called, Sue's being pronounced three times sonorously by Miss Traceley without eliciting an answer.

At a quarter past nine the seventy stood up to sing the 'Evening Hymn', and then knelt down to prayers. After prayers they went in to supper, and every girl's thought was, Where is Sue Bridehead? Some of the students, who had seen Jude from the window, felt that they would not mind risking her punishment for the pleasure of being kissed by such a kindly-faced young man. Hardly one among them believed in the cousinship.

Half-an-hour later they all lay in their cubicles, their tender feminine faces upturned to the flaring gas-jets which at intervals stretched down the long dormitories, every face bearing the legend

'The Weaker' upon it, as the penalty of the sex wherein they were moulded, which by no possible exertion of their willing hearts and abilities could be made strong while the inexorable laws of nature remain what they are. They formed a pretty, suggestive, pathetic sight, of whose pathos and beauty they were themselves unconscious, and would not discover till, amid the storms and strains of after-years, with their injustice, loneliness, child-bearing, and bereavement, their minds would revert to this experience as to something which had been allowed to slip past them insufficiently regarded.

One of the mistresses came in to turn out the lights, and before doing so gave a final glance at Sue's cot, which remained empty, and at her little dressing-table at the foot, which, like all the rest, was ornamented with various girlish trifles, framed photographs being not the least conspicuous among them. Sue's table had a moderate show, two men in their filigree and velvet frames standing together beside her looking-glass.

'Who are these men — did she ever say?' asked the mistress. 'Strictly speaking, relations' portraits only are allowed on these tables, you know.'

'One — the middle-aged man,' said a student in the next bed — 'is the schoolmaster she served under — Mr Phillotson.'

'And the other — this undergraduate in cap and gown — who is he?'

'He is a friend, or was. She has never told his name.'

'Was it either of these two who came for her?'

'No.'

'You are sure 'twas not the undergraduate?'

'Quite. He was a young man with a black beard.'

The lights were promptly extinguished, and till they fell asleep the girls indulged in conjectures about Sue, and wondered what games she had carried on in London and at Christminster before she came here, some of the more restless ones getting out of bed and looking from the mullioned windows at the vast west front of the Cathedral opposite, and the spire rising behind it.

When they awoke the next morning they glanced into Sue's nook, to find it still without a tenant. After the early lessons by gas-light, in half-toilet, and when they had come up to dress for breakfast, the bell of the entrance gate was heard to ring loudly. The mistress of the dormitory went away, and presently came back to say that the Principal's orders were that nobody was to speak to Bridehead without permission.

When, accordingly, Sue came into the dormitory to hastily tidy herself, looking flushed and tired, she went to her cubicle in silence, none of them coming out to greet her or to make inquiry. When they had gone downstairs they found that she did not follow them into the dining-hall to breakfast, and they then learnt that she had been severely reprimanded, and ordered to a solitary room for a week, there to be confined, and take her meals, and do all her reading.

At this the seventy murmured, the sentence being, they thought, too severe. A round robin was prepared and sent in to the Principal, asking for a remission of Sue's punishment. No notice was taken. Towards evening, when the geography mistress began dictating her subject, the girls in the class sat with folded arms.

'You mean that you are not going to work?' said the mistress at last. 'I may as well tell you that it has been ascertained that the young man Bridehead stayed out with was not her cousin, for the very good reason that she has no such relative. We have written to Christminster to ascertain.'

'We are willing to take her word,' said the head girl.

'This young man was discharged from his work at Christminster for drunkenness and blasphemy in public-houses, and he has come here to live, entirely to be near her.'

However, they remained stolid and motionless, and the mistress left the room to inquire from her superiors what was to be done.

Presently, towards dusk, the pupils, as they sat, heard exclamations from the first-year's girls in an adjoining class-room, and one rushed in to say that Sue Bridehead had got out of the back window of the room in which she had been confined, escaped in the dark across the lawn, and disappeared. How she had managed to get out of the garden nobody could tell, as it was bounded by the river at the bottom, and the side door was locked.

They went and looked at the empty room, the casement between the middle mullions of which stood open. The lawn was again searched with a lantern, every bush and shrub being examined, but she was nowhere hidden. Then the porter of the front gate was interrogated, and on reflection he said that he remembered hearing a sort of splashing in the stream at the back, but he had taken no notice, thinking some ducks had come down the river from above.

'She must have walked through the river!' said a mistress.

'Or drowned herself,' said the porter.

The mind of the matron was horrified — not so much at the possible death of Sue as at the possible half-column detailing that event in all the newspapers, which, added to the scandal of the year before, would give the College an unenviable notoriety for many months to come.

More lanterns were procured, and the river examined; and then, at last, on the opposite shore, which was open to the fields, some little boot-tracks were discerned in the mud, which left no doubt that the too excitable girl had waded through a depth of water reaching nearly to her shoulders — for this was the chief river of the county, and was mentioned in all the geography books with respect. As Sue had not brought disgrace upon the school by drowning herself, the matron began to speak superciliously of her, and to express gladness that she was gone.

On the self-same evening Jude sat in his lodgings by the Close Gate. Often at this hour after dusk he would enter the silent Close, and stand opposite the house that contained Sue, and watch the shadows of the girls' heads passing to and fro upon the blinds, and wish he had nothing else to do but to sit reading and learning all day what many of the thoughtless inmates despised. But to-night, having finished tea and brushed himself up, he was deep in the perusal of the Twenty-ninth Volume of Pusey's Library of the Fathers,* a set of books which he had purchased of a second-hand dealer at a price that seemed to him to be one of miraculous cheapness for that invaluable work. He fancied he heard something rattle lightly against his window; then he heard it again. Certainly somebody had thrown gravel. He rose and gently lifted the sash.

'Jude!' (from below).

'Sue!'

'Yes — it is! Can I come up without being seen?'

'O yes!'

'Then don't come down. Shut the window.'

Jude waited, knowing that she could enter easily enough, the front door being opened merely by a knob which anybody could turn, as in most old country towns. He palpitated at the thought that she had fled to him in her trouble as he had fled to her in his. What counterparts they were! He unlatched the door of his room, heard a stealthy rustle on the dark stairs, and in a moment she appeared in the light of his lamp. He went up to seize her hand, and found she was clammy as a marine deity, and that her clothes clung to her like the robes upon the figure in the Parthenon frieze.

'I'm so cold!' she said through her chattering teeth. 'Can I come by your fire, Jude?'

She crossed to his little grate and very little fire, but as the water dripped from her as she moved, the idea of drying herself was absurd. 'Whatever have you done, darling?' he asked, with alarm, the tender epithet slipping out unawares.

'Walked through the largest river in the county — that's what I've done! They locked me up for being out with you; and it seemed so unjust that I couldn't bear it, so I got out of the window and escaped across the stream!' She had begun the explanation in her usual slightly independent tones, but before she had finished the thin pink lips trembled, and she could hardly refrain from crying.

'Dear Sue!' he said. 'You must take off all your things! And let me see — you must borrow some from the landlady. I'll ask her.'

'No, no! Don't let her know, for God's sake! We are so near the school that they'll come after me!'

'Then you must put on mine. You don't mind?'

'O no.'

'My Sunday suit, you know. It is close here.' In fact, everything was close and handy in Jude's single chamber, because there was not room for it to be otherwise. He opened a drawer, took out his best dark suit, and giving the garments a shake, said, 'Now, how long shall I give you?'

'Ten minutes.'

Jude left the room and went into the street, where he walked up and down. A clock struck half-past seven, and he returned. Sitting in his only arm-chair he saw a slim and fragile being masquerading as himself on a Sunday, so pathetic in her defencelessness that his heart felt big with the sense of it. On two other chairs before the fire were her wet garments. She blushed as he sat down beside her, but only for a moment.

'I suppose, Jude, it is odd that you should see me like this and all my things hanging there? Yet what nonsense! They are only a woman's clothes — sexless cloth and linen. . . . I wish I didn't feel so ill and sick! Will you dry my clothes now? Please do, Jude, and I'll get a lodging by and by. It is not late yet.'

'No, you shan't, if you are ill. You must stay here. Dear, dear Sue, what can I get for you?'

'I don't know! I can't help shivering. I wish I could get warm.' Jude put on her his great-coat in addition, and then ran out to the nearest public-house, whence he returned with a little bottle in his hand. 'Here's six of best brandy,' he said. 'Now you drink it, dear; all of it.'

'I can't out of the bottle, can I?' Jude fetched the glass from the dressing-table, and administered the spirit in some water. She gasped a little, but gulped it down, and lay back in the arm-chair.

She then began to relate circumstantially her experiences since they had parted; but in the middle of her story her voice faltered, her head nodded, and she ceased. She was in a sound sleep. Jude, dying of anxiety lest she should have caught a chill which might permanently injure her, was glad to hear the regular breathing. He softly went nearer to her, and observed that a warm flush now rosed her hitherto blue cheeks, and felt that her hanging hand was no longer cold. Then he stood with his back to the fire regarding her, and saw in her almost a divinity.

CHAPTER FOUR

J UDE'S reverie was interrupted by the creak of footsteps ascending the stairs.

He whisked Sue's clothing from the chair where it was drying, thrust it under the bed, and sat down to his book. Somebody knocked and opened the door immediately. It was the landlady.

'O, I didn't know whether you was in or not, Mr Fawley. I wanted to know if you would require supper. I see you've a young gentleman—'

'Yes, ma'am. But I think I won't come down tonight. Will you bring supper up on a tray, and I'll have a cup of tea as well.'

It was Jude's custom to go downstairs to the kitchen, and eat his meals with the family, to save trouble. His landlady brought up the supper, however, on this occasion, and he took it from her at the door.

When she had descended he set the teapot on the hob, and drew out Sue's clothes anew; but they were far from dry. A thick woollen gown, he found, held a deal of water. So he hung them up again, and enlarged his fire and mused as the steam from the garments went up the chimney.

Suddenly she said, 'Jude!'

'Yes. All right. How do you feel now?'

'Better. Quite well. Why, I fell asleep, didn't I? What time is it? Not late surely?'

'It is past ten.'

'Is it really? What *shall* I do!' she said, starting up.

'Stay where you are.'

'Yes; that's what I want to do. But I don't know what they would say! And what will you do?'

'I am going to sit here by the fire all night, and read. To-morrow is Sunday, and I haven't to go out anywhere. Perhaps you will be saved a severe illness by resting there. Don't be frightened. I'm all right. Look here, what I have got for you. Some supper.'

When she had sat upright she breathed plaintively and said, 'I do feel rather weak still. I thought I was well; and I ought not to be here, ought I?' But the supper fortified her somewhat, and when she had had some tea and had lain back again she was bright and cheerful.

The tea must have been green, or too long drawn, for she seemed preternaturally wakeful afterwards, though Jude, who had not taken any, began to feel heavy; till her conversation fixed his attention.

'You called me a creature of civilization, or something, didn't you?' she said, breaking a silence. 'It was very odd you should have done that.'

'Why?'

'Well, because it is provokingly wrong. I am a sort of negation of it.'

'You are very philosophical. "A negation" is profound talking.'

'Is it? Do I strike you as being learned?' she asked, with a touch of raillery.

'No — not learned. Only you don't talk quite like a girl — well, a girl who has had no advantages.'

'I have had advantages. I don't know Latin and Greek, though I know the grammars of those tongues. But I know most of the Greek and Latin classics through translations, and other books too. I read Lemprière, Catullus, Martial, Juvenal, Lucian, Beaumont and Fletcher, Boccaccio, Scarron, De Brantôme, Sterne, De Foe, Smollett, Fielding, Shakespeare, the Bible, and other such; and found that all interest in the unwholesome part of those books ended with its mystery.'

'You have read more than I,' he said with a sigh. 'How came you to read some of those queerer ones?'

'Well,' she said thoughtfully, 'it was by accident. My life has been entirely shaped by what people call a peculiarity in me. I have no fear of men, as such, nor of their books. I have mixed with them — one or two of them particularly — almost as one of their own sex. I mean I have not felt about them as most women are taught to feel — to be on their guard against attacks on their virtue; for no average man — no man short of a sensual savage — will molest a woman by day or night, at home or abroad, unless she invites him. Until she says by a look "Come on" he is always afraid to, and if you never

say it, or look it, he never comes. However, what I was going to say
is that when I was eighteen I formed a friendly intimacy with an
undergraduate at Christminster, and he taught me a great deal, and
lent me books which I should never have got hold of otherwise.'

'Is your friendship broken off?'

'O yes. He died, poor fellow, two or three years after he had
taken his degree and left Christminster.'

'You saw a good deal of him, I suppose?'

'Yes. We used to go about together — on walking tours, reading
tours, and things of that sort — like two men almost. He asked me to
live with him, and I agreed to by letter. But when I joined him in
London I found he meant a different thing from what I meant. He
wanted me to be his mistress, in fact, but I wasn't in love with him —
and on my saying I should go away if he didn't agree to *my* plan, he
did so. We shared a sitting-room for fifteen months; and he became
a leader-writer for one of the greater London dailies; till he was
taken ill, and had to go abroad. He said I was breaking his heart by
holding out against him so long at such close quarters; he could
never have believed it of woman. I might play that game once too
often, he said. He came home merely to die. His death caused a
terrible remorse in me for my cruelty — though I hope he died of
consumption and not of me entirely. I went down to Sandbourne to
his funeral, and was his only mourner. He left me a little money —
because I broke his heart, I suppose. That's how men are — so much
better than women!'

'Good heavens! — what did you do then?'

'Ah — now you are angry with me!' she said, a contralto note of
tragedy coming suddenly into her silvery voice. 'I wouldn't have
told you if I had known!'

'No, I am not. Tell me all.'

'Well, I invested his money, poor fellow, in a bubble scheme, and
lost it. I lived about London by myself for some time, and then I
returned to Christminster, as my father — who was also in London,
and had started as an art metal-worker near Long-Acre — wouldn't
have me back; and I got that occupation in the artist-shop where
you found me. . . . I said you didn't know how bad I was!'

Jude looked round upon the arm-chair and its occupant, as if to
read more carefully the creature he had given shelter to. His voice

trembled as he said: 'However you have lived, Sue, I believe you are as innocent as you are unconventional!'

'I am not particularly innocent, as you see, now that I have

> "twitched the robe
> From that blank lay-figure your fancy draped",'*

said she, with an ostensible sneer, though he could hear that she was brimming with tears. 'But I have never yielded myself to any lover, if that's what you mean! I have remained as I began.'

'I quite believe you. But some women would not have remained as they began.'

'Perhaps not. Better women would not. People say I must be cold-natured — sexless — on account of it. But I won't have it! Some of the most passionately erotic poets have been the most self-contained in their daily lives.'

'Have you told Mr Phillotson about this University-scholar-friend?'

'Yes — long ago. I have never made any secret of it to anybody.'

'What did he say?'

'He did not pass any criticism — only said I was everything to him, whatever I did; and things like that.'

Jude felt much depressed; she seemed to get further and further away from him with her strange ways and curious unconsciousness of gender.

'Aren't you *really* vexed with me, dear Jude?' she suddenly asked, in a voice of such extraordinary tenderness that it hardly seemed to come from the same woman who had just told her story so lightly. 'I would rather offend anybody in the world than you, I think!'

'I don't know whether I am vexed or not. I know I care very much about you!'

'I care as much for you as for anybody I ever met.'

'You don't care *more*! There, I ought not to say that. Don't answer it!'

There was another long silence. He felt that she was treating him cruelly, though he could not quite say in what way. Her very helplessness seemed to make her so much stronger than he.

'I am awfully ignorant on general matters, although I have worked so hard,' he said, to turn the subject. 'I am absorbed in

Theology, you know. And what do you think I should be doing just about now, if you weren't here? I should be saying my evening prayers. I suppose you wouldn't like—'

'O no, no,' she answered, 'I would rather not, if you don't mind. I should seem so — such a hypocrite.'

'I thought you wouldn't join, so I didn't propose it. You must remember that I hope to be a useful minister some day.'

'To be ordained, I think you said?'

'Yes.'

'Then you haven't given up the idea? — I thought that perhaps you had by this time.'

'Of course not. I fondly thought at first that you felt as I do about that, as you were so mixed up in Christminster Anglicanism. And Mr Phillotson—'

'I have no respect for Christminster whatever, except, in a qualified degree, on its intellectual side,' said Sue Bridehead earnestly. 'My friend I spoke of took that out of me. He was the most irreligious man I ever knew, and the most moral. And intellect at Christminster is new wine in old bottles. The mediævalism of Christminster must go, be sloughed off, or Christminster itself will have to go. To be sure, at times one couldn't help having a sneaking liking for the traditions of the old faith, as preserved by a section of the thinkers there in touching and simple sincerity; but when I was in my saddest, rightest mind I always felt,

"O ghastly glories of saints, dead limbs of gibbeted Gods!" ' . . .*

'Sue, you are not a good friend of mine to talk like that!'

'Then I won't, dear Jude!' The emotional throat-note had come back, and she turned her face away.

'I still think Christminster has much that is glorious; though I was resentful because I couldn't get there.' He spoke gently, and resisted his impulse to pique her on to tears.

'It is an ignorant place, except as to the townspeople, artizans, drunkards, and paupers,' she said, perverse still at his differing from her. '*They* see life as it is, of course; but few of the people in the colleges do. You prove it in your own person. You are one of the very men Christminster was intended for when the colleges were founded; a man with a passion for learning, but no money, or opportunities, or friends. But you were elbowed off the pavement by the millionaires' sons.'

'Well, I can do without what it confers. I care for something higher.'

'And I for something broader, truer,' she insisted. 'At present intellect in Christminster is pushing one way, and religion the other; and so they stand stock-still, like two rams butting each other.'

'What would Mr Phillotson——'

'It is a place full of fetichists and ghost-seers!'

He noticed that whenever he tried to speak of the schoolmaster she turned the conversation to some generalizations about the offending University. Jude was extremely, morbidly, curious about her life as Phillotson's *protégée* and betrothed; yet she would not enlighten him.

'Well, that's just what I am, too,' he said. 'I am fearful of life, spectre-seeing always.'

'But you are good and dear!' she murmured.

His heart bumped, and he made no reply.

'You are in the Tractarian stage just now, are you not?' she added, putting on flippancy to hide real feeling, a common trick with her. 'Let me see — when was I there? — In the year eighteen hundred and——'

'There's a sarcasm in that which is rather unpleasant to me, Sue. Now will you do what I want you to? At this time I read a chapter, and then say prayers, as I told you. Now will you concentrate your attention on any book of these you like, and sit with your back to me, and leave me to my custom? You are sure you won't join me?'

'I'll look at you.'

'No. Don't tease, Sue!'

'Very well — I'll do just as you bid me, and I won't vex you, Jude,' she replied, in the tone of a child who was going to be good for ever after, turning her back upon him accordingly. A small Bible other than the one he was using lay near her, and during his retreat she took it up, and turned over the leaves.

'Jude,' she said brightly, when he had finished and come back to her; 'will you let me make you a *new* New Testament, like the one I made for myself at Christminster?'

'O yes. How was that made?'

'I altered my old one by cutting up all the Epistles and Gospels into separate *brochures*,* and re-arranging them in chronological order as written, beginning the book with Thessalonians, following on with the Epistles, and putting the Gospels much further on. Then I had the volume rebound. My University friend Mr—— — but never mind his name, poor boy — said it was an excellent idea. I know that reading it afterwards made it twice as interesting as before, and twice as understandable.'

'H'm!' said Jude, with a sense of sacrilege.

'And what a literary enormity this is,' she said, as she glanced into the pages of Solomon's Song. 'I mean the synopsis at the head of each chapter, explaining away the real nature of that rhapsody.* You needn't be alarmed: nobody claims inspiration for the chapter headings. Indeed, many divines treat them with contempt. It seems the drollest thing to think of the four-and-twenty elders, or bishops, or whatever number they were, sitting with long faces and writing down such stuff.'

Jude looked pained. 'You are quite Voltairean!' he murmured.

'Indeed? Then I won't say any more, except that people have no right to falsify the Bible! I *hate* such humbug as could attempt to plaster over with ecclesiastical abstractions such ecstatic, natural, human love as lies in that great and passionate song!' Her speech had grown spirited, and almost petulant at his rebuke, and her eyes moist. 'I *wish* I had a friend here to support me; but nobody is ever on my side!'

'But, my dear Sue, my very dear Sue, I am not against you!' he said, taking her hand, and surprised at her introducing personal feeling into mere argument.

'Yes you are, yes you are!' she cried, turning away her face that he might not see her brimming eyes. 'You are on the side of the people in the Training School — at least you seem almost to be! What I insist on is, that to explain such verses as this: "Whither is thy beloved gone, O thou fairest among women?" by the note: "*The Church professeth her faith*" is supremely ridiculous!'

'Well then, let it be! You make such a personal matter of everything! I am — only too inclined just now to apply the words profanely. You know *you* are fairest among women to me, come to that!'

'But you are not to say it now!' Sue replied, her voice changing to its softest note of severity. Then their eyes met, and they shook hands like cronies in a tavern, and Jude saw the absurdity of quarrelling on such a hypothetical subject, and she the silliness of crying about what was written in an old book like the Bible.

'I won't disturb your convictions — I really won't!' she went on soothingly, for now he was rather more ruffled than she. 'But I did want and long to ennoble some man to high aims; and when I saw you, and knew you wanted to be my comrade, I — shall I confess it? — thought that man might be you. But you take so much tradition on trust that I don't know what to say.'

'Well, dear; I suppose one must take some things on trust. Life isn't long enough to work out everything in Euclid problems before you believe it. I take Christianity.'

'Well, perhaps you might take something worse.'

'Indeed I might. Perhaps I have done so!' He thought of Arabella.

'I won't ask what, because we are going to be *very* nice with each other, aren't we, and never, never, vex each other any more?' She looked up trustfully, and her voice seemed trying to nestle in his breast.

'I shall always care for you!' said Jude.

'And I for you. Because you are single-hearted, and forgiving to your faulty and tiresome little Sue!'

He looked away, for that epicene tenderness of hers was too harrowing. Was it that which had broken the heart of the poor leader-writer; and was he to be the next one? . . . But Sue was so dear! . . . If he could only get over the sense of her sex, as she seemed to be able to do so easily of his, what a comrade she would make; for their difference of opinion on conjectural subjects only drew them closer together on matters of daily human experience. She was nearer to him than any other woman he had ever met, and he could scarcely believe that time, creed, or absence, would ever divide him from her.

But his grief at her incredulities returned. They sat on till she fell asleep again, and he nodded in his chair likewise. Whenever he aroused himself he turned her things, and made up the fire anew. About six o'clock he awoke completely, and lighting a candle, found that her clothes were dry. Her chair being a far more comfortable one than his she still slept on inside his coat, looking warm as a new bun and boyish as a Ganymedes.* Placing the garments by her and touching her on the shoulder he went downstairs, and washed himself by starlight in the yard.

CHAPTER FIVE

WHEN he returned she was dressed as usual.

'Now could I get out without anybody seeing me?' she asked. 'The town is not yet astir.'

'But you have had no breakfast.'

'O, I don't want any! I fear I ought not to have run away from that school! Things seem so different in the cold light of morning, don't they? What Mr Phillotson will say I don't know! It was quite by his wish that I went there. He is the only man in the world for whom I have any respect or fear. I hope he'll forgive me; but he'll scold me dreadfully, I expect!'

'I'll go to him and explain——' began Jude.

'O no, you shan't. I don't care for him! He may think what he likes – I shall do just as I choose!'

'But you just this moment said——'

'Well, if I did, I shall do as I like for all him! I have thought of what I shall do – go to the sister of one of my fellow-students in the Training School, who has asked me to visit her. She has a school near Shaston, about eighteen miles from here – and I shall stay there till this has blown over, and I get back to the Training School again.'

At the last moment he persuaded her to let him make her a cup of coffee, in a portable apparatus he kept in his room for use on rising to go to his work every day before the household was astir.

'Now a dew-bit * to eat with it,' he said; 'and off we go. You can have a regular breakfast when you get there.'

They went quietly out of the house, Jude accompanying her to the station. As they departed along the street a head was thrust out of an upper window of his lodging and quickly withdrawn. Sue still seemed sorry for her rashness, and to wish she had not rebelled; telling him at parting that she would let him know as soon as she got re-admitted to the Training School. They stood rather miserably together on the platform; and it was apparent that he wanted to say more.

'I want to tell you something — two things,' he said hurriedly as the train came up. 'One is a warm one, the other a cold one!'

'Jude,' she said. 'I know one of them. And you mustn't!'

'What?'

'You mustn't love me. You are to like me — that's all!'

Jude's face became so full of complicated glooms that hers was agitated in sympathy as she bade him adieu through the carriage window. And then the train moved on, and waving her pretty hand to him she vanished away.

Melchester was a dismal place enough for Jude that Sunday of her departure, and the Close so hateful that he did not go once to the Cathedral services. The next morning there came a letter from her, which, with her usual promptitude, she had written directly she had reached her friend's house. She told him of her safe arrival and comfortable quarters, and then added: —

'What I really write about, dear Jude, is something I said to you at parting. You had been so very good and kind to me that when you were out of sight I felt what a cruel and ungrateful woman I was to say it, and it has reproached me ever since. *If you want to love me, Jude, you may*: I don't mind at all; and I'll never say again that you mustn't!

'Now I won't write any more about that. You do forgive your thoughtless friend for her cruelty? and won't make her miserable by saying you don't? — Ever,   SUE'

It would be superfluous to say what his answer was; and how he thought what he would have done had he been free, which should have rendered a long residence with a female friend quite unnecessary for Sue. He felt he might have been pretty sure of his own victory if it had come to a conflict between Phillotson and himself for the possession of her.

Yet Jude was in danger of attaching more meaning to Sue's impulsive note than it really was intended to bear.

After the lapse of a few days he found himself hoping that she would write again. But he received no further communication; and in the intensity of his solicitude he sent another note, suggesting that he should pay her a visit some Sunday, the distance being under eighteen miles.

He expected a reply on the second morning after despatching his missive; but none came. The third morning arrived; the postman did not stop. This was Saturday, and in a feverish state of anxiety about her he sent off three brief lines stating that he was coming the following day, for he felt sure something had happened.

His first and natural thought had been that she was ill from her immersion; but it soon occurred to him that somebody would have written for her in such a case. Conjectures were put an end to by his arrival at the village school-house near Shaston on the bright morning of Sunday, between eleven and twelve o'clock, when the parish was as vacant as a desert, most of the inhabitants having gathered inside the church, whence their voices could occasionally be heard in unison.

A little girl opened the door. 'Miss Bridehead is upstairs,' she said. 'And will you please walk up to her?'

'Is she ill?' asked Jude hastily.

'Only a little – not very.'

Jude entered and ascended. On reaching the landing a voice told him which way to turn – the voice of Sue calling his name. He passed the doorway, and found her lying in a little bed in a room a dozen feet square.

'O Sue!' he cried, sitting down beside her and taking her hand. 'How is this! You couldn't write?'

'No – it wasn't that!' she answered. 'I did catch a bad cold – but I could have written. Only I wouldn't!'

'Why not? – frightening me like this!'

'Yes – that was what I was afraid of! But I had decided not to write to you any more. They won't have me back at the school – that's why I couldn't write. Not the fact, but the reason!'

'Well?'

'They not only won't have me, but they gave me a parting piece of advice—'

'What?'

She did not answer directly. 'I vowed I never would tell you, Jude – it is so vulgar and distressing!'

'Is it about us?'

'Yes.'

'But do tell me!'

'Well — somebody has sent them baseless reports about us, and they say you and I ought to marry as soon as possible, for the sake of my reputation! . . . There — now I have told you, and I wish I hadn't!'

'O poor Sue!'

'I don't think of you like that means! It did just *occur* to me to regard you in the way they think I do, but I hadn't begun to. I *have* recognized that the cousinship was merely nominal, since we met as total strangers. But my marrying you, dear Jude — why, of course, if I had reckoned upon marrying you I shouldn't have come to you so often! And I never supposed you thought of such a thing as marrying me till the other evening; when I began to fancy you did love me a little. Perhaps I ought not to have been so intimate with you. It is all my fault. Everything is my fault always!'

The speech seemed a little forced and unreal, and they regarded each other with a mutual distress.

'I was so blind at first!' she went on. 'I didn't see what you felt at all. O you have been unkind to me — you have — to look upon me as a sweetheart without saying a word, and leaving me to discover it myself! Your attitude to me has become known; and naturally they think we've been doing wrong! I'll never trust you again!'

'Yes, Sue,' he said simply; 'I am to blame — more than you think. I was quite aware that you did not suspect till within the last meeting or two what I was feeling about you. I admit that our meeting as strangers prevented a sense of relationship, and that it was a sort of subterfuge to avail myself of it. But don't you think I deserve a little consideration for concealing my wrong, very wrong, sentiments, since I couldn't help having them?'

She turned her eyes doubtfully towards him, and then looked away as if afraid she might forgive him.

By every law of nature and sex a kiss was the only rejoinder that fitted the mood and the moment, under the suasion of which Sue's undemonstrative regard of him might not inconceivably have changed its temperature. Some men would have cast scruples to the winds, and ventured it, oblivious both of Sue's declaration of her neutral feelings, and of the pair of autographs in the vestry chest of Arabella's parish church. Jude did not. He had, in fact, come in part to tell his own fatal story. It was upon his lips; yet at the hour of this distress he could not disclose it. He preferred to dwell upon the recognized barriers between them.

'Of course – I know you don't – care about me in any particular way,' he sorrowed. 'You ought not, and you are right. You belong to – Mr Phillotson. I suppose he has been to see you?'

'Yes,' she said shortly, her face changing a little. 'Though I didn't ask him to come. You are glad, of course, that he has been! But I shouldn't care if he didn't come any more!'

It was very perplexing to her lover that she should be piqued at his honest acquiescence in his rival, if Jude's feelings of love were deprecated by her. He went on to something else.

'This will blow over, dear Sue,' he said. 'The Training School authorities are not all the world. You can get to be a student in some other, no doubt.'

'I'll ask Mr Phillotson,' she said decisively.

Sue's kind hostess now returned from church, and there was no more intimate conversation. Jude left in the afternoon, hopelessly unhappy. But he had seen her, and sat with her. Such intercourse as that would have to content him for the remainder of his life. The lesson of renunciation it was necessary and proper that he, as a parish priest, should learn.

But the next morning when he awoke he felt rather vexed with her, and decided that she was rather unreasonable, not to say capricious. Then, in illustration of what he had begun to discern as one of her redeeming characteristics there came promptly a note, which she must have written almost immediately he had gone from her:

'Forgive me for my petulance yesterday! I was horrid to you; I know it, and I feel perfectly miserable at my horridness. It was so dear of you not to be angry! Jude, please still keep me as your friend and associate, with all my faults. I'll try not to be like it again.

'I am coming to Melchester on Saturday, to get my things away from the T.S., &c. I could walk with you for half-an-hour, if you would like? – Your repentant   SUE'

Jude forgave her straightway, and asked her to call for him at the Cathedral works when she came.

MEANWHILE a middle-aged man was dreaming a dream of great beauty concerning the writer of the above letter. He was Richard Phillotson, who had recently removed from the mixed village school at Lumsdon near Christminster to undertake a large boys' school in his native town of Shaston, which stood on a hill sixty miles to the south-west as the crow flies.

A glance at the place and its accessories was almost enough to reveal that the schoolmaster's plans and dreams so long indulged in had been abandoned for some new dream with which neither the Church nor literature had much in common. Essentially an unpractical man, he was now bent on making and saving money for a practical purpose – that of keeping a wife, who, if she chose, might conduct one of the girls' schools adjoining his own; for which purpose he had advised her to go into training, since she would not marry him off-hand.

About the time that Jude was removing from Marygreen to Melchester, and entering on adventures at the latter place with Sue, the schoolmaster was settling down in the new schoolhouse at Shaston. All the furniture being fixed, the books shelved, and the nails driven, he had begun to sit in his parlour during the dark winter nights and re-attempt some of his old studies – one branch of which had included Roman–Britannic antiquities – an unremunerative labour for a National schoolmaster* but a subject, that, after his abandonment of the University scheme, had interested him as being a comparatively unworked mine; practicable to those who, like himself, had lived in lonely spots where these remains were abundant, and were seen to compel inferences in startling contrast to accepted views on the civilization of that time.

A resumption of this investigation was the outward and apparent hobby of Phillotson at present – his ostensible reason for going alone into fields where causeways, dykes, and tumuli abounded, or shutting himself up in his house with a few urns, tiles, and mosaics he had collected, instead of calling round upon his new neighbours, who for their part had showed themselves willing enough to be friendly with him. But it was not the real, or the whole, reason, after all. Thus on a particular evening in the month, when it had grown quite late − to near midnight, indeed − and the light of his lamp, shining from his window at a salient angle of the hill-top town over infinite miles of valley westward, announced as by words a place and person given over to study, he was not exactly studying.

The interior of the room − the books, the furniture, the school-master's loose coat, his attitude at the table, even the flickering of the fire, bespoke the same dignified tale of undistracted research − more than creditable to a man who had had no advantages beyond those of his own making. And yet the tale, true enough till latterly, was not true now. What he was regarding was not history. They were historic notes, written in a bold womanly hand at his dictation some months before, and it was the clerical rendering of word after word that absorbed him.

He presently took from a drawer a carefully tied bundle of letters, few, very few, as correspondence counts nowadays. Each was in its envelope just as it had arrived, and the handwriting was of the same womanly character as the historic notes. He unfolded them one by one and read them musingly. At first sight there seemed in these small documents to be absolutely nothing to muse over. They were straightforward, frank letters, signed 'Sue B—'; just such ones as would be written during short absences, with no other thought than their speedy destruction, and chiefly concerning books in reading and other experiences of a Training School, forgotten doubtless by the writer with the passing of the day of their inditing. In one of them − quite a recent note − the young woman said that she had received his considerate letter, and that it was honourable and generous of him to say he would not come to see her oftener than she desired (the school being such an awkward place for callers, and because of her strong wish that her engagement to him should not be known, which it would infallibly be if he visited her often). Over these phrases the schoolmaster pored. What precise shade of satisfaction was to be gathered from a woman's gratitude that the man who loved her had not been often to see her? The problem occupied him, distracted him.

He opened another drawer, and found therein an envelope, from which he drew a photograph of Sue as a child, long before he had known her, standing under trellis-work with a little basket in her hand. There was another of her as a young woman, her dark eyes and hair making a very distinct and attractive picture of her, which just disclosed, too, the thoughtfulness that lay behind her lighter moods. It was a duplicate of the one she had given Jude, and would have given to any man. Phillotson brought it half-way to his lips, but withdrew it in doubt at her perplexing phrases: ultimately kissing the dead pasteboard with all the passionateness, and more than all the devotion, of a young man of eighteen.

The schoolmaster's was an unhealthy-looking, old-fashioned face, rendered more old-fashioned by his style of shaving. A certain gentlemanliness had been imparted to it by nature, suggesting an inherent wish to do rightly by all. His speech was a little slow, but his tones were sincere enough to make his hesitation no defect. His greying hair was curly, and radiated from a point in the middle of his crown. There were four lines across his forehead, and he only wore spectacles when reading at night. It was almost certainly a renunciation forced upon him by his academic purpose, rather than a distaste for women, which had hitherto kept him from closing with one of the sex in matrimony.

Such silent proceedings as those of this evening were repeated many and oft times when he was not under the eye of the boys, whose quick and penetrating regard would frequently become almost intolerable to the self-conscious master in his present anxious care for Sue, making him, in the grey hours of morning, dread to meet anew the gimlet glances, lest they should read what the dream within him was.

He had honourably acquiesced in Sue's announced wish that he was not often to visit her at the Training School; but at length, his patience being sorely tried, he set out one Saturday afternoon to pay her an unexpected call. There the news of her departure — expulsion as it might almost have been considered — was flashed upon him without warning or mitigation as he stood at the door expecting in a few minutes to behold her face; and when he turned away he could hardly see the road before him.

Sue had, in fact, never written a line to her suitor on the subject, although it was fourteen days old. A short reflection told him that this proved nothing, a natural delicacy being as ample a reason for silence as any degree of blameworthiness.

They had informed him at the school where she was living, and having no immediate anxiety about her comfort his thoughts took the direction of a burning indignation against the Training School Committee. In his bewilderment Phillotson entered the adjacent cathedral, just now in a direly dismantled state by reason of the repairs. He sat down on a block of freestone, regardless of the dusty imprint it made on his breeches; and his listless eyes following the movements of the workmen he presently became aware that the reputed culprit, Sue's lover Jude, was one amongst them.

Jude had never spoken to his former hero since the meeting by the model of Jerusalem. Having inadvertently witnessed Phillotson's tentative courtship of Sue in the lane there had grown up in the younger man's mind a curious dislike to think of the elder, to meet him, to communicate in any way with him; and since Phillotson's success in obtaining at least her promise had become known to Jude, he had frankly recognized that he did not wish to see or hear of his senior any more, learn anything of his pursuits, or even imagine again what excellencies might appertain to his character. On this very day of the schoolmaster's visit Jude was expecting Sue, as she had promised; and when therefore he saw the schoolmaster in the nave of the building, saw, moreover, that he was coming to speak to him, he felt no little embarrassment; which Phillotson's own embarrassment prevented his observing.

Jude joined him, and they both withdrew from the other workmen to the spot where Phillotson had been sitting. Jude offered him a piece of sackcloth for a cushion, and told him it was dangerous to sit on the bare block.

'Yes; yes,' said Phillotson abstractedly, as he reseated himself, his eyes resting on the ground as if he were trying to remember where he was. 'I won't keep you long. It was merely that I have heard that you have seen my little friend Sue recently. It occurred to me to speak to you on that account. I merely want to ask — about her.'

'I think I know what!' Jude hurriedly said. 'About her escaping from the Training School, and her coming to me?'

'Yes.'

'Well' — Jude for a moment felt an unprincipled and fiendish wish to annihilate his rival at all cost. By the exercise of that treachery which love for the same woman renders possible to men the most honourable in every other relation of life, he could send off Phillotson in agony and defeat by saying that the scandal was true, and that Sue had irretrievably committed herself with him. But his action did not respond for a moment to his animal instinct; and what he said was, 'I am glad of your kindness in coming to talk plainly to me about it. You know what they say? — that I ought to marry her.'

'What!'

'And I wish with all my soul I could!'

Phillotson trembled, and his naturally pale face acquired a corpse-like sharpness in its lines. 'I had no idea that it was of this nature! God forbid!'

'No, no!' said Jude aghast. 'I thought you understood? I mean that were I in a position to marry her, or some one, and settle down, instead of living in lodgings here and there, I should be glad!'

What he had really meant was simply that he loved her.

'But — since this painful matter has been opened up — what really happened?' asked Phillotson, with the firmness of a man who felt that a sharp smart now was better than a long agony of suspense hereafter. 'Cases arise, and this is one, when even ungenerous questions must be put to make false assumptions impossible, and to kill scandal.'

Jude explained readily; giving the whole series of adventures, including the night at the shepherd's, her wet arrival at his lodging, her indisposition from her immersion, their vigil of discussion, and his seeing her off next morning.

'Well now,' said Phillotson at the conclusion, 'I take it as your final word, and I know I can believe you, that the suspicion which led to her rustication is an absolutely baseless one?'

'It is,' said Jude solemnly. 'Absolutely. So help me God!'

The schoolmaster rose. Each of the twain felt that the interview could not comfortably merge in a friendly discussion of their recent experiences, after the manner of friends; and when Jude had taken him round, and shown him some features of the renovation which the old cathedral was undergoing, Phillotson bade the young man good-day and went away.

This visit took place about eleven o'clock in the morning; but no Sue appeared. When Jude went to his dinner at one he saw his beloved ahead of him in the street leading up from the North Gate, walking as if in no way looking for him. Speedily overtaking her he remarked that he had asked her to come to him at the Cathedral, and she had promised.

'I have been to get my things from the College,' she said – an observation which he was expected to take as an answer, though it was not one. Finding her to be in this evasive mood he felt inclined to give her the information so long withheld.

'You have not seen Mr Phillotson to-day?' he ventured to inquire.

'I have not. But I am not going to be cross-examined about him; and if you ask anything more I won't answer!'

'It is very odd that——' He stopped, regarding her.

'What?'

'That you are often not so nice in your real presence as you are in your letters!'

'Does it really seem so to you?' said she, smiling with quick curiosity. 'Well, that's strange; but I feel just the same about you, Jude. When you are gone away I seem such a cold-hearted——'

As she knew his sentiment towards her Jude saw that they were getting upon dangerous ground. It was now, he thought, that he must speak as an honest man.

But he did not speak, and she continued: 'It was that which made me write and say – I didn't mind your loving me, – if you wanted to, much!'

The exultation he might have felt at what that implied, or seemed to imply, was nullified by his intention, and he rested rigid till he began: 'I have never told you——'

'Yes you have,' murmured she.

'I mean, I have never told you my history – all of it.'

'But I guess it. I know nearly.'

Jude looked up. Could she possibly know of that morning performance of his with Arabella; which in a few months had ceased to be a marriage more completely than by death? He saw that she did not.

'I can't quite tell you here in the street,' he went on with a gloomy tongue. 'And you had better not come to my lodgings. Let us go in here.'

The building by which they stood was the market-house; it was the only place available; and they entered, the market being over, and the stalls and areas empty. He would have preferred a more congenial spot, but, as usually happens, in place of a romantic field or solemn aisle for his tale, it was told while they walked up and down over a floor littered with rotten cabbage-leaves, and amid all the usual squalors of decayed vegetable matter and unsaleable refuse. He began and finished his brief narrative, which merely led up to the information that he had married a wife some years earlier, and that his wife was living still. Almost before her countenance had time to change she hurried out the words,

'Why didn't you tell me before!'

'I couldn't. It seemed so cruel to tell it.'

'To yourself, Jude. So it was better to be cruel to me!'

'No, dear darling!' cried Jude passionately. He tried to take her hand, but she withdrew it. Their old relations of confidence seemed suddenly to have ended, and the antagonisms of sex to sex were left without any counterpoising predilections. She was his comrade, friend, unconscious sweetheart no longer; and her eyes regarded him in estranged silence.

'I was ashamed of the episode in my life which brought about the marriage,' he continued. 'I can't explain it precisely now. I could have done it if you had taken it differently!'

'But how can I?' she burst out. 'Here I have been saying, or writing, that — that you might love me, or something of the sort! — just out of charity — and all the time — O it is perfectly damnable how things are!' she said, stamping her foot in a nervous quiver.

'You take me wrong, Sue! I never thought you cared for me at all, till quite lately; so I felt it did not matter! Do you care for me, Sue? — you know how I mean? — I don't like "out of charity" at all!'

It was a question which in the circumstances Sue did not choose to answer.

'I suppose she — your wife — is — a very pretty woman, even if she's wicked?' she asked quickly.

'She's pretty enough, as far as that goes.'

'Prettier than I am, no doubt!'

'You are not the least alike. And I have never seen her for years. ... But she's sure to come back — they always do!'

'How strange of you to stay apart from her like this!' said Sue, her trembling lip and lumpy throat belying her irony. 'You, such a religious man. How will the demi-gods in your Pantheon – I mean those legendary persons you call Saints – intercede for you after this? Now if I had done such a thing it would have been different, and not remarkable, for I at least don't regard marriage as a Sacrament. Your theories are not so advanced as your practice!'

'Sue, you are terribly cutting when you like to be – a perfect Voltaire! But you must treat me as you will!'

When she saw how wretched he was she softened, and trying to blink away her sympathetic tears said with all the winning reproachfulness of a heart-hurt woman: 'Ah – you should have told me before you gave me that idea that you wanted to be allowed to love me! I had no feeling before that moment at the railway-station, except—' For once Sue was as miserable as he, in her attempts to keep herself free from emotion, and her less than half-success.

'Don't cry, dear!' he implored.

'I am – not crying – because I meant to – love you; but because of your want of – confidence!'

They were quite screened from the Market-square without, and he could not help putting out his arm towards her waist. His momentary desire was the means of her rallying. 'No, no!' she said, drawing back stringently, and wiping her eyes. 'Of course not! It would be hypocrisy to pretend that it would be meant as from my cousin; and it can't be in any other way.'

They moved on a dozen paces, and she showed herself recovered. It was distracting to Jude, and his heart would have ached less had she appeared anyhow but as she did appear; essentially large-minded and generous on reflection, despite a previous exercise of those narrow womanly humours on impulse that were necessary to give her sex.

'I don't blame you for what you couldn't help,' she said smiling. 'How should I be so foolish! I do blame you a little bit for not telling me before. But after all it doesn't matter. We should have had to keep apart, you see, even if this had not been in your life.'

'No, we shouldn't, Sue! This is the only obstacle!'

'You forget that I must have loved you, and wanted to be your wife, even if there had been no obstacle,' said Sue, with a gentle

seriousness which did not reveal her mind. 'And then we are
cousins, and it is bad for cousins to marry. And – I am engaged to
somebody else. As to our going on together as we were going, in a
sort of friendly way, the people round us would have made it unable
to continue. Their views of the relations of man and woman are
limited, as is proved by their expelling me from the school. Their
philosophy only recognizes relations based on animal desire. The
wide field of strong attachment where desire plays, at least, only a
secondary part, is ignored by them – the part of – who is it? –
Venus Urania.' *

Her being able to talk learnedly showed that she was mistress of
herself again; and before they parted she had almost regained her
vivacious glance, her reciprocity of tone, her gay manner, and her
second-thought attitude of critical largeness towards others of her
age and sex.

He could speak more freely now. 'There were several reasons
against my telling you rashly. One was what I have said; another,
that it was always impressed upon me that I ought not to marry –
that I belonged to an odd and peculiar family – the wrong breed for
marriage.'

'Ah – who used to say that to you?'

'My great-aunt. She said it always ended badly with us Fawleys.'

'That's strange. My father used to say the same to me!'

They stood possessed by the same thought, ugly enough, even as
an assumption: that a union between them, had such been possible,
would have meant a terrible intensification of unfitness – two bitters
in one dish.

'O but there can't be anything in it!' she said with nervous
lightness. 'Our family have been unlucky of late years in choosing
mates – that's all.'

And then they pretended to persuade themselves that all that had
happened was of no consequence, and that they could still be
cousins and friends and warm correspondents, and have happy
genial times when they met, even if they met less frequently than
before. Their parting was in good friendship, and yet Jude's last
look into her eyes was tinged with inquiry, for he felt that he did not
even now quite know her mind.

CHAPTER SEVEN

TIDINGS from Sue a day or two after passed across Jude like a withering blast.

Before reading the letter he was led to suspect that its contents were of a somewhat serious kind by catching sight of the signature – which was in her full name, never used in her correspondence with him since her first note:

'MY DEAR JUDE, – I have something to tell you which perhaps you will not be surprised to hear, though certainly it may strike you as being accelerated (as the railway companies say of their trains). Mr Phillotson and I are to be married quite soon – in three or four weeks. We had intended, as you know, to wait till I had gone through my course of training and obtained my certificate, so as to assist him, if necessary, in the teaching. But he generously says he does not see any object in waiting, now I am not at the Training School. It is so good of him, because the awkwardness of my situation has really come about by my fault in getting expelled.

'Wish me joy. Remember I say you are to, and you mustn't refuse! – Your affectionate cousin,

'SUSANNA FLORENCE MARY BRIDEHEAD'

Jude staggered under the news; could eat no breakfast; and kept on drinking tea because his mouth was so dry. Then presently he went back to his work and laughed the usual bitter laugh of a man so confronted. Everything seemed turning to satire. And yet, what could the poor girl do? he asked himself: and felt worse than shedding tears.

'O Susanna Florence Mary!' he said as he worked. 'You don't know what marriage means!'

Could it be possible that his announcement of his own marriage had pricked her on to this, just as his visit to her when in liquor may have pricked her on to her engagement? To be sure, there seemed to exist these other and sufficient reasons, practical and social, for her decision; but Sue was not a very practical or calculating person; and he was compelled to think that a pique at having his secret sprung upon her had moved her to give way to Phillotson's probable representations, that the best course to prove how unfounded were the suspicions of the school authorities would be to marry him off-hand, as in fulfilment of an ordinary engagement. Sue had, in fact, been placed in an awkward corner. Poor Sue!

He determined to play the Spartan; to make the best of it, and support her; but he could not write the requested good wishes for a day or two. Meanwhile there came another note from his impatient little dear:

'Jude, will you give me away? I have nobody else who could do it so conveniently as you, being the only married relation I have here on the spot, even if my father were friendly enough to be willing, which he isn't. I hope you won't think it a trouble? I have been looking at the marriage service in the Prayer-book, and it seems to me very humiliating that a giver-away should be required at all. According to the ceremony as there printed, my bridegroom chooses me of his own will and pleasure; but I don't choose him. Somebody *gives* me to him, like a she-ass or she-goat, or any other domestic animal. Bless your exalted views of woman, O Churchman! But I forget: I am no longer privileged to tease you. — Ever,
                        '**Susanna Florence Mary Bridehead**'

Jude screwed himself up to heroic key; and replied:

'**My dear Sue**, — Of course I wish you joy! And also of course I will give you away. What I suggest is that, as you have no house of your own, you do not marry from your school friend's, but from mine. It would be more proper, I think, since I am, as you say, the person nearest related to you in this part of the world.

'I don't see why you sign your letter in such a new and terribly formal way? Surely you care a bit about me still! — Ever your affectionate,
                                                        Jude'

What had jarred on him even more than the signature was a little sting he had been silent on — the phrase 'married relation' — What an idiot it made him seem as her lover! If Sue had written that in satire, he could hardly forgive her; if in suffering — ah, that was another thing!

His offer of his lodging must have commended itself to Phillotson at any rate, for the schoolmaster sent him a line of warm thanks, accepting the convenience. Sue also thanked him. Jude immediately moved into more commodious quarters, as much to escape the espionage of the suspicious landlady who had been one cause of Sue's unpleasant experience as for the sake of room.

Then Sue wrote to tell him the day fixed for the wedding; and Jude decided, after inquiry, that she should come into residence on the following Saturday, which would allow of a ten days' stay in the city prior to the ceremony, sufficiently representing a nominal residence of fifteen.*

She arrived by the ten o'clock train on the day aforesaid, Jude not going to meet her at the station, by her special request, that he should not lose a morning's work and pay, she said (if this were her true reason). But so well by this time did he know Sue that the remembrance of their mutual sensitiveness at emotional crises might, he thought, have weighed with her in this. When he came home to dinner she had taken possession of her apartment.

She lived in the same house with him, but on a different floor, and they saw each other little, an occasional supper being the only meal they took together, when Sue's manner was something that of a scared child. What she felt he did not know; their conversation was mechanical, though she did not look pale or ill. Phillotson came frequently, but mostly when Jude was absent. On the morning of the wedding, when Jude had given himself a holiday, Sue and her cousin had breakfast together for the first and last time during this curious interval; in his room — the parlour — which he had hired for the period of Sue's residence. Seeing, as women do, how helpless he was in making the place comfortable, she bustled about.

'What's the matter, Jude?' she said suddenly.

He was leaning with his elbows on the table and his chin on his hands, looking into a futurity which seemed to be sketched out on the tablecloth.

'O — nothing!'

'You are "father", you know. That's what they call the man who gives you away.'

Jude could have said 'Phillotson's age entitles him to be called that!' But he would not annoy her by such a cheap retort.

She talked incessantly, as if she dreaded his indulgence in reflection, and before the meal was over both he and she wished they had not put such confidence in their new view of things, and had taken breakfast apart. What oppressed Jude was the thought that, having done a wrong thing of this sort himself, he was aiding and abetting the woman he loved in doing a like wrong thing, instead of imploring and warning her against it. It was on his tongue to say, 'You have quite made up your mind?'

After breakfast they went out on an errand together moved by a mutual thought that it was the last opportunity they would have of indulging in unceremonious companionship. By the irony of fate, and the curious trick in Sue's nature of tempting Providence at critical times, she took his arm as they walked through the muddy street — a thing she had never done before in her life — and on turning the corner they found themselves close to a grey Perpendicular * church with a low-pitched roof — the church of St Thomas.

'That's the church,' said Jude.

'Where I am going to be married?'

'Yes.'

'Indeed!' she exclaimed with curiosity. 'How I should like to go in and see what the spot is like where I am so soon to kneel and do it.'

Again he said to himself, 'She does not realize what marriage means!'

He passively acquiesced in her wish to go in, and they entered by the western door. The only person inside the gloomy building was a charwoman cleaning. Sue still held Jude's arm, almost as if she loved him. Cruelly sweet, indeed, she had been to him that morning; but his thoughts of a penance in store for her were tempered by an ache:

> '. . . I can find no way
> How a blow should fall, such as falls on men,
> Nor prove too much for your womanhood!' *

They strolled undemonstratively up the nave towards the altar railing, which they stood against in silence, turning then and walking down the nave again, her hand still on his arm, precisely like a couple just married. The too suggestive incident, entirely of her making, nearly broke down Jude.

'I like to do things like this,' she said in the delicate voice of an epicure in emotions, which left no doubt that she spoke the truth.

'I know you do!' said Jude.

'They are interesting, because they have probably never been done before. I shall walk down the church like this with my husband in about two hours, shan't I!'

'No doubt you will!'

'Was it like this when you were married?'

'Good God, Sue – don't be so awfully merciless! . . . There, dear one, I didn't mean it!'

'Ah – you are vexed!' she said regretfully, as she blinked away an access of eye moisture. 'And I promised never to vex you! . . . I suppose I ought not to have asked you to bring me in here. O I oughtn't! I see it now. My curiosity to hunt up a new sensation always leads me into these scrapes. Forgive me! . . . You will, won't you, Jude?'

The appeal was so remorseful that Jude's eyes were even wetter than hers as he pressed her hand for Yes.

'Now we'll hurry away, and I won't do it any more!' she continued humbly; and they came out of the building, Sue intending to go on to the station to meet Phillotson. But the first person they encountered on entering the main street was the schoolmaster himself, whose train had arrived sooner than Sue expected. There was nothing really to demur to in her leaning on Jude's arm; but she withdrew her hand; and Jude thought that Phillotson had looked surprised.

'We have been doing such a funny thing!' said she, smiling candidly. 'We've been to the church, rehearsing as it were. Haven't we, Jude?'

'How?' said Phillotson curiously.

Jude inwardly deplored what he thought to be unnecessary frankness; but she had gone too far not to explain all, which she accordingly did, telling him how they had marched up to the altar.

Seeing how puzzled Phillotson seemed, Jude said as cheerfully as he could, 'I am going to buy her another little present. Will you both come to the shop with me?'

'No,' said Sue, 'I'll go on to the house with him'; and requesting her lover not to be a long time she departed with the schoolmaster.

Jude soon joined them at his rooms, and shortly after they prepared for the ceremony. Phillotson's hair was brushed to a

painful extent, and his shirt collar appeared stiffer than it had been
for the previous twenty years. Beyond this he looked dignified and
thoughtful, and altogether a man of whom it was not unsafe to
predict that he would make a kind and considerate husband. That he
adored Sue was obvious; and she could almost be seen to feel that
she was undeserving his adoration.

Although the distance was so short he had hired a fly from the
Red Lion, and six or seven women and children had gathered by the
door when they came out. The schoolmaster and Sue were unknown, though Jude was getting to be recognized as a citizen; and the
couple were judged to be some relations of his from a distance,
nobody supposing Sue to have been a recent pupil at the Training
School.

In the carriage Jude took from his pocket his extra little wedding-
present, which turned out to be two or three yards of white tulle,
which he threw over her bonnet and all, as a veil.

'It looks so odd over a bonnet,' she said. 'I'll take the bonnet off.'

'O no — let it stay,' said Phillotson. And she obeyed.

When they had passed up the church and were standing in their
places Jude found that the antecedent visit had certainly taken off
the edge of this performance, but by the time they were half way on
with the service he wished from his heart that he had not undertaken
the business of giving her away. How could Sue have had the
temerity to ask him to do it — a cruelty possibly to herself as well as
to him? Women were different from men in such matters. Was it
that they were, instead of more sensitive, as reputed, more callous,
and less romantic; or were they more heroic? Or was Sue simply so
perverse that she wilfully gave herself and him pain for the odd and
mournful luxury of practising long-suffering in her own person, and
of being touched with tender pity for him at having made him
practise it? He could perceive that her face was nervously set, and
when they reached the trying ordeal of Jude giving her to Phillotson
she could hardly command herself; rather, however, as it seemed,
from her knowledge of what her cousin must feel, whom she need
not have had there at all, than from self-consideration. Possibly she
would go on inflicting such pains again and again, and grieving for
the sufferer again and again, in all her colossal inconsistency.

Phillotson seemed not to notice, to be surrounded by a mist

which prevented his seeing the emotions of others. As soon as they
had signed their names and come away, and the suspense was over,
Jude felt relieved.

The meal at his lodging was a very simple affair, and at two
o'clock they went off. In crossing the pavement to the fly she looked
back; and there was a frightened light in her eyes. Could it be that
Sue had acted with such unusual foolishness as to plunge into she
knew not what for the sake of asserting her independence of him, of
retaliating on him for his secrecy? Perhaps Sue was thus venture-
some with men because she was childishly ignorant of that side of
their natures which wore out women's hearts and lives.

When her foot was on the carriage-step she turned round, saying
that she had forgotten something. Jude and the landlady offered to
get it.

'No,' she said, running back. 'It is my handkerchief. I know
where I left it.'

Jude followed her back. She had found it, and came holding it in
her hand. She looked into his eyes with her own teartul ones, and
her lips suddenly parted as if she were going to avow something. But
she went on; and whatever she had meant to say remained
unspoken.

JUDE wondered if she had really left her handkerchief behind; or whether it were that she had miserably wished to tell him of a love that at the last moment she could not bring herself to express.

He could not stay in his silent lodging when they were gone, and fearing that he might be tempted to drown his misery in alcohol he went upstairs, changed his dark clothes for his white, his thin boots for his thick, and proceeded to his customary work for the afternoon.

But in the cathedral he seemed to hear a voice behind him, and to be possessed with an idea that she would come back. She could not possibly go home with Phillotson, he fancied. The feeling grew and stirred. The moment that the clock struck the last of his working hours he threw down his tools and rushed homeward. 'Has anybody been for me?' he asked.

Nobody had been there.

As he could claim the downstairs sitting-room till twelve o'clock that night he sat in it all the evening; and even when the clock had struck eleven, and the family had retired, he could not shake off the feeling that she would come back and sleep in the little room adjoining his own, in which she had slept so many previous days. Her actions were always unpredictable: why should she not come? Gladly would he have compounded for the denial of her as a sweetheart and wife by having her live thus as a fellow-lodger and friend, even on the most distant terms. His supper still remained spread; and going to the front door, and softly setting it open, he returned to the room and sat as watchers sit on Old-Midsummer eves, expecting the phantom of the Beloved. But she did not come.

Having indulged in this wild hope he went upstairs, and looked out of the window, and pictured her through the evening journey to London, whither she and Phillotson had gone for their holiday; their rattling along through the damp night to their hotel, under the same sky of ribbed cloud as that he beheld, through which the moon

showed its position rather than its shape, and one or two of the
larger stars made themselves visible as faint nebulæ only. It was a
new beginning of Sue's history. He projected his mind into the
future, and saw her with children more or less in her own likeness
around her. But the consolation of regarding them as a continuation
of her identity was denied to him, as to all such dreamers, by the
wilfulness of Nature in not allowing issue from one parent alone.
Every desired renewal of an existence is debased by being half alloy.
'If at the estrangement or death of my lost love, I could go and see
her child — hers solely — there would be comfort in it!' said Jude.
And then he again uneasily saw, as he had latterly seen with more
and more frequency, the scorn of Nature for man's finer emotions,
and her lack of interest in his aspirations.

The oppressive strength of his affection for Sue showed itself on
the morrow and following days yet more clearly. He could no
longer endure the light of the Melchester lamps; the sunshine was as
drab paint; and the blue sky as zinc. Then he received news that his
old aunt was dangerously ill at Marygreen, which intelligence
almost coincided with a letter from his former employer at
Christminster, who offered him permanent work of a good class if
he would come back. The letters were almost a relief to him. He
started to visit Aunt Drusilla, and resolved to go onward to
Christminster to see what worth there might be in the builder's
offer.

Jude found his aunt even worse than the communication from the
Widow Edlin had led him to expect. There was every possibility of
her lingering on for weeks or months, though little likelihood. He
wrote to Sue informing her of the state of her aunt, and suggesting
that she might like to see her aged relative alive. He would meet her
at Alfredston Road, the following evening, Monday, on his way back
from Christminster, if she could come by the up-train which crossed
his down-train at that station. Next morning, accordingly, he went
on to Christminster, intending to return to Alfredston soon enough
to keep the suggested appointment with Sue.

The City of learning wore an estranged look, and he had lost all
feeling for its associations. Yet as the sun made vivid lights and
shades of the mullioned architecture of the façades, and drew pat-
terns of the crinkled battlements on the young turf of the quad-

rangles, Jude thought he had never seen the place look more
beautiful. He came to the street in which he had first beheld Sue.
The chair she had occupied when, leaning over her ecclesiastical
scrolls, a hog-hair brush in her hand, her girlish figure had arrested
the gaze of his inquiring eyes, stood precisely in its former spot,
empty. It was as if she were dead, and nobody had been found
capable of succeeding her in that artistic pursuit. Hers was now the
City phantom, while those of the intellectual and devotional
worthies who had once moved him to emotion were no longer able
to assert their presence there.

However, here he was; and in fulfilment of his intention he went
on to his former lodging in 'Beersheba', near the ritualistic church
of St Silas. The old landlady who opened the door seemed glad to
see him again, and bringing some lunch informed him that the
builder who had employed him had called to inquire his address.

Jude went on to the stone-yard where he had worked. But the old
sheds and bankers were distasteful to him; he felt it impossible to
engage himself to return and stay in this place of vanished dreams.
He longed for the hour of the homeward train to Alfredston, where
he might probably meet Sue.

Then, for one ghastly half-hour of depression caused by these
scenes, there returned upon him that feeling which had been his
undoing more than once – that he was not worth the trouble of
being taken care of either by himself or others; and during this half-
hour he met Tinker Taylor, the bankrupt ecclesiastical ironmonger,
at Fourways, who proposed that they should adjourn to a bar and
drink together. They walked along the street till they stood before
one of the great palpitating centres of Christminster life, the inn
wherein he formerly had responded to the challenge to rehearse the
Creed in Latin – now a popular tavern with a spacious and inviting
entrance, which gave admittance to a bar that had been entirely
renovated and refitted in modern style since Jude's residence here.

Tinker Taylor drank off his glass and departed, saying it was too
stylish a place now for him to feel at home in, unless he was drunker
than he had money to be just then. Jude was longer finishing his, and
stood abstractedly silent in the, for the minute, almost empty place.
The bar had been gutted and newly arranged throughout, mahogany
fixtures having taken the place of the old painted ones, while at the

back of the standing-space there were stuffed sofa-benches. The
room was divided into compartments in the approved manner,
between which were screens of ground glass in mahogany framing,
to prevent topers in one compartment being put to the blush by the
recognitions of those in the next. On the inside of the counter two
barmaids leant over the white-handled beer-engines, and the row of
little silvered taps inside, dripping into a pewter trough.

Feeling tired, and having nothing more to do till the train left,
Jude sat down on one of the sofas. At the back of the barmaids rose
bevel-edged mirrors, with glass shelves running along their front, on
which stood precious liquids that Jude did not know the name of, in
bottles of topaz, sapphire, ruby and amethyst. The moment was
enlivened by the entrance of some customers into the next compartment, and the starting of the mechanical tell-tale of monies received,
which emitted a ting-ting every time a coin was put in.

The barmaid attending to this compartment was invisible to
Jude's direct glance, though a reflection of her back in the glass
behind her was occasionally caught by his eyes. He had only
observed this listlessly, when she turned her face for a moment to
the glass to set her hair tidy. Then he was amazed to discover that
the face was Arabella's.

If she had come on to his compartment she would have seen him.
But she did not, this being presided over by the maiden on the other
side. Abby was in a black gown, with white linen cuffs and a broad
white collar, and her figure, more developed than formerly, was
accentuated by a bunch of daffodils that she wore on her left bosom.
In the compartment she served stood an electro-plated fountain of
water over a spirit-lamp, whose blue flame sent a steam from the
top, all this being visible to him only in the mirror behind her;
which also reflected the faces of the men she was attending to — one
of them a handsome, dissipated young fellow, possibly an undergraduate, who had been relating to her an experience of some
humorous sort.

'O, Mr Cockman, now! How can you tell such a tale to me in my
innocence!' she cried gaily. 'Mr Cockman, what do you use to make
your moustache curl so beautiful?' As the young man was clean
shaven the retort provoked a laugh at his expense.

'Come!' said he, 'I'll have a Curaçoa; and a light, please.'

She served the liqueur from one of the lovely bottles, and striking a match held it to his cigarette with ministering archness while he whiffed.

'Well, have you heard from your husband lately, my dear?' he asked.

'Not a sound,' said she.

'Where is he?'

'I left him in Australia; and I suppose he's there still.'

Jude's eyes grew rounder.

'What made you part from him?'

'Don't you ask questions, and you won't hear lies.'

'Come then, give me my change, which you've been keeping from me for the last quarter of an hour; and I'll romantically vanish up the street of this picturesque city.'

She handed the change over the counter, in taking which he caught her fingers and held them. There was a slight struggle and titter, and he bade her good-bye and left.

Jude had looked on with the eye of a dazed philosopher. It was extraordinary how far removed from his life Arabella now seemed to be. He could not realize their nominal closeness. And, this being the case, in his present frame of mind he was indifferent to the fact that Arabella was his wife indeed.

The compartment that she served emptied itself of visitors, and after a brief thought he entered it, and went forward to the counter. Arabella did not recognize him for a moment. Then their glances met. She started; till a humorous impudence sparkled in her eyes, and she spoke.

'Well, I'm blest! I thought you were underground years ago!'

'Oh!'

'I never heard anything of you, or I don't know that I should have come here. But never mind! What shall I treat you to this afternoon? A Scotch and soda? Come, anything that the house will afford, for old acquaintance' sake!'

'Thanks, Arabella,' said Jude without a smile. 'But I don't want anything more than I've had.' The fact was that her unexpected presence there had destroyed at a stroke his momentary taste for strong liquor as completely as if it had whisked him back to his milk-fed infancy.

'That's a pity, now you could get it for nothing.'

'How long have you been here?'

'About six weeks. I returned from Sydney three months ago. I always liked this business, you know.'

'I wonder you came to this place!'

'Well, as I say, I thought you were gone to glory, and being in London I saw the situation in an advertisement. Nobody was likely to know me here, even if I had minded, for I was never in Christminster in my growing up.'

'Why did you return from Australia?'

'Oh, I had my reasons. . . . Then you are not a Don yet?'

'No.'

'Not even a Reverend?'

'No.'

'Nor so much as a Rather Reverend dissenting gentleman?'

'I am as I was.'

'True — you look so.' She idly allowed her fingers to rest on the pull of the beer-engine as she inspected him critically. He observed that her hands were smaller and whiter than when he had lived with her, and that on the hand which pulled the engine she wore an ornamental ring set with what seemed to be real sapphires — which they were, indeed, and were much admired as such by the young men who frequented the bar.

'So you pass as having a living husband,' he continued.

'Yes. I thought it might be awkward if I called myself a widow, as I should have liked.'

'True. I am known here a little.'

'I didn't mean on that account — for as I said I didn't expect you. It was for other reasons.'

'What were they?'

'I don't care to go into them,' she replied evasively. 'I make a very good living, and I don't know that I want your company.'

Here a chappie with no chin, and a moustache like a lady's eyebrow, came and asked for a curiously compounded drink, and Arabella was obliged to go and attend to him. 'We can't talk here,' she said, stepping back a moment. 'Can't you wait till nine? Say yes, and don't be a fool. I can get off duty two hours sooner than usual, if I ask. I am not living in the house at present.'

He reflected and said gloomily, 'I'll come back. I suppose we'd better arrange something.'

'O bother arranging! I'm not going to arrange anything!'

'But I must know a thing or two; and, as you say, we can't talk here. Very well; I'll call for you.'

Depositing his unemptied glass he went out and walked up and down the street. Here was a rude flounce into the pellucid sentimentality of his sad attachment to Sue. Though Arabella's word was absolutely untrustworthy, he thought there might be some truth in her implication that she had not wished to disturb him, and had really supposed him dead. However, there was only one thing now to be done, and that was to play a straightforward part, the law being the law, and the woman between whom and himself there was no more unity than between east and west being in the eye of the Church one person with him.

Having to meet Arabella here, it was impossible to meet Sue at Alfredston as he had promised. At every thought of this a pang had gone through him; but the conjuncture could not be helped. Arabella was perhaps an intended intervention to punish him for his unauthorized love. Passing the evening, therefore, in a desultory waiting about the town wherein he avoided the precincts of every Cloister and Hall, because he could not bear to behold them, he repaired to the tavern bar while the hundred and one strokes were resounding from the Great Bell of Cardinal College, a coincidence which seemed to him gratuitous irony. The inn was now brilliantly lighted up, and the scene was altogether more brisk and gay. The faces of the barmaidens had risen in colour, each having a pink flush on her cheek; their manners were still more vivacious than before — more abandoned, more excited, more sensuous, and they expressed their sentiments and desires less euphemistically, laughing in a lackadaisical tone, without reserve.

The bar had been crowded with men of all sorts during the previous hour, and he had heard from without the hubbub of their voices; but the customers were fewer at last. He nodded to Arabella, and told her that she would find him outside the door when she came away.

'But you must have something with me first,' she said with great good-humour. 'Just an early nightcap: I always do. Then you can go out and wait a minute, as it is best we should not be seen going together.' She drew a couple of liqueur glasses of brandy; and though she had evidently, from her countenance, already taken in enough alcohol either by drinking or, more probably, from the atmosphere she had breathed for so many hours, she finished hers quickly. He also drank his, and went outside the house.

In a few minutes she came, in a thick jacket and a hat with a black feather. 'I live quite near,' she said, taking his arm, 'and can let myself in by a latch-key at any time. What arrangement do you want to come to?'

'O – none in particular,' he answered, thoroughly sick and tired, his thoughts again reverting to Alfredston, and the train he did not go by; the probable disappointment of Sue that he was not there when she arrived, and the missed pleasure of her company on the long and lonely climb by starlight up the hills to Marygreen. 'I ought to have gone back really! My aunt is on her deathbed, I fear.'

'I'll go over with you to-morrow morning. I think I could get a day off.'

There was something particularly uncongenial in the idea of Arabella, who had no more sympathy than a tigress with his relations or him, coming to the bedside of his dying aunt, and meeting Sue. Yet he said, 'Of course, if you'd like to, you can.'

'Well, that we'll consider. . . . Now, until we have come to some agreement it is awkward our being together here – where you are known, and I am getting known, though without any suspicion that I have anything to do with you. As we are going towards the station suppose we take the nine-forty train to Aldbrickham? We shall be there in little more than half-an-hour, and nobody will know us for one night, and we shall be quite free to act as we choose till we have made up our minds whether we'll make anything public or not.'

'As you like.'

'Then wait till I get two or three things. This is my lodging. Sometimes when late I sleep at the hotel where I am engaged, so nobody will think anything of my staying out.'

She speedily returned, and they went on to the railway, and made the half-hour's journey to Aldbrickham, where they entered a third-rate inn near the station in time for a late supper.

ON the morrow between nine and half-past they were journeying back to Christminster, the only two occupants of a compartment in a third-class railway-carriage. Having, like Jude, made rather a hasty toilet to catch the train, Arabella looked a little frowsy, and her face was very far from possessing the animation which had characterized it at the bar the night before. When they came out of the station she found that she still had half-an-hour to spare before she was due at the bar. They walked in silence a little way out of the town in the direction of Alfredston. Jude looked up the far highway.

'Ah ... poor feeble me!' he murmured at last.

'What?' said she.

'This is the very road by which I came into Christminster years ago full of plans!'

'Well, whatever the road is I think my time is nearly up, as I have to be in the bar by eleven o'clock. And as I said, I shan't ask for the day to go with you to see your aunt. So perhaps we had better part here. I'd sooner not walk up Chief Street* with you, since we've come to no conclusion at all.'

'Very well. But you said when we were getting up this morning that you had something you wished to tell me before I left?'

'So I had — two things — one in particular. But you wouldn't promise to keep it a secret. I'll tell you now if you promise? As an honest woman I wish you to know it. . . . It was what I began telling you in the night — about that gentleman who managed the Sydney hotel.' Arabella spoke somewhat hurriedly for her. 'You'll keep it close?'

'Yes — yes — I promise!' said Jude impatiently. 'Of course I don't want to reveal your secrets.'

'Whenever I met him out for a walk, he used to say that he was much taken with my looks, and he kept pressing me to marry him. I never thought of coming back to England again; and being out there in Australia, with no home of my own after leaving my father, I at last agreed, and did.'

'What — marry him?'

'Yes.'

'Regularly — legally — in church?'

'Yes. And lived with him till shortly before I left. It was stupid, I know; but I did! There, now I've told you. Don't round upon me! He talks of coming back to England, poor old chap. But if he does, he won't be likely to find me.'

Jude stood pale and fixed.

'Why the devil didn't you tell me last night !' he said.

'Well — I didn't. . . . Won't you make it up with me, then?'

'So in talking of "your husband" to the bar gentlemen you meant him, of course — not me!'

'Of course. . . . Come, don't fuss about it.'

'I have nothing more to say!' replied Jude. 'I have nothing at all to say about the — crime — you've confessed to!'

'Crime! Pooh. They don't think much of such as that over there! Lots of 'em do it. . . . Well, if you take it like that I shall go back to him! He was very fond of me, and we lived honourable enough, and as respectable as any married couple in the Colony! How did I know where you were?'

'I won't go blaming you. I could say a good deal; but perhaps it would be misplaced. What do you wish me to do?'

'Nothing. There was one thing more I wanted to tell you; but I fancy we've seen enough of one another for the present! I shall think over what you said about your circumstances, and let you know.'

Thus they parted. Jude watched her disappear in the direction of the hotel, and entered the railway station close by. Finding that it wanted three-quarters of an hour of the time at which he could get a train back to Alfredston, he strolled mechanically into the city as far as to the Fourways, where he stood as he had so often stood before, and surveyed Chief Street stretching ahead, with its college after college, in picturesqueness unrivalled except by such Continental vistas as the Street of Palaces in Genoa; the lines of the buildings being as distinct in the morning air as in an architectural drawing. But Jude was far from seeing or criticizing these things; they were hidden by an indescribable consciousness of Arabella's midnight contiguity, a sense of degradation at his revived experiences with her, of her appearance as she lay asleep at dawn, which set upon his motionless face a look as of one accurst. If he could only have felt resentment towards her he would have been less unhappy; but he pitied while he contemned her.

Jude turned and retraced his steps. Drawing again towards the station he started at hearing his name pronounced — less at the name than at the voice. To his great surprise no other than Sue stood like a vision before him — her look bodeful and anxious as in a dream, her little mouth nervous, and her strained eyes speaking reproachful inquiry.

'O Jude — I am so glad — to meet you like this!' she said in quick, uneven accents not far from a sob. Then she flushed as she observed his thought that they had not met since her marriage.

They looked away from each other to hide their emotion, took each other's hand without further speech, and went on together awhile, till she glanced at him with furtive solicitude. 'I arrived at Alfredston station last night, as you asked me to, and there was nobody to meet me! But I reached Marygreen alone, and they told me aunt was a trifle better. I sat up with her, and as you did not come all night I was frightened about you — I thought that perhaps, when you found yourself back in the old city, you were upset at — at thinking I was — married, and not there as I used to be; and that you had nobody to speak to; so you had tried to drown your gloom! — as you did at that former time when you were disappointed about entering as a student, and had forgotten your promise to me that you never would again. And this, I thought, was why you hadn't come to meet me!'

'And you came to hunt me up, and deliver me, like a good angel!'

'I thought I would come by the morning train and try to find you — in case — in case—'

'I did think of my promise to you, dear, continually! I shall never break out again as I did, I am sure. I may have been doing nothing better, but I was not doing that — I loathe the thought of it.'

'I am glad your staying had nothing to do with that. But,' she said, the faintest pout entering into her tone, 'you didn't come back last night and meet me, as you engaged to!'

'I didn't — I am sorry to say. I had an appointment at nine o'clock — too late for me to catch the train that would have met yours, or to get home at all.'

Looking at his loved one as she appeared to him now, in his tender thought the sweetest and most disinterested comrade that he had ever had, living largely in vivid imaginings, so ethereal a creature that her spirit could be seen trembling through her limbs, he felt heartily ashamed of his earthliness in spending the hours he had spent in Arabella's company. There was something rude and immoral in thrusting these recent facts of his life upon the mind of one who, to him, was so uncarnate as to seem at times impossible as a human wife to any average man. And yet she was Phillotson's. How she had become such, how she lived as such, passed his comprehension as he regarded her to-day.

'You'll go back with me?' he said. 'There's a train just now. I wonder how my aunt is by this time. . . . And so, Sue, you really came on my account all this way! At what an early time you must have started, poor thing!'

'Yes. Sitting up watching alone made me all nerves for you, and instead of going to bed when it got light I started. And now you won't frighten me like this again about your morals for nothing?'

He was not so sure that she had been frightened about his morals for nothing. He released her hand till they had entered the train, – it seemed the same carriage he had lately got out of with another – where they sat down side by side, Sue between him and the window. He regarded the delicate lines of her profile, and the small, tight, apple-like convexities of her bodice, so different from Arabella's amplitudes. Though she knew he was looking at her she did not turn to him, but kept her eyes forward, as if afraid that by meeting his own some troublous discussion would be initiated.

'Sue – you are married now, you know, like me; and yet we have been in such a hurry that we have not said a word about it!'

'There's no necessity,' she quickly returned.

'O well – perhaps not. . . . But I wish—'

'Jude – don't talk about *me* – I wish you wouldn't!' she entreated. 'It distresses me, rather. Forgive my saying it! . . . Where did you stay last night?'

She had asked the question in perfect innocence, to change the topic. He knew that, and said merely, 'At an inn,' though it would have been a relief to tell her of his meeting with an unexpected one.

But the latter's final announcement of her marriage in Australia bewildered him lest what he might say should do his ignorant wife an injury.

Their talk proceeded but awkwardly till they reached Alfredston. That Sue was not as she had been, but was labelled 'Phillotson', paralyzed Jude whenever he wanted to commune with her as an individual. Yet she seemed unaltered – he could not say why. There remained the five-mile extra journey into the country, which it was just as easy to walk as to drive, the greater part of it being uphill. Jude had never before in his life gone that road with Sue, though he had with another. It was now as if he carried a bright light which temporarily banished the shady associations of the earlier time.

Sue talked; but Jude noticed that she still kept the conversation from herself. At length he inquired if her husband were well.

'O yes,' she said. 'He is obliged to be in the school all the day, or he would have come with me. He is so good and kind that to accompany me he would have dismissed the school for once, even against his principles – for he is strongly opposed to giving casual holidays – only I wouldn't let him. I felt it would be better to come alone. Aunt Drusilla, I knew, was so very eccentric; and his being almost a stranger to her now would have made it irksome to both. Since it turns out that she is hardly conscious I am glad I did not ask him.'

Jude had walked moodily while this praise of Phillotson was being expressed. 'Mr Phillotson obliges you in everything, as he ought,' he said.

'Of course.'

'You ought to be a happy wife.'

'And of course I am.'

'Bride, I might almost have said, as yet. It is not so many weeks since I gave 'you to him, and—'

'Yes, I know! I know!' There was something in her face which belied her late assuring words, so strictly proper and so lifelessly spoken that they might have been taken from a list of model speeches in 'The Wife's Guide to Conduct'. Jude knew the quality of every vibration in Sue's voice, could read every symptom of her mental condition; and he was convinced that she was unhappy, although she had not been a month married. But her rushing away thus from home, to see the last of a relative whom she had hardly known in her life, proved nothing; for Sue naturally did such things as those.

'Well, you have my good wishes now as always, Mrs Phillotson.'

She reproached him by a glance.

'No, you are not Mrs Phillotson,' murmured Jude. 'You are dear, free Sue Bridehead, only you don't know it! Wifedom has not yet squashed up and digested you in its vast maw as an atom which has no further individuality.'

Sue put on a look of being offended, till she answered, 'Nor has husbandom you, so far as I can see!'

'But it has!' he said, shaking his head sadly.

When they reached the lone cottage under the firs, between the Brown House and Marygreen, in which Jude and Arabella had lived and quarrelled, he turned to look at it. A squalid family lived there now. He could not help saying to Sue: 'That's the house my wife and I occupied the whole of the time we lived together. I brought her home to that house.'

She looked at it. 'That to you was what the school-house at Shaston is to me.'

'Yes; but I was not very happy there, as you are in yours.'

She closed her lips in retortive silence, and they walked some way till she glanced at him to see how he was taking it. 'Of course I may have exaggerated your happiness — one never knows,' he continued blandly.

'Don't think that, Jude, for a moment, even though you may have said it to sting me! He's as good to me as a man can be, and gives me perfect liberty — which elderly husbands don't do in general. . . . If you think I am not happy because he's too old for me, you are wrong.'

'I don't think anything against him — to you, dear.'

'And you won't say things to distress me, will you?'

'I will not.'

He said no more, but he knew that, from some cause or other, in taking Phillotson as a husband, Sue felt that she had done what she ought not to have done.

They plunged into the concave field on the other side of which rose the village — the field wherein Jude had received a thrashing from the farmer many years earlier. On ascending to the village and approaching the house they found Mrs Edlin standing at the door, who at sight of them lifted her hands deprecatingly. 'She's downstairs, if you'll believe me!' cried the widow. 'Out o' bed she got, and nothing could turn her. What will come o't I do not know!'

On entering, there indeed by the fireplace sat the old woman, wrapped in blankets, and turning upon them a countenance like that of Sebastiano's Lazarus.* They must have looked their amazement, for she said in a hollow voice:

'Ah – sceered ye, have I! I wasn't going to bide up there no longer, to please nobody! 'Tis more than flesh and blood can bear, to be ordered to do this and that by a feller that don't know half as well as you do yourself! . . . Ah – you'll rue this marrying as well as he!' she added, turning to Sue. 'All our family do, – and nearly all everybody else's. You should have done as I did, you simpleton! And Phillotson the schoolmaster, of all men! What made 'ee marry him?'

'What makes most women marry, aunt?'

'Ah! You mean to say you loved the man!'

'I don't mean to say anything definite.'

'Do ye love un?'

'Don't ask me, aunt.'

'I can mind the man very well. A very civil, honourable liver; but Lord! – I don't want to wownd your feelings, but – there be certain men here and there that no woman of any niceness can stomach. I should have said he was one. I don't say so now, since you must ha' known better than I, – but that's what I should have said!'

Sue jumped up and went out. Jude followed her, and found her in the outhouse, crying.

'Don't cry, dear!' said Jude in distress. 'She means well, but is very crusty and queer now, you know.'

'O no – it isn't that!' said Sue, trying to dry her eyes. 'I don't mind her roughness one bit.'

'What is it, then?'

'It is that what she says is – is true!'

'God – what – you don't like him?' asked Jude.

'I don't mean that!' she said hastily. 'That I ought – perhaps I ought not to have married!'

He wondered if she had really been going to say that at first. They went back, and the subject was smoothed over, and her aunt took rather kindly to Sue, telling her that not many young women newly married would have come so far to see a sick old crone like her. In the afternoon Sue prepared to depart, Jude hiring a neighbour to drive her to Alfredston.

'I'll go with you to the station, if you'd like?' he said.

She would not let him. The man came round with the trap, and Jude helped her into it, perhaps with unnecessary attention, for she looked at him prohibitively.

'I suppose — I may come to see you some day, when I am back again at Melchester?' he half-crossly observed.

She bent down and said softly: 'No, dear — you are not to come yet. I don't think you are in a good mood.'

'Very well,' said Jude. 'Good-bye!'

'Good-bye!' She waved her hand and was gone.

'She's right! I won't go!' he murmured.

He passed the evening and following days in mortifying by every possible means his wish to see her, nearly starving himself in attempts to extinguish by fasting his passionate tendency to love her. He read sermons on discipline; and hunted up passages in Church history that treated of the Ascetics of the second century. Before he had returned from Marygreen to Melchester there arrived a letter from Arabella. The sight of it revived a stronger feeling of self-condemnation for his brief return to her society than for his attachment to Sue.

The letter, he perceived, bore a London postmark instead of the Christminster one. Arabella informed him that a few days after their parting in the morning at Christminster, she had been surprised by an affectionate letter from her Australian husband, formerly manager of the hotel in Sydney. He had come to England on purpose to find her; and had taken a free, fully-licensed public, in Lambeth, where he wished her to join him in conducting the business, which was likely to be a very thriving one, the house being situated in an excellent, densely populated, gin-drinking neighbourhood, and already doing a trade of £200 a month, which could be easily doubled.

As he had said that he loved her very much still, and implored

her to tell him where she was, and as they had only parted in a slight
tiff, and as her engagement in Christminster was only temporary,
she had just gone to join him as he urged. She could not help feeling
that she belonged to him more than to Jude, since she had properly
married him, and had lived with him much longer than with her first
husband. In thus wishing Jude good-bye she bore him no ill-will,
and trusted he would not turn upon her, a weak woman, and inform
against her, and bring her to ruin now that she had a chance of
improving her circumstances and leading a genteel life.

JUDE returned to Melchester, which had the questionable recommendation of being only a dozen and a half miles from his Sue's now permanent residence. At first he felt that this nearness was a distinct reason for not going southward at all; but Christminster was too sad a place to bear, while the proximity of Shaston to Melchester might afford him the glory of worsting the Enemy in a close engagement, such as was deliberately sought by the priests and virgins of the early Church, who, disdaining an ignominious flight from temptation, became even chamber-partners with impunity. Jude did not pause to remember that, in the laconic words of the historian, 'insulted Nature sometimes vindicated her rights'* in such circumstances.

He now returned with feverish desperation to his study for the priesthood — in the recognition that the single-mindedness of his aims, and his fidelity to the cause, had been more than questionable of late. His passion for Sue troubled his soul; yet his lawful abandonment to the society of Arabella for twelve hours seemed instinctively a worse thing — even though she had not told him of her Sydney husband till afterwards. He had, he verily believed, overcome all tendency to fly to liquor — which, indeed, he had never done from taste, but merely as an escape from intolerable misery of mind. Yet he perceived with despondency that, taken all round, he was a man of too many passions to make a good clergyman; the utmost he could hope for was that in a life of constant internal warfare between flesh and spirit the former might not always be victorious.

As a hobby, auxiliary to his readings in Divinity, he developed his slight skill in church-music and thorough-bass, till he could join in part-singing from notation with some accuracy. A mile or two from Melchester there was a restored village church, to which Jude had originally gone to fix the new columns and capitals. By this means he had become acquainted with the organist, and the ultimate result was that he joined the choir as a bass voice.

He walked out to this parish twice every Sunday, and sometimes in the week. One evening about Easter the choir met for practice, and a new hymn which Jude had heard of as being by a Wessex composer was to be tried and prepared for the following week. It turned out to be a strangely emotional composition. As they all sang it over and over again its harmonies grew upon Jude, and moved him exceedingly.

When they had finished he went round to the organist to make inquiries. The score was in manuscript, the name of the composer being at the head, together with the title of the hymn: 'The Foot of the Cross'.

'Yes,' said the organist. 'He is a local man. He is a professional musician at Kennetbridge – between here and Christminster. The vicar knows him. He was brought up and educated in Christminster traditions, which accounts for the quality of the piece. I think he plays in the large church there, and has a surpliced choir. He comes to Melchester sometimes, and once tried to get the Cathedral organ when the post was vacant. The hymn is getting about everywhere this Easter.'

As he walked humming the air on his way home, Jude fell to musing on its composer, and the reasons why he composed it. What a man of sympathies he must be! Perplexed and harassed as he himself was about Sue and Arabella, and troubled as was his conscience by the complication of his position, how he would like to know that man! 'He of all men would understand my difficulties,' said the impulsive Jude. If there were any person in the world to choose as a confidant, this composer would be the one, for he must have suffered, and throbbed, and yearned.

In brief, ill as he could afford the time and money for the journey, Fawley resolved, like the child that he was, to go to Kennetbridge the very next Sunday. He duly started, early in the morning, for it was only by a series of crooked railways that he could get to the town. About mid-day he reached it, and crossing the bridge into the quaint old borough he inquired for the house of the composer.

They told him it was a red brick building some little way further on. Also that the gentleman himself had just passed along the street not five minutes before.

'Which way?' asked Jude with alacrity.

'Straight along homeward from church.'

Jude hastened on, and soon had the pleasure of observing a man in a black coat and a black slouched felt hat no considerable distance ahead. Stretching out his legs yet more widely he stalked after. 'A hungry soul in pursuit of a full soul!' he said. 'I must speak to that man!'

He could not, however, overtake the musician before he had entered his own house, and then arose the question if this were an expedient time to call. Whether or not he decided to do so there and then, now that he had got here, the distance home being too great for him to wait till late in the afternoon. This man of soul would understand scant ceremony, and might be quite a perfect adviser in a case in which an earthly and illegitimate passion had cunningly obtained entrance into his heart through the opening afforded for religion.

Jude accordingly rang the bell, and was admitted.

The musician came to him in a moment, and being respectably dressed, good-looking, and frank in manner, Jude obtained a favourable reception. He was nevertheless conscious that there would be a certain awkwardness in explaining his errand.

'I have been singing in the choir of a little church near Melchester,' he said. 'And we have this week practised "The Foot of the Cross", which I understand, sir, that you composed?'

'I did — a year or so ago.'

'I — like it. I think it supremely beautiful!'

'Ah well — other people have said so too. Yes, there's money in it, if I could only see about getting it published. I have other compositions to go with it, too; I wish I could bring them out; for I haven't made a five-pound note out of any of them yet. These publishing people — they want the copyright of an obscure composer's work, such as mine is, for almost less than I should have to pay a person for making a fair manuscript copy of the score. The one you speak of I have lent to various friends about here and Melchester, and so it has got to be sung a little. But music is a poor staff to lean on — I am giving it up entirely. You must go into trade if

you want to make money nowadays. The wine business is what I am
thinking of. This is my forthcoming list – it is not issued yet – but
you can take one.'

He handed Jude an advertisement list of several pages in booklet
shape, ornamentally margined with a red line, in which were set
forth the various clarets, champagnes, ports, sherries, and other
wines with which he purposed to initiate his new venture. It took
Jude more than by surprise that the man with the soul was thus and
thus; and he felt that he could not open up his confidences.

They talked a little longer, but constrainedly, for when the
musician found that Jude was a poor man his manner changed from
what it had been while Jude's appearance and address deceived him
as to his position and pursuits. Jude stammered out something about
his feelings in wishing to congratulate the author on such an exalted
composition, and took an embarrassed leave.

All the way home by the slow Sunday train, sitting in the fireless
waiting-rooms on this cold spring day, he was depressed enough at
his simplicity in taking such a journey. But no sooner did he reach
his Melchester lodging than he found awaiting him a letter which
had arrived that morning a few minutes after he had left the house.
It was a contrite little note from Sue, in which she said, with sweet
humility, that she felt she had been horrid in telling him he was not
to come to see her; that she despised herself for having been so
conventional; and that he was to be sure to come by the eleven-
forty-five train that very Sunday, and have dinner with them at half-
past one.

Jude almost tore his hair at having missed this letter till it was too
late to act upon its contents; but he had chastened himself considerably of late, and at last his chimerical expedition to
Kennetbridge really did seem to have been another special intervention of Providence to keep him away from temptation. But a growing impatience of faith, which he had noticed in himself more than
once of late, made him pass over in ridicule the idea that God sent
people on fools' errands. He longed to see her; he was angry at
having missed her: and he wrote instantly, telling her what had
happened, and saying he had not enough patience to wait till the
following Sunday, but would come any day in the week that she
liked to name.

Since he wrote a little over-ardently, Sue, as her manner was, delayed her reply till Thursday before Good Friday, when she said he might come that afternoon if he wished, this being the earliest day on which she could welcome him, for she was now assistant-teacher in her husband's school. Jude therefore got leave from the Cathedral works at the trifling expense of a stoppage of pay, and went.

PART FOURTH

At Shaston

'Whoso prefers either Matrimony or other Ordinance before the Good of Man and the plain Exigence of Charity, let him profess Papist, or Protestant, or what he will, he is no better than a Pharisee.' — J. MILTON

CHAPTER ONE

SHASTON, the ancient British Palladour,

'From whose foundation first such strange reports arise',*

(as Drayton sang it), was, and is, in itself the city of a dream. Vague imaginings of its castle, its three mints, its magnificent apsidal Abbey, the chief glory of South Wessex, its twelve churches, its shrines, chantries, hospitals, its gabled freestone mansions – all now ruthlessly swept away – throw the visitor, even against his will, into a pensive melancholy, which the stimulating atmosphere and limitless landscape around him can scarcely dispel. The spot was the burial-place of a king and a queen, of abbots and abbesses, saints and bishops, knights and squires. The bones of King Edward 'the Martyr', * carefully removed hither for holy preservation, brought Shaston a renown which made it the resort of pilgrims from every part of Europe, and enabled it to maintain a reputation extending far beyond English shores. To this fair creation of the great Middle-Age the Dissolution was, as historians tell us, the death-knell. With the destruction of the enormous abbey the whole place collapsed in a general ruin: the Martyr's bones met with the fate of the sacred pile that held them, and not a stone is now left to tell where they lie.

The natural picturesqueness and singularity of the town still remain; but strange to say these qualities, which were noted by many writers in ages when scenic beauty is said to have been unappreciated, are passed over in this, and one of the queerest and quaintest spots in England stands virtually unvisited to-day.

It has a unique position on the summit of a steep and imposing scarp, rising on the north, south, and west sides of the borough out of the deep alluvial Vale of Blackmoor, the view from the Castle Green over three counties of verdant pasture – South, Mid, and Nether Wessex – being as sudden a surprise to the unexpectant traveller's eyes as the medicinal air is to his lungs. Impossible to a railway, it can best be reached on foot, next best by light vehicles;

and it is hardly accessible to these but by a sort of isthmus on the north-east, that connects it with the high chalk table-land on that side.

Such is, and such was, the now world-forgotten Shaston or Palladour. Its situation rendered water the great want of the town; and within living memory horses, donkeys and men may have been seen toiling up the winding ways to the top of the height, laden with tubs and barrels filled from the wells beneath the mountain, and hawkers retailing their contents at the price of a halfpenny a bucket-ful.

This difficulty in the water supply, together with two other odd facts, namely, that the chief graveyard slopes up as steeply as a roof behind the church, and that in former times the town passed through a curious period of corruption, conventual and domestic, gave rise to the saying that Shaston was remarkable for three consolations to man, such as the world afforded not elsewhere. It was a place where the churchyard lay nearer heaven than the church steeple, where beer was more plentiful than water, and where there were more wanton women than honest wives and maids. It is also said that after the middle ages the inhabitants were too poor to pay their priests, and hence were compelled to pull down their churches, and refrain altogether from the public worship of God; a necessity which they bemoaned over their cups in the settles of their inns on Sunday afternoons. In those days the Shastonians were apparently not without a sense of humour.

There was another peculiarity — this a modern one — which Shaston appeared to owe to its site. It was the resting-place and headquarters of the proprietors of wandering vans, shows, shooting-galleries, and other itinerant concerns, whose business lay largely at fairs and markets. As strange wild birds are seen assembled on some lofty promontory, meditatively pausing for longer flights, or to return by the course they followed thither, so here, in this cliff-town, stood in stultified silence the yellow and green caravans bearing names not local, as if surprised by a change in the landscape so violent as to hinder their further progress; and here they usually remained all the winter till they turned to seek again their old tracks in the following spring.

It was to this breezy and whimsical spot that Jude ascended from the nearest station for the first time in his life about four o'clock one afternoon, and entering on the summit of the peak after a toilsome climb, passed the first houses of the aerial town; and drew towards the school-house. The hour was too early; the pupils were still in school, humming small, like a swarm of gnats; and he withdrew a few steps along Abbey Walk, whence he regarded the spot which fate had made the home of all he loved best in the world. In front of the schools, which were extensive and stone-built, grew two enormous beeches with smooth mouse-coloured trunks, as such trees only will grow on chalk uplands.* Within the mullioned and transomed windows he could see the black, brown, and flaxen crowns of the scholars over the sills, and to pass the time away he walked down to the level terrace where the Abbey gardens once had spread, his heart throbbing in spite of him.

Unwilling to enter till the children were dismissed he remained here till young voices could be heard in the open air, and girls in white pinafores over red and blue frocks appeared dancing along the paths which the abbess, prioress, sub-prioress, and fifty nuns had demurely paced three centuries earlier. Retracing his steps he found that he had waited too long, and that Sue had gone out into the town at the heels of the last scholar, Mr Phillotson having been absent all the afternoon at a teachers' meeting at Shottsford.

Jude went into the empty schoolroom and sat down, the girl who was sweeping the floor having informed him that Mrs Phillotson would be back again in a few minutes. A piano stood near — actually the old piano that Phillotson had possessed at Marygreen — and though the dark afternoon almost prevented him seeing the notes Jude touched them in his humble way, and could not help modulating into the hymn which had so affected him in the previous week.

A figure moved behind him, and thinking it was still the girl with the broom Jude took no notice, till the person came close and laid her fingers lightly upon his bass hand. The imposed hand was a little one he seemed to know, and he turned.

'Don't stop,' said Sue. 'I like it. I learnt it before I left Melchester. They used to play it in the Training School.'

'I can't strum before you! Play it for me.'

'O well — I don't mind.'

Sue sat down, and her rendering of the piece, though not remarkable, seemed divine as compared with his own. She, like him, was evidently touched – to her own surprise – by the recalled air; and when she had finished, and he moved his hand towards hers, it met his own half-way. Jude grasped it – just as he had done before her marriage.

'It is odd,' she said, in a voice quite changed, 'that I should care about that air; because—'

'Because what?'

'I am not that sort – quite.'

'Not easily moved?'

'I didn't quite mean that.'

'O, but you *are* one of that sort, for you are just like me at heart!'

'But not at head.'

She played on, and suddenly turned round; and by an unpremeditated instinct each clasped the other's hand again.

She uttered a forced little laugh as she relinquished his quickly. 'How funny!' she said. 'I wonder what we both did that for?'

'I suppose because we are both alike, as I said before.'

'Not in our thoughts! Perhaps a little in our feelings.'

'And they rule thoughts. . . . Isn't it enough to make one blaspheme that the composer of that hymn is one of the most commonplace men I ever met!'

'What – you know him?'

'I went to see him.'

'O you goose – to do just what I should have done! Why did you?'

'Because we are not alike,' he said drily.

'Now we'll have some tea,' said Sue. 'Shall we have it here instead of in my house? It is no trouble to get the kettle and things brought in. We don't live at the school, you know, but in that ancient dwelling across the way called Old-Grove Place.* It is so antique and dismal that it depresses me dreadfully. Such houses are very well to visit, but not to live in – I feel crushed into the earth by the weight of so many previous lives there spent. In a new place like these schools there is only your own life to support. Sit down, and I'll tell Ada to bring the tea-things across.'

He waited in the light of the stove, the door of which she flung open before going out, and when she returned, followed by the maiden with tea, they sat down by the same light, assisted by the blue rays of a spirit-lamp under the brass kettle on the stand.

'This is one of your wedding-presents to me,' she said, signifying the latter.

'Yes,' said Jude.

The kettle of his gift sang with some satire in its note, to his mind; and to change the subject he said, 'Do you know of any good readable edition of the uncanonical books of the New Testament? You don't read them in the school, I suppose?'

'O dear no! — 'twould alarm the neighbourhood. . . . Yes, there is one. I am not familiar with it now, though I was interested in it when my former friend was alive. Cowper's *Apocryphal Gospels.*'*

'That sounds like what I want.' His thoughts, however, reverted with a twinge to the 'former friend' — by whom she meant, as he knew, the University comrade of her earlier days. He wondered if she talked of him to Phillotson.

'The Gospel of Nicodemus is very nice,' she went on, to keep him from his jealous thoughts, which she read clearly, as she always did. Indeed when they talked on an indifferent subject, as now, there was ever a second silent conversation passing between their emotions, so perfect was the reciprocity between them. 'It is quite like the genuine article. All cut up into verses, too; so that it is like one of the other evangelists read in a dream, when things are the same, yet not the same. But, Jude, do you take an interest in those questions still? Are you getting up *Apologetica*?'*

'Yes. I am reading Divinity harder than ever.'

She regarded him curiously.

'Why do you look at me like that?' said Jude.

'Oh — why do you want to know?'

'I am sure you can tell me anything I may be ignorant of in that subject. You must have learnt a lot of everything from your dear dead friend!'

'We won't get on to that now!' she coaxed. 'Will you be carving out at that church again next week, where you learnt the pretty hymn?'

'Yes, perhaps.'

'That will be very nice. Shall I come and see you there? It is in this direction, and I could come any afternoon by train for half-an-hour?'

'No. Don't come!'

'What — aren't we going to be friends, then, any longer, as we used to be?'

'No.'

'I didn't know that. I thought you were always going to be kind to me!'

'No, I am not.'

'What have I done, then? I am sure I thought we two——' The *tremolo* in her voice caused her to break off.

'Sue, I sometimes think you are a flirt,' said he abruptly.

There was a momentary pause, till she suddenly jumped up; and to his surprise he saw by the kettle-flame that her face was flushed.

'I can't talk to you any longer, Jude!' she said, the tragic contralto note having come back as of old. 'It is getting too dark to stay together like this, after playing morbid Good Friday tunes that make one feel what one shouldn't! . . . We mustn't sit and talk in this way any more. Yes — you must go away, for you mistake me! I am very much the reverse of what you say so cruelly — O Jude, it *was* cruel to say that! Yet I can't tell you the truth — I should shock you by letting you know how I give way to my impulses, and how much I feel that I shouldn't have been provided with attractiveness unless it were meant to be exercised! Some women's love of being loved is insatiable; and so, often, is their love of loving; and in the last case they may find that they can't give it continuously to the chamber-officer appointed by the bishop's licence to receive it. But you are so straightforward, Jude, that you can't understand me! . . . Now you must go. I am sorry my husband is not at home.'

'Are you?'

'I perceive I have said that in mere convention! Honestly I don't think I am sorry. It does not matter, either way, sad to say!'

As they had overdone the grasp of hands some time sooner, she touched his fingers but lightly when he went out now. He had hardly gone from the door when, with a dissatisfied look, she jumped on a form and opened the iron casement of a window beneath which he was passing in the path without. 'When do you leave here to catch your train, Jude?' she asked.

He looked up in some surprise. 'The coach that runs to meet it goes in three-quarters of an hour or so.'

'What will you do with yourself for the time?'

'O – wander about, I suppose. Perhaps I shall go and sit in the old church.'

'It does seem hard of me to pack you off so! You have thought enough of churches, Heaven knows, without going into one in the dark. Stay there.'

'Where?'

'Where you are. I can talk to you better like this than when you were inside. . . . It was so kind and tender of you to give up half a day's work to come to see me! . . . You are Joseph the dreamer of dreams,* dear Jude. And a tragic Don Quixote. And sometimes you are St Stephen, who, while they were stoning him, could see Heaven opened. O my poor friend and comrade, you'll suffer yet!'

Now that the high window-sill was between them, so that he could not get at her, she seemed not to mind indulging in a frankness she had feared at close quarters. 'I have been thinking,' she continued, still in the tone of one brimful of feeling, 'that the social moulds civilization fits us into have no more relation to our actual shapes than the conventional shapes of the constellations have to the real star-patterns. I am called Mrs Richard Phillotson, living a calm wedded life with my counterpart of that name. But I am not really Mrs Richard Phillotson, but a woman tossed about, all alone, with aberrant passions, and unaccountable antipathies. . . . Now you mustn't wait longer, or you will lose the coach. Come and see me again. You must come to the house then.'

'Yes!' said Jude. 'When shall it be?'

'To-morrow week. Good-bye – good-bye!' She stretched out her hand and stroked his forehead pitifully – just once. Jude said good-bye, and went away into the darkness.

Passing along Bimport Street he thought he heard the wheels of the coach departing, and, truly enough, when he reached the Duke's Arms in the Market Place the coach had gone. It was impossible for him to get to the station on foot in time for this train, and he settled himself perforce to wait for the next – the last to Melchester that night.

He wandered about awhile, obtained something to eat; and then, having another half-hour on his hands, his feet involuntarily took him through the venerable graveyard of Trinity Church, with its avenues of limes, in the direction of the schools again. They were entirely in darkness. She had said she lived over the way at Old-Grove Place, a house which he soon discovered from her description of its antiquity.

A glimmering candle-light shone from a front window, the shutters being yet unclosed. He could see the interior clearly — the floor sinking a couple of steps below the road without, which had become raised during the centuries since the house was built. Sue, evidently just come in, was standing with her hat on in this front parlour or sitting-room, whose walls were lined with wainscoting of panelled oak reaching from floor to ceiling, the latter being crossed by huge moulded beams only a little way above her head. The mantelpiece was of the same heavy description, carved with Jacobean pilasters and scroll-work. The centuries did, indeed, ponderously overhang a young wife who passed her time here.

She had opened a rosewood work-box, and was looking at a photograph. Having contemplated it a little while she pressed it against her bosom, and put it again in its place.

Then becoming aware that she had not obscured the windows she came forward to do so, candle in hand. It was too dark for her to see Jude without, but he could see her face distinctly, and there was an unmistakable tearfulness about the dark, long-lashed eyes.

She closed the shutters, and Jude turned away to pursue his solitary journey home. 'Whose photograph was she looking at?' he said. He had once given her his; but she had others, he knew. Yet it was his, surely?

He knew he should go to see her again, according to her invitation. Those earnest men he read of, the saints, whom Sue, with gentle irreverence, called his demi-gods, would have shunned such encounters if they doubted their own strength. But he could not. He might fast and pray during the whole interval, but the human was more powerful in him than the Divine.

HOWEVER, if God disposed not, woman did. The next morning but one brought him this note from her:

'Don't come next week. On your own account, don't! We were too free, under the influence of that morbid hymn and the twilight. Think no more than you can help of   SUSANNA FLORENCE MARY'

The disappointment was keen. He knew her mood, the look of her face, when she subscribed herself at length thus. But whatever her mood he could not say she was wrong in her view. He replied:

'I acquiesce. You are right. It is a lesson in renunciation which I suppose I ought to learn at this season.   JUDE'

He despatched the note on Easter Eve, and there seemed a finality in their decisions. But other forces and laws than theirs were in operation. On Easter Monday morning he received a message from the Widow Edlin, whom he had directed to telegraph if anything serious happened:

'Your aunt is sinking. Come at once.'

He threw down his tools and went. Three and a half hours later he was crossing the downs about Marygreen, and presently plunged into the concave field across which the short cut was made to the village. As he ascended on the other side a labouring man, who had been watching his approach from a gate across the path, moved uneasily, and prepared to speak. 'I can see in his face that she is dead,' said Jude. 'Poor Aunt Drusilla!'

It was as he had supposed, and Mrs Edlin had sent out the man to break the news to him.

'She wouldn't have knowed 'ee. She lay like a doll wi' glass eyes; so it didn't matter that you wasn't here,' said he.

Jude went on to the house, and in the afternoon, when everything was done, and the layers-out had finished their beer, and gone, he sat down alone in the silent place. It was absolutely necessary to communicate with Sue, though two or three days earlier they had agreed to mutual severance. He wrote in the briefest terms:

'Aunt Drusilla is dead, having been taken almost suddenly. The funeral is on Friday afternoon.'

He remained in and about Marygreen through the intervening days, went out on Friday morning to see that the grave was finished, and wondered if Sue would come. She had not written, and that seemed to signify rather that she would come than that she would not. Having timed her by her only possible train, he locked the door about mid-day, and crossed the hollow field to the verge of the upland by the Brown House, where he stood and looked over the vast prospect northwards, and over the nearer landscape in which Alfredston stood. Two miles behind it a jet of white steam was travelling from the left to the right of the picture.

There was a long time to wait, even now, till he would know if she had arrived. He did wait, however, and at last a small hired vehicle pulled up at the bottom of the hill, and a person alighted, the conveyance going back, while the passenger began ascending the hill. He knew her; and she looked so slender to-day that it seemed as if she might be crushed in the intensity of a too passionate embrace — such as it was not for him to give. Two-thirds of the way up her head suddenly took a solicitous poise, and he knew that she had at that moment recognized him. Her face soon began a pensive smile, which lasted till, having descended a little way, he met her.

'I thought,' she began with nervous quickness, 'that it would be so sad to let you attend the funeral alone! And so — at the last moment — I came.'

'Dear faithful Sue!' murmured Jude.

With the elusiveness of her curious double nature, however, Sue did not stand still for any further greeting, though it wanted some time to the burial. A pathos so unusually compounded as that which attached to this hour was unlikely to repeat itself for years, if ever, and Jude would have paused, and meditated, and conversed. But Sue either saw it not at all, or, seeing it more than he, would not allow herself to feel it.

The sad and simple ceremony was soon over, their progress to the church being almost at a trot, the bustling undertaker having a more important funeral an hour later, three miles off. Drusilla was put into the new ground, quite away from her ancestors. Sue and Jude had gone side by side to the grave, and now sat down to tea in the familiar house; their lives united at least in this last attention to the dead.

'She was opposed to marriage, from first to last, you say?' murmured Sue.

'Yes. Particularly for members of our family.'

Her eyes met his, and remained on him awhile.

'We are rather a sad family, don't you think, Jude?'

'She said we made bad husbands and wives. Certainly we make unhappy ones. At all events, I do, for one!'

Sue was silent. 'Is it wrong, Jude,' she said with a tentative tremor, 'for a husband or wife to tell a third person that they are unhappy in their marriage? If a marriage ceremony is a religious thing, it is possibly wrong; but if it is only a sordid contract, based on material convenience in householding, rating, and taxing, and the inheritance of land and money by children, making it necessary that the male parent should be known — which it seems to be — why surely a person may say, even proclaim upon the housetops, that it hurts and grieves him or her?'

'I have said so, anyhow, to you.'

Presently she went on: 'Are there many couples, do you think, where one dislikes the other for no definite fault?'

'Yes, I suppose. If either cares for another person, for instance.'

'But even apart from that? Wouldn't the woman, for example, be very bad-natured if she didn't like to live with her husband; merely' — her voice undulated, and he guessed things — 'merely because she had a personal feeling against it — a physical objection — a fastidiousness, or whatever it may be called — although she might respect and be grateful to him? I am merely putting a case. Ought she to try to overcome her pruderies?'

Jude threw a troubled look at her. He said, looking away: 'It would be just one of those cases in which my experiences go contrary to my dogmas. Speaking as an order-loving man — which I hope I am, though I fear I am not — I should say, yes. Speaking from experience and unbiased nature, I should say, no. . . . Sue, I believe you are not happy!'

'Of course I am!' she contradicted. 'How can a woman be unhappy who has only been married eight weeks to a man she chose freely?'

'"Chose freely!"'

'Why do you repeat it? . . . But I have to go back by the six o'clock train. You will be staying on here, I suppose?'

'For a few days to wind up aunt's affairs. This house is gone now. Shall I go to the train with you?'

A little laugh of objection came from Sue. 'I think not. You may come part of the way.'

'But stop — you can't go to-night! That train won't take you to Shaston. You must stay and go back to-morrow. Mrs Edlin has plenty of room, if you don't like to stay here?'

'Very well,' she said dubiously. 'I didn't tell him I would come for certain.'

Jude went to the widow's house adjoining, to let her know; and returning in a few minutes sat down again.

'It is horrible how we are circumstanced, Sue — horrible!' he said abruptly, with his eyes bent to the floor.

'No! Why?'

'I can't tell you all my part of the gloom. Your part is that you ought not to have married him. I saw it before you had done it, but I thought I mustn't interfere. I was wrong. I ought to have!'

'But what makes you assume all this, dear?'

'Because — I can see you through your feathers, my poor little bird!'

Her hand lay on the table, and Jude put his upon it. Sue drew hers away.

'That's absurd, Sue,' cried he, 'after what we've been talking about! I am more strict and formal than you, if it comes to that; and that you should object to such an innocent action shows that you are ridiculously inconsistent!'

'Perhaps it was too prudish,' she said repentantly. 'Only I have fancied it was a sort of trick of ours — too frequent perhaps. There, you may hold it as much as you like. Is that good of me?'

'Yes; very.'

'But I must tell him.'

'Who?'

'Richard.'

'O – of course, if you think it necessary. But as it means nothing it may be bothering him needlessly.'

'Well – are you sure you mean it only as my cousin?'

'Absolutely sure. I have no feelings of love left in me.'

'That's news. How has it come to be?'

'I've seen Arabella.'

She winced at the hit; then said curiously, 'When did you see her?'

'When I was at Christminster.'

'So she's come back; and you never told me! I suppose you will live with her now?'

'Of course – just as you live with your husband.'

She looked at the window pots with the geraniums and cactuses, withered for want of attention, and through them at the outer distance, till her eyes began to grow moist. 'What is it?' said Jude, in a softened tone.

'Why should you be so glad to go back to her if – if – what you used to say to me is still true – I mean if it were true then! Of course it is not now! How could your heart go back to Arabella so soon?'

'A special Providence, I suppose, helped it on its way.'

'Ah – it isn't true!' she said with gentle resentment. 'You are teasing me – that's all – because you think I am not happy!'

'I don't know. I don't wish to know.'

'If I were unhappy it would be my fault, my wickedness; not that I should have a right to dislike him! He is considerate to me in everything; and he is very interesting, from the amount of general knowledge he has acquired by reading everything that comes in his way. . . . Do you think, Jude, that a man ought to marry a woman his own age, or one younger than himself – eighteen years – as I am than he?'

'It depends upon what they feel for each other.'

He gave her no opportunity of self-satisfaction, and she had to go on unaided, which she did in a vanquished tone, verging on tears:

'I – I think I must be equally honest with you as you have been with me. Perhaps you have seen what it is I want to say? – that though I like Mr Phillotson as a friend, I don't like him – it is a

torture to me to — live with him as a husband! — There, now I have
let it out — I couldn't help it, although I have been — pretending I am
happy. — Now you'll have a contempt for me for ever, I suppose!'
She bent down her face upon her hands as they lay upon the cloth,
and silently sobbed in little jerks that made the fragile three-legged
table quiver.

'I have only been married a month or two!' she went on, still
remaining bent upon the table, and sobbing into her hands. 'And it
is said that what a woman shrinks from — in the early days of her
marriage — she shakes down to with comfortable indifference in
half-a-dozen years. But that is much like saying that the amputation
of a limb is no affliction, since a person gets comfortably accustomed
to the use of a wooden leg or arm in the course of time!'

Jude could hardly speak, but he said, 'I thought there was something wrong, Sue! O, I thought there was!'

'But it is not as you think! — there is nothing wrong except my
own wickedness, I suppose you'd call it — a repugnance on my part,
for a reason I cannot disclose, and what would not be admitted as
one by the world in general! . . . What tortures me so much is the
necessity of being responsive to this man whenever he wishes, good
as he is morally! — the dreadful contract to feel in a particular way
in a matter whose essence is its voluntariness! . . . I wish he would
beat me, or be faithless to me, or do some open thing that I could
talk about as a justification for feeling as I do! But he does nothing,
except that he has grown a little cold since he has found out how I
feel. That's why he didn't come to the funeral. . . . O, I am very
miserable — I don't know what to do! . . . Don't come near me, Jude,
because you mustn't. Don't — don't!'

But he had jumped up and put his face against hers — or rather
against her ear, her face being inaccessible.

'I told you not to, Jude!'

'I know you did — I only wish to — console you! It all arose
through my being married before we met, didn't it? You would have
been my wife, Sue, wouldn't you, if it hadn't been for that?'

Instead of replying she rose quickly, and saying she was going to
walk to her aunt's grave in the churchyard to recover herself, went
out of the house. Jude did not follow her. Twenty minutes later he
saw her cross the village green towards Mrs Edlin's, and soon she

sent a little girl to fetch her bag, and tell him she was too tired to see him again that night.

In the lonely room of his aunt's house Jude sat watching the cottage of the Widow Edlin as it disappeared behind the night shade. He knew that Sue was sitting within its walls equally lonely and disheartened; and again questioned his devotional motto that all was for the best.

He retired to rest early, but his sleep was fitful from the sense that Sue was so near at hand. At some time near two o'clock, when he was beginning to sleep more soundly, he was aroused by a shrill squeak that had been familiar enough to him when he lived regularly at Marygreen. It was the cry of a rabbit caught in a gin.* As was the little creature's habit, it did not soon repeat its cry; and probably would not do so more than once or twice; but would remain bearing its torture till the morrow, when the trapper would come and knock it on the head.

He who in his childhood had saved the lives of the earthworms now began to picture the agonies of the rabbit from its lacerated leg. If it were a 'bad catch' by the hind-leg, the animal would tug during the ensuing six hours till the iron teeth of the trap had stripped the leg-bone of its flesh, when, should a weak-springed instrument enable it to escape, it would die in the fields from the mortification of the limb. If it were a 'good catch', namely, by the fore-leg, the bone would be broken, and the limb nearly torn in two in attempts at an impossible escape.

Almost half-an-hour passed, and the rabbit repeated its cry. Jude could rest no longer till he had put it out of its pain, so dressing himself quickly he descended, and by the light of the moon went across the green in the direction of the sound. He reached the hedge bordering the widow's garden, when he stood still. The faint click of the trap as dragged about by the writhing animal guided him now, and reaching the spot he struck the rabbit on the back of the neck with the side of his palm, and it stretched itself out dead.

He was turning away when he saw a woman looking out of the open casement at a window on the ground floor of the adjacent cottage. 'Jude!' said a voice timidly — Sue's voice. 'It is you — is it not?'

'Yes, dear!'

'I haven't been able to sleep at all, and then I heard the rabbit, and couldn't help thinking of what it suffered, till I felt I must come down and kill it! But I am so glad you got there first. . . . They ought not to be allowed to set these steel traps, ought they!'

Jude had reached the window, which was quite a low one, so that she was visible down to her waist. She let go the casement-stay and put her hand upon his, her moonlit face regarding him wistfully.

'Did it keep you awake?' he said.

'No — I was awake.'

'How was that?'

'O, you know — now! I know you, with your religious doctrines, think that a married woman in trouble of a kind like mine commits a mortal sin in making a man the confidant of it, as I did you. I wish I hadn't, now!'

'Don't wish it, dear,' he said. 'That may have *been* my view; but my doctrines and I begin to part company.'

'I knew it — I knew it! And that's why I vowed I wouldn't disturb your beliefs. But — I am *so glad* to see you! — and, O, I didn't mean to see you again, now the last tie between us, Aunt Drusilla, is dead!'

Jude seized her hand and kissed it. 'There is a stronger one left!' he said. 'I'll never care about my doctrines or my religion any more! Let them go! Let me help you, even if I do love you, and even if you. . . .'

'Don't say it! — I know what you mean; but I can't admit so much as that. There! Guess what you like, but don't press me to answer questions!'

'I wish you were happy, whatever I may be!'

'I *can't* be! So few could enter into my feeling — they would say 'twas my fanciful fastidiousness, or something of that sort, and condemn me. . . . It is none of the natural tragedies of love that's love's usual tragedy in civilized life, but a tragedy artificially manufactured for people who in a natural state would find relief in parting! . . . It would have been wrong, perhaps, for me to tell my distress to you, if I had been able to tell it to anybody else. But I have nobody. And I *must* tell somebody! Jude, before I married him I had never thought out fully what marriage meant, even though I knew. It was idiotic of me — there is no excuse. I was old enough, and I thought I was very experienced. So I rushed on, when I had got into that Training School scrape, with all the cock-sureness of the fool that I was! ... I am certain one ought to be allowed to undo what one has done so ignorantly! I daresay it happens to lots of women; only they submit, and I kick. ... When people of a later age look back upon the barbarous customs and superstitions of the times that we have the unhappiness to live in, what *will* they say!'

'You are very bitter, darling Sue! How I wish — I wish—'

'You must go in now!'

In a moment of impulse she bent over the sill, and laid her face upon his hair, weeping, and then imprinting a scarcely perceptible little kiss upon the top of his head, withdrawing quickly, so that he could not put his arms round her, as otherwise he unquestionably would have done. She shut the casement, and he returned to his cottage.

SUE's distressful confession recurred to Jude's mind all the night as being a sorrow indeed.

The morning after, when it was time for her to go, the neighbours saw her companion and herself disappearing on foot down the hill path which led into the lonely road to Alfredston. An hour passed before he returned along the same route, and in his face there was a look of exaltation not unmixed with recklessness. An incident had occurred.

They had stood parting in the silent highway, and their tense and passionate moods had led to bewildered inquiries of each other on how far their intimacy ought to go; till they had almost quarrelled, and she had said tearfully that it was hardly proper of him as a parson in embryo to think of such a thing as kissing her even in farewell, as he now wished to do. Then she had conceded that the fact of the kiss would be nothing: all would depend upon the spirit of it. If given in the spirit of a cousin and a friend she saw no objection: if in the spirit of a lover she could not permit it. 'Will you swear that it will not be in that spirit?' she had said.

No: he would not. And then they had turned from each other in estrangement, and gone their several ways, till at a distance of twenty or thirty yards both had looked round simultaneously. That look behind was fatal to the reserve hitherto more or less maintained. They had quickly run back, and met, and embracing most unpremeditatedly, kissed close and long. When they parted for good it was with flushed cheeks on her side, and a beating heart on his.

The kiss was a turning-point in Jude's career. Back again in the cottage, and left to reflection, he saw one thing: that though his kiss of that aerial being had seemed the purest moment of his faultful life, as long as he nourished this unlicensed tenderness it was glaringly inconsistent for him to pursue the idea of becoming the soldier and servant of a religion in which sexual love was regarded as at its best a frailty, and at its worst damnation. What Sue had said in warmth was really the cold truth. When to defend his affection tooth and nail, to persist with headlong force in impassioned attentions to her, was all he thought of, he was condemned *ipso facto* as a professor of the accepted school of morals. He was as unfit, obviously, by nature, as he had been by social position, to fill the part of a propounder of accredited dogma.

Strange that his first aspiration – towards academical proficiency – had been checked by a woman, and that his second aspiration – towards apostleship – had also been checked by a woman. 'Is it,' he said, 'that the women are to blame; or is it the artificial system of things, under which the normal sex-impulses are turned into devilish domestic gins and springes to noose and hold back those who want to progress?'

It had been his standing desire to become a prophet, however humble, to his struggling fellow-creatures, without any thought of personal gain. Yet with a wife living away from him with another husband, and himself in love erratically, the loved one's revolt against her state being possibly on his account, he had sunk to be barely respectable according to regulation views.

It was not for him to consider further: he had only to confront the obvious, which was that he had made himself quite an impostor as a law-abiding religious teacher.

At dusk that evening he went into the garden and dug a shallow hole, to which he brought out all the theological and ethical works that he possessed, and had stored here. He knew that, in this country of true believers, most of them were not saleable at a much higher price than waste-paper value, and preferred to get rid of them in his own way, even if he should sacrifice a little money to the sentiment of thus destroying them. Lighting some loose pamphlets to begin with, he cut the volumes into pieces as well as he could, and with a three-pronged fork shook them over the flames. They kindled, and lighted up the back of the house, the pigsty, and his own face, till they were more or less consumed.

Though he was almost a stranger here now, passing cottagers talked to him over the garden hedge.

'Burning up your awld aunt's rubbidge, I suppose? Ay; a lot gets heaped up in nooks and corners when you've lived eighty years in one house.'

It was nearly one o'clock in the morning before the leaves, covers, and binding of Jeremy Taylor, Butler, Doddridge, Paley, Pusey, Newman and the rest had gone to ashes; but the night was quiet, and as he turned and turned the paper shreds with the fork, the sense of being no longer a hypocrite to himself afforded his mind a relief which gave him calm. He might go on believing as before, but he professed nothing, and no longer owned and exhibited engines of faith which, as their proprietor, he might naturally be supposed to exercise on himself first of all. In his passion for Sue he could now stand as an ordinary sinner, and not as a whited sepulchre.

Meanwhile Sue, after parting from him earlier in the day, had gone along to the station, with tears in her eyes for having run back and let him kiss her. Jude ought not to have pretended that he was not a lover, and made her give way to an impulse to act unconventionally, if not wrongly. She was inclined to call it the latter; for Sue's logic was extraordinarily compounded, and seemed to maintain that before a thing was done it might be right to do, but that being done it became wrong; or, in other words, that things which were right in theory were wrong in practice.

'I have been too weak, I think!' she jerked out as she pranced on, shaking down tear-drops now and then. 'It was burning, like a lover's — O it was! And I won't write to him any more, or at least for a long time, to impress him with my dignity! And I hope it will hurt him very much — expecting a letter to-morrow morning, and the next, and the next, and no letter coming. He'll suffer then with suspense — won't he, that's all! — and I am very glad of it!' — Tears of pity for Jude's approaching sufferings at her hands mingled with those which had surged up in pity for herself.

Then the slim little wife of a husband whose person was disagreeable to her, the ethereal, fine-nerved, sensitive girl, quite unfitted by temperament and instinct to fulfil the conditions of the matrimonial relation with Phillotson, possibly with scarce any man, walked fitfully along, and panted, and brought weariness into her eyes by gazing and worrying hopelessly.

Phillotson met her at the arrival station, and, seeing that she was troubled, thought it must be owing to the depressing effect of her aunt's death and funeral. He began telling her of his day's doings,

and how his friend Gillingham, a neighbouring schoolmaster whom
he had not seen for years, had called upon him. While ascending to
the town, seated on the top of the omnibus beside him, she said
suddenly and with an air of self-chastisement, regarding the white
road and its bordering bushes of hazel:

'Richard — I let Mr Fawley hold my hand a long while. I don't
know whether you think it wrong?'

He, waking apparently from thoughts of far different mould, said
vaguely, 'O, did you? What did you do that for?'

'I don't know. He wanted to, and I let him.'

'I hope it pleased him. I should think it was hardly a novelty.'

They lapsed into silence. Had this been a case in the court of an
omniscient judge he might have entered on his notes the curious fact
that Sue had placed the minor for the major indiscretion, and had
not said a word about the kiss.

After tea that evening Phillotson sat balancing the school regis-
ters. She remained in an unusually silent, tense, and restless condition, and at last, saying she was tired, went to bed early. When
Phillotson arrived upstairs, weary with the drudgery of the atten-
dance-numbers, it was a quarter to twelve o'clock. Entering their
chamber, which by day commanded a view of some thirty or forty
miles over the Vale of Blackmoor, and even into Outer Wessex, he
went to the window, and, pressing his face against the pane, gazed
with hard-breathing fixity into the mysterious darkness which now
covered the far-reaching scene. He was musing. 'I think,' he said at
last, without turning his head, 'that I must get the Committee to
change the school-stationer. All the copybooks are sent wrong this
time.'

There was no reply. Thinking Sue was dozing he went on:

'And there must be a re-arrangement of that ventilator in the
class-room. The wind blows down upon my head unmercifully, and
gives me the earache.'

As the silence seemed more absolute than ordinarily he turned
round. The heavy, gloomy oak wainscot which extended over the
walls upstairs and down in the dilapidated 'Old-Grove Place', and
the massive chimney-piece reaching to the ceiling, stood in odd
contrast to the new and shining brass bedstead, and the new suite of
birch furniture that he had bought for her, the two styles seeming to

nod to each other across three centuries upon the shaking floor.

'Soo!' he said (this being the way in which he pronounced her name).

She was not in the bed, though she had apparently been there — the clothes on her side being flung back. Thinking she might have forgotten some kitchen detail and gone downstairs for a moment to see to it, he pulled off his coat and idled quietly enough for a few minutes, when, finding she did not come, he went out upon the landing, candle in hand, and said again 'Soo!'

'Yes!' came back to him in her voice, from the distant kitchen quarter.

'What are you doing down there at midnight — tiring yourself out for nothing!'

'I am not sleepy; I am reading; and there is a larger fire here.'

He went to bed. Some time in the night he awoke. She was not there, even now. Lighting a candle he hastily stepped out upon the landing, and again called her name.

She answered 'Yes!' as before; but the tones were small and confined, and whence they came he would not at first understand. Under the staircase was a large clothes-closet, without a window; they seemed to come from it. The door was shut, but there was no lock or other fastening. Phillotson, alarmed, went towards it, wondering if she had suddenly become deranged.

'What are you doing in there?' he asked.

'Not to disturb you I came here, as it was so late.'

'But there's no bed, is there? And no ventilation! Why, you'll be suffocated if you stay all night!'

'O no, I think not. Don't trouble about me.'

'But—' Phillotson seized the knob and pulled at the door. She had fastened it inside with a piece of string, which broke at his pull. There being no bedstead she had flung down some rugs and made a little nest for herself in the very cramped quarters the closet afforded.

When he looked in upon her she sprang out of her lair, great-eyed and trembling.

'You ought not to have pulled open the door!' she cried excitedly. 'It is not becoming in you! O, will you go away; please will you!'

She looked so pitiful and pleading in her white night-gown

against the shadowy lumber-hole that he was quite worried. She continued to beseech him not to disturb her.

He said: 'I've been kind to you, and given you every liberty; and it is monstrous that you should feel in this way!'

'Yes,' said she, weeping. 'I know that! It is wrong and wicked of me, I suppose! I am very sorry. But it is not I altogether that am to blame!'

'Who is then? Am I?'

'No — I don't know! The universe, I suppose — things in general, because they are so horrid and cruel!'

'Well, it is no use talking like that. Making a man's house so unseemly at this time o' night! Eliza will hear, if we don't mind.' (He meant the servant.) 'Just think if either of the parsons in this town was to see us now! I hate such eccentricities, Sue. There's no order or regularity in your sentiments! . . . But I won't intrude on you further; only I would advise you not to shut the door too tight, or I shall find you stifled to-morrow.'

On rising the next morning he immediately looked into the closet, but Sue had already gone downstairs. There was a little nest where she had lain, and spiders' webs hung overhead. 'What must a woman's aversion be when it is stronger than her fear of spiders!' he said bitterly.

He found her sitting at the breakfast-table, and the meal began almost in silence, the burghers walking past upon the pavement — or rather roadway, pavements being scarce here — which was two or three feet above the level of the parlour floor. They nodded down to the happy couple their morning greetings, as they went on.

'Richard,' she said all at once; 'would you mind my living away from you?'

'Away from me? Why, that's what you were doing when I married you. What then was the meaning of marrying at all?'

'You wouldn't like me any the better for telling you.'

'I don't object to know.'

'Because I thought I could do nothing else. You had got my promise a long time before that, remember. Then, as time went on, I regretted I had promised you, and was trying to see an honourable way to break it off. But as I couldn't I became rather reckless and careless about the conventions. Then you know what scandals were

spread, and how I was turned out of the Training School you had
taken such time and trouble to prepare me for and get me into; and
this frightened me, and it seemed then that the one thing I could do
would be to let the engagement stand. Of course I, of all people,
ought not to have cared what was said, for it was just what I fancied
I never did care for. But I was a coward – as so many women are –
and my theoretic unconventionality broke down. If that had not
entered into the case it would have been better to have hurt your
feelings once for all then, than to marry you and hurt them all my
life after. . . . And you were so generous in never giving credit for a
moment to the rumour.'

'I am bound in honesty to tell you that I weighed its probability,
and inquired of your cousin about it.'

'Ah!' she said with pained surprise.

'I didn't doubt you.'

'But you inquired!'

'I took his word.'

Her eyes had filled. '*He* wouldn't have inquired!' she said. 'But
you haven't answered me. Will you let me go away? I know how
irregular it is of me to ask it—'

'It is irregular.'

'But I do ask it! Domestic laws should be made according to
temperaments, which should be classified. If people are at all
peculiar in character they have to suffer from the very rules that
produce comfort in others! . . . Will you let me?'

'But we married—'

'What is the use of thinking of laws and ordinances,' she burst
out, 'if they make you miserable when you know you are committing no sin?'

'But you are committing a sin in not liking me.'

'I *do* like you! But I didn't reflect it would be – that it would be so
much more than that. . . . For a man and woman to live on intimate
terms when one feels as I do is adultery, in any circumstances,
however legal. There – I've said it! . . . Will you let me, Richard?'

'You distress me, Susanna, by such importunity!'

'Why can't we agree to free each other? We made the compact,
and surely we can cancel it – not legally, of course; but we can
morally, especially as no new interests, in the shape of children, have

arisen to be looked after. Then we might be friends, and meet without pain to either. O Richard, be my friend and have pity! We shall both be dead in a few years, and then what will it matter to anybody that you relieved me from constraint for a little while? I daresay you think me eccentric, or super-sensitive, or something absurd. Well – why should I suffer for what I was born to be, if it doesn't hurt other people?'

'But it does – it hurts *me!* And you vowed to love me.'

'Yes – that's it! I am in the wrong. I always am! It is as culpable to bind yourself to love always as to believe a creed always, and as silly as to vow always to like a particular food or drink!'

'And do you mean, by living away from me, living by yourself?'

'Well, if you insisted, yes. But I meant living with Jude.'

'As his wife?'

'As I choose.'

Phillotson writhed.

Sue continued: 'She, or he, "who lets the world, or his own portion of it, choose his plan of life for him, has no need of any other faculty than the ape-like one of imitation".* J. S. Mill's words, those are. I have been reading it up. Why can't you act upon them? I wish to, always.'

'What do I care about J. S. Mill!' moaned he. 'I only want to lead a quiet life! Do you mind my saying that I have guessed what never once occurred to me before our marriage – that you were in love, and are in love, with Jude Fawley!'

'You may go on guessing that I am, since you have begun. But do you suppose that if I had been I should have asked you to let me go and live with him?'

The ringing of the school bell saved Phillotson from the necessity of replying at present to what apparently did not strike him as being such a convincing *argumentum ad verecundiam* * as she, in her loss of courage at the last moment, meant it to appear. She was beginning to be so puzzling and unstateable that he was ready to throw in with her other little peculiarities the extremest request which a wife could make.

They proceeded to the schools that morning as usual, Sue entering the class-room, where he could see the back of her head through the glass partition whenever he turned his eyes that way. As he went on giving and hearing lessons his forehead and eyebrows twitched from concentrated agitation of thought; till at length he tore a scrap from a sheet of scribbling paper and wrote:

'Your request prevents my attending to work at all. I don't know what I am doing! Was it seriously made?'

He folded the piece of paper very small, and gave it to a little boy to take to Sue. The child toddled off into the class-room. Phillotson saw his wife turn and take the note, and the bend of her pretty head as she read it, her lips slightly crisped, to prevent undue expression under fire of so many young eyes. He could not see her hands, but she changed her position, and soon the child returned, bringing nothing in reply. In a few minutes, however, one of Sue's class appeared, with a little note similar to his own. These words only were pencilled therein:

'I am sincerely sorry to say that it was seriously made.'

Phillotson looked more disturbed than before, and the meeting-place of his brows twitched again. In ten minutes he called up the child he had just sent to her, and despatched another missive:

'God knows I don't want to thwart you in any reasonable way. My whole thought is to make you comfortable and happy. But I cannot agree to such a preposterous notion as your going to live with your lover. You would lose everybody's respect and regard; and so should I!'

After an interval a similar part was enacted in the class-room, and an answer came:

'I know you mean my good. But I don't want to be respectable! To produce "Human development in its richest diversity" * (to quote your Humboldt) is to my mind far above respectability. No doubt my tastes are low — in your view hopelessly low! If you won't let me go to him, will you grant me this one request — allow me to live in your house in a separate way?'

To this he returned no answer.

She wrote again:

'I know what you think. But cannot you have pity on me? I beg you to; I implore you to be merciful! I would not ask if I were not almost compelled by what I can't bear! No poor woman has ever wished more than I that Eve had not fallen, so that (as the primitive Christians believed) some harmless mode of vegetation might have peopled Paradise. But I won't trifle! Be kind to me — even though I have not been kind to you! I will go away, go abroad, anywhere, and never trouble you.'

Nearly an hour passed, and then he returned an answer:

'I do not wish to pain you. How well you *know* I don't! Give me a little time. I am disposed to agree to your last request.'

One line from her:

'Thank you from my heart, Richard. I do not deserve your kindness.'

All day Phillotson bent a dazed regard upon her through the glazed partition; and he felt as lonely as when he had not known her.

But he was as good as his word, and consented to her living apart in the house. At first, when they met at meals, she had seemed more composed under the new arrangement; but the irksomeness of their position worked on her temperament, and the fibres of her nature seemed strained like harp-strings. She talked vaguely and indiscriminately to prevent his talking pertinently.

PHILLOTSON was sitting up late, as was often his custom, trying to get together the materials for his long-neglected hobby of Roman antiquities. For the first time since reviving the subject he felt a return of his old interest in it. He forgot time and place, and when he remembered himself and ascended to rest it was nearly two o'clock.

His preoccupation was such that, though he now slept on the other side of the house, he mechanically went to the room that he and his wife had occupied when he first became a tenant of Old-Grove Place, which since his differences with Sue had been hers exclusively. He entered, and unconsciously began to undress.

There was a cry from the bed, and a quick movement. Before the schoolmaster had realized where he was he perceived Sue starting up half-awake, staring wildly, and springing out upon the floor on the side away from him, which was towards the window. This was somewhat hidden by the canopy of the bedstead, and in a moment he heard her flinging up the sash. Before he had thought that she meant to do more than get air she had mounted upon the sill and leapt out. She disappeared in the darkness, and he heard her fall below.

Phillotson, horrified, ran downstairs, striking himself sharply against the newel * in his haste. Opening the heavy door he ascended the two or three steps to the level of the ground, and there on the gravel before him lay a white heap. Phillotson seized it in his arms, and bringing Sue into the hall seated her on a chair, where he gazed at her by the flapping light of the candle which he had set down in the draught on the bottom stair.

She had certainly not broken her neck. She looked at him with eyes that seemed not to take him in; and though not particularly large in general they appeared so now. She pressed her side and rubbed her arm, as if conscious of pain; then stood up, averting her face, in evident distress at his gaze.

'Thank God — you are not killed! Though it's not for want of trying – not much hurt I hope?'

Her fall, in fact, had not been a serious one, probably owing to the lowness of the old rooms and to the high level of the ground without. Beyond a scraped elbow and a blow in the side she had apparently incurred little harm.

'I was asleep, I think!' she began, her pale face still turned away from him. 'And something frightened me – a terrible dream – I thought I saw you—' The actual circumstances seemed to come back to her, and she was silent.

Her cloak was hanging at the back of the door, and the wretched Phillotson flung it round her. 'Shall I help you upstairs?' he asked drearily; for the significance of all this sickened him of himself and of everything.

'No thank you, Richard. I am very little hurt. I can walk.'

'You ought to lock your door,' he mechanically said, as if lecturing in school. 'Then no one could intrude even by accident.'

'I have tried – it won't lock. All the doors are out of order.'

The aspect of things was not improved by her admission. She ascended the staircase slowly, the waving light of the candle shining on her. Phillotson did not approach her, or attempt to ascend himself till he heard her enter her room. Then he fastened up the front door, and returning sat down on the lower stairs, holding the newel with one hand, and bowing his face into the other. Thus he remained for a long long time – a pitiable object enough to one who had seen him; till, raising his head and sighing a sigh which seemed to say that the business of his life must be carried on, whether he had a wife or no, he took the candle and went upstairs to his lonely room on the other side of the landing.

No further incident touching the matter between them occurred till the following evening, when, immediately school was over, Phillotson walked out of Shaston, saying he required no tea, and not informing Sue where he was going. He descended from the town level by a steep road in a north-westerly direction, and continued to move downwards till the soil changed from its white dryness to a tough brown clay. He was now on the low alluvial beds

'Where Duncliffe is the traveller's mark,
And cloty Stour's a-rolling dark.'*

More than once he looked back in the increasing obscurity of evening. Against the sky was Shaston, dimly visible

'On the grey-topp'd height
Of Paladore, as pale day wore
Away....'[1]*

The new-lit lights from its windows burnt with a steady shine as if watching him, one of which windows was his own. Above it he could just discern the pinnacled tower of Trinity Church. The air down here, tempered by the thick damp bed of tenacious clay, was not as it had been above, but soft and relaxing, so that when he had walked a mile or two he was obliged to wipe his face with his handkerchief.

Leaving Duncliffe Hill on the left he proceeded without hesitation through the shade, as a man goes on, night or day, in a district over which he has played as a boy. He had walked altogether about four and a half miles

'Where Stour receives her strength,
From six cleere fountains fed',[2]*

when he crossed a tributary of the Stour, and reached Leddenton – a little town of three or four thousand inhabitants – where he went on to the boys' school, and knocked at the door of the master's residence.

A boy pupil-teacher opened it, and to Phillotson's inquiry if Mr Gillingham was at home replied that he was, going at once off to his own house, and leaving Phillotson to find his way in as he could. He discovered his friend putting away some books from which he had been giving evening lessons. The light of the paraffin lamp fell on Phillotson's face – pale and wretched by contrast with his friend's, who had a cool, practical look. They had been schoolmates in boyhood, and fellow-students at Wintoncester Training College, many years before this time.

'Glad to see you, Dick! But you don't look well? Nothing the matter?'

Phillotson advanced without replying, and Gillingham closed the cupboard and pulled up beside his visitor.

'Why you haven't been here – let me see – since you were

---

[1] William Barnes.   [2] Drayton.

married? I called, you know, but you were out; and upon my word
it is such a climb after dark that I have been waiting till the days are
longer before lumpering up again. I am glad you didn't wait, however.'

Though well-trained and even proficient masters, they occasionally used a dialect-word of their boyhood to each other in private.

'I've come, George, to explain to you my reasons for taking a step
that I am about to take, so that you, at least, will understand my
motives if other people question them anywhen — as they may,
indeed certainly will. . . . But anything is better than the present
condition of things. God forbid that you should ever have such an
experience as mine!'

'Sit down. You don't mean — anything wrong between you and
Mrs Phillotson?'

'I do. . . . My wretched state is that I've a wife I love, who not
only does not love me, but — but— Well, I won't say. I know her
feeling! I should prefer hatred from her!'

'Ssh!'

'And the sad part of it is that she is not so much to blame as I.
She was a pupil-teacher under me, as you know, and I took advantage of her inexperience, and toled * her out for walks, and got her
to agree to a long engagement before she well knew her own mind.
Afterwards she saw somebody else, but she blindly fulfilled her
engagement.'

'Loving the other?'

'Yes; with a curious tender solicitude seemingly; though her
exact feeling for him is a riddle to me — and to him too, I think —
possibly to herself. She is one of the oddest creatures I ever met.
However, I have been struck with these two facts; the extraordinary
sympathy, or similarity, between the pair. He is her cousin, which
perhaps accounts for some of it. They seem to be one person split in
two! And with her unconquerable aversion to myself as a husband,
even though she may like me as a friend, 'tis too much to bear
longer. She has conscientiously struggled against it, but to no
purpose. I cannot bear it — I cannot! I can't answer her arguments —
she has read ten times as much as I. Her intellect sparkles like
diamonds, while mine smoulders like brown paper. . . . She's one too
many for me!'

'She'll get over it, good-now?'*

'Never! It is — but I won't go into it — there are reasons why she never will. At last she calmly and firmly asked if she might leave me and go to him. The climax came last night, when, owing to my entering her room by accident, she jumped out of window — so strong was her dread of me! She pretended it was a dream, but that was to soothe me. Now when a woman jumps out of window without caring whether she breaks her neck or no, she's not to be mistaken; and this being the case I have come to a conclusion: that it is wrong to so torture a fellow-creature any longer; and I won't be the inhuman wretch to do it, cost what it may!'

'What — you'll let her go? And with her lover?'

'Whom with is her matter. I shall let her go; with him certainly, if she wishes. I know I may be wrong — I know I can't logically, or religiously, defend my concession to such a wish of hers; or harmonize it with the doctrines I was brought up in. Only I know one thing· something within me tells me I am doing wrong in refusing her. I, like other men, profess to hold that if a husband gets such a so-called preposterous request from his wife, the only course that can possibly be regarded as right and proper and honourable in him is to refuse it, and put her virtuously under lock and key, and murder her lover perhaps. But is that essentially right, and proper, and honourable, or is it contemptibly mean and selfish? I don't profess to decide. I simply am going to act by instinct, and let principles take care of themselves. If a person who has blindly walked into a quagmire cries for help, I am inclined to give it, if possible.'

'But — you see, there's the question of neighbours and society — what will happen if everybody—'

'O, I am not going to be a philosopher any longer! I only see what's under my eyes.'

'Well — I don't agree with your instinct, Dick!' said Gillingham gravely. 'I am quite amazed, to tell the truth, that such a sedate, plodding fellow as you should have entertained such a craze for a moment. You said when I called that she was puzzling and peculiar: I think you are!'

'Have you ever stood before a woman whom you know to be intrinsically a good woman, while she has pleaded for release — been the man she has knelt to and implored indulgence of?'

'I am thankful to say I haven't.'

'Then I don't think you are in a position to give an opinion. I have been that man, and it makes all the difference in the world, if one has any manliness or chivalry in him. I had not the remotest idea — living apart from women as I have done for so many years — that merely taking a woman to church and putting a ring upon her finger could by any possibility involve one in such a daily, continuous tragedy as that now shared by her and me!'

'Well, I could admit some excuse for letting her leave you, provided she kept to herself. But to go attended by a cavalier — that makes a difference.'

'Not a bit. Suppose, as I believe, she would rather endure her present misery than be made to promise to keep apart from him? All that is a question for herself. It is not the same thing at all as the treachery of living on with a husband and playing him false. . . . However, she has not distinctly implied living with him as wife, though I think she means to. . . . And to the best of my understanding it is not an ignoble, merely animal, feeling between the two: that is the worst of it; because it makes me think their affection will be enduring. I did not mean to confess to you that in the first jealous weeks of my marriage, before I had come to my right mind, I hid myself in the school one evening when they were together there, and I heard what they said. I am ashamed of it now, though I suppose I was only exercising a legal right. I found from their manner that an extraordinary affinity, or sympathy, entered into their attachment, which somehow took away all flavour of grossness. Their supreme desire is to be together — to share each other's emotions, and fancies, and dreams.'

'Platonic!'

'Well no. Shelleyan would be nearer to it. They remind me of — what are their names — Laon and Cythna.* Also of Paul and Virginia* a little. The more I reflect, the more *entirely* I am on their side!'

'But if people did as you want to do, there'd be a general domestic disintegration. The family would no longer be the social unit.'

'Yes — I am all abroad,* I suppose!' said Phillotson sadly. 'I was never a very bright reasoner, you remember. . . . And yet, I don't see why the woman and the children should not be the unit without the man.'

'By the Lord Harry! — Matriarchy! ... Does *she* say all this too?'

'O no. She little thinks I have out-Sued Sue in this — all in the last twelve hours!'

'It will upset all received opinion hereabout. Good God — what will Shaston say!'

'I don't say that it won't. I don't know — I don't know! ... As I say, I am only a feeler, not a reasoner.'

'Now,' said Gillingham, 'let us take it quietly, and have something to drink over it.' He went under the stairs, and produced a bottle of cider-wine, of which they drank a rummer* each. 'I think you are rafted,* and not yourself,' he continued. 'Do go back and make up your mind to put up with a few whims. But keep her. I hear on all sides that she's a charming young thing.'

'Ah yes! That's the bitterness of it! Well, I won't stay. I have a long walk before me.'

Gillingham accompanied his friend a mile on his way, and at parting expressed his hope that this consultation, singular as its subject was, would be the renewal of their old comradeship. 'Stick to her!' were his last words, flung into the darkness after Phillotson; from which his friend answered 'Ay, ay!'

But when Phillotson was alone under the clouds of night, and no sound was audible but that of the purling tributaries of the Stour, he said, 'So Gillingham, my friend, you had no stronger arguments against it than those!'

'I think she ought to be smacked, and brought to her senses — that's what I think!' murmured Gillingham, as he walked back alone.

The next morning came, and at breakfast Phillotson told Sue:

'You may go — with whom you will. I absolutely and unconditionally agree.'

Having once come to this conclusion it seemed to Phillotson more and more indubitably the true one. His mild serenity at the sense that he was doing his duty by a woman who was at his mercy almost overpowered his grief at relinquishing her.

Some days passed, and the evening of their last meal together had come — a cloudy evening with wind — which indeed was very seldom absent in this elevated place. How permanently it was imprinted upon his vision; that look of her as she glided into the parlour to tea; a slim flexible figure; a face, strained from its roundness, and marked by the pallors of restless days and nights, suggesting tragic possibilities quite at variance with her times of buoyancy; a trying of this morsel and that, and an inability to eat either. Her nervous manner, begotten of a fear lest he should be injured by her course, might have been interpreted by a stranger as displeasure that Phillotson intruded his presence on her for the few brief minutes that remained.

'You had better have a slice of ham, or an egg, or something with your tea? You can't travel on a mouthful of bread and butter.'

She took the slice he helped her to; and they discussed as they sat trivial questions of housekeeping, such as where he would find the key of this or that cupboard, what little bills were paid, and what not.

'I am a bachelor by nature, as you know, Sue,' he said, in a heroic attempt to put her at her ease. 'So that being without a wife will not really be irksome to me, as it might be to other men who have had one a little while. I have, too, this grand hobby in my head of writing "The Roman Antiquities of Wessex", which will occupy all my spare hours.'

'If you will send me some of the manuscript to copy at any time, as you used to, I will do it with so much pleasure!' she said with amenable gentleness. 'I should much like to be some help to you still — as a — friend.'

Phillotson mused, and said: 'No, I think we ought to be really separate, if we are to be at all. And for this reason, that I don't wish to ask you any questions, and particularly wish you not to give me information as to your movements, or even your address. . . . Now, what money do you want? You must have some, you know.'

'O, of course, Richard, I couldn't think of having any of *your* money to go away from you with! I don't want any either. I have enough of my own to last me for a long while, and Jude will let me have—'

'I would rather not know anything about him, if you don't mind. You are free, absolutely; and your course is your own.'

'Very well. But I'll just say that I have packed only a change or two of my own personal clothing, and one or two little things besides that are my very own. I wish you would look into my trunk before it is closed. Besides that I have only a small parcel that will go into Jude's portmanteau.'

'Of course I shall do no such thing as examine your luggage! I wish you would take three-quarters of the household furniture. I don't want to be bothered with it. I have a sort of affection for a little of it that belonged to my poor mother and father. But the rest you are welcome to whenever you like to send for it.'

'That I shall never do.'

'You go by the six-thirty train, don't you? It is now a quarter to six.'

'You ... You don't seem very sorry I am going, Richard!'

'O no – perhaps not.'

'I like you much for how you have behaved. It is a curious thing that directly I have begun to regard you as not my husband, but as my old teacher, I like you. I won't be so affected as to say I love you, because you know I don't, except as a friend. But you do seem that to me!'

Sue was for a few moments a little tearful at these reflections, and then the station omnibus came round to take her up. Phillotson saw her things put on the top, handed her in, and was obliged to make an appearance of kissing her as he wished her good-bye, which she quite understood and imitated. From the cheerful manner in which they parted the omnibus-man had no other idea than that she was going for a short visit.

When Phillotson got back into the house he went upstairs and opened the window in the direction the omnibus had taken. Soon the noise of its wheels died away. He came down then, his face compressed like that of one bearing pain; he put on his hat and went out, following by the same route for nearly a mile. Suddenly turning round he came home.

He had no sooner entered than the voice of his friend Gillingham greeted him from the front room.

'I could make nobody hear; so finding your door open I walked in, and made myself comfortable. I said I would call, you remember.'

'Yes. I am much obliged to you, Gillingham, particularly for coming to-night.'

'How is Mrs—'

'She is quite well. She is gone — just gone. That's her tea-cup, that she drank out of only an hour ago. And that's the plate she—' Phillotson's throat got choked up, and he could not go on. He turned and pushed the tea-things aside.

'Have you had any tea, by-the-bye?' he asked presently. in a renewed voice.

'No — yes — never mind,' said Gillingham, preoccupied. 'Gone, you say she is?'

'Yes. . . . I would have died for her; but I wouldn't be cruel to her in the name of the law. She is, as I understand, gone to join her lover. What they are going to do I cannot say. Whatever it may be she has my full consent to.'

There was a stability, a ballast, in Phillotson's pronouncement which restrained his friend's comment. 'Shall I — leave you?' he asked.

'No, no. It is a mercy to me that you have come. I have some articles to arrange and clear away. Would you help me?'

Gillingham assented; and having gone to the upper rooms the schoolmaster opened drawers, and began taking out all Sue's things that she had left behind, and laying them in a large box. 'She wouldn't take all I wanted her to,' he continued. 'But when I made up my mind to her going to live in her own way I did make up my mind.'

'Some men would have stopped at an agreement to separate.'

'I've gone into all that, and don't wish to argue it. I was, and am, the most old-fashioned man in the world on the question of marriage — in fact I had never thought critically about its ethics at all. But certain facts stared me in the face, and I couldn't go against them.'

They went on with the packing silently. When it was done Phillotson closed the box and turned the key.

'There,' he said. 'To adorn her in somebody's eyes; never again in mine!'

FOUR-AND-TWENTY hours before this time Sue had written the following note to Jude:

'It is as I told you; and I am leaving to-morrow evening. Richard and I thought it could be done with less obtrusiveness after dark. I feel rather frightened, and therefore ask you to be sure you are on the Melchester platform to meet me. I arrive at a little to seven. I know you will, of course, dear Jude; but I feel so timid that I can't help begging you to be punctual. He has been so *very* kind to me through it all!

'Now to our meeting!   S.'

As she was carried by the omnibus further and further down from the mountain town — the single passenger that evening — she regarded the receding road with a sad face. But no hesitation was apparent therein.

The up-train by which she was departing stopped by signal only. To Sue it seemed strange that such a powerful organization as a railway-train should be brought to a standstill on purpose for her — a fugitive from her lawful home.

The twenty minutes' journey drew towards its close, and Sue began gathering her things together to alight. At the moment that the train came to a standstill by the Melchester platform a hand was laid on the door and she beheld Jude. He entered the compartment promptly. He had a black bag in his hand, and was dressed in the dark suit he wore on Sundays and in the evening after work. Altogether he looked a very handsome young fellow, his ardent affection for her burning in his eyes.

'O Jude!' She clasped his hand with both hers, and her tense state caused her to simmer over in a little succession of dry sobs. 'I — I am so glad! I get out here?'

'No. I get in, dear one! I've packed. Besides this bag I've only a big box which is labelled.'

'But don't I get out? Aren't we going to stay here?'

'We couldn't possibly, don't you see. We are known here — I, at

any rate, am well known. I've booked for Aldbrickham; and here's
your ticket for the same place, as you have only one to here.'

'I thought we should have stayed here,' she repeated.

'It wouldn't have done at all.'

'Ah! – Perhaps not.'

'There wasn't time for me to write and say the place I had decided
on. Aldbrickham is a much bigger town – sixty or seventy thousand
inhabitants – and nobody knows anything about us there.'

'And you have given up your Cathedral work here?'

'Yes. It was rather sudden – your message coming unexpectedly.
Strictly, I might have been made to finish out the week. But I
pleaded urgency and I was let off. I would have deserted any day at
your command, dear Sue. I have deserted more than that for you!'

'I fear I am doing you a lot of harm. Ruining your prospects of
the Church; ruining your progress in your trade; everything!'

'The Church is no more to me. Let it lie! *I* am not to be one of

> "The soldier-saints who, row on row,
>   Burn upward each to his point of bliss",*

if any such there be! My point of bliss is not upward, but here.'

'O I seem so bad – upsetting men's courses like this!' said she,
taking up in her voice the emotion that had begun in his. But she
recovered her equanimity by the time they had travelled a dozen
miles.

'He has been so good in letting me go,' she resumed. 'And here's
a note I found on my dressing-table, addressed to you.'

'Yes. He's not an unworthy fellow,' said Jude, glancing at the
note. 'And I am ashamed of myself for hating him because he
married you.'

'According to the rule of women's whims I suppose I ought to
suddenly love him, because he has let me go so generously and
unexpectedly,' she answered smiling. 'But I am so cold, or devoid of
gratitude, or so something, that even this generosity hasn't made me
love him, or repent, or want to stay with him as his wife; although I
do feel I like his large-mindedness, and respect him more than ever.'

'It may not work so well for us as if he had been less kind, and
you had run away against his will,' murmured Jude.

'That I *never* would have done.'

Jude's eyes rested musingly on her face. Then he suddenly kissed her; and was going to kiss her again. 'No — only once now — please, Jude!'

'That's rather cruel,' he answered; but acquiesced. 'Such a strange thing has happened to me,' Jude continued after a silence. 'Arabella has actually written to ask me to get a divorce from her — in kindness to her, she says. She wants to honestly and legally marry that man she has already married virtually; and begs me to enable her to do it.'

'What have you done?'

'I have agreed. I thought at first I couldn't do it without getting her into trouble about that second marriage, and I don't want to injure her in any way. Perhaps she's no worse than I am, after all! But nobody knows about it over here, and I find it will not be a difficult proceeding at all. If she wants to start afresh I have only too obvious reasons for not hindering her.'

'Then you'll be free?'

'Yes, I shall be free.'

'Where are we booked for?' she asked, with the discontinuity that marked her to-night.

'Aldbrickham, as I said.'

'But it will be very late when we get there?'

'Yes. I thought of that, and I wired for a room for us at the Temperance Hotel there.'

'One?'

'Yes — one.'

She looked at him. 'O Jude!' Sue bent her forehead against the corner of the compartment. 'I thought you might do it; and that I was deceiving you. But I didn't mean that!'

In the pause which followed, Jude's eyes fixed themselves with a stultified expression on the opposite seat. 'Well!' he said. . . . 'Well!'

He remained in silence; and seeing how discomfited he was she put her face against his cheek, murmuring, 'Don't be vexed, dear!'

'Oh — there's no harm done,' he said. 'But — I understood it like that. . . . Is this a sudden change of mind?'

'You have no right to ask me such a question; and I shan't answer!' she said smiling.

'My dear one, your happiness is more to me than anything —

although we seem to verge on quarrelling so often! — and your will
is law to me. I am something more than a mere — selfish fellow, I
hope. Have it as you wish!' On reflection his brow showed perplexity. 'But perhaps it is that you don't love me — not that you have
become conventional! Much as, under your teaching, I hate convention, I hope it *is* that, not the other terrible alternative!'

Even at this obvious moment for candour Sue could not be quite
candid as to the state of that mystery, her heart. 'Put it down to my
timidity,' she said with hurried evasiveness; 'to a woman's natural
timidity when the crisis comes. I *may* feel as well as you that I have
a perfect right to live with you as you thought — from this moment. I
may hold the opinion that, in a proper state of society, the father of
a woman's child will be as much a private matter of hers as the cut
of her under-linen, on whom nobody will have any right to question
her. But partly, perhaps, because it is by his generosity that I am
now free, I would rather not be other than a little rigid. If there had
been a rope-ladder, and he had run after us with pistols, it would
have seemed different, and I may have acted otherwise. But don't
press me and criticize me, Jude! Assume that I haven't the courage
of my opinions. I know I am a poor miserable creature. My nature
is not so passionate as yours!'

He repeated simply: 'I thought — what I naturally thought. But if
we are not lovers, we are not. Phillotson thought so, I am sure. See,
here is what he has written to me.' He opened the letter she had
brought, and read:

'I make only one condition — that you are tender and kind to her.
I know you love her. But even love may be cruel at times. You are
made for each other: it is obvious, palpable, to any unbiased older
person. You were all along "the shadowy third"* in my short life
with her. I repeat, take care of Sue.'

'He's a good fellow, isn't he!' she said with latent tears. On
reconsideration she added, 'He was very resigned to letting me go —
too resigned almost! I never was so near being in love with him as
when he made such thoughtful arrangements for my being comfortable on my journey, and offering to provide money. Yet I was not. If
I loved him ever so little as a wife, I'd go back to him even now.'

'But you don't, do you?'

'It is true — O so terribly true! — I don't.'

'Nor me neither, I half fear!' he said pettishly. 'Nor anybody perhaps! — Sue, sometimes, when I am vexed with you, I think you are incapable of real love.'

'That's not good and loyal of you!' she said, and drawing away from him as far as she could, looked severely out into the darkness. She added in hurt tones, without turning round: 'My liking for you is not as some women's perhaps. But it is a delight in being with you, of a supremely delicate kind, and I don't want to go further and risk it by — an attempt to intensify it! I quite realized that, as woman with man, it was a risk to come. But, as *me* with *you*, I resolved to trust you to set my wishes above your gratification. Don't discuss it further, dear Jude!'

'Of course, if it would make you reproach yourself . . . but you do like me very much, Sue? say you do! Say that you do a quarter, a tenth, as much as I do you; and I'll be content!'

'I've let you kiss me, and that tells enough.'

'Just once or so!'

'Well — don't be a greedy boy.'

He leant back, and did not look at her for a long time. That episode in her past history of which she had told him — of the poor Christminster graduate whom she had handled thus, returned to Jude's mind; and he saw himself as a possible second in such a torturing destiny.

'This is a queer elopement!' he murmured. 'Perhaps you are making a cat's-paw of me with Phillotson all this time. Upon my word it almost seems so — to see you sitting up there so prim!'

'Now you mustn't be angry — I won't let you!' she coaxed, turning and moving nearer to him. 'You did kiss me just now, you know; and I didn't dislike you to, I own it, Jude. Only I don't want to let you do it again, just yet — considering how we are circumstanced, don't you see!'

He could never resist her when she pleaded (as she well knew). And they sat side by side with joined hands, till she aroused herself at some thought.

'I can't possibly go to that Temperance Inn, after your telegraphing that message!'

'Why not?'

'You can see well enough!'

'Very well; there'll be some other one open, no doubt. I have sometimes thought, since your marrying Phillotson because of a stupid scandal, that under the affectation of independent views you are as enslaved to the social code as any woman I know!'

'Not mentally. But I haven't the courage of my views, as I said before. I didn't marry him altogether because of the scandal. But sometimes a woman's *love of being loved* gets the better of her conscience, and though she is agonized at the thought of treating a man cruelly, she encourages him to love her while she doesn't love him at all. Then, when she sees him suffering, her remorse sets in, and she does what she can to repair the wrong.'

'You simply mean that you flirted outrageously with him, poor old chap, and then repented, and to make reparation, married him, though you tortured yourself to death by doing it.'

'Well − if you will put it brutally! − it was a little like that − that and the scandal together − and your concealing from me what you ought to have told me before!'

He could see that she was distressed and tearful at his criticisms, and soothed her, saying: 'There, dear; don't mind! Crucify me, if you will! You know you are all the world to me, whatever you do!'

'I am very bad and unprincipled − I know you think that!' she said, trying to blink away her tears.

'I think and know you are my dear Sue, from whom neither length nor breadth, nor things present nor things to come, can divide me!' *

Though so sophisticated in many things she was such a child in others that this satisfied her, and they reached the end of their journey on the best of terms. It was about ten o'clock when they arrived at Aldbrickham, the county town of North Wessex. As she would not go to the Temperance Hotel because of the form of his telegram, Jude inquired for another; and a youth who volunteered to find one wheeled their luggage to The George further on, which proved to be the inn at which Jude had stayed with Arabella on that one occasion of their meeting after their division for years.

Owing, however, to their now entering it by another door, and to his preoccupation, he did not at first recognize the place. When they had engaged their respective rooms they went down to a late supper. During Jude's temporary absence the waiting-maid spoke to Sue.

'I think, ma'am, I remember your relation, or friend, or whatever he is, coming here once before – late, just like this, with his wife – a lady, at any rate, that wasn't you by no manner of means – jest as med be with you now.'

'O do you?' said Sue, with a certain sickness of heart. 'Though I think you must be mistaken! How long ago was it?'

'About a month or two. A handsome, full-figured woman. They had this room.'

When Jude came back and sat down to supper Sue seemed moping and miserable. 'Jude,' she said to him plaintively, at their parting that night upon the landing, 'it is not so nice and pleasant as it used to be with us! And I don't like it here – I can't bear the place! And I don't like you so well as I did!'

'How fidgeted you seem, dear! Why do you change like this?'

'Because it was cruel to bring me here!'

'Why?'

'You were lately here with Arabella. There, now I have said it!'

'Dear me, why—' said Jude looking round him. 'Yes – it is the same! I really didn't know it, Sue. Well – it is not cruel, since we have come as we have – two relations staying together.'

'How long ago was it you were here? Tell me, tell me!'

'The day before I met you in Christminster, when we went back to Marygreen together. I told you I had met her.'

'Yes, you said you had met her, but you didn't tell me all. Your story was that you had met as estranged people, who were not husband and wife at all in Heaven's sight – not that you had made it up with her.'

'We didn't make it up,' he said sadly. 'I can't explain, Sue.'

'You've been false to me; you, my last hope! And I shall never forget it, never!'

'But by your own wish, dear Sue, we are only to be friends, not lovers! It is so very inconsistent of you to—'

'Friends can be jealous!'

'I don't see that. You concede nothing to me and I have to concede everything to you. After all, you were on good terms with your husband at that time.'

'No, I wasn't, Jude. O how can you think so! And you have taken me in, even if you didn't intend to.' She was so mortified that he was obliged to take her into her room and close the door lest the people should hear. 'Was it this room? Yes it was — I see by your look it was! I won't have it for mine! O it was treacherous of you to have her again! *I* jumped out of the window!'

'But Sue, she was, after all, my legal wife, if not—'

Slipping down on her knees Sue buried her face in the bed and wept.

'I never knew such an unreasonable — such a dog-in-the-manger feeling,' said Jude. 'I am not to approach you, nor anybody else!'

'O don't you *understand* my feeling! *Why* don't you! Why are you so gross! *I* jumped out of the window!'

'Jumped out of window?'

'I can't explain!'

It was true that he did not understand her feeling very well. But he did a little; and began to love her none the less.

'I — I thought you cared for nobody — desired nobody in the world but me at that time — and ever since!' continued Sue.

'It is true. I did not, and don't now!' said Jude, as distressed as she.

'But you must have thought much of her! Or—'

'No — I need not — you don't understand me either — women never do! Why should you get into such a tantrum about nothing?'

Looking up from the quilt she pouted provokingly: 'If it hadn't been for that, perhaps I would have gone on to the Temperance Hotel, after all, as you proposed; for I was beginning to think I did belong to you!'

'O, it is of no consequence!' said Jude distantly.

'I thought, of course, that she had never been really your wife since she left you of her own accord years and years ago! My sense of it was, that a parting such as yours from her, and mine from him, ended the marriage.'

'I can't say more without speaking against her, and I don't want to do that,' said he. 'Yet I must tell you one thing, which would settle the matter in any case. She has married another man — really married him! I knew nothing about it till after the visit we made here.'

'Married another? . . . It is a crime — as the world treats it, but does not believe.'

'There — now you are yourself again. Yes, it is a crime — as you don't hold, but would fearfully concede. But I shall never inform against her! and it is evidently a prick of conscience in her that has led her to urge me to get a divorce, that she may re-marry this man legally. So you perceive I shall not be likely to see her again.'

'And you didn't really know anything of this when you saw her?' said Sue more gently, as she rose.

'I did not. Considering all things, I don't think you ought to be angry, darling!'

'I am not. But I shan't go to the Temperance Hotel!'

He laughed. 'Never mind!' he said. 'So that I am near you, I am comparatively happy. It is more than this earthly wretch called Me deserves — you spirit, you disembodied creature, you dear, sweet, tantalizing phantom — hardly flesh at all; so that when I put my arms round you I almost expect them to pass through you as through air! Forgive me for being gross, as you call it! Remember that our calling cousins when really strangers was a snare. The enmity of our parents gave a piquancy to you in my eyes that was intenser even than the novelty of ordinary new acquaintance.'

'Say those pretty lines, then, from Shelley's "Epipsychidion" as if they meant me!' she solicited, slanting up closer to him as they stood. 'Don't you know them?'

'I know hardly any poetry,' he replied mournfully.

'Don't you? These are some of them:

> "There was a Being whom my spirit oft
>   Met on its visioned wanderings far aloft.
>
>   .   .   .
>
>   A seraph of Heaven, too gentle to be human,
>   Veiling beneath that radiant form of woman. . . ."

O it is too flattering, so I won't go on! But say it's me! — say it's me!'

'It *is* you, dear; exactly like you!'

'Now I forgive you! And you shall kiss me just once there — not very long.' She put the tip of her finger gingerly to her cheek; and he did as commanded. 'You do care for me very much, don't you, in spite of my not — you know?'

'Yes, sweet!' he said with a sigh; and bade her good-night.

IN returning to his native town of Shaston as schoolmaster Phillotson had won the interest and awakened the memories of the inhabitants, who, though they did not honour him for his miscellaneous acquirements as he would have been honoured elsewhere, retained for him a sincere regard. When, shortly after his arrival, he brought home a pretty wife — awkwardly pretty for him, if he did not take care, they said — they were glad to have her settle among them.

For some time after her flight from that home Sue's absence did not excite comment. Her place as monitor in the school was taken by another young woman within a few days of her vacating it, which substitution also passed without remark, Sue's services having been of a provisional nature only. When, however, a month had passed, and Phillotson casually admitted to acquaintance that he did not know where his wife was staying, curiosity began to be aroused; till, jumping to conclusions, people ventured to affirm that Sue had played him false and run away from him. The schoolmaster's growing languor and listlessness over his work gave countenance to the idea.

Though Phillotson had held his tongue as long as he could, except to his friend Gillingham, his honesty and directness would not allow him to do so when misapprehensions as to Sue's conduct spread abroad. On a Monday morning the chairman of the School Committee called, and after attending to the business of the school drew Phillotson aside out of earshot of the children.

'You'll excuse my asking, Phillotson, since everybody is talking of it: is this true as to your domestic affairs — that your wife's going away was on no visit, but a secret elopement with a lover? If so, I condole with you.'

'Don't,' said Phillotson. 'There was no secret about it.'

'She has gone to visit friends?'

'No.'

'Then what has happened?'

'She has gone away under circumstances that usually call for condolence with the husband. But I gave my consent.'

The chairman looked as if he had not apprehended the remark.

'What I say is quite true,' Phillotson continued testily. 'She asked leave to go away with her lover, and I let her. Why shouldn't I? A woman of full age, it was a question for her own conscience — not for me. I was not her gaoler. I can't explain any further. I don't wish to be questioned.'

The children observed that much seriousness marked the faces of the two men, and went home and told their parents that something new had happened about Mrs Phillotson. Then Phillotson's little maidservant, who was a schoolgirl just out of her standards,* said that Mr Phillotson had helped in his wife's packing, had offered her what money she required, and had written a friendly letter to her young man, telling him to take care of her. The chairman of committee thought the matter over, and talked to the other managers of the school, till a request came to Phillotson to meet them privately. The meeting lasted a long time, and at the end the schoolmaster came home, looking as usual pale and worn. Gillingham was sitting in his house awaiting him.

'Well; it is as you said,' observed Phillotson, flinging himself down wearily in a chair. 'They have requested me to send in my resignation on account of my scandalous conduct in giving my tortured wife her liberty — or, as they call it, condoning her adultery. But I shan't resign!'

'I think I would.'

'I won't. It is no business of theirs. It doesn't affect me in my public capacity at all. They may expel me if they like.'

'If you make a fuss it will get into the papers, and you'll never get appointed to another school. You see, they have to consider what you did as done by a teacher of youth — and its effects as such upon the morals of the town; and, to ordinary opinion, your position is indefensible. You must let me say that.'

To this good advice, however, Phillotson would not listen.

'I don't care,' he said. 'I don't go unless I am turned out. And for this reason; that by resigning I acknowledge I have acted wrongly by her; when I am more and more convinced every day that in the sight of Heaven and by all natural, straightforward humanity, I have acted rightly.'

Gillingham saw that his rather headstrong friend would not be able to maintain such a position as this; but he said nothing further, and in due time — indeed, in a quarter of an hour — the formal letter of dismissal arrived, the managers having remained behind to write it after Phillotson's withdrawal. The latter replied that he should not accept dismissal; and called a public meeting, which he attended, although he looked so weak and ill that his friend implored him to stay at home. When he stood up to give his reasons for contesting the decision of the managers he advanced them firmly, as he had done to his friend, and contended, moreover, that the matter was a domestic theory which did not concern them. This they overruled, insisting that the private eccentricities of a teacher came quite within their sphere of control, as it touched the morals of those he taught. Phillotson replied that he did not see how an act of natural charity could injure morals.

All the respectable inhabitants and well-to-do fellow-natives of the town were against Phillotson to a man. But, somewhat to his surprise, some dozen or more champions rose up in his defence as from the ground.

It has been stated that Shaston was the anchorage of a curious and interesting group of itinerants, who frequented the numerous fairs and markets held up and down Wessex during the summer and autumn months. Although Phillotson had never spoken to one of these gentlemen they now nobly led the forlorn hope in his defence. The body included two cheapjacks, a shooting-gallery proprietor and the ladies who loaded the guns, a pair of boxing-masters, a steam-roundabout manager, two travelling broom-makers, who called themselves widows, a gingerbread-stall keeper, a swing-boat owner, and a 'test-your-strength' man.

This generous phalanx of supporters, and a few others of independent judgment, whose own domestic experiences had been not without vicissitude, came up and warmly shook hands with Phillotson; after which they expressed their thoughts so strongly to the meeting that issue was joined, the result being a general scuffle, wherein a blackboard was split, three panes of the school-windows were broken, an inkbottle was spilled over a town-councillor's shirt-front, a churchwarden was dealt such a topper★ with the map of Palestine that his head went right through Samaria, and many black eyes and bleeding noses were given, one of which, to everybody's horror, was the venerable incumbent's, owing to the zeal of an emancipated chimney-sweep, who took the side of Phillotson's party. When Phillotson saw the blood running down the rector's face he deplored almost in groans the untoward and degrading circumstances, regretted that he had not resigned when called upon, and went home so ill that next morning he could not leave his bed.

The farcical yet melancholy event was the beginning of a serious illness for him; and he lay in his lonely bed in the pathetic state of mind of a middle-aged man who perceives at length that his life, intellectual and domestic, is tending to failure and gloom. Gillingham came to see him in the evenings, and on one occasion mentioned Sue's name.

'She doesn't care anything about me!' said Phillotson. 'Why should she?'

'She doesn't know you are ill.'

'So much the better for both of us.'

'Where are her lover and she living?'

'At Melchester — I suppose; at least he was living there some time ago.'

When Gillingham reached home he sat and reflected, and at last wrote an anonymous line to Sue, on the bare chance of its reaching her, the letter being enclosed in an envelope addressed to Jude at the diocesan capital. Arriving at that place it was forwarded to Marygreen in North Wessex, and thence to Aldbrickham by the only person who knew his present address — the widow who had nursed his aunt.

Three days later, in the evening, when the sun was going down in splendour over the lowlands of Blackmoor, and making the Shaston windows like tongues of fire to the eyes of the rustics in that Vale, the sick man fancied that he heard somebody come to the house, and a few minutes after there was a tap at the bedroom door. Phillotson did not speak; the door was hesitatingly opened, and there entered — Sue.

She was in light spring clothing, and her advent seemed ghostly — like the flitting in of a moth. He turned his eyes upon her, and flushed; but appeared to check his primary impulse to speak.

'I have no business here,' she said, bending her frightened face to him. 'But I heard you were ill — very ill; and — and as I know that you recognize other feelings between man and woman than physical love, I have come.'

'I am not very ill, my dear friend. Only unwell.'

'I didn't know that; and I am afraid that only a severe illness would have justified my coming!'

'Yes ... yes. And I almost wish you had not come! It is a little too soon — that's all I mean. Still, let us make the best of it. You haven't heard about the school, I suppose?'

'No — what about it?'

'Only that I am going away from here to another place. The managers and I don't agree, and we are going to part — that's all.'

Sue did not for a moment, either now or later, suspect what troubles had resulted to him from letting her go; it never once seemed to cross her mind, and she had received no news whatever from Shaston. They talked on slight and ephemeral subjects, and when his tea was brought up he told the amazed little servant that a cup was to be set for Sue. That young person was much more interested in their history than they supposed, and as she descended the stairs she lifted her eyes and hands in grotesque amazement. While they sipped Sue went to the window and thoughtfully said, 'It is such a beautiful sunset, Richard.'

'They are mostly beautiful from here, owing to the rays crossing the mist of the Vale. But I lose them all, as they don't shine into this gloomy corner where I lie.'

'Wouldn't you like to see this particular one? It is like heaven opened.'

'Ah yes! But I can't.'

'I'll help you to.'

'No — the bedstead can't be shifted.'

'But see how I mean.'

She went to where a swing-glass stood, and taking it in her hands carried it to a spot by the window where it could catch the sunshine, moving the glass till the beams were reflected into Phillotson's face.

'There — you can see the great red sun now!' she said. 'And I am sure it will cheer you — I do so hope it will!' She spoke with a childlike, repentant kindness, as if she could not do too much for him.

Phillotson smiled sadly. 'You are an odd creature!' he murmured as the sun glowed in his eyes. 'The idea of your coming to see me after what has passed!'

'Don't let us go back upon that!' she said quickly. 'I have to catch the omnibus for the train, as Jude doesn't know I have come; he was out when I started; so I must return home almost directly. Richard, I am so very glad you are better. You don't hate me, do you? You have been such a kind friend to me!'

'I am glad to know you think so,' said Phillotson huskily. 'No. I don't hate you!'

It grew dusk quickly in the gloomy room during their intermittent chat, and when candles were brought and it was time to leave she put her hand in his — or rather allowed it to flit through his; for she was significantly light in touch. She had nearly closed the door when he said, 'Sue!' He had noticed that, in turning away from him, tears were on her face and a quiver in her lip.

It was bad policy to recall her — he knew it while he pursued it. But he could not help it. She came back.

'Sue,' he murmured, 'do you wish to make it up, and stay? I'll forgive you and condone everything!'

'O you can't, you can't!' she said hastily. 'You can't condone it now!'

'*He* is your husband now, in effect, you mean, of course?'

'You may assume it. He is obtaining a divorce from his wife Arabella.'

'His wife! It is altogether news to me that he has a wife.'

'It was a bad marriage.'

'Like yours.'

'Like mine. He is not doing it so much on his own account as on hers. She wrote and told him it would be a kindness to her, since then she could marry and live respectably. And Jude has agreed.'

'A wife. . . . A kindness to her. Ah, yes; a kindness to her to release her altogether. . . . But I don't like the sound of it. *I* can forgive, Sue.'

'No, no! You can't have me back now I have been so wicked — as to do what I have done!'

There had arisen in Sue's face that incipient fright which showed itself whenever he changed from friend to husband, and which made her adopt any line of defence against marital feeling in him. 'I *must* go now. I'll come again – may I?'

'I don't ask you to go, even now. I ask you to stay.'

'I thank you, Richard; but I must. As you are not so ill as I thought, I *cannot* stay!'

'She's his – his from lips to heel!' said Phillotson; but so faintly that in closing the door she did not hear it. The dread of a reactionary change in the schoolmaster's sentiments, coupled, perhaps, with a faint shamefacedness at letting even him know what a slipshod lack of thoroughness, from a man's point of view, characterized her transferred allegiance, prevented her telling him of her, thus far, incomplete relations with Jude; and Phillotson lay writhing like a man in hell as he pictured the prettily dressed, maddening compound of sympathy and averseness who bore his name, returning impatiently to the home of her lover.

Gillingham was so interested in Phillotson's affairs, and so seriously concerned about him, that he walked up the hillside to Shaston two or three times a week, although, there and back, it was a journey of nine miles, which had to be performed between tea and supper, after a hard day's work in school. When he called on the next occasion after Sue's visit his friend was downstairs, and Gillingham noticed that his restless mood had been supplanted by a more fixed and composed one.

'She's been here since you called last,' said Phillotson.

'Not Mrs Phillotson?'

'Yes.'

'Ah! You have made it up?'

'No. .... She just came, patted my pillow with her little white hand, played the thoughtful nurse for half-an-hour, and went away.'

'Well – I'm hanged! A little hussy!'

'What do you say?'

'O – nothing!'

'What do you mean?'

'I mean, what a tantalizing, capricious little woman! If she were not your wife—'

'She is not; she's another man's except in name and law. And I have been thinking – it was suggested to me by a conversation I had with her — that, in kindness to her, I ought to dissolve the legal tie altogether; which, singularly enough, I think I can do, now she has been back, and refused my request to stay after I said I had forgiven her. I believe that fact would afford me opportunity of doing it, though I did not see it at the moment. What's the use of keeping her chained on me if she doesn't belong to me? I know — I feel absolutely certain — that she would welcome my taking such a step as the greatest charity to her. For though as a fellow-creature she sympathizes with, and pities me, and even weeps for me, as a husband she cannot endure me — she loathes me — there's no use in mincing words — she loathes me, and my only manly, and dignified, and merciful course is to complete what I have begun. . . . And for worldly reasons, too, it will be better for her to be independent. I have hopelessly ruined my prospects because of my decision as to what was best for us, though she does not know it; I see only dire poverty ahead from my feet to the grave; for I can be accepted as teacher no more. I shall probably have enough to do to make both ends meet during the remainder of my life, now my occupation's gone; and I shall be better able to bear it alone. I may as well tell you that what has suggested my letting her go is some news she brought me — the news that Fawley is doing the same.'

'O — he had a spouse, too? A queer couple, these lovers!'

'Well — I don't want your opinion on that. What I was going to say is that my liberating her can do her no possible harm, and will open up a chance of happiness for her which she has never dreamt of hitherto. For then they'll be able to marry, as they ought to have done at first.'

Gillingham did not hurry to reply. 'I may disagree with your motive,' he said gently, for he respected views he could not share. 'But I think you are right in your determination — if you can carry it out. I doubt, however, if you can.'

PART FIFTH

At Aldbrickham and Elsewhere

'*Thy aerial part, and all the fiery parts which are mingled in thee, though by nature they have an upward tendency, still in obedience to the disposition of the universe they are over-powered here in the compound mass the body.*'
— M. ANTONINUS (Long)

How Gillingham's doubts were disposed of will most quickly appear by passing over the series of dreary months and incidents that followed the events of the last chapter, and coming on to a Sunday in the February of the year following.

Sue and Jude were living in Aldbrickham, in precisely the same relations that they had established between themselves when she left Shaston to join him the year before. The proceedings in the Law-Courts had reached their consciousness but as a distant sound, and an occasional missive which they hardly understood.

They had met, as usual, to breakfast together in the little house with Jude's name on it, that he had taken at fifteen pounds a year, with three-pounds-ten extra for rates and taxes, and furnished with his aunt's ancient and lumbering goods, which had cost him about their full value to bring all the way from Marygreen. Sue kept house, and managed everything.

As he entered the room this morning Sue held up a letter she had just received.

'Well; and what is it about?' he said after kissing her.

'That the decree *nisi* in the case of Phillotson *versus* Phillotson and Fawley, pronounced six months ago, has just been made absolute.'

'Ah,' said Jude, as he sat down.

The same concluding incident in Jude's suit against Arabella had occurred about a month or two earlier. Both cases had been too insignificant to be reported in the papers, further than by name in a long list of other undefended cases.

'Now then, Sue, at any rate, you can do what you like!' He looked at his sweetheart curiously.

'Are we – you and I – just as free now as if we had never married at all?'

'Just as free — except, I believe, that a clergyman may object personally to re-marry you, and hand the job on to somebody else.'

'But I wonder — do you think it is really so with us? I know it is generally. But I have an uncomfortable feeling that my freedom has been obtained under false pretences!'

'How?'

'Well — if the truth about us had been known, the decree wouldn't have been pronounced. It is only, is it, because we have made no defence, and have led them into a false supposition? Therefore is my freedom lawful, however proper it may be?'

'Well — why did you let it be under false pretences? You have only yourself to blame,' he said mischievously.

'Jude — don't! You ought not to be touchy about that still. You must take me as I am.'

'Very well, darling: so I will. Perhaps you were right. As to your question, we were not obliged to prove anything. That was their business. Anyhow we are living together.'

'Yes. Though not in their sense.'

'One thing is certain, that however the decree may be brought about, a marriage is dissolved when it is dissolved. There is this advantage in being poor obscure people like us — that these things are done for us in a rough and ready fashion. It was the same with me and Arabella. I was afraid her criminal second marriage would have been discovered, and she punished; but nobody took any interest in her — nobody inquired, nobody suspected it. If we'd been patented nobilities we should have had infinite trouble, and days and weeks would have been spent in investigations.'

By degrees Sue acquired her lover's cheerfulness at the sense of freedom, and proposed that they should take a walk in the fields, even if they had to put up with a cold dinner on account of it. Jude agreed, and Sue went upstairs and prepared to start, putting on a joyful coloured gown in observance of her liberty; seeing which Jude put on a lighter tie.

'Now we'll strut arm and arm,' he said, 'like any other engaged couple. We've a legal right to.'

They rambled out of the town, and along a path over the low-lying lands that bordered it, though these were frosty now, and the extensive seed-fields were bare of colour and produce. The pair, however, were so absorbed in their own situation that their surroundings were little in their consciousness.

'Well, my dearest, the result of all this is that we can marry after a decent interval.'

'Yes; I suppose we can,' said Sue, without enthusiasm.

'And aren't we going to?'

'I don't like to say no, dear Jude; but I feel just the same about it now as I have done all along. I have just the same dread lest an iron contract should extinguish your tenderness for me, and mine for you, as it did between our unfortunate parents.'

'Still, what can we do? I do love you, as you know, Sue.'

'I know it abundantly. But I think I would much rather go on living always as lovers, as we are living now, and only meeting by day. It is so much sweeter — for the woman at least, and when she is sure of the man. And henceforward we needn't be so particular as we have been about appearances.'

'Our experiences of matrimony with others have not been encouraging, I own,' said he with some gloom; 'either owing to our own dissatisfied, unpractical natures, or by our misfortune. But we two—'

'Should be two dissatisfied ones linked together, which would be twice as bad as before. . . . I think I should begin to be afraid of you, Jude, the moment you had contracted to cherish me under a Government stamp, and I was licensed to be loved on the premises by you — Ugh, how horrible and sordid! Although, as you are, free, I trust you more than any other man in the world.'

'No, no — don't say I should change!' he expostulated; yet there was misgiving in his own voice also.

'Apart from ourselves, and our unhappy peculiarities, it is foreign to a man's nature to go on loving a person when he is told that he must and shall be that person's lover. There would be a much likelier chance of his doing it if he were told not to love. If the marriage ceremony consisted in an oath and signed contract between the parties to cease loving from that day forward, in consideration of personal possession being given, and to avoid each other's society as much as possible in public, there would be more loving couples than there are now. Fancy the secret meetings between the perjuring husband and wife, the denials of having seen each other, the clambering in at bedroom windows, and the hiding in closets! There'd be little cooling then.'

'Yes; but admitting this, or something like it, to be true, you are not the only one in the world to see it, dear little Sue. People go on marrying because they can't resist natural forces, although many of them may know perfectly well that they are possibly buying a month's pleasure with a life's discomfort. No doubt my father and mother, and your father and mother, saw it, if they at all resembled us in habits of observation. But then they went and married just the same, because they had ordinary passions. But you, Sue, are such a phantasmal, bodiless creature, one who — if you'll allow me to say it — has so little animal passion in you, that you can act upon reason in the matter, when we poor unfortunate wretches of grosser substance can't.'

'Well,' she sighed, 'you've owned that it would probably end in misery for us. And I am not so exceptional a woman as you think. Fewer women like marriage than you suppose, only they enter into it for the dignity it is assumed to confer, and the social advantages it gains them sometimes — a dignity and an advantage that I am quite willing to do without.'

Jude fell back upon his old complaint — that, intimate as they were, he had never once had from her an honest, candid declaration that she loved or could love him. 'I really fear sometimes that you cannot,' he said, with a dubiousness approaching anger. 'And you are so reticent. I know that women are taught by other women that they must never admit the full truth to a man. But the highest form of affection is based on full sincerity on both sides. Not being men, these women don't know that in looking back on those he has had tender relations with, a man's heart returns closest to her who was the soul of truth in her conduct. The better class of man, even if caught by airy affectations of dodging and parrying, is not retained by them. A Nemesis attends the woman who plays the game of elusiveness too often, in the utter contempt for her that, sooner or later, her old admirers feel; under which they allow her to go unlamented to her grave.'

Sue, who was regarding the distance, had acquired a guilty look; and she suddenly replied in a tragic voice: 'I don't think I like you to-day so well as I did, Jude!'

'Don't you? Why?'

'O, well — you are not nice — too sermony. Though I suppose I am so bad and worthless that I deserve the utmost rigour of lecturing!'

'No, you are not bad. You are a dear. But as slippery as an eel when I want to get a confession from you.'

'O yes I am bad, and obstinate, and all sorts! It is no use your pretending I am not! People who are good don't want scolding as I do. . . . But now that I have nobody but you, and nobody to defend me, it is *very* hard that I mustn't have my own way in deciding how I'll live with you, and whether I'll be married or no!'

'Sue, my own comrade and sweetheart, I don't want to force you either to marry or to do the other thing — of course I don't! It is too wicked of you to be so pettish! Now we won't say any more about it, and go on just the same as we have done; and during the rest of our walk we'll talk of the meadows only, and the floods, and the prospect of the farmers this coming year.'

After this the subject of marriage was not mentioned by them for several ·days, though living as they were with only a landing between them it was constantly in their minds. Sue was assisting Jude very materially now: he had latterly occupied himself on his own account in working and lettering headstones, which he kept in a little yard at the back of his little house, where in the intervals of domestic duties she marked out the letters full size for him, and blacked them in after he had cut them. It was a lower class of handicraft than were his former performances as a cathedral mason, and his only patrons were the poor people who lived in his own neighbourhood, and knew what a cheap man this 'Jude Fawley: Monumental Mason' (as he called himself on his front door) was to employ for the simple memorials they required for their dead. But he seemed more independent than before, and it was the only arrangement under which Sue, who particularly wished to be no burden on him, could render any assistance.

IT was an evening at the end of the month, and Jude had just returned home from hearing a lecture on ancient history in the public hall not far off. When he entered Sue, who had been keeping indoors during his absence, laid out supper for him. Contrary to custom she did not speak. Jude had taken up some illustrated paper, which he perused till, raising his eyes, he saw that her face was troubled.

'Are you depressed, Sue?' he said.

She paused a moment. 'I have a message for you,' she answered.

'Somebody has called?'

'Yes. A woman.' Sue's voice quavered as she spoke, and she suddenly sat down from her preparations, laid her hands in her lap, and looked into the fire. 'I don't know whether I did right or not!' she continued. 'I said you were not at home, and when she said she would wait, I said I thought you might not be able to see her.'

'Why did you say that, dear? I suppose she wanted a headstone. Was she in mourning?'

'No. She wasn't in mourning, and she didn't want a headstone; and I thought you couldn't see her.' Sue looked critically and imploringly at him.

'But who was she? Didn't she say?'

'No. She wouldn't give her name. But I know who she was — I think I do! It was Arabella!'

'Heaven save us! What should Arabella come for? What made you think it was she?'

'O, I can hardly tell. But I know it was! I feel perfectly certain it was — by the light in her eyes as she looked at me. She was a fleshy, coarse woman.'

'Well — I should not have called Arabella coarse exactly, except in speech, though she may be getting so by this time under the duties of the public-house. She was rather handsome when I knew her.'

'Handsome! But yes! — so she is!'

'I think I heard a quiver in your little mouth. Well, waiving that, as she is nothing to me, and virtuously married to another man, why should she come troubling us?'

'Are you sure she's married? Have you definite news of it?'

'No – not definite news. But that was why she asked me to release her. She and the man both wanted to lead a proper life, as I understood.'

'O Jude – it was, it *was* Arabella!' cried Sue, covering her eyes with her hand. 'And I am so miserable! It seems such an ill-omen, whatever she may have come for. You could not possibly see her, could you?'

'I don't really think I could. It would be so very painful to talk to her now – for her as much as for me. However, she's gone. Did she say she would come again?'

'No. But she went away very reluctantly.'

Sue, whom the least thing upset, could not eat any supper, and when Jude had finished his he prepared to go to bed. He had no sooner raked out the fire, fastened the doors, and got to the top of the stairs than there came a knock. Sue instantly emerged from her room, which she had but just entered.

'There she is again!' Sue whispered in appalled accents.

'How do you know?'

'She knocked like that last time.'

They listened, and the knocking came again. No servant was kept in the house, and if the summons were to be responded to one of them would have to do it in person. 'I'll open a window,' said Jude. 'Whoever it is cannot be expected to be let in at this time.'

He accordingly went into his bedroom and lifted the sash. The lonely street of early retiring workpeople was empty from end to end save of one figure – that of a woman walking up and down by the lamp a few yards off.

'Who's there?' he asked.

'Is that Mr Fawley?' came up from the woman, in a voice which was unmistakably Arabella's.

Jude replied that it was.

'Is it she?' asked Sue from the door, with lips apart.

'Yes, dear,' said Jude. 'What do you want, Arabella?' he inquired.

'I beg your pardon, Jude, for disturbing you,' said Arabella humbly. 'But I called earlier — I wanted particularly to see you to-night, if I could. I am in trouble, and have nobody to help me!'

'In trouble, are you?'

'Yes.'

There was a silence. An inconvenient sympathy seemed to be rising in Jude's breast at the appeal. 'But aren't you married?' he said.

Arabella hesitated. 'No, Jude, I am not,' she returned. 'He wouldn't, after all. And I am in great difficulty. I hope to get another situation as barmaid soon. But it takes time, and I really am in great distress, because of a sudden responsibility that's been sprung upon me from Australia; or I wouldn't trouble you — believe me I wouldn't. I want to tell you about it.'

Sue remained at gaze, in painful tension, hearing every word, but speaking none.

'You are not really in want of money, Arabella?' he asked, in a distinctly softened tone.

'I have enough to pay for the night's lodging I have obtained, but barely enough to take me back again.'

'Where are you living?'

'In London still.' She was about to give the address, but she said, 'I am afraid somebody may hear, so I don't like to call out particulars of myself so loud. If you could come down and walk a little way with me towards the Prince Inn, where I am staying to-night, I would explain all. You may as well, for old time's sake!'

'Poor thing! — I must do her the kindness of hearing what's the matter, I suppose,' said Jude in much perplexity. 'As she's going back to-morrow it can't make much difference.'

'But you can go and see her to-morrow, Jude! Don't go now, Jude!' came in plaintive accents from the doorway. 'O, it is only to entrap you, I know it is, as she did before! Don't, don't go, dear! She is such a low-passioned woman — I can see it in her shape, and hear it in her voice!'

'But I shall go,' said Jude. 'Don't attempt to detain me, Sue. God knows I love her little enough now, but I don't want to be cruel to her.' He turned to the stairs.

'But she's not your wife!' cried Sue distractedly. 'And I—'

'And you are not either, dear, yet,' said Jude.

'O, but are you going to her? Don't! Stay at home! Please, please stay at home, Jude, and not go to her, now she's not your wife any more than I!'

'Well, she is, rather more than you, come to that,' he said, taking his hat determinedly. 'I've wanted you to be, and I've waited with the patience of Job, and I don't see that I've got anything by my self-denial. I shall certainly give her something, and hear what it is she is so anxious to tell me; no man could do less!'

There was that in his manner which she knew it would be futile to oppose. She said no more, but, turning to her room as meekly as a martyr, heard him go downstairs, unbolt the door, and close it behind him. With a woman's disregard of her dignity when in the presence of nobody but herself, she also trotted down, sobbing articulately as she went. She listened. She knew exactly how far it was to the inn that Arabella had named as her lodging. It would occupy about seven minutes to get there at an ordinary walking pace; seven to come back again. If he did not return in fourteen minutes he would have lingered. She looked at the clock. It was twenty-five minutes to eleven. He *might* enter the inn with Arabella, as they would reach it before closing time; she might get him to drink with her; and Heaven only knew what disasters would befall him then.

In a still suspense she waited on. It seemed as if the whole time had nearly elapsed when the door was opened again, and Jude appeared.

Sue gave a little ecstatic cry. 'O, I knew I could trust you! — how good you are!' — she began.

'I can't find her anywhere in this street, and I went out in my slippers only. She has walked on, thinking I've been so hard-hearted as to refuse her requests entirely, poor woman. I've come back for my boots, as it is beginning to rain.'

'O, but why should you take such trouble for a woman who has served you so badly!' said Sue in a jealous burst of disappointment.

'But, Sue, she's a woman, and I once cared for her; and one can't be a brute in such circumstances.'

'She isn't your wife any longer!' exclaimed Sue, passionately excited. 'You *mustn't* go out to find her! It isn't right! You *can't* join her, now she's a stranger to you. How can you forget such a thing, my dear, dear one!'

'She seems much the same as ever — an erring, careless, unreflecting fellow-creature,' he said, continuing to pull on his boots. 'What those legal fellows have been playing at in London makes no difference in my real relations to her. If she was my wife while she was away in Australia with another husband she's my wife now.'

'But she wasn't! That's just what I hold! There's the absurdity! — Well — you'll come straight back, after a few minutes, won't you dear? She is too low, too coarse for you to talk to long, Jude, and was always!'

'Perhaps I am coarse too, worse luck! I have the germs of every human infirmity in me, I verily believe — that was why I saw it was so preposterous of me to think of being a curate. I have cured myself of drunkenness I think; but I never know in what new form a suppressed vice will break out in me! I do love you, Sue, though I have danced attendance on you so long for such poor returns! All that's best and noblest in me loves you, and your freedom from everything that's gross has elevated me, and enabled me to do what I should never have dreamt myself capable of, or any man, a year or two ago. It is all very well to preach about self-control, and the wickedness of coercing a woman. But I should just like a few virtuous people who have condemned me in the past, about Arabella and other things, to have been in my tantalizing position with you through these late weeks! — they'd believe, I think, that I have exercised some little restraint in always giving in to your wishes — living here in one house, and not a soul between us.'

'Yes, you have been good to me, Jude; I know you have, my dear protector.'

'Well — Arabella has appealed to me for help. I must go out and speak to her, Sue, at least!'

'I can't say any more! — O, if you must, you must!' she said, bursting out into sobs that seemed to tear her heart. 'I have nobody but you, Jude, and you are deserting me! I didn't know you were like this — I can't bear it, I can't! If she were yours it would be different!'

'Or if you were.'

'Very well then — if I must I must. Since you will have it so, I agree! I will be. Only I didn't mean to! And I didn't want to marry

again, either! . . . But, yes — I agree, I agree! I do love you. I ought to
have known that you would conquer in the long run, living like
this!'

She ran across and flung her arms round his neck. 'I am not a
cold-natured, sexless creature, am I, for keeping you at such a
distance? I am sure you don't think so! Wait and see! I do belong to
you, don't I! I give in!'

'And I'll arrange for our marriage to-morrow, or as soon as ever
you wish.'

'Yes, Jude.'

'Then I'll let her go,' said he, embracing Sue softly, 'I do feel that
it would be unfair to you to see her, and perhaps unfair to her. She is
not like you, my darling, and never was: it is only bare justice to say
that. Don't cry any more. There; and there; and there!' He kissed
her on one side, and on the other, and in the middle, and rebolted
the front door.

The next morning it was wet.

'Now, dear,' said Jude gaily at breakfast; 'as this is Saturday I
mean to call about the banns at once, so as to get the first publishing
done to-morrow, or we shall lose a week. Banns will do? We shall
save a pound or two.'

Sue absently agreed to banns. But her mind for the moment was
running on something else. A glow had passed away from her, and
depression sat upon her features.

'I feel I was wickedly selfish last night!' she murmured. 'It was
sheer unkindness in me — or worse — to treat Arabella as I did. I
didn't care about her being in trouble, and what she wished to tell
you! Perhaps it was really something she was justified in telling you.
That's some more of my badness, I suppose! Love has its own dark
morality when rivalry enters in — at least, mine has, if other people's
hasn't. . . . I wonder how she got on? I hope she reached the inn all
right, poor woman.'

'O yes: she got on all right,' said Jude placidly.

'I hope she wasn't shut out, and that she hadn't to walk the streets
in the rain. Do you mind my putting on my waterproof and going to
see if she got in? I've been thinking of her all the morning.'

'Well — is it necessary? You haven't the least idea how Arabella is able to shift for herself. Still, darling, if you want to go and inquire you can.'

There was no limit to the strange and unnecessary penances which Sue would meekly undertake when in a contrite mood; and this going to see all sorts of extraordinary persons whose relation to her was precisely of a kind that would have made other people shun them, was her instinct ever, so that the request did not surprise him.

'And when you come back,' he added, 'I'll be ready to go about the banns. You'll come with me?'

Sue agreed, and went off under cloak and umbrella, letting Jude kiss her freely, and returning his kisses in a way she had never done before. Times had decidedly changed. 'The little bird is caught at last!' she said, a sadness showing in her smile.

'No – only nested,' he assured her.

She walked along the muddy street till she reached the public-house mentioned by Arabella, which was not so very far off. She was informed that Arabella had not yet left, and in doubt how to announce herself so that her predecessor in Jude's affections would recognize her, she sent up word that a friend from Spring Street had called, naming the place of Jude's residence. She was asked to step upstairs, and on being shown into a room found that it was Arabella's bedroom, and that the latter had not yet risen. She halted on the turn of her toe till Arabella cried from the bed, 'Come in and shut the door,' which Sue accordingly did.

Arabella lay facing the window, and did not at once turn her head: and Sue was wicked enough, despite her penitence, to wish for a moment that Jude could behold her forerunner now, with the daylight full upon her. She may have seemed handsome enough in profile under the lamps, but a frowsiness was apparent this morning; and the sight of her own fresh charms in the looking-glass made Sue's manner bright, till she reflected what a meanly sexual emotion this was in her, and hated herself for it.

'I've just looked in to see if you got back comfortably last night, that's all,' she said gently. 'I was afraid afterwards that you might have met with any mishap?'

'O – how stupid this is! I thought my visitor was – your friend – your husband – Mrs Fawley, as I suppose you call yourself?' said Arabella, flinging her head back upon the pillows with a disappointed toss, and ceasing to retain the dimple she had just taken the trouble to produce.

'Indeed I don't,' said Sue.

'O, I thought you might have, even if he's not really yours. Decency is decency, any hour of the twenty-four.'

'I don't know what you mean,' said Sue stiffly. 'He is mine, if you come to that!'

'He wasn't yesterday.'

Sue coloured roseate, and said 'How do you know?'

'From your manner when you talked to me at the door. Well, my dear, you've been quick about it, and I expect my visit last night helped it on — ha-ha! But I don't want to get him away from you.'

Sue looked out at the rain, and at the dirty toilet-cover, and at the detached tail of Arabella's hair hanging on the looking-glass, just as it had done in Jude's time; and wished she had not come. In the pause there was a knock at the door, and the chambermaid brought in a telegram for 'Mrs Cartlett'.

Arabella opened it as she lay, and her ruffled look disappeared.

'I am much obliged to you for your anxiety about me,' she said blandly when the maid had gone; 'but it is not necessary you should feel it. My man finds he can't do without me after all, and agrees to stand by the promise to marry again over here that he has made me all along. See here! This is in answer to one from me.' She held out the telegram for Sue to read, but Sue did not take it. 'He asks me to come back. His little corner public in Lambeth would go to pieces without me, he says. But he isn't going to knock me about when he has had a drop, any more after we are spliced by English law than before! ... As for you, I should coax Jude to take me before the parson straight off, and have done with it, if I were in your place. I say it as a friend, my dear.'

'He's waiting to, any day,' returned Sue, with frigid pride.

'Then let him, in Heaven's name. Life with a man is more business-like after it, and money matters work better. And then, you see, if you have rows, and he turns you out of doors, you can get the law to protect you, which you can't otherwise, unless he half runs you through with a knife, or cracks your noddle with a poker. And if he bolts away from you — I say it friendly, as woman to woman, for there's never any knowing what a man med do — you'll have the sticks o' furniture, and won't be looked upon as a thief. I shall marry my man over again, now he's willing, as there was a little flaw in the first ceremony. In my telegram last night which this is an answer to, I told him I had almost made it up with Jude; and that frightened him, I expect! Perhaps I should quite have done it if it hadn't been for you,' she said laughing; 'and then how different our histories might have been from to-day! Never such a tender fool as Jude is if a woman seems in trouble, and coaxes him a bit! Just as he used to be about birds and things. However, as it happens, it is just as well as if I had made it up, and I forgive you. And, as I say, I'd advise you to get the business legally done as soon as possible. You'll find it an awful bother later on if you don't.'

'I have told you he is asking me to marry him — to make our natural marriage a legal one,' said Sue, with yet more dignity. 'It was quite by my wish that he didn't the moment I was free.'

'Ah, yes — you are a oneyer* too, like myself,' said Arabella, eyeing her visitor with humorous criticism. 'Bolted from your first, didn't you, like me?'

'Good morning! — I must go,' said Sue hastily.

'And I, too, must up and off!' replied the other, springing out of bed so suddenly that the soft parts of her person shook. Sue jumped aside in trepidation. 'Lord, I am only a woman — not a six-foot sojer! . . . Just a moment, dear,' she continued, putting her hand on Sue's arm. 'I really did want to consult Jude on a little matter of business, as I told him. I came about that more than anything else. Would he run up to speak to me at the station as I am going? You think not. Well, I'll write to him about it. I didn't want to write it, but never mind — I will.'

WHEN Sue reached home Jude was awaiting her at the door to take the initial step towards their marriage. She clasped his arm, and they went along silently together, as true comrades ofttimes do. He saw that she was preoccupied, and forbore to question her.

'O Jude — I've been talking to her,' she said at last. 'I wish I hadn't! And yet it is best to be reminded of things.'

'I hope she was civil.'

'Yes. I — I can't help liking her — just a little bit! She's not an ungenerous nature; and I am so glad her difficulties have all suddenly ended.' She explained how Arabella had been summoned back, and would be enabled to retrieve her position. 'I was referring to our old question. What Arabella has been saying to me has made me feel more than ever how hopelessly vulgar an institution legal marriage is — a sort of trap to catch a man — I can't bear to think of it. I wish I hadn't promised to let you put up the banns this morning!'

'O, don't mind me. Any time will do for me. I thought you might like to get it over quickly, now.'

'Indeed, I don't feel any more anxious now than I did before. Perhaps with any other man I might be a little anxious; but among the very few virtues possessed by your family and mine, dear, I think I may set staunchness. So I am not a bit frightened about losing you, now I really am yours and you really are mine. In fact, I am easier in my mind than I was, for my conscience is clear about Richard, who now has a right to his freedom. I felt we were deceiving him before.'

'Sue, you seem when you are like this to be one of the women of some grand old civilization, whom I used to read about in my bygone, wasted, classical days, rather than a denizen of a mere Christian country. I almost expect you to say at these times that you have just been talking to some friend whom you met in the Via Sacra,* about the latest news of Octavia* or Livia;* or have been listening to Aspasia's* eloquence, or have been watching Praxiteles chiselling away at his latest Venus, while Phryne* made complaint that she was tired of posing.'

They had now reached the house of the parish-clerk. Sue stood back, while her lover went up to the door. His hand was raised to knock when she said: 'Jude!'

He looked round.

'Wait a minute, would you mind?'

He came back to her.

'Just let us think,' she said timidly. 'I had such a horrid dream one night! . . . And Arabella—'

'What did Arabella say to you?' he asked.

'O, she said that when people were tied up you could get the law of a man better if he beat you — and how when couples quarrelled. . . . Jude, do you think that when you *must* have me with you by law, we shall be so happy as we are now? The men and women of our family are very generous when everything depends upon their good-will, but they always kick against compulsion. Don't you dread the attitude that insensibly arises out of legal obligation? Don't you think it is destructive to a passion whose essence is its gratuitousness?'

'Upon my word, love, you are beginning to frighten me, too, with all this foreboding! Well, let's go back and think it over.'

Her face brightened. 'Yes — so we will!' said she. And they turned from the clerk's door, Sue taking his arm and murmuring as they walked on homeward:

> "Can you keep the bee from ranging,
>   Or the ring-dove's neck from changing?
>   No! Nor fetter'd love. . . ."*

They thought it over, or postponed thinking. Certainly they postponed action, and seemed to live on in a dreamy paradise. At the end of a fortnight or three weeks matters remained unadvanced, and no banns were announced to the ears of any Aldbrickham congregation.

Whilst they were postponing and postponing thus a letter and a newspaper arrived before breakfast one morning from Arabella. Seeing the handwriting Jude went up to Sue's room and told her, and as soon as she was dressed she hastened down. Sue opened the news-

paper; Jude the letter. After glancing at the paper she held
across the first page to him with her finger on a paragraph; but he
was so absorbed in his letter that he did not turn awhile.

'Look!' said she.

He looked and read. The paper was one that circulated in South
London only, and the marked advertisement was simply the announcement of a marriage at St John's Church, Waterloo Road,
under the names, 'CARTLETT—DONN'; the united pair being Arabella
and the innkeeper.

'Well, it is satisfactory,' said Sue complacently. 'Though, after
this, it seems rather low to do likewise, and I am glad— However,
she is provided for now in a way, I suppose, whatever her faults,
poor thing. It is nicer that we are able to think that, than to be
uneasy about her. I ought, too, to write to Richard and ask him how
he is getting on, perhaps?'

But Jude's attention was still absorbed. Having merely glanced at
the announcement he said in a disturbed voice: 'Listen to this letter.
What shall I say or do?'

"THE THREE HORNS, LAMBETH
"DEAR JUDE (I won't be so distant as to call you Mr Fawley),—I send to-
day a newspaper, from which useful document you will learn that I was
married over again to Cartlett last Tuesday. So that business is settled right
and tight at last. But what I write about more particular is that private affair
I wanted to speak to you on when I came down to Aldbrickham. I couldn't
very well tell it to your lady friend, and should much have liked to let you
know it by word of mouth, as I could have explained better than by letter.
The fact is, Jude, that, though I have never informed you before, there was a
boy born of our marriage, eight months after I left you, when I was at
Sydney, living with my father and mother. All that is easily provable. As I
had separated from your before I thought such a thing was going to happen,
and I was over there, and our quarrel had been sharp, I did not think it
convenient to write about the birth. I was then looking out for a good
situation, so my parents took the child, and he has been with them ever
since. That was why I did not mention it when I met you in Christminster,
nor at the law proceedings. He is now of an intelligent age, of course, and
my mother and father have lately written to say that, as they have rather a
hard struggle over there, and I am settled comfortably here, they don't see
why they should be encumbered with the child any longer, his parents being
alive. I would have him with me here in a moment, but he is not old enough
to be of any use in the bar, nor will be for years and years, and naturally

Cartlett might think him in the way. They have, however, packed him off to me in charge of some friends who happened to be coming home, and I must ask you to take him when he arrives, for I don't know what to do with him. He is lawfully yours, that I solemnly swear. If anybody says he isn't, call them brimstone liars, for my sake. Whatever I may have done before or afterwards, I was honest to you from the time we were married till I went away, and I remain, yours, &c.,   ARABELLA CARTLETT" '

Sue's look was one of dismay. 'What will you do, dear?' she asked faintly.

Jude did not reply, and Sue watched him anxiously, with heavy breaths.

'It hits me hard!' said he in an under-voice. 'It *may* be true! I can't make it out. Certainly, if his birth was exactly when she says, he's mine. I cannot think why she didn't tell me when I met her at Christminster, and came on here that evening with her! . . . Ah — I do remember now that she said something about having a thing on her mind that she would like me to know, if ever we lived together again.'

'The poor child seems to be wanted by nobody!' Sue replied, and her eyes filled.

Jude had by this time come to himself. 'What a view of life he must have, mine or not mine!' he said. 'I must say that, if I were better off, I should not stop for a moment to think whose he might be. I would take him and bring him up. The beggarly question of parentage — what is it, after all? What does it matter, when you come to think of it, whether a child is yours by blood or not? All the little ones of our time are collectively the children of us adults of the time, and entitled to our general care. That excessive regard of parents for their own children, and their dislike of other people's is, like class-feeling, patriotism, save-your-own-soul-ism, and other virtues, a mean exclusiveness at bottom.'

Sue jumped up and kissed Jude with passionate devotion. 'Yes — so it is, dearest! And we'll have him here! And if he isn't yours it makes it all the better. I do hope he isn't — though perhaps I ought not to feel quite that! If he isn't, I should like so much for us to have him as an adopted child!'

'Well, you must assume about him what is most pleasing to you, my curious little comrade!' he said. 'I feel that, anyhow, I don't like

to leave the unfortunate little fellow to neglect. Just think of his life
in a Lambeth pothouse, and all its evil influences, with a parent who
doesn't want him, and has, indeed, hardly seen him, and a stepfather
who doesn't know him. "Let the day perish wherein I was born, and
the night in which it was said, There is a man child conceived!" *
That's what the boy — *my* boy, perhaps, will find himself saying
before long!'

'O no!'

'As I was the petitioner, I am really entitled to his custody, I
suppose.'

'Whether or no, we must have him. I see that. I'll do the best I can
to be a mother to him, and we can afford to keep him somehow. I'll
work harder. I wonder when he'll arrive?'

'In the course of a few weeks, I suppose.'

'I wish — When shall we have courage to marry, Jude?'

'Whenever you have it, I think I shall. It remains with you
entirely, dear. Only say the word, and it's done.'

'Before the boy comes?'

'Certainly.'

'It would make a more natural home for him, perhaps,' she
murmured.

Jude thereupon wrote in purely formal terms to request that the
boy should be sent on to them as soon as he arrived, making no
remark whatever on the surprising nature of Arabella's information,
nor vouchsafing a single word of opinion on the boy's paternity, nor
on whether, had he known all this, his conduct towards her would
have been quite the same.

In the down train that was timed to reach Aldbrickham station
about ten o'clock the next evening, a small, pale child's face could be
seen in the gloom of a third-class carriage. He had large, frightened
eyes, and wore a white woollen cravat, over which a key was
suspended round his neck by a piece of common string: the key
attracting attention by its occasional shine in the lamplight. In the
band of his hat his half-ticket was stuck. His eyes remained mostly
fixed on the back of the seat opposite, and never turned to the
window even when a station was reached and called. On the other

seat were two or three passengers, one of them a working woman
who held a basket on her lap, in which was a tabby kitten. The
woman opened the cover now and then, whereupon the kitten would
put out its head, and indulge in playful antics. At these the fellow-
passengers laughed, except the solitary boy bearing the key and
ticket, who, regarding the kitten with his saucer eyes, seemed mutely
to say: 'All laughing comes from misapprehension. Rightly looked
at there is no laughable thing under the sun.'

Occasionally at a stoppage the guard would look into the compartment and say to the boy, 'All right, my man. Your box is safe in
the van.' The boy would say, 'Yes,' without animation, would try to
smile, and fail.

He was Age masquerading as Juvenility, and doing it so badly
that his real self showed through crevices. A ground swell from
ancient years of night seemed now and then to lift the child in this
his morning-life, when his face took a back view over some great
Atlantic of Time, and appeared not to care about what it saw.

When the other travellers closed their eyes, which they did one
by one — even the kitten curling itself up in the basket, weary of its
too circumscribed play — the boy remained just as before. He then
seemed to be doubly awake, like an enslaved and dwarfed Divinity,
sitting passive and regarding his companions as if he saw their
whole rounded lives rather than their immediate figures.

This was Arabella's boy. With her usual carelessness she had
postponed writing to Jude about him till the eve of his landing, when
she could absolutely postpone no longer, though she had known for
weeks of his approaching arrival, and had, as she truly said, visited
Aldbrickham mainly to reveal the boy's existence and his near
home-coming to Jude. This very day on which she had received her
former husband's answer at some time in the afternoon, the child
reached the London Docks, and the family in whose charge he had
come, having put him into a cab for Lambeth, and directed the
cabman to his mother's house, bade him good-bye, and went their
way.

On his arrival at the Three Horns, Arabella had looked him over
with an expression that was as good as saying, 'You are very much
what I expected you to be,' had given him a good meal, a little

money, and, late as it was getting, despatched him to Jude by the next train, wishing her husband Cartlett, who was out, not to see him.

The train reached Aldbrickham, and the boy was deposited on the lonely platform beside his box. The collector took his ticket and, with a meditative sense of the unfitness of things, asked him where he was going by himself at that time of night.

'Going to Spring Street,' said the little one impassively.

'Why, that's a long way from here; a'most out in the country; and the folks will be gone to bed.'

'I've got to go there.'

'You must have a fly * for your box.'

'No. I must walk.'

'O well: you'd better leave your box here and send for it. There's a 'bus goes half-way, but you'll have to walk the rest.'

'I am not afraid.'

'Why didn't your friends come to meet 'ee?'

'I suppose they didn't know I was coming.'

'Who is your friends?'

'Mother didn't wish me to say.'

'All I can do, then, is to take charge of this. Now walk as fast as you can.'

Saying nothing further the boy came out into the street, looking round to see that nobody followed or observed him. When he had walked some little distance he asked for the street of his destination. He was told to go straight on quite into the outskirts of the place.

The child fell into a steady mechanical creep which had in it an impersonal quality – the movement of the wave, or of the breeze, or of the cloud. He followed his directions literally, without an inquiring gaze at anything. It could have been seen that the boy's ideas of life were different from those of the local boys. Children begin with detail, and learn up to the general; they begin with the contiguous, and gradually comprehend the universal. The boy seemed to have begun with the generals of life, and never to have concerned himself with the particulars. To him the houses, the willows, the obscure fields beyond, were apparently regarded not as brick residences, pollards, meadows; but as human dwellings in the abstract, vegetation, and the wide dark world.

He found the way to the little lane, and knocked at the door of Jude's house. Jude had just retired to bed, and Sue was about to enter her chamber adjoining when she heard the knock and came down.

'Is this where father lives?' asked the child.

'Who?'

'Mr Fawley, that's his name.'

Sue ran up to Jude's room and told him, and he hurried down as soon as he could, though to her impatience he seemed long.

'What — is it he — so soon?' she asked as Jude came.

She scrutinized the child's features, and suddenly went away into the little sitting-room adjoining. Jude lifted the boy to a level with himself, keenly regarded him with gloomy tenderness, and telling him he would have been met if they had known of his coming so soon, set him provisionally in a chair whilst he went to look for Sue, whose super-sensitiveness was disturbed, as he knew. He found her in the dark, bending over an arm-chair. He enclosed her with his arm, and putting his face by hers, whispered, 'What's the matter?'

'What Arabella says is true — true! I see you in him!'

'Well: that's one thing in my life as it should be, at any rate.'

'But the other half of him is — she! And that's what I can't bear! But I ought to — I'll try to get used to it; yes, I ought!'

'Jealous little Sue! I withdraw all remarks about your sexlessness. Never mind! Time may right things. . . . And Sue, darling; I have an idea! We'll educate and train him with a view to the University. What I couldn't accomplish in my own person perhaps I can carry out through him? They are making it easier for poor students now, you know.'

'O you dreamer!' said she, and holding his hand returned to the child with him. The boy looked at her as she had looked at him. 'Is it you who's my *real* mother at last?' he inquired.

'Why? Do I look like your father's wife?'

'Well, yes; 'cept he seems fond of you, and you of him. Can I call you mother?'

Then a yearning look came over the child and he began to cry. Sue thereupon could not refrain from instantly doing likewise, being a harp which the least wind of emotion from another's heart could make to vibrate as readily as a radical stir in her own.

'You may call me mother, if you wish to, my poor dear!' she said, bending her cheek against his to hide her tears.

'What's this round your neck?' asked Jude with affected calmness.

'The key of my box that's at the station.'

They bustled about and got him some supper, and made him up a temporary bed, where he soon fell asleep. Both went and looked at him as he lay.

'He called you mother two or three times before he dropped off,' murmured Jude. 'Wasn't it odd that he should have wanted to!'

'Well — it was significant,' said Sue. 'There's more for us to think about in that one little hungry heart than in all the stars of the sky.... I suppose, dear, we *must* pluck up courage, and get that ceremony over? It is no use struggling against the current, and I feel myself getting intertwined with my kind. O Jude, you'll love me dearly, won't you, afterwards! I do want to be kind to this child, and to be a mother to him; and our adding the legal form to our marriage might make it easier for me.'

THEIR next and second attempt thereat was more deliberately made, though it was begun on the morning following the singular child's arrival at their home.

Him they found to be in the habit of sitting silent, his quaint and weird face set, and his eyes resting on things they did not see in the substantial world.

'His face is like the tragic mask of Melpomene,'* said Sue. 'What is your name, dear? Did you tell us?'

'Little Father Time is what they always called me. It is a nickname; because I look so aged, they say.'

'And you talk so, too,' said Sue tenderly. 'It is strange, Jude, that these preternaturally old boys almost always come from new countries. But what were you christened?'

'I never was.'

'Why was that?'

'Because, if I died in damnation, 'twould save the expense of a Christian funeral.'

'O — your name is not Jude, then?' said his father with some disappointment.

The boy shook his head. 'Never heerd on it.'

'Of course not,' said Sue quickly; 'since she was hating you all the time!'

'We'll have him christened,' said Jude; and privately to Sue: 'The day we are married.' Yet the advent of the child disturbed him.

Their position lent them shyness, and having an impression that a marriage at a Superintendent Registrar's office was more private than an ecclesiastical one, they decided to avoid a church this time. Both Sue and Jude together went to the office of the district to give notice: they had become such companions that they could hardly do anything of importance except in each other's company.

Jude Fawley signed the form of notice, Sue looking over his shoulder and watching his hand as it traced the words. As she read

the four-square undertaking, never before seen by her, into which
her own and Jude's names were inserted, and by which that very
volatile essence, their love for each other, was supposed to be made
permanent, her face seemed to grow painfully apprehensive. 'Names
and Surnames of the Parties' — (they were to be parties now, not
lovers, she thought). 'Condition' — (a horrid idea) — 'Rank or
Occupation' — 'Age' — 'Dwelling at' — 'Length of Residence' —
'Church or Building in which the Marriage is to be solemnized' —
'District and County in which the Parties respectively dwell.'

'It spoils the sentiment, doesn't it!' she said on their way home. 'It
seems making a more sordid business of it even than signing the
contract in a vestry. There is a little poetry in a church. But we'll try
to get through with it, dearest, now.'

'We will. "For what man is he that hath betrothed a wife and hath
not taken her? Let him go and return unto his house, lest he die in
the battle, and another man take her."* So said the Jewish law-
giver.'

'How you know the Scriptures, Jude! You really ought to have
been a parson. I can only quote profane writers!'

During the interval before the issuing of the certificate Sue, in her
housekeeping errands, sometimes walked past the office, and fur-
tively glancing in saw affixed to the wall the notice of the purposed
clinch to their union. She could not bear its aspect. Coming after
her previous experience of matrimony, all the romance of their
attachment seemed to be starved away by placing her present case in
the same category. She was usually leading little Father Time by the
hand, and fancied that people thought him hers, and regarded the
intended ceremony as the patching up of an old error.

Meanwhile Jude decided to link his present with his past in some
slight degree by inviting to the wedding the only person remaining
on earth who was associated with his early life at Marygreen — the
aged widow Mrs Edlin, who had been his great-aunt's friend and
nurse in her last illness. He hardly expected that she would come;
but she did, bringing singular presents, in the form of apples, jam,
brass snuffers, an ancient pewter dish, a warming-pan, and an
enormous bag of goose feathers towards a bed. She was allotted the
spare room in Jude's house, whither she retired early, and where
they could hear her through the ceiling below, honestly saying the

Lord's Prayer in a loud voice, as the Rubric directed.

As, however, she could not sleep, and discovered that Sue and Jude were still sitting up — it being in fact only ten o'clock — she dressed herself again, and came down; and they all sat by the fire till a late hour — Father Time included; though, as he never spoke, they were hardly conscious of him.

'Well, I bain't set against marrying as your great-aunt was,' said the widow. 'And I hope 'twill be a jocund wedding for ye in all respects this time. Nobody can hope it more, knowing what I do of your families, which is more, I suppose, than anybody else now living. For they have been unlucky that way, God knows.'

Sue breathed uneasily.

'They was always good-hearted people, too — wouldn't kill a fly if they knowed it,' continued the wedding guest. 'But things happened to thwart 'em, and if everything wasn't vitty * they were upset. No doubt that's how he that the tale is told of came to do what 'a did — if he *were* one of your family.'

'What was that?' said Jude.

'Well — that tale, ye know; he that was gibbeted just on the brow of the hill by the Brown House — not far from the milestone between Marygreen and Alfredston, where the other road branches off. But Lord, 'twas in my grandfather's time; and it medn' have been one of your folk at all.'

'I know where the gibbet is said to have stood, very well,' murmured Jude. 'But I never heard of this. What — did this man — my ancestor and Sue's — kill his wife?'

' 'Twer not that exactly. She ran away from him, with their child, to her friends; and while she was there the child died. He wanted the body, to bury it where his people lay, but she wouldn't give it up. Her husband then came in the night with a cart, and broke into the house to steal the coffin away; but he was catched, and being obstinate, wouldn't tell what he broke in for. They brought it in burglary, and that's why he was hanged and gibbeted on Brown House Hill. His wife went mad after he was dead. But it medn' be true that he belonged to ye more than to me.'

A small slow voice rose from the shade of the fireside, as if out of the earth: 'If I was you, mother, I wouldn't marry father!' It came from little Time, and they started, for they had forgotten him.

'O, it is only a tale,' said Sue cheeringly.

After this exhilarating tradition from the widow on the eve of the solemnization they rose, and, wishing their guest good-night, retired.

The next morning Sue, whose nervousness intensified with the hours, took Jude privately into the sitting-room before starting. 'Jude, I want you to kiss me, as a lover, incorporeally,' she said, tremulously nestling up to him, with damp lashes. 'It won't be ever like this any more, will it! I wish we hadn't begun the business. But I suppose we must go on. How horrid that story was last night! It spoilt my thoughts of to-day. It makes me feel as if a tragic doom overhung our family, as it did the house of Atreus.'*

'Or the house of Jeroboam,'* said the quondam theologian.

'Yes. And it seems awful temerity in us two to go marrying! I am going to vow to you in the same words I vowed in to my other husband, and you to me in the same as you used to your other wife; regardless of the deterrent lesson we were taught by those experiments!'

'If you are uneasy I am made unhappy,' said he. 'I had hoped you would feel quite joyful. But if you don't, you don't. It is no use pretending. It is a dismal business to you, and that makes it so to me!'

'It is unpleasantly like that other morning — that's all,' she murmured. 'Let us go on now.'

They started arm in arm for the office aforesaid, no witness accompanying them except the Widow Edlin. The day was chilly and dull, and a clammy fog blew through the town from 'Royal-tower'd Thame'.* On the steps of the office there were the muddy footmarks of people who had entered, and in the entry were damp umbrellas. Within the office several persons were gathered, and our couple perceived that a marriage between a soldier and a young woman was just in progress. Sue, Jude, and the widow stood in the background while this was going on, Sue reading the notices of marriage on the wall. The room was a dreary place to two of their temperament, though to its usual frequenters it doubtless seemed ordinary enough. Law-books in musty calf covered one wall, and elsewhere were Post-Office Directories, and other books of reference. Papers in packets tied with red tape were pigeon-holed around, and some iron safes filled a recess; while the bare wood floor was, like the doorstep, stained by previous visitors.

The soldier was sullen and reluctant: the bride sad and timid; she was soon, obviously, to become a mother, and she had a black eye. Their little business was soon done, and the twain and their friends straggled out, one of the witnesses saying casually to Jude and Sue in passing, as if he had known them before: 'See the couple just come in? Ha, ha! That fellow is just out of gaol this morning. She met him at the gaol gates, and brought him straight here. She's paying for everything.'

Sue turned her head and saw an ill-favoured man, closely cropped, with a broad-faced, pock-marked woman on his arm, ruddy with liquor and the satisfaction of being on the brink of a gratified desire. They jocosely saluted the outgoing couple, and went forward in front of Jude and Sue, whose diffidence was increasing. The latter drew back and turned to her lover, her mouth shaping itself like that of a child about to give way to grief:

'Jude — I don't like it here! I wish we hadn't come! The place gives me the horrors: it seems so unnatural as the climax of our love! I wish it had been at church, if it had to be at all. It is not so vulgar there!'

'Dear little girl,' said Jude. 'How troubled and pale you look!'

'It must be performed here now, I suppose?'

'No — perhaps not necessarily.'

He spoke to the clerk, and came back. 'No — we need not marry here or anywhere, unless we like, even now,' he said. 'We can be married in a church, if not with the same certificate with another he'll give us, I think. Anyhow, let us go out till you are calmer, dear, and I too, and talk it over.'

They went out stealthily and guiltily, as if they had committed a misdemeanour, closing the door without noise, and telling the widow, who had remained in the entry, to go home and await them; that they would call in any casual passers as witnesses, if necessary. When in the street they turned into an unfrequented side alley, where they walked up and down as they had done long ago in the Market-house at Melchester.

'Now, darling, what shall we do? We are making a mess of it, it strikes me. Still, *anything* that pleases you will please me.'

'But Jude, dearest, I am worrying you! You wanted it to be there, didn't you?'

'Well, to tell the truth, when I got inside I felt as if I didn't care much about it. The place depressed me almost as much as it did you — it was ugly. And then I thought of what you had said this morning as to whether we ought.'

They walked on vaguely, till she paused, and her little voice began anew: 'It seems so weak, too, to vacillate like this! And yet how much better than to act rashly a second time. . . . How terrible that scene was to me! The expression in that flabby woman's face, leading her on to give herself to that gaol-bird, not for a few hours, as she would, but for a lifetime, as she must. And the other poor soul — to escape a nominal shame which was owing to the weakness of her character, degrading herself to the real shame of bondage to a tyrant who scorned her — a man whom to avoid for ever was her only chance of salvation. . . . This is our parish church, isn't it? This is where it would have to be, if we did it in the usual way? A service or something seems to be going on.'

Jude went up and looked in at the door. 'Why — it is a wedding here too,' he said. 'Everybody seems to be on our tack to-day.'

Sue said she supposed it was because Lent was just over, when there was always a crowd of marriages. 'Let us listen,' she said, 'and find how it feels to us when performed in a church.'

They stepped in, and entered a back seat, and watched the proceedings at the altar. The contracting couple appeared to belong to the well-to-do middle class, and the wedding altogether was of ordinary prettiness and interest. They could see the flowers tremble in the bride's hand, even at that distance, and could hear her mechanical murmur of words whose meaning her brain seemed to gather not at all under the pressure of her self-consciousness. Sue and Jude listened, and severally saw themselves in time past going through the same form of self-committal.

'It is not the same to her, poor thing, as it would be to me doing it over again with my present knowledge,' Sue whispered. 'You see, they are fresh to it, and take the proceedings as a matter of course. But having been awakened to its awful solemnity as we have, or at least as I have, by experience, and to my own too squeamish feelings perhaps sometimes, it really does seem immoral in me to go and undertake the same thing again with open eyes. Coming in here and seeing this has frightened me from a church wedding as much as the other did from a registry one. . . . We are a weak, tremulous pair, Jude, and what others may feel confident in I feel doubts of — my being proof against the sordid conditions of a business contract again!'

Then they tried to laugh, and went on debating in whispers the object-lesson before them. And Jude said he also thought they were both too thin-skinned — that they ought never to have been born — much less have come together for the most preposterous of all joint-ventures for *them* — matrimony.

His betrothed shuddered; and asked him earnestly if he indeed felt that they ought not to go in cold blood and sign that life-undertaking again? 'It is awful if you think we have found ourselves not strong enough for it, and knowing this, are proposing to perjure ourselves,' she said.

'I fancy I do think it — since you ask me,' said Jude. 'Remember I'll do it if you wish, own darling.' While she hesitated he went on to confess that, though he thought they ought to be able to do it, he felt checked by the dread of incompetency just as she did — from their peculiarities, perhaps, because they were unlike other people. 'We are horribly sensitive; that's really what's the matter with us, Sue!' he declared.

'I fancy more are like us than we think!'

'Well, I don't know. The intention of the contract is good, and right for many, no doubt; but in our case it may defeat its own ends because we are the queer sort of people we are — folk in whom domestic ties of a forced kind snuff out cordiality and spontaneousness.'

Sue still held that there was not much queer or exceptional in them: that all were so. 'Everybody is getting to feel as we do. We are a little beforehand, that's all. In fifty, a hundred, years the descendants of these two will act and feel worse than we. They will see weltering humanity still more vividly than we do now, as

Shapes like our own selves hideously multiplied,*

and will be afraid to reproduce them.'

'What a terrible line of poetry! . . . though I have felt it myself about my fellow-creatures, at morbid times.'

Thus they murmured on, till Sue said more brightly:

'Well – the general question is not our business, and why should
we plague ourselves about it? However different our reasons are we
come to the same conclusion; that for us particular two, an irrevocable oath is risky. Then, Jude, let us go home without killing our
dream! Yes? How good you are, my friend: you give way to all my
whims!'

'They accord very much with my own.'

He gave her a little kiss behind a pillar while the attention of
everybody present was taken up in observing the bridal procession
entering the vestry; and then they came outside the building. By the
door they waited till two or three carriages, which had gone away
for a while, returned, and the new husband and wife came into the
open daylight. Sue sighed.

'The flowers in the bride's hand are sadly like the garland which
decked the heifers of sacrifice in old times!'

'Still, Sue, it is no worse for the woman than for the man. That's
what some women fail to see, and instead of protesting against the
conditions they protest against the man, the other victim; just as a
woman in a crowd will abuse the man who crushes against her,
when he is only the helpless transmitter of the pressure put upon
him.'

'Yes – some are like that, instead of uniting with the man against
the common enemy, coercion.' The bride and bridegroom had by
this time driven off, and the two moved away with the rest of the
idlers. 'No – don't let's do it,' she continued. 'At least just now.'

They reached home, and passing the window arm in arm saw the
widow looking out at them. 'Well,' cried their guest when they
entered, 'I said to myself when I zeed ye coming so loving up to the
door, "They made up their minds at last, then!"'

They briefly hinted that they had not.

'What – and ha'n't ye really done it? Chok' it all, that I should
have lived to see a good old saying like "marry in haste and repent
at leisure" spoiled like this by you two! 'Tis time I got back again to
Marygreen – sakes if tidden * – if this is what the new notions be
leading us to! Nobody thought o' being afeard o' matrimony in my
time, nor of much else but a cannon-ball or empty cupboard! Why

when I and my poor man were married we thought no more o't than of a game o' dibs!' *

'Don't tell the child when he comes in,' whispered Sue nervously. 'He'll think it has all gone on right, and it will be better that he should not be surprised and puzzled. Of course it is only put off for reconsideration. If we are happy as we are, what does it matter to anybody?'

THE purpose of a chronicler of moods and deeds does not require him to express his personal views upon the grave controversy above given. That the twain were happy — between their times of sadness — was indubitable. And when the unexpected apparition of Jude's child in the house had shown itself to be no such disturbing event as it had looked, but one that brought into their lives a new and tender interest of an ennobling and unselfish kind, it rather helped than injured their happiness.

To be sure, with such pleasing anxious beings * as they were, the boy's coming also brought with it much thought for the future, particularly as he seemed at present to be singularly deficient in all the usual hopes of childhood. But the pair tried to dismiss, for a while at least, a too strenuously forward view.

There is in Upper Wessex an old town of nine or ten thousand souls; the town may be called Stoke-Barehills. It stands with its gaunt, unattractive, ancient church, and its new red brick suburb, amid the open, chalk-soiled cornlands, near the middle of an imaginary triangle which has for its three corners the towns of Aldbrickham and Wintoncester, and the important military station of Quartershot. The great western highway from London passes through it, near a point where the road branches into two, merely to unite again some twenty miles further westward. Out of this bifurcation and reunion there used to arise among wheeled travellers, before railway days, endless questions of choice between the respective ways. But the question is now as dead as the scot-and-lot freeholder, * the road waggoner, and the mail coachman who disputed it; and probably not a single inhabitant of Stoke-Barehills is now even aware that the two roads which part in his town ever meet again; for nobody now drives up and down the great western highway daily.

The most familiar object in Stoke-Barehills nowadays is its cemetery, standing among some picturesque mediæval ruins beside the railway; the modern chapels, modern tombs, and modern shrubs, having a look of intrusiveness amid the crumbling and ivy-covered decay of the ancient walls.

On a certain day, however, in the particular year which has now been reached by this narrative – the month being early June – the features of the town excite little interest, though many visitors arrive by the trains; some down trains, in especial, nearly emptying themselves here. It is the week of the Great Wessex Agricultural Show, whose vast encampment spreads over the open outskirts of the town like the tents of an investing army. Rows of marquees, huts, booths, pavilions, arcades, porticoes – every kind of structure short of a permanent one – cover the green field for the space of a square half-mile, and the crowds of arrivals walk through the town in a mass, and make straight for the exhibition ground. The way thereto is lined with shows, stalls, and hawkers on foot, who make a market-place of the whole roadway to the show proper, and lead some of the improvident to lighten their pockets appreciably before they reach the gates of the exhibition they came expressly to see.

It is the popular day, the shilling day, and of the fast arriving excursion trains two from different directions enter the two contiguous railway-stations at almost the same minute. One, like several which have preceded it, comes from London: the other by a cross-line from Aldbrickham; and from the London train alights a couple; a short, rather bloated man, with a globular stomach and small legs, resembling a top on two pegs, accompanied by a woman of rather fine figure and rather red face, dressed in black material, and covered with beads from bonnet to skirt, that made her glisten as if clad in chain-mail.

They cast their eyes around. The man was about to hire a fly as some others had done, when the woman said, 'Don't be in such a hurry, Cartlett. It isn't so very far to the show-yard. Let us walk down the street into the place. Perhaps I can pick up a cheap bit of furniture or old china. It is years since I was here – never since I lived as a girl at Aldbrickham, and used to come across for a trip sometimes with my young man.'

'You can't carry home furniture by excursion train,' said, in a thick voice, her husband, the landlord of The Three Horns, Lambeth; for they had both come down from the tavern in that 'excellent, densely populated, gin-drinking neighbourhood,' which they had occupied ever since the advertisement in those words had attracted them thither. The configuration of the landlord showed that he, too, like his customers, was becoming affected by the liquors he retailed.

'Then I'll get it sent, if I see any worth having,' said his wife.

They sauntered on, but had barely entered the town when her attention was attracted by a young couple leading a child, who had come out from the second platform, into which the train from Aldbrickham had steamed. They were walking just in front of the innkeepers.

'Sakes alive!' said Arabella.

'What's that?' said Cartlett.

'Who do you think that couple is? Don't you recognize the man?'

'No.'

'Not from the photos I have showed you?'

'Is it Fawley?'

'Yes – of course.'

'Oh, well. I suppose he was inclined for a little sight-seeing like the rest of us.' Cartlett's interest in Jude, whatever it might have been when Arabella was new to him, had plainly flagged since her charms and her idiosyncrasies, her supernumerary hair-coils, and her optional dimples, were becoming as a tale that is told.*

Arabella so regulated her pace and her husband's as to keep just in the rear of the other three, which it was easy to do without notice in such a stream of pedestrians. Her answers to Cartlett's remarks were vague and slight, for the group in front interested her more than all the rest of the spectacle.

'They are rather fond of one another and of their child, seemingly,' continued the publican.

'*Their* child! 'Tisn't their child,' said Arabella with a curious, sudden covetousness. 'They haven't been married long enough for it to be theirs!'

But although the smouldering maternal instinct was strong enough in her to lead her to quash her husband's conjecture, she was not disposed on second thoughts to be more candid than necessary. Mr Cartlett had no other idea than that his wife's child by her first husband was with his grandparents at the Antipodes.

'O I suppose not. She looks quite a girl.'

'They are only lovers, or lately married, and have the child in charge, as anybody can see.'

All continued to move ahead. The unwitting Sue and Jude, the couple in question, had determined to make this Agricultural Exhibition within twenty miles of their own town the occasion of a day's excursion which should combine exercise and amusement with instruction, at small expense. Not regardful of themselves alone, they had taken care to bring Father Time, to try every means of making him kindle and laugh like other boys, though he was to some extent a hindrance to the delightfully unreserved intercourse in their pilgrimages which they so much enjoyed. But they soon ceased to consider him an observer, and went along with that tender attention to each other which the shyest can scarcely disguise, and which these, among entire strangers as they imagined, took less trouble to disguise than they might have done at home. Sue, in her new summer clothes, flexible and light as a bird, her little thumb stuck up by the stem of her white cotton sunshade, went along as if she hardly touched ground, and as if a moderately strong puff of wind would float her over the hedge into the next field. Jude, in his light grey holiday-suit, was really proud of her companionship, not more for her external attractiveness than for her sympathetic words and ways. That complete mutual understanding, in which every glance and movement was as effectual as speech for conveying intelligence between them, made them almost the two parts of a single whole.

The pair with their charge passed through the turnstiles, Arabella and her husband not far behind them. When inside the enclosure the publican's wife could see that the two ahead began to take trouble with the youngster, pointing out and explaining the many objects of interest, alive and dead; and a passing sadness would touch their faces at their every failure to disturb his indifference.

'How she sticks to him!' said Arabella. 'O no — I fancy they are not married, or they wouldn't be so much to one another as that. ... I wonder!'

'But I thought you said he did marry her?'

'I heard he was going to — that's all, going to make another attempt, after putting it off once or twice.... As far as they

themselves are concerned they are the only two in the show. I
should be ashamed of making myself so silly if I were he!'

'I don't see as how there's anything remarkable in their
behaviour. I should never have noticed their being in love, if you
hadn't said so.'

'You never see anything,' she rejoined. Nevertheless Cartlett's
view of the lovers' or married pair's conduct was undoubtedly that
of the general crowd, whose attention seemed to be in no way
attracted by what Arabella's sharpened vision discerned.

'He's charmed by her as if she were some fairy!' continued
Arabella. 'See how he looks round at her, and lets his eyes rest on
her. I am inclined to think that she don't care for him quite so much
as he does for her. She's not a particular warm-hearted creature to
my thinking, though she cares for him pretty middling much — as
much as she's able to; and he could make her heart ache a bit if he
liked to try — which he's too simple to do. There — now they are
going across to the cart-horse sheds. Come along.'

'I don't want to see the cart-horses. It is no business of ours to
follow these two. If we have come to see the show let us see it in our
own way, as they do in theirs.'

'Well — suppose we agree to meet somewhere in an hour's time —
say at that refreshment tent over there, and go about independent?
Then you can look at what you choose to, and so can I.'

Cartlett was not loth to agree to this, and they parted — he
proceeding to the shed where malting processes were being exhibited, and Arabella in the direction taken by Jude and Sue. Before,
however, she had regained their wake a laughing face met her own,
and she was confronted by Anny, the friend of her girlhood.

Anny had burst out in hearty laughter at the mere fact of the
chance rencounter. 'I am still living down there,' she said, as soon as
she was composed. 'I am soon going to be married, but my intended
couldn't come up here to-day. But there's lots of us come by
excursion, though I've lost the rest of 'em for the present.'

'Have you met Jude and his young woman, or wife, or whatever
she is? I saw 'em by now.'

'No. Not a glimpse of un for years!'

'Well, they are close by here somewhere. Yes — there they are —
by that grey horse!'

'O, that's his present young woman — wife did you say? Has he married again?'

'I don't know.'

'She's pretty, isn't she!'

'Yes — nothing to complain of; or jump at. Not much to depend on, though; a slim, fidgety little thing like that.'

'He's a nice-looking chap, too! You ought to ha' stuck to un, Arabella.'

'I don't know but I ought,' murmured she.

Anny laughed. 'That's you, Arabella! Always wanting another man than your own.'

'Well, and what woman don't I should like to know? As for that body with him — she don't know what love is — at least what I call love! I can see in her face she don't.'

'And perhaps, Abby dear, you don't know what she calls love.'

'I'm sure I don't wish to! . . . Ah — they are making for the Art Department. I should like to see some pictures myself. Suppose we go that way? — Why, if all Wessex isn't here, I verily believe! There's Dr Vilbert. Haven't seen him for years, and he's not looking a day older than when I used to know him. How do you do, Physician? I was just saying that you don't look a day older than when you knew me as a girl.'

'Simply the result of taking my own pills regular, ma'am. Only two and threepence a box — warranted efficacious by the Government stamp. Now let me advise you to purchase the same immunity from the ravages of Time by following my example? Only two-and-three.'

The physician had produced a box from his waistcoat pocket, and Arabella was induced to make the purchase.

'At the same time,' continued he, when the pills were paid for, 'you have the advantage of me, Mrs— Surely not Mrs Fawley, once Miss Donn, of the vicinity of Marygreen?'

'Yes. But Mrs Cartlett now.'

'Ah — you lost him, then? Promising young fellow! A pupil of mine, you know— I taught him the dead languages. And believe me, he soon knew nearly as much as I.'

'I lost him; but not as you think,' said Arabella drily. 'The lawyers untied us. There he is, look, alive and lusty; along with that young woman, entering the Art exhibition.'

'Ah – dear me! Fond of her, apparently.'

'They *say* they are cousins.'

'Cousinship is a great convenience to their feelings, I should say?'

'Yes. So her husband thought, no doubt, when he divorced her. ... Shall we look at the pictures, too?'

The trio followed across the green and entered. Jude and Sue, with the child, unaware of the interest they were exciting, had gone up to a model at one end of the building, which they regarded with considerable attention for a long while before they went on. Arabella and her friends came to it in due course, and the inscription it bore was: 'Model of Cardinal College, Christminster; by J. Fawley and S. F. M. Bridehead.'

'Admiring their own work,' said Arabella. 'How like Jude – always thinking of Colleges and Christminster, instead of attending to his business!'

They glanced cursorily at the pictures, and proceeded to the band-stand. When they had stood a little while listening to the music of the military performers, Jude, Sue, and the child came up on the other side, Arabella did not care if they should recognize her; but they were too deeply absorbed in their own lives, as translated into emotion by the military band, to perceive her under her beaded veil. She walked round the outside of the listening throng, passing behind the lovers, whose movements had an unexpected fascination for her to-day. Scrutinizing them narrowly from the rear she noticed that Jude's hand sought Sue's as they stood, the two standing close together so as to conceal, as they supposed, this tacit expression of their mutual responsiveness.

'Silly fools – like two children!' Arabella whispered to herself morosely, as she rejoined her companions, with whom she preserved a preoccupied silence.

Anny meanwhile had jokingly remarked to Vilbert on Arabella's hankering interest in her first husband.

'Now,' said the physician to Arabella, apart; 'do you want anything such as this, Mrs Cartlett? It is not compounded out of my regular pharmacopœia, but I am sometimes asked for such a thing.' He produced a small phial of clear liquid. 'A love-philtre, such as was used by the Ancients with great effect. I found it out by study of their writings, and have never known it to fail.'

'What is it made of?' asked Arabella curiously.

'Well — a distillation of the juices of doves' hearts — otherwise pigeons' — is one of the ingredients. It took nearly a hundred hearts to produce that small bottle full.'

'How do you get pigeons enough?'

'To tell a secret, I get a piece of rock-salt, of which pigeons are inordinately fond, and place it in a dovecote on my roof. In a few hours the birds come to it from all points of the compass — east, west, north, and south — and thus I secure as many as I require. You use the liquid by contriving that the desired man shall take about ten drops of it in his drink. But remember, all this is told you because I gather from your questions that you mean to be a purchaser. You must keep faith with me?'

'Very well — I don't mind a bottle — to give some friend or other to try it on her young man.' She produced five shillings, the price asked, and slipped the phial in her capacious bosom. Saying presently that she was due at an appointment with her husband she sauntered away towards the refreshment bar, Jude, his companion, and the child having gone on to the horticultural tent, where Arabella caught a glimpse of them standing before a group of roses in bloom.

She waited a few minutes observing them, and then proceeded to join her spouse with no very amiable sentiments. She found him seated on a stool by the bar, talking to one of the gaily dressed maids who had served him with spirits.

'I should think you had enough of this business at home!' Arabella remarked gloomily. 'Surely you didn't come fifty miles from your own bar to stick in another? Come, take me round the show, as other men do their wives! Dammy, one would think you were a young bachelor, with nobody to look after but yourself!'

'But we agreed to meet here; and what could I do but wait?'

'Well, now we have met, come along,' she returned, ready to quarrel with the sun for shining on her. And they left the tent together, this pot-bellied man and florid woman, in the antipathetic, recriminatory mood of the average husband and wife of Christendom.

In the meantime the more exceptional couple and the boy still lingered in the pavilion of flowers — an enchanted palace to their appreciative taste — Sue's usually pale cheeks reflecting the pink of the tinted roses at which she gazed; for the gay sights, the air, the music, and the excitement of a day's outing with Jude, had quickened her blood and made her eyes sparkle with vivacity. She adored roses, and what Arabella had witnessed was Sue detaining Jude almost against his will while she learnt the names of this variety and that, and put her face within an inch of their blooms to smell them.

'I should like to push my face quite into them – the dears!' she had said. 'But I suppose it is against the rules to touch them – isn't it, Jude?'

'Yes, you baby,' said he: and then playfully gave her a little push, so that her nose went among the petals.

'The policemen will be down on us, and I shall say it was my husband's fault!'

Then she looked up at him, and smiled in a way that told so much to Arabella.

'Happy?' he murmured.

She nodded.

'Why? Because you have come to the great Wessex Agricultural Show – or because *we* have come?'

'You are always trying to make me confess to all sorts of absurdities. Because I am improving my mind, of course, by seeing all these steam-ploughs, and threshing-machines, and chaff-cutters, and cows, and pigs, and sheep.'

Jude was quite content with a baffle from his ever evasive companion. But when he had forgotten that he had put the question, and because he no longer wished for an answer, she went on: 'I feel that we have returned to Greek joyousness, and have blinded ourselves to sickness and sorrow, and have forgotten what twenty-five centuries have taught the race since their time, as one of your Christminster luminaries says. . . . There is one immediate shadow, however, – only one.' And she looked at the aged child, whom, though they had taken him to everything likely to attract a young intelligence, they had utterly failed to interest.

He knew what they were saying and thinking. 'I am very, very sorry, father and mother,' he said. 'But please don't mind! – I can't help it. I should like the flowers very very much, if I didn't keep on thinking they'd be all withered in a few days!'

THE unnoticed lives that the pair had hitherto led began, from the day of the suspended wedding onwards, to be observed and discussed by other persons than Arabella. The society of Spring Street and the neighbourhood generally did not understand, and probably could not have been made to understand, Sue and Jude's private minds, emotions, positions, and fears. The curious facts of a child coming to them unexpectedly, who called Jude father, and Sue mother, and a hitch in a marriage ceremony intended for quietness to be performed at a registrar's office, together with rumours of the undefended cases in law-courts, bore only one translation to plain minds.

Little Time — for though he was formally turned into 'Jude', the apt nickname stuck to him — would come home from school in the evening, and repeat inquiries and remarks that had been made to him by the other boys; and cause Sue, and Jude when he heard them, a great deal of pain and sadness.

The result was that shortly after the attempt at the registrar's the pair went off — to London it was believed — for several days, hiring somebody to look to the boy. When they came back they let it be understood indirectly, and with total indifference and weariness of mien, that they were legally married at last. Sue, who had previously been called Mrs Bridehead, now openly adopted the name of Mrs Fawley. Her dull, cowed, and listless manner for days seemed to substantiate all this.

But the mistake (as it was called) of their going away so secretly to do the business, kept up much of the mystery of their lives; and they found that they made not such advances with their neighbours as they had expected to do thereby. A living mystery was not much less interesting than a dead scandal.

The baker's lad and the grocer's boy, who at first had used to lift their hats gallantly to Sue when they came to execute their errands, these days no longer took the trouble to render her that homage,

and the neighbouring artizans' wives looked straight along the
pavement when they encountered her.

Nobody molested them, it is true; but an oppressive atmosphere
began to encircle their souls, particularly after their excursion to the
Show, as if that visit had brought some evil influence to bear on
them. And their temperaments were precisely of a kind to suffer
from this atmosphere, and to be indisposed to lighten it by vigorous
and open statements. Their apparent attempt at reparation had come
too late to be effective.

The headstone and epitaph orders fell off: and two or three
months later, when autumn came, Jude perceived that he would
have to return to journey-work again, a course all the more unfortunate now, in that he had not as yet cleared off the debt he had
unavoidably incurred in the payment of the law-costs of the
previous year.

One evening he sat down to share the common meal with Sue and
the child as usual. 'I am thinking,' he said to her, 'that I'll hold on
here no longer. The life suits us, certainly; but if we could get away
to a place where we are unknown, we should be lighter hearted, and
have a better chance. And so I am afraid we must break it up here,
however awkward for you, poor dear!'

Sue was always much affected at a picture of herself as an object
of pity, and she saddened.

'Well – I am not sorry,' said she presently. 'I am much depressed
by the way they look at me here. And you have been keeping on this
house and furniture entirely for me and the boy! You don't want it
yourself, and the expense is unnecessary. But whatever we do,
wherever we go, you won't take him away from me, Jude dear? I
could not let him go now! The cloud upon his young mind makes
him so pathetic to me; I do hope to lift it some day! And he loves
me so. You won't take him away from me?'

'Certainly I won't, dear little girl! We'll get nice lodgings, wherever we go. I shall be moving about probably – getting a job here
and a job there.'

'I shall do something too, of course, till – till— Well, now I can't
be useful in the lettering it behoves me to turn my hand to something else.'

'Don't hurry about getting employment,' he said regretfully. 'I don't want you to do that. I wish you wouldn't, Sue. The boy and yourself are enough for you to attend to.'

There was a knock at the door, and Jude answered it. Sue could hear the conversation:

'Is Mr Fawley at home? . . . Biles and Willis the building contractors sent me to know if you'll undertake the relettering of the Ten Commandments in a little church they've been restoring lately in the country near here.'

Jude reflected, and said he could undertake it.

'It is not a very artistic job,' continued the messenger. 'The clergyman is a very old-fashioned chap, and he has refused to let anything more be done to the church than cleaning and repairing.'

'Excellent old man!' said Sue to herself, who was sentimentally opposed to the horrors of over-restoration.

'The Ten Commandments are fixed to the east end,' the messenger went on, 'and they want doing up with the rest of the wall there, since he won't have them carted off as old materials belonging to the contractor, in the usual way of the trade.'

A bargain as to terms was struck, and Jude came indoors. 'There, you see,' he said cheerfully. 'One more job yet, at any rate, and you can help in it — at least you can try. We shall have all the church to ourselves, as the rest of the work is finished.'

Next day Jude went out to the church, which was only two miles off. He found that what the contractor's clerk had said was true. The tables of the Jewish law towered sternly over the utensils of Christian grace, as the chief ornament of the chancel end, in the fine dry style of the last century. And as their framework was constructed of ornamental plaster they could not be taken down for repair. A portion, crumbled by damp, required renewal; and when this had been done, and the whole cleansed, he began to renew the lettering. On the second morning Sue came to see what assistance she could render, and also because they liked to be together.

The silence and emptiness of the building gave her confidence, and, standing on a safe low platform erected by Jude, which she was nevertheless timid at mounting, she began painting in the letters of the first Table while he set about mending a portion of the second. She was quite pleased at her powers; she had acquired them in the days she painted illumined texts for the church-fitting shop at

Christminster. Nobody seemed likely to disturb them; and the pleasant twitter of birds, and rustle of October leafage, came in through an open window, and mingled with their talk.

They were not, however, to be left thus snug and peaceful for long. About half-past twelve there came footsteps on the gravel without. The old vicar and his churchwarden entered, and, coming up to see what was being done, seemed surprised to discover that a young woman was assisting. They passed on into an aisle, at which time the door again opened, and another figure entered − a small one, that of little Time, who was crying. Sue had told him where he might find her between school-hours, if he wished. She came down from her perch, and said, 'What's the matter, my dear?'

'I couldn't stay to eat my dinner in school, because they said—' He described how some boys had taunted him about his nominal mother, and Sue, grieved, expressed her indignation to Jude aloft. The child went into the churchyard, and Sue returned to her work. Meanwhile the door had opened again, and there shuffled in with a business-like air the white-aproned woman who cleaned the church. Sue recognized her as one who had friends in Spring Street, whom she visited. The church-cleaner looked at Sue, gaped, and lifted her hands; she had evidently recognized Jude's companion as the latter had recognized her. Next came two ladies, and after talking to the charwoman they also moved forward, and as Sue stood reaching upward, watched her hand tracing the letters, and critically regarded her person in relief against the white wall, till she grew so nervous that she trembled visibly.

They went back to where the others were standing, talking in undertones: and one said − Sue could not hear which − 'She's his wife, I suppose?'

'Some say Yes: some say No,' was the reply from the char-woman.

'Not? Then she ought to be, or somebody's − that's very clear!'

'They've only been married a very few weeks, whether or no.'

'A strange pair to be painting the Two Tables! I wonder Biles and Willis could think of such a thing as hiring those!'

The churchwarden supposed that Biles and Willis knew of nothing wrong, and then the other, who had been talking to the old woman, explained what she meant by calling them strange people.

The probable drift of the subdued conversation which followed was made plain by the churchwarden breaking into an anecdote, in a voice that everybody in the church could hear, though obviously suggested by the present situation:

'Well, now, it is a curious thing, but my grandfather told me a strange tale of a most immoral case that happened at the painting of the Commandments in a church out by Gaymead — which is quite within a walk of this one. In them days Commandments were mostly done in gilt letters on a black ground, and that's how they were out where I say, before the owld church was rebuilded. It must have been somewhere about a hundred years ago that them Commandments wanted doing up, just as ours do here, and they had to get men from Aldbrickham to do 'em. Now they wished to get the job finished by a particular Sunday, so the men had to work late Saturday night, against their will, for over-time was not paid then as 'tis now. There was no true religion in the country at that date, neither among pa'sons, clerks, nor people, and to keep the men up to their work the vicar had to let 'em have plenty of drink during the afternoon. As evening drawed on they sent for some more themselves; rum, by all account. It got later and later, and they got more and more fuddled, till at last they went a-putting their rum-bottle and rummers upon the Communion table, and drawed up a trestle or two, and sate round comfortable, and poured out again right hearty bumpers. No sooner had they tossed off their glasses than, so the story goes, they fell down senseless, one and all. How long they bode so they didn't know, but when they came to themselves there was a terrible thunderstorm a-raging, and they seemed to see in the gloom a dark figure with very thin legs and a curious voot,* a-standing on the ladder, and finishing their work. When it got daylight they could see that the work was really finished, and couldn't at all mind * finishing it themselves. They went home, and the next thing they heard was that a great scandal had been caused in the church that Sunday morning, for when the people came and service began, all saw that the Ten Commandments wez painted with the "Nots" left out. Decent people wouldn't attend service there for a long time, and the Bishop had to be sent for to re-consecrate the church. That's the tradition as I used to hear it as a child. You must take it for what it is wo'th, but this case to-day has reminded me o't, as I say.'

The visitors gave one more glance, as if to see whether Jude and Sue had left the Nots out likewise, and then severally left the church, even the old woman at last. Sue and Jude, who had not stopped working, sent back the child to school, and remained without speaking; till, looking at her narrowly, he found she had been crying silently.

'Never mind, comrade!' he said. 'I know what it is!'

'I can't *bear* that they, and everybody, should think people wicked because they may have chosen to live their own way! It is really these opinions that make the best intentioned people reckless, and actually become immoral!'

'Never be cast down! It was only a funny story.'

'Ah, but we suggested it! I am afraid I have done you mischief, Jude, instead of helping you by coming!'

To have suggested such a story was certainly not very exhilarating, in a serious view of their position. However, in a few minutes Sue seemed to see that their position this morning had a ludicrous side, and wiping her eyes she laughed.

'It is droll, after all,' she said, 'that we two, of all people, with our queer history, should happen to be here painting the Ten Commandments! You a reprobate, and I – in my condition. . . . O dear!' . . . And with her hand over her eyes she laughed again silently and intermittently, till she was quite weak.

'That's better,' said Jude gaily. 'Now we are right again, aren't we, little girl!'

'O but it is serious, all the same!' she sighed as she took up the brush and righted herself. 'But do you see they don't think we are married? They *won't* believe it! It is extraordinary!'

'I don't care whether they think so or not,' said Jude. 'I shan't take any more trouble to make them.'

They sat down to lunch – which they had brought with them not to hinder time – and having eaten it were about to set to work anew when a man entered the church, and Jude recognized in him the contractor Willis. He beckoned to Jude, and spoke to him apart.

'Here – I've just had a complaint about this,' he said, with rather breathless awkwardness. 'I don't wish to go into the matter – as of course I didn't know what was going on – but I am afraid I must ask you and her to leave off, and let somebody else finish this! It is best, to avoid all unpleasantness. I'll pay you for the week, all the same.'

Jude was too independent to make any fuss; and the contractor paid him, and left. Jude picked up his tools, and Sue cleansed her brush. Then their eyes met.

'How could we be so simple as to suppose we might do this!' said she, dropping to her tragic note. 'Of course we ought not — I ought not — to have come!'

'I had no idea that anybody was going to intrude into such a lonely place and see us!' Jude returned. 'Well, it can't be helped, dear; and of course I wouldn't wish to injure Willis's trade-connection by staying.' They sat down passively for a few minutes, proceeded out of the church, and overtaking the boy pursued their thoughtful way to Aldbrickham.

Fawley had still a pretty zeal in the cause of education, and, as was natural with his experiences, he was active in furthering 'equality of opportunity' by any humble means open to him. He had joined an Artizans' Mutual Improvement Society established in the town about the time of his arrival there; its members being young men of all creeds and denominations, including Churchmen, Congregationalists, Baptists, Unitarians, Positivists, and others — Agnostics had scarcely been heard of at this time — their one common wish to enlarge their minds forming a sufficiently close bond of union. The subscription was small, and the room homely; and Jude's activity, uncustomary acquirements, and above all, singular intuition on what to read and how to set about it — begotten of his years of struggle against malignant stars — had led to his being placed on the committee.

A few evenings after his dismissal from the church repairs, and before he had obtained any more work to do, he went to attend a meeting of the aforesaid committee. It was late when he arrived: all the others had come, and as he entered they looked dubiously at him, and hardly uttered a word of greeting. He guessed that something bearing on himself had been either discussed or mooted. Some ordinary business was transacted, and it was disclosed that the number of subscriptions had shown a sudden falling off for that quarter. One member — a really well-meaning and upright man — began speaking in enigmas about certain possible causes: that it behoved them to look well into their constitution; for if the committee were not respected, and had not at least, in their differences, a common standard of *conduct*, they would bring the institution to the ground. Nothing further was said in Jude's presence, but he knew what this meant; and turning to the table wrote a note resigning his office there and then.

Thus the supersensitive couple were more and more impelled to go away. And then bills were sent in, and the question arose, what could Jude do with his great-aunt's heavy old furniture, if he left the town to travel he knew not whither? This, and the necessity of ready money, compelled him to decide on an auction, much as he would have preferred to keep the venerable goods.

The day of the sale came on; and Sue for the last time cooked her own, the child's, and Jude's breakfast in the little house he had furnished. It chanced to be a wet day; moreover Sue was unwell, and not wishing to desert her poor Jude in such gloomy circumstances, for he was compelled to stay awhile, she acted on the suggestion of the auctioneer's man, and ensconced herself in an upper room, which could be emptied of its effects, and so kept closed to the bidders. Here Jude discovered her; and with the child, and their few trunks, baskets, and bundles, and two chairs and a table that were not in the sale, the two sat in meditative talk.

Footsteps began stamping up and down the bare stairs, the comers inspecting the goods, some of which were of so quaint and ancient a make as to acquire an adventitious value as art. Their door was tried once or twice, and to guard themselves against intrusion Jude wrote 'Private' on a scrap of paper, and stuck it upon the panel.

They soon found that, instead of the furniture, their own personal histories and past conduct began to be discussed to an unexpected and intolerable extent by the intending bidders. It was not till now that they really discovered what a fools' paradise of supposed unrecognition they had been living in of late. Sue silently took her companion's hand, and with eyes on each other they heard these passing remarks — the quaint and mysterious personality of Father Time being a subject which formed a large ingredient in the hints and innuendoes. At length the auction began in the room below, whence they could hear each familiar article knocked down, the highly prized ones cheaply, the unconsidered at an unexpected price.

'People don't understand us,' he sighed heavily. 'I am glad we have decided to go.'

'The question is, where to?'

'It ought to be to London. There one can live as one chooses.'

'No — not London, dear! I know it well. We should be unhappy there.'

'Why?'

'Can't you think?'

'Because Arabella is there?'

'That's the chief reason.'

'But in the country I shall always be uneasy lest there should be some more of our late experience. And I don't care to lessen it by explaining, for one thing, all about the boy's history. To cut him off from his past I have determined to keep silent. I am sickened of ecclesiastical work now; and I shouldn't like to accept it, if offered me!'

'You ought to have learnt Classic. Gothic is barbaric art, after all. Pugin * was wrong, and Wren was right. Remember the interior of Christminster Cathedral — almost the first place in which we looked in each other's faces. Under the picturesqueness of those Norman details one can see the grotesque childishness of uncouth people trying to imitate the vanished Roman forms, remembered by dim tradition only.'

'Yes — you have half converted me to that view by what you have said before. But one can work, and despise what one does. I must do something, if not church-gothic.'

'I wish we could both follow an occupation in which personal circumstances don't count,' she said, smiling up wistfully. 'I am as disqualified for teaching as you are for ecclesiastical art. You must fall back upon railway stations, bridges, theatres, music-halls, hotels — everything that has no connection with conduct.'

'I am not skilled in those. . . . . I ought to take to bread-baking. I grew up in the baking business with aunt, you know. But even a baker must be conventional, to get customers.'

'Unless he keeps a cake and gingerbread stall at markets and fairs, where people are gloriously indifferent to everything except the quality of the goods.'

Their thoughts were diverted by the voice of the auctioneer:

'Now this antique oak settle – a unique example of old English furniture, worthy the attention of all collectors!'

'That was my great-grandfather's,' said Jude. 'I wish we could have kept the poor old thing!'

One by one the articles went, and the afternoon passed away. Jude and the other two were getting tired and hungry, but after the conversation they had heard they were shy of going out while the purchasers were in their line of retreat. However, the later lots drew on, and it became necessary to emerge into the rain soon, to take on Sue's things to their temporary lodging.

'Now the next lot: two pairs of pigeons, all alive and plump – a nice pie for somebody for next Sunday's dinner!'

The impending sale of these birds had been the most trying suspense of the whole afternoon. They were Sue's pets, and when it was found that they could not possibly be kept, more sadness was caused than by parting from all the furniture. Sue tried to think away her tears as she heard the trifling sum that her dears were deemed to be worth advanced by small stages to the price at which they were finally knocked down. The purchaser was a neighbouring poulterer, and they were unquestionably doomed to die before the next market day.

Noting her dissembled distress Jude kissed her, and said it was time to go and see if the lodgings were ready. He would go on with the boy, and fetch her soon.

When she was left alone she waited patiently, but Jude did not come back. At last she started, the coast being clear, and on passing the poulterer's shop, not far off, she saw her pigeons in a hamper by the door. An emotion at sight of them, assisted by the growing dusk of evening, caused her to act on impulse, and first looking around her quickly, she pulled out the peg which fastened down the cover, and went on. The cover was lifted from within, and the pigeons flew away with a clatter that brought the chagrined poulterer cursing and swearing to the door.

Sue reached the lodging trembling, and found Jude and the boy making it comfortable for her. 'Do the buyers pay before they bring away the things?' she asked breathlessly.

'Yes, I think. Why?'

'Because, then, I've done such a wicked thing!' And she explained, in bitter contrition.

'I shall have to pay the poulterer for them, if he doesn't catch them,' said Jude. 'But never mind. Don't fret about it, dear.'

'It was so foolish of me! O why should Nature's law be mutual butchery!'

'Is it so, mother?' asked the boy intently.

'Yes!' said Sue vehemently.

'Well, they must take their chance, now, poor things,' said Jude. 'As soon as the sale-account is wound up, and our bills paid, we go.'

'Where do we go to?' asked Time, in suspense.

'We must sail under sealed orders, that nobody may trace us. . . . We mustn't go to Alfredston, or to Melchester, or to Shaston, or to Christminster. Apart from those we may go anywhere.'

'Why mustn't we go there, father?'

'Because of a cloud that has gathered over us; though "we have wronged no man, corrupted no man, defrauded no man!" * Though perhaps we have "done that which was right in our own eyes".'*

CHAPTER SEVEN

FROM that week Jude Fawley and Sue walked no more in the town of Aldbrickham.

Whither they had gone nobody knew, chiefly because nobody cared to know. Any one sufficiently curious to trace the steps of such an obscure pair might have discovered without great trouble that they had taken advantage of his adaptive craftsmanship to enter on a shifting, almost nomadic, life, which was not without its pleasantness for a time.

Wherever Jude heard of freestone work to be done, thither he went, choosing by preference places remote from his old haunts and Sue's. He laboured at a job, long or briefly, till it was finished; and then moved on.

Two whole years and a half passed thus. Sometimes he might have been found shaping the mullions of a country mansion, sometimes setting the parapet of a town-hall, sometimes ashlaring* an hotel at Sandbourne, sometimes a museum at Casterbridge, sometimes as far down as Exonbury, sometimes at Stoke-Barehills. Later still he was at Kennetbridge, a thriving town not more than a dozen miles south of Marygreen, this being his nearest approach to the village where he was known; for he had a sensitive dread of being questioned as to his life and fortunes by those who had been acquainted with him during his ardent young manhood of study and promise, and his brief and unhappy married life at that time.

At some of these places he would be detained for months, at others only a few weeks. His curious and sudden antipathy to ecclesiastical work, both episcopal and nonconformist, which had risen in him when suffering under a smarting sense of misconception, remained with him in cold blood, less from any fear of renewed censure than from an ultra-conscientiousness which would not allow him to seek a living out of those who would disapprove of his ways; also, too, from a sense of inconsistency between his former dogmas and his present practice, hardly a shred of the beliefs with

which he had first gone up to Christminster now remaining with
him. He was mentally approaching the position which Sue had
occupied when he first met her.

On a Saturday evening in May, nearly three years after
Arabella's recognition of Sue and himself at the Agricultural Show,
some of those who there encountered each other met again.

It was the spring fair at Kennetbridge, and, though this ancient
trade-meeting had much dwindled from its dimensions of former
times, the long straight street of the borough presented a lively scene
about midday. At this hour a light trap, among other vehicles, was
driven into the town by the north road, and up to the door of a
temperance inn. There alighted two women, one the driver, an
ordinary country person, the other a finely built figure in the deep
mourning of a widow. Her sombre suit, of pronounced cut, caused
her to appear a little out of place in the medley and bustle of a
provincial fair.

'I will just find out where it is, Anny,' said the widow-lady to her
companion, when the horse and cart had been taken by a man who
came forward: 'and then I'll come back, and meet you here; and
we'll go in and have something to eat and drink. I begin to feel quite
a sinking.'

'With all my heart,' said the other. 'Though I would sooner have
put up at the Chequers or the Jack. You can't get much at these
temperance houses.'

'Now, don't you give way to gluttonous desires, my child,' said
the woman in weeds reprovingly. 'This is the proper place. Very
well: we'll meet in half-an-hour, unless you come with me to find out
where the site of the new chapel is?'

'I don't care to. You can tell me.'

The companions then went their several ways, the one in crape
walking firmly along with a mien of disconnection from her miscellaneous surroundings. Making inquiries she came to a hoarding,
within which were excavations denoting the foundations of a building; and on the boards without one or two large posters announcing
that the foundation-stone of the chapel about to be erected would be
laid that afternoon at three o'clock by a London preacher of great
popularity among his body.

Having ascertained thus much the immensely weeded widow

retraced her steps, and gave herself leisure to observe the movements of the fair. By and by her attention was arrested by a little stall of cakes and gingerbreads, standing between the more pretentious erections of trestles and canvas. It was covered with an immaculate cloth, and tended by a young woman apparently unused to the business, she being accompanied by a boy with an octogenarian face, who assisted her.

'Upon my — senses!' murmured the widow to herself. 'His wife Sue — if she is so!' She drew nearer to the stall. 'How do you do, Mrs Fawley?' she said blandly.

Sue changed colour and recognized Arabella through the crape veil.

'How are you, Mrs Cartlett?' she said stiffly. And then perceiving Arabella's garb her voice grew sympathetic in spite of herself. 'What? — you have lost—'

'My poor husband. Yes. He died suddenly, six weeks ago, leaving me none too well off, though he was a kind husband to me. But whatever profit there is in public-house keeping goes to them that brew the liquors, and not to them that retail 'em. . . . And you, my little old man! You don't know me, I expect?'

'Yes, I do. You be the woman I thought wer my mother for a bit, till I found you wasn't,' replied Father Time, who had learned to use the Wessex tongue quite naturally by now.

'All right. Never mind. I am a friend.'

'Juey,' said Sue suddenly, 'go down to the station platform with this tray — there's another train coming in, I think.'

When he was gone Arabella continued: 'He'll never be a beauty, will he, poor chap! Does he know I am his mother really?'

'No. He thinks there is some mystery about his parentage — that's all. Jude is going to tell him when he is a little older.'

'But how do you come to be doing this? I am surprised.'

'It is only a temporary occupation — a fancy of ours while we are in a difficulty.'

'Then you are living with him still?'

'Yes.'

'Married?'

'Of course.'

'Any children?'

'Two.'

'And another coming soon, I see.'

Sue writhed under the hard and direct questioning, and her tender little mouth began to quiver.

'Lord – I mean goodness gracious – what is there to cry about? Some folks would be proud enough!'

'It is not that I am ashamed – not as you think! But it seems such a terribly tragic thing to bring beings into the world – so presumptuous – that I question my right to do it sometimes!'

'Take it easy, my dear. . . . But you don't tell me why you do such a thing as this? Jude used to be a proud sort of chap – above any business almost, leave alone keeping a standing.' *

'Perhaps my husband has altered a little since then. I am sure he is not proud now!' And Sue's lips quivered again. 'I am doing this because he caught a chill early in the year while putting up some stone-work of a music-hall, at Quartershot, which he had to do in the rain, the work having to be executed by a fixed day. He is better than he was; but it has been a long, weary time! We have had an old widow friend with us to help us through it; but she's leaving soon.'

'Well, I am respectable too, thank God, and of a serious way of thinking since my loss. Why did you choose to sell gingerbreads?'

'That's a pure accident. He was brought up to the baking business, and it occurred to him to try his hand at these, which he can make without coming out of doors. We call them Christminster cakes. They are a great success.'

'I never saw any like 'em. Why, they are windows and towers, and pinnacles! And upon my word they are very nice.' She had helped herself, and was unceremoniously munching one of the cakes.

'Yes. They are reminiscences of the Christminster Colleges. Traceried windows, and cloisters, you see. It was a whim of his to do them in pastry.'

'Still harping on Christminster – even in his cakes!' laughed Arabella. 'Just like Jude. A ruling passion. What a queer fellow he is, and always will be!'

Sue sighed, and she looked her distress at hearing him criticized.

'Don't you think he is? Come now; you do, though you are so fond of him!'

'Of course Christminster is a sort of fixed vision with him, which I suppose he'll never be cured of believing in. He still thinks it a great centre of high and fearless thought, instead of what it is, a nest of commonplace schoolmasters whose characteristic is timid obsequiousness to tradition.'

Arabella was quizzing Sue with more regard of how she was speaking than of what she was saying. 'How odd to hear a woman selling cakes talk like that!' she said. 'Why don't you go back to schoolkeeping?'

Sue shook her head. 'They won't have me.'

'Because of the divorce, I suppose?'

'That and other things. And there is no reason to wish it. We gave up all ambition, and were never so happy in our lives till his illness came.'

'Where are you living?'

'I don't care to say.'

'Here in Kennetbridge?'

Sue's manner showed Arabella that her random guess was right.

'Here comes the boy back again,' continued Arabella. 'My boy and Jude's!'

Sue's eyes darted a spark. 'You needn't throw that in my face!' she cried.

'Very well — though I half feel as if I should like to have him with me! . . . But Lord, I don't want to take him from 'ee — ever I should sin to speak so profane — though I should think you must have enough of your own! He's in very good hands, that I know; and I am not the woman to find fault with what the Lord has ordained. I've reached a more resigned frame of mind.'

'Indeed! I wish I had been able to do so.'

'You should try,' replied the widow, from the serene heights of a soul conscious not only of spiritual but of social superiority. 'I make no boast of my awakening, but I'm not what I was. After Cartlett's death I was passing the chapel in the street next ours, and went into it for shelter from a shower of rain. I felt a need of some sort of support under my loss, and, as 'twas righter than gin, I took to going there regular, and found it a great comfort. But I've left London now, you know, and at present I am living at Alfredston, with my friend Anny, to be near my own old country. I'm not come here to the fair to-day. There's to be the foundation-stone of a new chapel laid this afternoon by a popular London preacher, and I drove over with Anny. Now I must go back to meet her.'

Then Arabella wished Sue good-bye, and went on.

CHAPTER EIGHT

MICHAELMAS came and passed, and Jude and his wife, who had lived but a short time in her father's house after their re-marriage, were in lodgings on the top floor of a dwelling nearer to the centre of the city.

He had done a few days' work during the two or three months since the event, but his health had been indifferent, and it was now precarious. He was sitting in an arm-chair before the fire, and coughed a good deal.

'I've got a bargain for my trouble in marrying thee over again!' Arabella was saying to him. 'I shall have to keep 'ee entirely, — that's what 'twill come to! I shall have to make black-pot and sausages, and hawk 'em about the street, all to support an invalid husband I'd no business to be saddled with at all. Why didn't you keep your health, deceiving one like this? You were well enough when the wedding was!'

'Ah, yes!' said he, laughing acridly. 'I have been thinking of my foolish feeling about the pig you and I killed during our first marriage. I feel now that the greatest mercy that could be vouchsafed to me would be that something should serve me as I served that animal.'

This was the sort of discourse that went on between them every day now. The landlord of the lodging, who had heard that they were a queer couple, had doubted if they were married at all, especially as he had seen Arabella kiss Jude one evening when she had taken a little cordial; and he was about to give them notice to quit, till by chance overhearing her one night haranguing Jude in rattling terms, and ultimately flinging a shoe at his head, he recognized the note of genuine wedlock; and concluding that they must be respectable, said no more.

Jude did not get any better, and one day he requested Arabella with considerable hesitation, to execute a commission for him. She asked him indifferently what it was.

In the afternoon Sue and the other people bustling about Kennetbridge fair could hear singing inside the placarded hoarding further down the street. Those who peeped through the opening saw a crowd of persons in broadcloth, with hymn-books in their hands, standing round the excavations for the new chapel-walls. Arabella Cartlett and her weeds stood among them. She had a clear, powerful voice, which could be distinctly heard with the rest, rising and falling to the tune, her breast's superb abundance being also seen doing likewise.

It was two hours later on the same day that Anny and Mrs Cartlett, having had tea at the Temperance hotel, started on their return journey across the high and open country which stretches between Kennetbridge and Alfredston. Arabella was in a thoughtful mood; but her thoughts were not of the new chapel, as Anny at first surmised.

'No — it is something else,' at last said Arabella sullenly. 'I came here to-day never thinking of anybody but poor Cartlett, or of anything but spreading the Gospel by means of this new tabernacle they've begun this afternoon. But something has happened to turn my mind another way quite. Anny, I've heard of un again, and I've seen *her*!'

'Who?'

'I've heard of Jude, and I've seen his wife. And ever since, do what I will, and though I sung the hymns wi' all my strength, I have not been able to help thinking about 'n; which I've no right to do as a chapel member.'

'Can't ye fix your mind upon what was said by the London preacher to-day, and try to get rid of your wandering fancies that way?'

'I do. But my wicked heart will ramble off in spite of myself!'

'Well — I know what it is to have a wanton wind o' my own, too! If you on'y knew what I do dream sometimes o' nights quite against my wishes, you'd say I had my struggles!' (Anny, too, had grown rather serious of late, her lover having jilted her.)

'What shall I do about it?' urged Arabella morbidly.

'You could take a lock of your late-lost husband's hair, and have it made into a mourning brooch, and look at it every hour of the day.'

'I haven't a morsel! – and if I had 'twould be no good. . . . After all that's said about the comforts of this religion, I wish I had Jude back again!'

'You must fight valiant against the feeling, since he's another's. And I've heard that another good thing for it, when it afflicts volupshious widows, is to go to your husband's grave in the dusk of evening, and stand a long while a-bowed down.'

'Pooh! I know as well as you what I should do; only I don't do it!'

They drove in silence along the straight road till they were within the horizon of Marygreen, which lay not far to the left of their route. They came to the junction of the highway and the cross-lane leading to that village, whose church-tower could be seen athwart the hollow. When they got yet further on, and were passing the lonely house in which Arabella and Jude had lived during the first months of their marriage, and where the pig-killing had taken place, she could control herself no longer.

'He's more mine than hers!' she burst out. 'What right has she to him, I should like to know! I'd take him from her if I could!'

'Fie, Abby! And your husband only six weeks gone! Pray against it!'

'Be damned if I do! Feelings are feelings! I won't be a creeping hypocrite any longer – so there!'

Arabella had hastily drawn from her pocket a bundle of tracts which she had brought with her to distribute at the fair, and of which she had given away several. As she spoke she flung the whole remainder of the packet into the hedge. 'I've tried that sort o' physic and have failed wi' it. I must be as I was born!'

'Hush! You be excited, dear! Now you come along home quiet, and have a cup of tea, and don't let us talk about un no more. We won't come out this road again, as it leads to where he is, because it inflames 'ee so. You'll be all right again soon.'

Arabella did calm herself down by degrees; and they crossed the Ridge-way. When they began to descend the long, straight hill, they

saw plodding along in front of them an elderly man of spare stature
and thoughtful gait. In his hand he carried a basket; and there was a
touch of slovenliness in his attire, together with that indefinable
something in his whole appearance which suggested one who was
his own housekeeper, purveyor, confidant, and friend, through possessing nobody else at all in the world to act in those capacities for
him. The remainder of the journey was down-hill, and guessing him
to be going to Alfredston they offered him a lift, which he accepted.

Arabella looked at him, and looked again, till at length she spoke.
'If I don't mistake I am talking to Mr Phillotson?'

The wayfarer faced round and regarded her in turn. 'Yes; my
name is Phillotson,' he said. 'But I don't recognize you, ma'am.'

'I remember you well enough when you used to be schoolmaster
out at Marygreen, and I one of your scholars. I used to walk up
there from Cresscombe every day, because we had only a mistress
down at our place, and you taught better. But you wouldn't remember me as I should you? — Arabella Donn.'

He shook his head. 'No,' he said politely, 'I don't recall the name.
And I should hardly recognize in your present portly self the slim
school child no doubt you were then.'

'Well, I always had plenty of flesh on my bones. However, I am
staying down here with some friends at present. You know, I
suppose, who I married?'

'No.'

'Jude Fawley — also a scholar of yours — at least a night scholar —
for some little time I think? And known to you afterwards, if I am
not mistaken.'

'Dear me, dear me,' said Phillotson, starting out of his stiffness.
'*You* Fawley's wife? To be sure — he had a wife! And he — I
understood—'

'Divorced her — as you did yours — perhaps for better reasons.'

'Indeed?'

'Well — he med have been right in doing it — right for both; for I
soon married again, and all went pretty straight till my husband
died lately. But you — you were decidedly wrong!'

'No,' said Phillotson, with sudden testiness. 'I would rather not
talk of this, but — I am convinced I did only what was right, and just,

and moral. I have suffered for my act and opinions, but I hold to them; though her loss was a loss to me in more ways than one!'

'You lost your school and good income through her, did you not?'

'I don't care to talk of it. I have recently come back here – to Marygreen, I mean.'

'You are keeping the school there again, just as formerly?'

The pressure of a sadness that would out unsealed him. 'I am there,' he replied. 'Just as formerly, no. Merely on sufferance. It was a last resource – a small thing to return to after my move upwards, and my long indulged hopes – a returning to zero, with all its humiliations. But it is a refuge. I like the seclusion of the place, and the vicar having known me before my so-called eccentric conduct towards my wife had ruined my reputation as a schoolmaster, he accepted my services when all other schools were closed against me. However, although I take fifty pounds a year here after taking above two hundred elsewhere, I prefer it to running the risk of having my old domestic experiences raked up against me, as I should do if I tried to make a move.'

'Right you are. A contented mind is a continual feast. She has done no better.'

'She is not doing well, you mean?'

'I met her by accident at Kennetbridge this very day, and she is anything but thriving. Her husband is ill, and she anxious. You made a fool of a mistake about her, I tell 'ee again, and the harm you did yourself by dirting your own nest serves you right, excusing the liberty.'

'How?'

'She was innocent.'

'But nonsense! They did not even defend the case!'

'That was because they didn't care to. She was quite innocent of what obtained you your freedom, at the time you obtained it. I saw her just afterwards, and proved it to myself completely by talking to her.'

Phillotson grasped the edge of the spring-cart, and appeared to be much stressed and worried by the information. 'Still – she wanted to go,' he said.

'Yes. But you shouldn't have let her. That's the only way with these fanciful women that chaw high * — innocent or guilty. She'd have come round in time. We all do! Custom does it! it's all the same in the end! However, I think she's fond of her man still — whatever he med be of her. You were too quick about her. *I* shouldn't have let her go! I should have kept her chained on — her spirit for kicking would have been broke soon enough! There's nothing like bondage and a stone-deaf taskmaster for taming us women. Besides, you've got the laws on your side. Moses knew. Don't you call to mind what he says?'

'Not for the moment, ma'am, I regret to say.'

'Call yourself a schoolmaster! I used to think o't when they read it in church, and I was carrying on a bit. "Then shall the man be guiltless; but the woman shall bear her iniquity." * Damn rough on us women; but we must grin and put up wi' it! — Haw haw! — Well; she's got her deserts now.'

'Yes,' said Phillotson, with biting sadness. 'Cruelty is the law pervading all nature and society; and we can't get out of it if we would!'

'Well — don't you forget to try it next time, old man.'

'I cannot answer you, madam. I have never known much of womankind.'

They had now reached the low levels bordering Alfredston, and passing through the outskirts approached a mill, to which Phillotson said his errand led him; whereupon they drew up, and he alighted, bidding them good-night in a preoccupied mood.

In the meantime Sue, though remarkably successful in her cake-selling experiment at Kennetbridge fair, had lost the temporary brightness which had begun to sit upon her sadness on account of that success. When all her 'Christminster' cakes had been disposed of she took upon her arm the empty basket, and the cloth which had covered the standing she had hired, and giving the other things to the boy left the street with him. They followed a lane to a distance of half a mile, till they met an old woman carrying a child in short clothes, and leading a toddler in the other hand.

Sue kissed the children, and said, 'How is he now?'

'Still better!' returned Mrs Edlin cheerfully. 'Before you are upstairs again your husband will be well enough – don't 'ee trouble.'

They turned, and came to some old, dun-tiled cottages with gardens and fruit-trees. Into one of these they entered by lifting the latch without knocking, and were at once in the general living-room. Here they greeted Jude, who was sitting in an armchair, the increased delicacy of his normally delicate features, and the childishly expectant look in his eyes, being alone sufficient to show that he had been passing through a severe illness.

'What – you have sold them all?' he said, a gleam of interest lighting up his face.

'Yes. Arcades, gables, east windows and all.' She told him the pecuniary results, and then hesitated. At last, when they were left alone, she informed him of the unexpected meeting with Arabella, and the latter's widowhood.

Jude was discomposed. 'What – is she living here?' he said.

'No; at Alfredston,' said Sue.

Jude's countenance remained clouded. 'I thought I had better tell you?' she continued, kissing him anxiously.

'Yes. . . . Dear me! Arabella not in the depths of London, but down here! It is only a little over a dozen miles across the country to Alfredston. What is she doing there?'

She told him all she knew. 'She has taken to chapel-going,' Sue added, 'and talks accordingly.'

'Well,' said Jude, 'perhaps it is for the best that we have almost decided to move on. I feel much better to-day, and shall be well enough to leave in a week or two. Then Mrs Edlin can go home again – dear faithful old soul – the only friend we have in the world!'

'Where do you think to go to?' Sue asked, a troublousness in her tones.

Then Jude confessed what was in his mind. He said it would surprise her, perhaps, after his having resolutely avoided all the old places for so long. But one thing and another had made him think a great deal of Christminster lately, and, if she didn't mind, he would like to go back there. Why should they care if they were known? It was over-sensitive of them to mind so much. They could go on selling cakes there, for that matter, if he couldn't work. He had no sense of shame at mere poverty; and perhaps he would be as strong as ever soon, and able to set up stone-cutting for himself there.

'Why should you care so much for Christminster?' she said pensively. 'Christminster cares nothing for you, poor dear!'

'Well, I do, I can't help it. I love the place — although I know how it hates all men like me — the so-called Self-taught, — how it scorns our laboured acquisitions, when it should be the first to respect them; how it sneers at our false quantities and mispronunciations, when it should say, I see you want help, my poor friend! . . . Nevertheless, it is the centre of the universe to me, because of my early dream: and nothing can alter it. Perhaps it will soon wake up, and be generous. I pray so! . . . I should like to go back to live there — perhaps to die there! In two or three weeks I might, I think. It will then be June, and I should like to be there by a particular day.'

His hope that he was recovering proved so far well grounded that in three weeks they had arrived in the city of many memories; were actually treading its pavements, receiving the reflection of the sunshine from its wasting walls.

PART SIXTH

At Christminster again

'...And she humbled her body greatly, and all the places of her joy she filled with her torn hair.' — ESTHER (Apoc.)

'There are two who decline, a woman and I,
And enjoy our death in the darkness here.' — R. BROWNING

ON their arrival the station was lively with straw-hatted young men, welcoming young girls who bore a remarkable family likeness to their welcomers, and who were dressed up in the brightest and lightest of raiment.

'The place seems gay,' said Sue. 'Why — it is Remembrance Day!* — Jude — how sly of you — you came to-day on purpose!'

'Yes,' said Jude quietly, as he took charge of the small child, and told Arabella's boy to keep close to them, Sue attending to their own eldest. 'I thought we might as well come to-day as on any other.'

'But I am afraid it will depress you!' she said, looking anxiously at him up and down.

'O, I mustn't let it interfere with our business; and we have a good deal to do before we shall be settled here. The first thing is lodgings.'

Having left their luggage and his tools at the station they proceeded on foot up the familiar street, the holiday people all drifting in the same direction. Reaching the Fourways they were about to turn off to where accommodation was likely to be found when, looking at the clock and the hurrying crowd, Jude said: 'Let us go and see the procession, and never mind the lodgings just now? We can get them afterwards.'

'Oughtn't we to get a house over our heads first?' she asked.

But his soul seemed full of the anniversary, and together they went down Chief Street, their smallest child in Jude's arms, Sue leading her little girl, and Arabella's boy walking thoughtfully and silently beside them. Crowds of pretty sisters in airy costumes, and meekly ignorant parents who had known no College in their youth, were under convoy in the same direction by brothers and sons bearing the opinion written large on them, that no properly qualified human beings had lived on earth till they came to grace it here and now.

'My failure is reflected on me by every one of those young

fellows,' said Jude. 'A lesson on presumption is awaiting me to-day! — Humiliation Day for me! ... If you, my dear darling, hadn't come to my rescue, I should have gone to the dogs with despair!'

She saw from his face that he was getting into one of his tempestuous, self-harrowing moods. 'It would have been better if we had gone at once about our own affairs, dear,' she answered. 'I am sure this sight will awaken old sorrows in you, and do no good!'

'Well – we are near; we will see it now,' said he.

They turned in on the left by the church with the Italian porch,* whose helical columns were heavily draped with creepers, and pursued the lane till there arose on Jude's sight the circular theatre with that well-known lantern above it, which stood in his mind as the sad symbol of his abandoned hopes; for it was from that outlook that he had finally surveyed the City of Colleges on the afternoon of his great meditation, which convinced him at last of the futility of his attempt to be a son of the University.

To-day, in the open space stretching between this building and the nearest college, stood a crowd of expectant people. A passage was kept clear through their midst by two barriers of timber, extending from the door of the college to the door of the large building between it and the theatre.

'Here is the place – they are just going to pass!' cried Jude in sudden excitement. And pushing his way to the front he took up a position close to the barrier, still hugging the youngest child in his arms, while Sue and the others kept immediately behind him. The crowd filled in at their back, and fell to talking, joking, and laughing as carriage after carriage drew up at the lower door of the college, and solemn stately figures in blood-red robes began to alight. The sky had grown overcast and livid, and thunder rumbled now and then.

Father Time shuddered. 'It do seem like the Judgment Day!' he whispered.

'They are only learned Doctors,' said Sue.

While they waited big drops of rain fell on their heads and shoulders, and the delay grew tedious. Sue again wished not to stay.

'They won't be long now,' said Jude, without turning his head.

But the procession did not come forth, and somebody in the crowd, to pass the time, looked at the façade of the nearest college, and said he wondered what was meant by the Latin inscription in its midst. Jude, who stood near the inquirer, explained it, and finding that the people all round him were listening with interest, went on to describe the carving of the frieze (which he had studied years before), and to criticize some details of masonry in other college fronts about the city.

The idle crowd, including the two policemen at the doors, stared like the Lycaonians* at Paul, for Jude was apt to get too enthusiastic over any subject in hand, and they seemed to wonder how the stranger should know more about the buildings of their town than they themselves did; till one of them said: 'Why, I know that man; he used to work here years ago — Jude Fawley, that's his name! Don't you mind he used to be nicknamed Tutor of St Slums, d'ye mind? — because he aimed at that line o' business? He's married, I suppose, then, and that's his child he's carrying. Taylor would know him, as he knows everybody.'

The speaker was a man named Jack Stagg, with whom Jude had formerly worked in repairing the college masonries; Tinker Taylor was seen to be standing near. Having his attention called the latter cried across the barriers to Jude: 'You've honoured us by coming back again, my friend!'

Jude nodded.

'An' you don't seem to have done any great things for yourself by going away?'

Jude assented to this also.

'Except found more mouths to fill!' This came in a new voice, and Jude recognized its owner to be Uncle Joe, another mason whom he had known.

Jude replied good-humouredly that he could not dispute it; and from remark to remark something like a general conversation arose between him and the crowd of idlers, during which Tinker Taylor asked Jude if he remembered the Apostles' Creed in Latin still, and the night of the challenge in the public-house.

'But Fortune didn't lie that way?' threw in Joe. 'Yer powers wasn't enough to carry 'ee through?'

'Don't answer them any more!' entreated Sue.

'I don't think I like Christminster!' murmured little Time mournfully, as he stood submerged and invisible in the crowd.

But finding himself the centre of curiosity, quizzing, and comment, Jude was not inclined to shrink from open declarations of what he had no great reason to be ashamed of; and in a little while was stimulated to say in a loud voice to the listening throng generally:

'It is a difficult question, my friends, for any young man — that question I had to grapple with, and which thousands are weighing at the present moment in these uprising times — whether to follow uncritically the track he finds himself in, without considering his aptness for it, or to consider what his aptness or bent may be, and re-shape his course accordingly. I tried to do the latter, and I failed. But I don't admit that my failure proved my view to be a wrong one, or that my success would have made it a right one; though that's how we appraise such attempts nowadays — I mean, not by their essential soundness, but by their accidental outcomes. If I had ended by becoming like one of these gentlemen in red and black that we saw dropping in here by now, everybody would have said: "See how wise that young man was, to follow the bent of his nature!" But having ended no better than I began they say: "See what a fool that fellow was in following a freak of his fancy!"

'However it was my poverty and not my will that consented to be beaten. It takes two or three generations to do what I tried to do in one; and my impulses — affections — vices perhaps they should be called — were too strong not to hamper a man without advantages; who should be as cold-blooded as a fish and as selfish as a pig to have a really good chance of being one of his country's worthies. You may ridicule me — I am quite willing that you should — I am a fit subject, no doubt. But I think if you knew what I have gone through these last few years you would rather pity me. And if they knew' — he nodded towards the college at which the Dons were severally arriving — 'it is just possible they would do the same.'

'He do look ill and worn-out, it is true!' said a woman.

Sue's face grew more emotional; but though she stood close to Jude she was screened.

'I may do some good before I am dead — be a sort of success as a frightful example of what not to do; and so illustrate a moral story,' continued Jude, beginning to grow bitter, though he had opened serenely enough. 'I was, perhaps, after all, a paltry victim to the spirit of mental and social restlessness, that makes so many unhappy in these days!'

'Don't tell them that!' whispered Sue with tears, at perceiving Jude's state of mind. 'You weren't that. You struggled nobly to acquire knowledge, and only the meanest souls in the world would blame you!'

Jude shifted the child into a more easy position on his arm, and concluded: 'And what I appear, a sick and poor man, is not the worst of me. I am in a chaos of principles — groping in the dark — acting by instinct and not after example. Eight or nine years ago when I came here first, I had a neat stock of fixed opinions, but they dropped away one by one; and the further I get the less sure I am. I doubt if I have anything more for my present rule of life than following inclinations which do me and nobody else any harm, and actually give pleasure to those I love best. There, gentlemen, since you wanted to know how I was getting on, I have told you. Much good may it do you! I cannot explain further here. I perceive there is something wrong somewhere in our social formulas: what it is can only be discovered by men or women with greater insight than mine, — if, indeed, they ever discover it — at least in our time. "For who knoweth what is good for man in this life? — and who can tell a man what shall be after him under the sun?" '*

'Hear, hear,' said the populace.

'Well preached!' said Tinker Taylor. And privately to his neighbours: 'Why, one of them jobbing pa'sons swarming about here, that takes the services when our head Reverends want a holiday, wouldn't ha' discoursed such doctrine for less than a guinea down? Hey? I'll take my oath not one o' 'em would! And then he must have had it wrote down for 'n. And this only a working man!'

As a sort of objective commentary on Jude's remarks there drove up at this moment with a belated Doctor, robed and panting, a cab whose horse failed to stop at the exact point required for setting down the hirer, who jumped out and entered the door. The driver, alighting, began to kick the animal in the belly.

'If that can be done,' said Jude, 'at college gates in the most religious and educational city in the world, what shall we say as to how far we've got?'

'Order!' said one of the policemen, who had been engaged with a comrade in opening the large doors opposite the college. 'Keep yer tongue quiet, my man, while the procession passes.' The rain came on more heavily, and all who had umbrellas opened them. Jude was not one of these, and Sue only possessed a small one, half sunshade. She had grown pale, though Jude did not notice it then.

'Let us go on, dear,' she whispered, endeavouring to shelter him. 'We haven't any lodgings yet, remember, and all our things are at the station; and you are by no means well yet. I am afraid this wet will hurt you!'

'They are coming now. Just a moment, and I'll go!' said he.

A peal of six bells struck out, human faces began to crowd the windows around, and the procession of Heads of Houses and new Doctors emerged, their red and black gowned forms passing across the field of Jude's vision like inaccessible planets across an object glass.*

As they went their names were called by knowing informants; and when they reached the old round theatre of Wren a cheer rose high.

'Let's go that way!' cried Jude, and though it now rained steadily he seemed not to know it, and took them round to the Theatre. Here they stood upon the straw that was laid to drown the discordant noise of wheels, where the quaint and frost-eaten stone busts encircling the building looked with pallid grimness on the proceedings, and in particular at the bedraggled Jude, Sue, and their children, as at ludicrous persons who had no business there.

'I wish I could get in!' he said to her fervidly. 'Listen — I may catch a few words of the Latin speech by staying here; the windows are open.'

However, beyond the peals of the organ, and the shouts and hurrahs between each piece of oratory, Jude's standing in the wet did not bring much Latin to his intelligence more than, now and then, a sonorous word in *um* or *ibus*.

'Well — I'm an outsider to the end of my days!' he sighed after a while. 'Now I'll go, my patient Sue. How good of you to wait in the rain all this time — to gratify my infatuation! I'll never care any more about the infernal cursed place, upon my soul I won't! But what made you tremble so when we were at the barrier? And how pale you are, Sue!'

'I saw Richard amongst the people on the other side.'

'Ah – did you!'

'He is evidently come up to Jerusalem to see the festival like the rest of us: and on that account is probably living not so very far away. He had the same hankering for the University that you had, in a milder form. I don't think he saw me, though he must have heard you speaking to the crowd. But he seemed not to notice.'

'Well – suppose he did. Your mind is free from worries about him now, my Sue?'

'Yes, I suppose so. But I am weak. Although I know it is all right with our plans, I felt a curious dread of him; an awe, or terror, of conventions I don't believe in. It comes over me at times like a sort of creeping paralysis, and makes me so sad!'

'You are getting tired, Sue. O – I forgot, darling! Yes, we'll go on at once.'

They started in quest of the lodging, and at last found something that seemed to promise well, in Mildew Lane – a spot which to Jude was irresistible – though to Sue it was not so fascinating – a narrow lane close to the back of a college, but having no communication with it. The little houses were darkened to gloom by the high collegiate buildings, within which life was so far removed from that of the people in the lane as if it had been on opposite sides of the globe; yet only a thickness of wall divided them. Two or three of the houses had notices of rooms to let, and the newcomers knocked at the door of one, which a woman opened.

'Ah – listen!' said Jude suddenly, instead of addressing her.

'What?'

'Why the bells – what church can that be? The tones are familiar.'

Another peal of bells had begun to sound out at some distance off.

'I don't know!' said the landlady tartly. 'Did you knock to ask that?'

'No; for lodgings,' said Jude, coming to himself.

The householder scrutinized Sue's figure a moment. 'We haven't any to let,' said she, shutting the door.

Jude looked discomfited, and the boy distressed. 'Now, Jude,' said Sue, 'let me try. You don't know the way.'

They found a second place hard by; but here the occupier, observing not only Sue, but the boy and the small children, said civilly, 'I am sorry to say we don't let where there are children'; and also closed the door.

The small child squared its mouth and cried silently, with an instinct that trouble loomed. The boy sighed. 'I don't like Christminster!' he said. 'Are the great old houses gaols?'

'No; colleges,' said Jude; 'which perhaps you'll study in some day.'

'I'd rather not!' the boy rejoined.

'Now we'll try again,' said Sue. 'I'll pull my cloak more round me. . . . Leaving Kennetbridge for this place is like coming from Caiaphas to Pilate! . . .* How do I look now, dear?'

'Nobody would notice it now,' said Jude.

There was one other house, and they tried a third time. The woman here was more amiable; but she had little room to spare, and could only agree to take in Sue and the children if her husband could go elsewhere. This arrangement they perforce adopted, in the stress from delaying their search till so late. They came to terms with her, though her price was rather high for their pockets. But they could not afford to be critical till Jude had time to get a more permanent abode; and in this house took possession of a back room on the second floor with an inner closet-room for the children. Jude stayed and had a cup of tea; and was pleased to find that the window commanded the back of another of the colleges. Kissing all four he went to get a few necessaries and look for lodgings for himself.

When he was gone the landlady came up to talk a little with Sue, and gather something of the circumstances of the family she had taken in. Sue had not the art of prevarication, and, after admitting several facts as to their late difficulties and wanderings, she was startled by the landlady saying suddenly:

'Are you really a married woman?'

Sue hesitated; and then impulsively told the woman that her husband and herself had each been unhappy in their first marriages, after which, terrified at the thought of a second irrevocable union, and lest the conditions of the contract should kill their love, yet wishing to be together, they had literally not found the courage to repeat it, though they had attempted it two or three times. There-

fore, though in her own sense of the words she was a married
woman, in the landlady's sense she was not.

The housewife looked embarrassed, and went downstairs. Sue sat
by the window in a reverie, watching the rain. Her quiet was broken
by the noise of some one entering the house, and then the voices of a
man and woman in conversation in the passage below. The landlady's husband had arrived, and she was explaining to him the
incoming of the lodgers during his absence.

His voice rose in sudden anger. 'Now who wants such a woman
here? and perhaps a confinement! . . . Besides, didn't I say I
wouldn't have children? The hall and stairs fresh painted, to be
kicked about by them! You must have known all was not straight
with 'em — coming like that. Taking in a family when I said a single
man.'

The wife expostulated, but, as it seemed, the husband insisted on
his point; for presently a tap came to Sue's door, and the woman
appeared.

'I am sorry to tell you, ma'am,' she said, 'that I can't let you have
the room for the week after all. My husband objects; and therefore I
must ask you to go. I don't mind your staying over to-night, as it is
getting late in the afternoon; but I shall be glad if you can leave
early in the morning.'

Though she knew that she was entitled to the lodging for a week,
Sue did not wish to create a disturbance between the wife and
husband, and she said she would leave as requested. When the
landlady had gone Sue looked out of the window again. Finding that
the rain had ceased she proposed to the boy that, after putting the
little ones to bed, they should go out and search about for another
place, and bespeak it for the morrow, so as not to be so hard driven
then as they had been that day.

Therefore, instead of unpacking her boxes, just been sent on from
the station by Jude, they sallied out into the damp though not
unpleasant streets, Sue resolving not to disturb her husband with the
news of her notice to quit while he was perhaps worried in obtaining
a lodging for himself. In the company of the boy she wandered into
this street and into that; but though she tried a dozen different
houses she fared far worse alone than she had fared in Jude's
company, and could get nobody to promise her a room for the

following day. Every householder looked askance at such a woman and child inquiring for accommodation in the gloom.

'I ought not to be born, ought I?' said the boy with misgiving.

Thoroughly tired at last Sue returned to the place where she was not welcome, but where at least she had temporary shelter. In her absence Jude had left his address; but knowing how weak he still was she adhered to her determination not to disturb him till the next day.

SUE sat looking at the bare floor of the room, the house being little more than an old intramural cottage, and then she regarded the scene outside the uncurtained window. At some distance opposite, the outer walls of Sarcophagus College ⋆ — silent, black and windowless — threw their four centuries of gloom, bigotry, and decay into the little room she occupied, shutting out the moonlight by night and the sun by day. The outlines of Rubric College ⋆ also were discernible beyond the other, and the tower of a third further off still. She thought of the strange operation of a simple-minded man's ruling passion, that it should have led Jude, who loved her and the children so tenderly, to place them here in this depressing purlieu, because he was still haunted by his dream. Even now he did not distinctly hear the freezing negative that those scholared walls had echoed to his desire.

The failure to find another lodging, and the lack of room in this house for his father, had made a deep impression on the boy; — a brooding undemonstrative horror seemed to have seized him. The silence was broken by his saying: 'Mother, *what* shall we do tomorrow!'

'I don't know!' said Sue despondently. 'I am afraid this will trouble your father.'

'I wish father was quite well, and there had been room for him! Then it wouldn't matter so much! Poor father!'

'It wouldn't!'

'Can I do anything?'

'No! All is trouble, adversity and suffering!'

'Father went away to give us children room, didn't he?'

'Partly.'

'It would be better to be out o' the world than in it, wouldn't it?'

'It would almost, dear.'

' 'Tis because of us children, too, isn't it, that you can't get a good lodging?'

'Well – people do object to children sometimes.'

'Then if children make so much trouble, why do people have 'em?'

'O – because it is a law of nature.'

'But we don't ask to be born?'

'No indeed.'

'And what makes it worse with me is that you are not my real mother, and you needn't have had me unless you liked. I oughtn't to have come to 'ee – that's the real truth! I troubled 'em in Australia, and I trouble folk here. I wish I hadn't been born!'

'You couldn't help it, my dear.'

'I think that whenever children be born that are not wanted they should be killed directly, before their souls come to 'em, and not allowed to grow big and walk about!'

Sue did not reply. She was doubtfully pondering how to treat this too reflective child.

She at last concluded that, so far as circumstances permitted, she would be honest and candid with one who entered into her difficulties like an aged friend.

'There is going to be another in our family soon,' she hesitatingly remarked.

'How?'

'There is going to be another baby.'

'What!' The boy jumped up wildly. 'O God, mother, you've never a-sent for another; and such trouble with what you've got!'

'Yes, I have, I am sorry to say!' murmured Sue, her eyes glistening with suspended tears.

The boy burst out weeping. 'O you don't care, you don't care!' he cried in bitter reproach. 'How *ever* could you, mother, be so wicked and cruel as this, when you needn't have done it till we was better off, and father well! – To bring us all into *more* trouble! No room for us, and father a-forced to go away, and we turned out to-morrow; and yet you be going to have another of us soon! . . . Tis done o' purpose! – 'tis – 'tis!' He walked up and down sobbing.

'Y-you must forgive me, little Jude!' she pleaded, her bosom heaving now as much as the boy's. 'I can't explain – I will when you are older. It does seem – as if I had done it on purpose, now we are in these difficulties! I can't explain, dear! But it – is not quite on purpose — I can't help it!'

'Yes it is — it must be! For nobody would interfere with us, like that, unless you agreed! I won't forgive you, ever, ever! I'll never believe you care for me, or father, or any of us any more!'

He got up, and went away into the closet adjoining her room, in which a bed had been spread on the floor. There she heard him say: 'If we children was gone there'd be no trouble at all!'

'Don't think that, dear,' she cried, rather peremptorily. 'But go to sleep!'

The following morning she awoke at a little past six, and decided to get up and run across before breakfast to the inn which Jude had informed her to be his quarters, to tell him what had happened before he went out. She arose softly, to avoid disturbing the children, who, as she knew, must be fatigued by their exertions of yesterday.

She found Jude at breakfast in the obscure tavern he had chosen as a counterpoise to the expense of her lodging: and she explained to him her homelessness. He had been so anxious about her all night, he said. Somehow, now it was morning, the request to leave the lodgings did not seem such a depressing incident as it had seemed the night before, nor did even her failure to find another place affect her so deeply as at first. Jude agreed with her that it would not be worth while to insist upon her right to stay a week, but to take immediate steps for removal.

'You must all come to this inn for a day or two,' he said. 'It is a rough place, and it will not be so nice for the children, but we shall have more time to look round. There are plenty of lodgings in the suburbs — in my old quarter of Beersheba. Have breakfast with me now you are here, my bird. You are sure you are well? There will be plenty of time to get back and prepare the children's meal before they wake. In fact, I'll go with you.'

She joined Jude in a hasty meal, and in a quarter of an hour they started together, resolving to clear out from Sue's too respectable lodging immediately. On reaching the place and going upstairs she found that all was quiet in the children's room, and called to the landlady in timorous tones to please bring up the tea-kettle and something for their breakfast. This was perfunctorily done, and producing a couple of eggs which she had brought with her she put them into the boiling kettle, and summoned Jude to watch them for the youngsters, while she went to call them, it being now about half-past eight o'clock.

Jude stood bending over the kettle, with his watch in his hand, timing the eggs so that his back was turned to the little inner chamber where the children lay. A shriek from Sue suddenly caused him to start round. He saw that the door of the room, or rather closet — which had seemed to go heavily upon its hinges as she pushed it back — was open, and that Sue had sunk to the floor just within it. Hastening forward to pick her up he turned his eyes to the little bed spread on the boards; no children were there. He looked in bewilderment round the room. At the back of the door were fixed two hooks for hanging garments, and from these the forms of the two youngest children were suspended, by a piece of box-cord round each of their necks, while from a nail a few yards off the body of little Jude was hanging in a similar manner. An overturned chair was near the elder boy, and his glazed eyes were slanted into the room; but those of the girl and the baby boy were closed.

Half paralyzed by the strange and consummate horror of the scene he let Sue lie, cut the cords with his pocket-knife and threw the three children on the bed; but the feel of their bodies in the momentary handling seemed to say that they were dead. He caught up Sue, who was in fainting fits, and put her on the bed in the other room, after which he breathlessly summoned the landlady and ran out for a doctor.

When he got back Sue had come to herself, and the two helpless women, bending over the children in wild efforts to restore them, and the triplet of little corpses, formed a sight which overthrew his self-command. The nearest surgeon came in, but, as Jude had inferred, his presence was superfluous. The children were past saving, for though their bodies were still barely cold it was conjectured that they had been hanging more than an hour. The probability held by the parents later on, when they were able to reason on the case, was that the elder boy, on waking, looked into the outer room for Sue, and, finding her absent, was thrown into a fit of aggravated despondency that the events and information of the evening before had induced in his morbid temperament. Moreover a piece of paper was found upon the floor, on which was written, in the boy's hand, with the bit of lead pencil that he carried:

'Done because we are too menny.'

At sight of this Sue's nerves utterly gave way, an awful conviction that her discourse with the boy had been the main cause of the tragedy, throwing her into a convulsive agony which knew no abatement. They carried her away against her wish to a room on the lower floor; and there she lay, her slight figure shaken with her gasps, and her eyes staring at the ceiling, the woman of the house vainly trying to soothe her.

They could hear from this chamber the people moving about above, and she implored to be allowed to go back, and was only kept from doing so by the assurance that, if there were any hope, her presence might do harm, and the reminder that it was necessary to take care of herself lest she should endanger a coming life. Her inquiries were incessant, and at last Jude came down and told her there was no hope. As soon as she could speak she informed him what she had said to the boy, and how she thought herself the cause of this.

'No,' said Jude. 'It was in his nature to do it. The doctor says there are such boys springing up amongst us — boys of a sort unknown in the last generation — the outcome of new views of life. They seem to see all its terrors before they are old enough to have staying power to resist them. He says it is the beginning of the coming universal wish not to live.* He's an advanced man, the doctor: but he can give no consolation to—'

Jude had kept back his own grief on account of her; but he now broke down; and this stimulated Sue to efforts of sympathy which in some degree distracted her from her poignant self-reproach. When everybody was gone, she was allowed to see the children.

The boy's face expressed the whole tale of their situation. On that little shape had converged all the inauspiciousness and shadow which had darkened the first union of Jude, and all the accidents, mistakes, fears, errors of the last. He was their nodal point, their focus, their expression in a single term. For the rashness of those parents he had groaned, for their ill-assortment he had quaked, and for the misfortunes of these he had died.

When the house was silent, and they could do nothing but await the coroner's inquest, a subdued, large, low voice spread into the air of the room from behind the heavy walls at the back.

'What is it?' said Sue, her spasmodic breathing suspended.

'The organ of the College chapel. The organist practising I suppose. It's the anthem from the seventy-third Psalm; "Truly God is loving unto Israel." '

She sobbed again. 'O, O my babies! They had done no harm! Why should they have been taken away, and not I!'

There was another stillness — broken at last by two persons in conversation somewhere without.

'They are talking about us, no doubt!' moaned Sue. ' "We are made a spectacle unto the world, and to angels, and to men!" '

Jude listened — 'No — they are not talking of us,' he said. 'They are two clergymen of different views, arguing about the eastward position.* Good God — the eastward position, and all creation groaning!'

Then another silence, till she was seized with another uncontrollable fit of grief. 'There is something external to us which says, "You shan't!" First it said, "You shan't learn!" Then it said, "You shan't labour!" Now it says, "You shan't love!" '

He tried to soothe her by saying, 'That's bitter of you, darling.'

'But it's true!'

Thus they waited, and she went back again to her room. The baby's frock, shoes, and socks, which had been lying on a chair at the time of his death, she would not now have removed, though Jude would fain have got them out of her sight. But whenever he touched them she implored him to let them lie, and burst out almost savagely at the woman of the house when she also attempted to put them away.

Jude dreaded her dull apathetic silences almost more than her paroxysms. 'Why don't you speak to me, Jude?' she cried out, after one of these. 'Don't turn away from me! I can't *bear* the loneliness of being out of your looks!'

'There, dear; here I am,' he said, putting his face close to hers.

'Yes. . . . O my comrade, our perfect union — our two-in-oneness — is now stained with blood!'

'Shadowed by death — that's all.'

'Ah; but it was I who incited him really, though I didn't know I was doing it! I talked to the child as one should only talk to people of mature age. I said the world was against us, that it was better to be out of life than in it at this price; and he took it literally. And I told him I was going to have another child. It upset him. O how bitterly he upbraided me!'

'Why did you do it, Sue?'

'I can't tell. It was that I wanted to be truthful. I couldn't bear deceiving him as to the facts of life. And yet I wasn't truthful, for with a false delicacy I told him too obscurely. — Why was I half wiser than my fellow-women? and not entirely wiser! Why didn't I tell him pleasant untruths, instead of half realities? It was my want of self-control, so that I could neither conceal things nor reveal them!'

'Your plan might have been a good one for the majority of cases; only in our peculiar case it chanced to work badly perhaps. He must have known sooner or later.'

'And I was just making my baby darling a new frock; and now I shall never see him in it, and never talk to him any more! . . . My eyes are so swollen that I can scarcely see; and yet little more than a year ago I called myself happy! We went about loving each other too much — indulging ourselves to utter selfishness with each other! We said — do you remember? — that we would make a virtue of joy. I said it was Nature's intention, Nature's law and *raison d'être* that we should be joyful in what instincts she afforded us — instincts which civilization had taken upon itself to thwart. What dreadful things I said! And now Fate has given us this stab in the back for being such fools as to take Nature at her word!'

She sank into a quiet contemplation, till she said, 'It is best, perhaps, that they should be gone. — Yes — I see it is! Better that they should be plucked fresh than stay to wither away miserably!'

'Yes,' replied Jude. 'Some say that the elders should rejoice when their children die in infancy.'

'But they don't know! . . . O my babies, my babies, could you be alive now! You may say the boy wished to be out of life, or he wouldn't have done it. It was not unreasonable for him to die: it was part of his incurably sad nature, poor little fellow! But then the others — my *own* children and yours!'

Again Sue looked at the hanging little frock, and at the socks and shoes; and her figure quivered like a string. 'I am a pitiable creature,' she said, 'good neither for earth nor heaven any more! I am driven out of my mind by things! What ought to be done?' She stared at Jude, and tightly held his hand.

'Nothing can be done,' he replied. 'Things are as they are, and will be brought to their destined issue.'

She paused. 'Yes! Who said that?' she asked heavily.

'It comes in the chorus of the *Agamemnon*.* It has been in my mind continually since this happened.'

'My poor Jude — how you've missed everything! — you more than I, for I did get you! To think you should know that by your unassisted reading, and yet be in poverty and despair!'

After such momentary diversions her grief would return in a wave.

The jury duly came and viewed the bodies, the inquest was held; and next arrived the melancholy morning of the funeral. Accounts in the newspapers had brought to the spot curious idlers, who stood apparently counting the window-panes and the stones of the walls. Doubt of the real relations of the couple added zest to their curiosity. Sue had declared that she would follow the two little ones to the grave, but at the last moment she gave way, and the coffins were quietly carried out of the house while she was lying down. Jude got into the vehicle, and it drove away, much to the relief of the landlord, who now had only Sue and her luggage remaining on his hands, which he hoped to be also clear of later on in the day, and so to have freed his house from the exasperating notoriety it had acquired during the week through his wife's unlucky admission of these strangers. In the afternoon he privately consulted with the owner of the house, and they agreed that if any objection to it arose from the tragedy which had occurred there they would try to get its number changed.

When Jude had seen the two little boxes — one containing little Jude, and the other the two smallest — deposited in the earth he hastened back to Sue, who was still in her room, and he therefore did not disturb her just then. Feeling anxious, however, he went again about four o'clock. The woman thought she was still lying

down, but returned to him to say that she was not in her bedroom
after all. Her hat and jacket, too, were missing: she had gone out.
Jude hurried off to the public-house where he was sleeping. She had
not been there. Then bethinking himself of possibilities he went
along the road to the cemetery, which he entered, and crossed to
where the interments had recently taken place. The idlers who had
followed to the spot by reason of the tragedy were all gone now. A
man with a shovel in his hands was attempting to earth in the
common grave of the three children, but his arm was held back by
an expostulating woman who stood in the half-filled hole. It was Sue,
whose coloured clothing, which she had never thought of changing
for the mourning he had bought, suggested to the eye a deeper grief
than the conventional garb of bereavement could express.

'He's filling them in, and he shan't till I've seen my little ones
again!' she cried wildly when she saw Jude. 'I want to see them once
more. O Jude – please Jude – I want to see them! I didn't know you
would let them be taken away while I was asleep! You said perhaps I
should see them once more before they were screwed down; and
then you didn't, but took them away! O Jude, you are cruel to me
too!'

'She's been wanting me to dig out the grave again, and let her get
to the coffins,' said the man with the spade. 'She ought to be took
home, by the look o' her. She is hardly responsible, poor thing,
seemingly. Can't dig 'em up again now, ma'am. Do ye go home with
your husband, and take it quiet, and thank God that there'll be
another soon to swage* yer grief.'

But Sue kept asking piteously: 'Can't I see them once more – just
once! Can't I? Only just one little minute, Jude? It would not take
long! And I should be so glad, Jude! I will be so good, and not
disobey you ever any more, Jude, if you will let me? I would go
home quietly afterwards, and not want to see them any more! Can't
I? Why can't I?'

Thus she went on. Jude was thrown into such acute sorrow that
he almost felt he would try to get the man to accede. But it could do
no good, and might make her still worse; and he saw that it was
imperative to get her home at once. So he coaxed her, and whispered
tenderly, and put his arm round her to support her; till she helplessly gave in, and was induced to leave the cemetery.

He wished to obtain a fly to take her back in, but economy being so imperative she deprecated his doing so, and they walked along slowly, Jude in black crape, she in brown and red clothing. They were to have gone to a new lodging that afternoon, but Jude saw that it was not practicable, and in course of time they entered the now hated house. Sue was once got to bed, and the doctor sent for.

Jude waited all the evening downstairs. At a very late hour the intelligence was brought to him that a child had been prematurely born, and that it, like the others, was a corpse.

SUE was convalescent, though she had hoped for death, and Jude had again obtained work at his old trade. They were in other lodgings now, in the direction of Beersheba, and not far from the Church of Ceremonies – Saint Silas.

They would sit silent, more bodeful of the direct antagonism of things than of their insensate and stolid obstructiveness. Vague and quaint imaginings had haunted Sue in the days when her intellect scintillated like a star, that the world resembled a stanza or melody composed in a dream; it was wonderfully excellent to the half-aroused intelligence, but hopelessly absurd at the full waking; that the First Cause worked automatically like a somnambulist, and not reflectively like a sage; that at the framing of the terrestrial conditions there seemed never to have been contemplated such a development of emotional perceptiveness among the creatures subject to those conditions as that reached by thinking and educated humanity. But affliction makes opposing forces loom anthropomorphous; and those ideas were now exchanged for a sense of Jude and herself fleeing from a persecutor.

'We must conform!' she said mournfully. 'All the ancient wrath of the Power above us has been vented upon us, His poor creatures, and we must submit. There is no choice. We must. It is no use fighting against God!'

'It is only against man and senseless circumstance,' said Jude.

'True!' she murmured. 'What have I been thinking of! I am getting as superstitious as a savage! . . . But whoever or whatever our foe may be, I am cowed into submission. I have no more fighting strength left; ho more enterprise. I am beaten, beaten! . . . "We are made a spectacle unto the world, and to angels, and to men!" ∗ I am always saying that now.'

'I feel the same!'

'What shall we do? You are in work now; but remember, it may only be because our history and relations are not absolutely known.

'... Possibly, if they knew our marriage had not been formalized they would turn you out of your job as they did at Aldbrickham!'

'I hardly know. Perhaps they would hardly do that. However, I think that we ought to make it legal now — as soon as you are able to go out.'

'You think we ought?'

'Certainly.'

And Jude fell into thought. 'I have seemed to myself lately,' he said, 'to belong to that vast band of men shunned by the virtuous — the men called seducers. It amazes me when I think of it! I have not been conscious of it, or of any wrong-doing towards you, whom I love more than myself. Yet I *am* one of those men! I wonder if any other of them are the same purblind, simple creatures as I? ... Yes, Sue — that's what I am. I seduced you. ... You were a distinct type — a refined creature, intended by Nature to be left intact. But I couldn't leave you alone!'

'No, no, Jude!' she said quickly. 'Don't reproach yourself with being what you are not. If anybody is to blame it is I.'

'I supported you in your resolve to leave Phillotson; and without me perhaps you wouldn't have urged him to let you go.'

'I should have, just the same. As to ourselves the fact of our not having entered into a legal contract is the saving feature in our union. We have thereby avoided insulting, as it were, the solemnity of our first marriages.'

'Solemnity?' Jude looked at her with some surprise, and grew conscious that she was not the Sue of their earlier time.

'Yes,' she said, with a little quiver in her words, 'I have had dreadful fears, a dreadful sense of my own insolence of action. I have thought — that I am still his wife!'

'Whose?'

'Richard's.'

'Good God, dearest! — why?'

'O I can't explain! Only the thought comes to me.'

'It is your weakness — a sick fancy, without reason or meaning! Don't let it trouble you.'

Sue sighed uneasily.

As a set-off against such discussions as these there had come an improvement in their pecuniary position, which earlier in their

experience would have made them cheerful. Jude had quite unexpectedly found good employment at his old trade almost directly he
arrived, the summer weather suiting his fragile constitution; and
outwardly his days went on with that monotonous uniformity which
is in itself so grateful after vicissitude. People seemed to have
forgotten that he had ever shown any awkward aberrancies: and he
daily mounted to the parapets and copings of colleges he could
never enter, and renewed the crumbling freestones of mullioned
windows he would never look from, as if he had known no wish to
do otherwise.

There was this change in him; that he did not often go to any
service at the churches now. One thing troubled him more than any
other; that Sue and himself had mentally travelled in opposite
directions since the tragedy: events which had enlarged his own
views of life, laws, customs, and dogmas, had not operated in the
same manner on Sue's. She was no longer the same as in the
independent days, when her intellect played like lambent lightning
over conventions and formalities which he at that time respected,
though he did not now.

On a particular Sunday evening he came in rather late. She was
not at home, but she soon returned, when he found her silent and
meditative.

'What are you thinking of, little woman?' he asked curiously.

'O I can't tell clearly! I have thought that we have been selfish,
careless, even impious, in our courses, you and I. Our life has been a
vain attempt at self-delight. But self-abnegation is the higher road.
We should mortify the flesh — the terrible flesh — the curse of
Adam!'

'Sue!' he murmured. 'What has come over you?'

'We ought to be continually sacrificing ourselves on the altar of
duty! But I have always striven to do what has pleased me. I well
deserved the scourging I have got! I wish something would take the
evil right out of me, and all my monstrous errors, and all my sinful
ways!'

'Sue — my own too suffering dear! — there's no evil woman in
you. Your natural instincts are perfectly healthy; not quite so
impassioned, perhaps, as I could wish; but good, and dear, and pure.
And as I have often said, you are absolutely the most ethereal, least

sensual woman I ever knew to exist without inhuman sexlessness. Why do you talk in such a changed way? We have not been selfish, except when no one could profit by our being otherwise. You used to say that human nature was noble and long-suffering, not vile and corrupt, and at last I thought you spoke truly. And now you seem to take such a much lower view!'

'I want a humble heart; and a chastened mind; and I have never had them yet!'

'You have been fearless, both as a thinker and as a feeler, and you deserved more admiration than I gave. I was too full of narrow dogmas at that time to see it.'

'Don't say that, Jude! I wish my every fearless word and thought could be rooted out of my history. Self-renunciation – that's everything! I cannot humiliate myself too much. I should like to prick myself all over with pins and bleed out the badness that's in me!'

'Hush!' he said, pressing her little face against his breast as if she were an infant. 'It is bereavement that has brought you to this! Such remorse is not for you, my sensitive plant,* but for the wicked ones of the earth – who never feel it!'

'I ought not to stay like this,' she murmured, when she had remained in the position a long while.

'Why not?'

'It is indulgence.'

'Still on the same tack! But is there anything better on earth than that we should love one another?'

'Yes. It depends on the sort of love; and yours – ours – is the wrong.'

'I won't have it, Sue! Come, when do you wish our marriage to be signed in a vestry?'

She paused, and looked up uneasily. 'Never,' she whispered.

Not knowing the whole of her meaning he took the objection serenely, and said nothing. Several minutes elapsed, and he thought she had fallen asleep; but he spoke softly, and found that she was wide awake all the time. She sat upright and sighed.

'There is a strange, indescribable perfume or atmosphere about you to-night, Sue,' he said. 'I mean not only mentally, but about your clothes, also. A sort of vegetable scent, which I seem to know, yet cannot remember.'

366   JUDE THE OBSCURE

'It is incense.'

'Incense?'

'I have been to the service at St Silas', and I was in the fumes of it.'

'Oh – St Silas'.'

'Yes. I go there sometimes.'

'Indeed. You go there!'

'You see, Jude, it is lonely here in the week-day mornings, when you are at work, and I think and think of – of my—' She stopped till she could control the lumpiness of her throat. 'And I have taken to go in there, as it is so near.'

'O well – of course, I say nothing against it. Only it is odd, for you. They little think what sort of chiel is amang them!' *

'What do you mean, Jude?'

'Well – a sceptic, to be plain.'

'How can you pain me so, dear Jude, in my trouble! Yet I know you didn't mean it. But you ought not to say that.'

'I won't. But I am much surprised!'

'Well – I want to tell you something else, Jude. You won't be angry, will you? I have thought of it a good deal since my babies died. I don't think I ought to be your wife – or as your wife – any longer.'

'What? ... But you *are*!'

'From your point of view; but—'

'Of course we were afraid of the ceremony, and a good many others would have been in our places, with such strong reasons for fears. But experience has proved how we misjudged ourselves, and overrated our infirmities; and if you are beginning to respect rites and ceremonies, as you seem to be, I wonder you don't say it shall be carried out instantly? You certainly *are* my wife, Sue, in all but law. What do you mean by what you said?'

'I don't think I am!'

'Not? But suppose we *had* gone through the ceremony? Would you feel that you were then?'

'No. I should not feel even then that I was. I should feel worse than I do now.'

'Why so – in the name of all that's perverse, my dear?'

Because I am Richard's.'

'Ah — you hinted that absurd fancy to me before!'

'It was only an impression with me then; I feel more and more convinced as time goes on that — I belong to him, or to nobody.'

'My good heavens — how we are changing places!'

'Yes. Perhaps so.'

Some few days later, in the dusk of the summer evening, they were sitting in the same small room downstairs, when a knock came to the front door of the carpenter's house where they were lodging, and in a few moments there was a tap at the door of their room. Before they could open it the comer did so, and a woman's form appeared.

'Is Mr Fawley here?'

Jude and Sue started as he mechanically replied in the affirmative, for the voice was Arabella's.

He formally requested her to come in, and she sat down in the window bench, where they could distinctly see her outline against the light; but no characteristic that enabled them to estimate her general aspect and air. Yet something seemed to denote that she was not quite so comfortably circumstanced, nor so bouncingly attired, as she had been during Cartlett's life-time.

The three attempted an awkward conversation about the tragedy, of which Jude had felt it to be his duty to inform her immediately, though she had never replied to his letter.

'I have just come from the cemetery,' she said. 'I inquired and found the child's grave. I couldn't come to the funeral — thank you for inviting me all the same. I read all about it in the papers, and I felt I wasn't wanted. ... No — I couldn't come to the funeral,' repeated Arabella, who, seeming utterly unable to reach the ideal of a catastrophic manner, fumbled with iterations. 'But I am glad I found the grave. As 'tis your trade, Jude, you'll be able to put up a handsome stone to 'em.'

'I shall put up a headstone,' said Jude drearily.

'He was my child, and naturally I feel for him.'

'I hope so. We all did.'

'The others that weren't mine I didn't feel so much for, as was natural.'

'Of course.'

A sigh came from the dark corner where Sue sat.

'I had often wished I had mine with me,' continued Mrs Cartlett. 'Perhaps 'twouldn't have happened then! But of course I didn't wish to take him away from your wife.'

'I am not his wife,' came from Sue.

The unexpectedness of her words struck Jude silent.

'O I beg your pardon, I'm sure,' said Arabella. 'I thought you were!'

Jude had known from the quality of Sue's tone that her new and transcendental views lurked in her words; but all except their obvious meaning was, naturally, missed by Arabella. The latter, after evincing that she was struck by Sue's avowal, recovered herself, and went on to talk with placid bluntness about 'her' boy, for whom, though in his lifetime she had shown no care at all, she now exhibited a ceremonial mournfulness that was apparently sustaining to the conscience. She alluded to the past, and in making some remark appealed again to Sue. There was no answer: Sue had invisibly left the room.

'She said she was not your wife?' resumed Arabella in another voice. 'Why should she do that?'

'I cannot inform you,' said Jude shortly.

'She is, isn't she? She once told me so.'

'I don't criticize what she says.'

'Ah – I see! Well, my time is up. I am staying here to-night, and thought I could do no less than call, after our mutual affliction. I am sleeping at the place where I used to be barmaid, and to-morrow I go back to Alfredston. Father is come home again, and I am living with him.'

'He has returned from Australia?' said Jude with languid curiosity.

'Yes. Couldn't get on there. Had a rough time of it. Mother died of dys – what do you call it – in the hot weather, and father and two of the young ones have just got back. He has got a cottage near the old place, and for the present I am keeping house for him.'

Jude's former wife had maintained a stereotyped manner of strict good breeding even now that Sue was gone, and limited her stay to a number of minutes that should accord with the highest respectability. When she had departed Jude, much relieved, went to the stairs and called Sue – feeling anxious as to what had become of her.

There was no answer, and the carpenter who kept the lodgings said she had not come in. Jude was puzzled, and became quite alarmed at her absence, for the hour was growing late. The carpenter called his wife, who conjectured that Sue might have gone to St Silas' church, as she often went there.

'Surely not at this time o' night?' said Jude. 'It is shut.'

'She knows somebody who keeps the key, and she has it whenever she wants it.'

'How long has she been going on with this?'

'Oh, some few weeks, I think.'

Jude went vaguely in the direction of the church, which he had never once approached since he lived out that way years before, when his young opinions were more mystical than they were now. The spot was deserted, but the door was certainly unfastened; he lifted the latch without noise, and pushing to the door behind him, stood absolutely still inside. The prevalent silence seemed to contain a faint sound, explicable as a breathing, or a sobbing, which came from the other end of the building. The floor-cloth deadened his footsteps as he moved in that direction through the obscurity, which was broken only by the faintest reflected night-light from without.

High overhead, above the chancel steps, Jude could discern a huge, solidly constructed Latin cross — as large, probably, as the original it was designed to commemorate. It seemed to be suspended in the air by invisible wires; it was set with large jewels, which faintly glimmered in some weak ray caught from outside, as the cross swayed to and fro in a silent and scarcely perceptible motion. Underneath, upon the floor, lay what appeared to be a heap of black clothes, and from this was repeated the sobbing that he had heard before. It was his Sue's form, prostrate on the paving.

'Sue!' he whispered.

Something white disclosed itself; she had turned up her face.

'What — do you want with me here, Jude?' she said almost sharply. 'You shouldn't come! I wanted to be alone! Why did you intrude here?'

'How can you ask!' he retorted in quick reproach, for his full heart was wounded to its centre at this attitude of hers towards him. 'Why do I come? Who has a right to come, I should like to know, if I have not! I, who love you better than my own self — better — O far

better — than you have loved me! What made you leave me to come
here alone?'

'Don't criticize me, Jude — I can't bear it! — I have often told you
so. You must take me as I am. I am a wretch — broken by my
distractions! I couldn't *bear* it when Arabella came — I felt so utterly
miserable I had to come away. She seems to be your wife still, and
Richard to be my husband!'

'But they are nothing to us!'

'Yes, dear friend, they are. I see marriage differently now. My
babies have been taken from me to show me this! Arabella's child
killing mine was a judgment — the right slaying the wrong. What,
what shall I do! I am such a vile creature — too worthless to mix
with ordinary human beings!'

'This is terrible!' said Jude, verging on tears. 'It is monstrous and
unnatural for you to be so remorseful when you have done no
wrong!'

'Ah — you don't know my badness!'

He returned vehemently: 'I do! Every atom and dreg of it! You
make me hate Christianity, or mysticism, or Sacerdotalism, or
whatever it may be called, if it's that which has caused this deterior-
ation in you. That a woman-poet, a woman-seer, a woman whose
soul shone like a diamond — whom all the wise of the world would
have been proud of, if they could have known you — should degrade
herself like this! I am glad I had nothing to do with Divinity — damn
glad — if it's going to ruin you in this way!'

'You are angry, Jude, and unkind to me, and don't see how things
are.'

'Then come along home with me, dearest, and perhaps I shall. I
am over-burdened — and you, too, are unhinged just now.' He put
his arm round her and lifted her; but though she came, she preferred
to walk without his support.

'I don't dislike you, Jude,' she said in a sweet and imploring
voice. 'I love you as much as ever! Only — I ought not to love you —
any more. O I must not any more!'

'I can't own it.'

'But I have made up my mind that I am not your wife! I belong to
him — I sacramentally joined myself to him for life. Nothing can
alter it!'

'But surely we are man and wife, if ever two people were in this world? Nature's own marriage it is, unquestionably!'

'But not Heaven's. Another was made for me there, and ratified eternally in the church at Melchester.'

'Sue, Sue — affliction has brought you to this unreasonable state! After converting me to your views on so many things, to find you suddenly turn to the right-about like this — for no reason whatever, confounding all you have formerly said through sentiment merely! You root out of me what little affection and reverence I had left in me for the Church as an old acquaintance. . . . What I can't understand in you is your extraordinary blindness now to your old logic. Is it peculiar to you, or is it common to woman? Is a woman a thinking unit at all, or a fraction always wanting its integer? How you argued that marriage was only a clumsy contract — which it is — how you showed all the objections to it — all the absurdities! If two and two made four when we were happy together, surely they make four now? I can't understand it, I repeat!'

'Ah, dear Jude; that's because you are like a totally deaf man observing people listening to music. You say "What are they regarding? Nothing is there." But something is.'

'That is a hard saying from you; and not a true parallel! You threw off old husks of prejudices, and taught me to do it; and now you go back upon yourself. I confess I am utterly stultified in my estimate of you.'

'Dear friend, my only friend, don't be hard with me! I can't help being as I am, I am convinced I am right — that I see the light at last. But O, how to profit by it!'

They walked along a few more steps till they were outside the building, and she had returned the key. 'Can this be the girl,' said Jude when she came back, feeling a slight renewal of elasticity now that he was in the open street; 'can this be the girl who brought the Pagan deities into this most Christian city? — who mimicked Miss Fontover when she crushed them with her heel? — quoted Gibbon, and Shelley, and Mill? Where are dear Apollo, and dear Venus now!'

'O don't, don't be so cruel to me, Jude, and I so unhappy!' she sobbed. 'I can't bear it! I was in error — I cannot reason with you. I was wrong — proud in my own conceit! Arabella's coming was the finish. Don't satirize me: it cuts like a knife!'

He flung his arms round her and kissed her passionately there in the silent street, before she could hinder him. They went on till they came to a little coffee-house. 'Jude,' she said with suppressed tears, 'would you mind getting a lodging here?'

'I will — if, if you really wish? But do you? Let me go to our door and understand you.'

He went and conducted her in. She said she wanted no supper, and went in the dark upstairs and struck a light. Turning she found that Jude had followed her, and was standing at the chamber door. She went to him, put her hand in his, and said 'Good-night.'

'But Sue! Don't we live here?'

'You said you would do as I wished!'

'Yes. Very well! ... Perhaps it was wrong of me to argue distastefully as I have done! Perhaps as we couldn't conscientiously marry at first in the old-fashioned way, we ought to have parted. Perhaps the world is not illuminated enough for such experiments as ours! Who were we, to think we could act as pioneers!'

'I am so glad you see that much, at any rate. I never deliberately meant to do as I did. I slipped into my false position through jealousy and agitation!'

'But surely through love — you loved me?'

'Yes. But I wanted to let it stop there, and go on always as mere lovers; until—'

'But people in love couldn't live for ever like that!'

'Women could: men can't, because they — won't. An average woman is in this superior to an average man — that she never instigates, only responds. We ought to have lived in mental comunion, and no more.'

'I was the unhappy cause of the change, as I have said before! ... Well, as you will! ... But human nature can't help being itself.'

'O yes — that's just what it has to learn — self-mastery.'

'I repeat — if either were to blame it was not you but I.'

'No — it was I. Your wickedness was only the natural man's desire to possess the woman. Mine was not the reciprocal wish till envy stimulated me to oust Arabella. I had thought I ought in charity to let you approach me — that it was damnably selfish to torture you as I did my other friend. But I shouldn't have given way if you hadn't broken me down by making me fear you would go back to her. . . . But don't let us say any more about it! Jude, will you leave me to myself now?'

'Yes. . . . But Sue — my wife, as you are!' he burst out; 'my old reproach to you was, after all, a true one. You have never loved me as I love you — never — never! Yours is not a passionate heart — your heart does not burn in a flame! You are, upon the whole, a sort of fay, or sprite — not a woman!'

'At first I did not love you, Jude; that I own. When I first knew you I merely wanted you to love me. I did not exactly flirt with you; but that inborn craving which undermines some women's morals almost more than unbridled passion — the craving to attract and captivate, regardless of the injury it may do the man — was in me; and when I found I had caught you, I was frightened. And then — I don't know how it was — I couldn't bear to let you go — possibly to Arabella again — and so I got to love you, Jude. But you see, however fondly it ended, it began in the selfish and cruel wish to make your heart ache for me without letting mine ache for you.'

'And now you add to your cruelty by leaving me!'

'Ah — yes! The further I flounder, the more harm I do!'

'O Sue!' said he with a sudden sense of his own danger. 'Do not do an immoral thing for moral reasons! You have been my social salvation. Stay with me for humanity's sake! You know what a weak fellow I am. My two Arch Enemies you know — my weakness for womankind and my impulse to strong liquor. Don't abandon me to them, Sue, to save your own soul only! They have been kept entirely at a distance since you became my guardian-angel! Since I have had you I have been able to go into any temptations of the sort, without risk. Isn't my safety worth a little sacrifice of dogmatic principle? I am in terror lest, if you leave me, it will be with me another case of the pig that was washed turning back to his wallowing in the mire!'

Sue burst out weeping. 'O but you must not, Jude! You won't! I'll pray for you night and day!'

'Well — never mind; don't grieve,' said Jude generously. 'I did suffer, God knows, about you at that time; and now I suffer again. But perhaps not so much as you. The woman mostly gets the worst of it in the long run!'

'She does.'

'Unless she is absolutely worthless and contemptible. And this one is not that, anyhow!'

Sue drew a nervous breath or two. 'She is — I fear! ... Now Jude — good-night, — please!'

'I mustn't stay? — Not just once more? As it has been so many times — O Sue, my wife, why not!'

'No — no — not wife! ... I am in your hands, Jude — don't tempt me back now I have advanced so far!'

'Very well. I do your bidding. I owe that to you, darling, in penance for how I over-ruled it at the first time. My God, how selfish I was! Perhaps — perhaps I spoilt one of the highest and purest loves that ever existed between man and woman! ... Then let the veil of our temple be rent in two from this hour!' *

He went to the bed, removed one of the pair of pillows thereon, and flung it to the floor.

Sue looked at him, and bending over the bed-rail wept silently. 'You don't see that it is a matter of conscience with me, and not of dislike to you!' she brokenly murmured. 'Dislike to you! But I can't say any more — it breaks my heart — it will be undoing all I have begun! Jude — good-night!'

'Good-night,' he said, and turned to go.

'O but you shall kiss me!' said she, starting up. 'I can't — bear—!'

He clasped her, and kissed her weeping face as he had scarcely ever done before, and they remained in silence till she said, 'Good-bye, good-bye!' And then gently pressing him away she got free, trying to mitigate the sadness by saying: 'We'll be dear friends just the same, Jude, won't we? And we'll see each other sometimes — Yes! — and forget all this, and try to be as we were long ago?'

Jude did not permit himself to speak, but turned and descended the stairs.

THE man whom Sue, in her mental volte-face, was now regarding as her inseparable husband, lived still at Marygreen.

On the day before the tragedy of the children, Phillotson had seen both her and Jude as they stood in the rain at Christminster watching the procession to the Theatre. But he had said nothing of it at the moment to his companion Gillingham, who, being an old friend, was staying with him at the village aforesaid, and had, indeed, suggested the day's trip to Christminster.

'What are you thinking of?' said Gillingham, as they went home. 'The University degree you never obtained?'

'No, no,' said Phillotson gruffly. 'Of somebody I saw to-day.' In a moment he added, 'Susanna.'

'I saw her, too,'

'You said nothing.'

'I didn't wish to draw your attention to her. But, as you did see her, you should have said: "How d'ye do, my dear-that-was?"'

'Ah, well. I might have. But what do you think of this: I have good reason for supposing that she was innocent when I divorced her — that I was all wrong. Yes, indeed! Awkward, isn't it?'

'She has taken care to set you right since, anyhow, apparently.'

'H'm. That's a cheap sneer. I ought to have waited, unquestionably.'

At the end of the week, when Gillingham had gone back to his school near Shaston, Phillotson, as was his custom, went to Alfredston market; ruminating again on Arabella's intelligence as he walked down the long hill which he had known before Jude knew it, though his history had not beaten so intensely upon its incline. Arrived in the town he bought his usual weekly local paper; and when he had sat down in an inn to refresh himself for the five miles' walk back, he pulled the paper from his pocket and read awhile. The account of the 'Strange suicide of a stone-mason's children' met his eye.

Unimpassioned as he was, it impressed him painfully, and puzzled him not a little, for he could not understand the age of the elder child being what it was stated to be. However, there was no doubt that the newspaper report was in some way true.

'Their cup of sorrow is now full!' he said: and thought and thought of Sue, and what she had gained by leaving him.

Arabella having made her home at Alfredston, and the schoolmaster coming to market there every Saturday, it was not wonderful that in a few weeks they met again — the precise time being just after her return from Christminster, where she had stayed much longer than she had at first intended, keeping an interested eye on Jude, though Jude had seen no more of her. Phillotson was on his way homeward when he encountered Arabella, and she was approaching the town.

'You like walking out this way, Mrs Cartlett?' he said.

'I've just begun to again,' she replied. 'It is where I lived as maid and wife, and all the past things of my life that are interesting to my feelings are mixed up with this road. And they have been stirred up in me too, lately; for I've been visiting at Christminster. Yes; I've seen Jude.'

'Ah! How do they bear their terrible affliction?'

'In a ve-ry strange way — ve-ry strange! She don't live with him any longer. I only heard of it as a certainty just before I left; though I had thought things were drifting that way from their manner when I called on them.'

'Not live with her husband? Why, I should have thought 'twould have united them more.'

'He's not her husband, after all. She has never really married him although they have passed as man and wife so long. And now, instead of this sad event making 'em hurry up, and get the thing done legally, she's took in a queer religious way, just as I was in my affliction at losing Cartlett, only hers is of a more 'sterical sort than mine. And she says, so I was told, that she's your wife in the eye of Heaven and the Church — yours only; and can't be anybody else's by any act of man.'

'Ah — indeed? . . . Separated, have they!'

'You see, the eldest boy was mine——'

'O — yours!'

'Yes, poor little fellow – born in lawful wedlock, thank God. And perhaps she feels, over and above other things, that I ought to have been in her place. I can't say. However, as for me, I am soon off from here. I've got father to look after now, and we can't live in such a humdrum place as this. I hope soon to be in a bar again at Christminster, or some other big town.'

They parted. When Phillotson had ascended the hill a few steps he stopped, hastened back, and called her.

'What is, or was, their address?'

Arabella gave it.

'Thank you. Good afternoon.'

Arabella smiled grimly as she resumed her way, and practised dimple-making all along the road from where the pollard windows begin to the old almshouses in the first street of the town.

Meanwhile Phillotson ascended to Marygreen, and for the first time during a lengthened period he lived with a forward eye. On crossing under the large trees of the green to the humble school-house to which he had been reduced he stood a moment, and pictured Sue coming out of the door to meet him. No man had ever suffered more inconvenience from his own charity, Christian or heathen, than Phillotson had done in letting Sue go. He had been knocked about from pillar to post at the hands of the virtuous almost beyond endurance; he had been nearly starved, and was now dependent entirely upon the very small stipend from the school of this village (where the parson had got ill-spoken of for befriending him). He had often thought of Arabella's remarks that he should have been more severe with Sue, that her recalcitrant spirit would soon have been broken. Yet such was his obstinate and illogical disregard of opinion, and of the principles in which he had been trained, that his convictions on the rightness of his course with his wife had not been disturbed.

Principles which could be subverted by feeling in one direction were liable to the same catastrophe in another. The instincts which had allowed him to give Sue her liberty now enabled him to regard her as none the worse for her life with Jude. He wished for her still, in his curious way, if he did not love her, and, apart from policy, soon felt that he would be gratified to have her again as his, always provided that she came willingly.

But artifice was necessary, he had found, for stemming the cold
and inhumane blast of the world's contempt. And here were the
materials ready made. By getting Sue back and re-marrying her on
the respectable plea of having entertained erroneous views of her,
and gained his divorce wrongfully, he might acquire some comfort,
resume his old courses, perhaps return to the Shaston school, if not
even to the Church as a licentiate.

He thought he would write to Gillingham to inquire his views,
and what he thought of his, Phillotson's, sending a letter to her.
Gillingham replied, naturally, that now she was gone it were best to
let her be; and considered that if she were anybody's wife she was
the wife of the man to whom she had borne three children and owed
such tragical adventures. Probably, as his attachment to her seemed
unusually strong, the singular pair would make their union legal in
course of time, and all would be well, and decent, and in order.

'But they won't — Sue won't!' exclaimed Phillotson to himself.
'Gillingham is so matter-of-fact. She's affected by Christminster
sentiment and teaching. I can see her views on the indissolubility of
marriage well enough, and I know where she got them. They are not
mine; but I shall make use of them to further mine.'

He wrote a brief reply to Gillingham. 'I know I am entirely
wrong, but I don't agree with you. As to her having lived with and
had three children by him, my feeling is (though I can advance no
logical or moral defence of it, on the old lines) that it has done little
more than finish her education. I shall write to her, and learn
whether what that woman said is true or no.'

As he had made up his mind to do this before he had written to
his friend, there had not been much reason for writing to the latter
at all. However, it was Phillotson's way to act thus.

He accordingly addressed a carefully considered epistle to Sue,
and, knowing her emotional temperament, threw a Rhadamanthine
strictness * into the lines here and there, carefully hiding his heter-
odox feelings, not to frighten her. He stated that, it having come to
his knowledge that her views had considerably changed, he felt
compelled to say that his own, too, were largely modified by events
subsequent to their parting. He would not conceal from her that
passionate love had little to do with his communication. It arose
from a wish to make their lives, if not a success, at least no such

disastrous failure as they threatened to become, through his acting on what he had considered at the time a principle of justice, charity, and reason.

To indulge one's instinctive and uncontrolled sense of justice and right, was not, he had found, permitted with impunity in an old civilization like ours. It was necessary to act under an acquired and cultivated sense of the same, if you wished to enjoy an average share of comfort and honour; and to let crude loving-kindness take care of itself.

He suggested that she should come to him there at Marygreen.

On second thoughts he took out the last paragraph but one; and having re-written the letter he despatched it immediately, and in some excitement awaited the issue.

A few days after a figure moved through the white fog which enveloped the Beersheba suburb of Christminster, towards the quarter in which Jude Fawley had taken up his lodging since his division from Sue. A timid knock sounded upon the door of his abode.

It was evening – so he was at home; and by a species of divination he jumped up and rushed to the door himself.

'Will you come out with me? I would rather not come in. I want to – to talk with you – and to go with you to the cemetery.'

It had been in the trembling accents of Sue that these words came. Jude put on his hat. 'It is dreary for you to be out,' he said. 'But if you prefer not to come in, I don't mind.'

'Yes – I do. I shall not keep you long.'

Jude was too much affected to go on talking at first; she, too, was now such a mere cluster of nerves that all initiatory power seemed to have left her, and they proceeded through the fog like Acherontic shades * for a long while, without sound or gesture.

'I want to tell you,' she presently said, her voice now quick, now slow, 'so that you may not hear of it by chance. I am going back to Richard. He has – so magnanimously – agreed to forgive all.'

'Going back? How can you go—'

'He is going to marry me again. That is for form's sake, and to satisfy the world, which does not see things as they are. But of course I *am* his wife already. Nothing has changed that.'

He turned upon her with an anguish that was well-nigh fierce.

'But you are *my* wife! Yes, you are. You know it. I have always regretted that feint of ours in going away and pretending to come back legally married, to save appearances. I loved you, and you loved me; and we closed with each other; and that made the marriage. We still love — you as well as I — I *know* it, Sue! Therefore our marriage is not cancelled.'

'Yes; I know how you see it,' she answered with despairing self-suppression. 'But I am going to marry him again, as it would be called by you. Strictly speaking you too, — don't mind my saying it, Jude! — you should take back — Arabella.'

'I should? Good God — what next! But how if you and I had married legally, as we were on the point of doing?'

'I should have felt just the same — that ours was not a marriage. And I would go back to Richard without repeating the sacrament, if he asked me. But "the world and its ways have a certain worth" * (I suppose): therefore I concede a repetition of the ceremony.... Don't crush all the life out of me by satire and argument, I implore you! I was strongest once, I know, and perhaps I treated you cruelly. But Jude, return good for evil! I am the weaker now. Don't retaliate upon me, but be kind. O be kind to me — a poor wicked woman who is trying to mend!'

He shook his head hopelessly, his eyes wet. The blow of her bereavement seemed to have destroyed her reasoning faculty. The once keen vision was dimmed. 'All wrong, all wrong!' he said huskily. 'Error — perversity! It drives me out of my senses. Do you care for him? Do you love him? You know you don't! It will be a fanatic prostitution — God forgive me, yes — that's what it will be!'

'I don't love him — I must, must, own it, in deepest remorse! But I shall try to learn to love him by obeying him.'

Jude argued, urged, implored; but her conviction was proof against all. It seemed to be the one thing on earth on which she was firm, and that her firmness in this had left her tottering in every other impulse and wish she possessed.

'I have been considerate enough to let you know the whole truth, and to tell it you myself,' she said in cut tones; 'that you might not consider yourself slighted by hearing of it at second-hand. I have even owned the extreme fact that I do not love him. I did not think you would be so rough with me for doing so! I was going to ask you. . . .'

'To give you away?'

'No. To send — my boxes to me — if you would. But I suppose you won't.'

'Why, of course I will. What — isn't he coming to fetch you — to marry you from here? He won't condescend to do that?'

'No — I won't let him. I go to him voluntarily, just as I went away from him. We are to be married at his little church at Marygreen.'

She was so sadly sweet in what he called her wrong-headedness that Jude could not help being moved to tears more than once for pity of her. 'I never knew such a woman for doing impulsive penances as you, Sue! No sooner does one expect you to go straight on, as the one rational proceeding, than you double round the corner!'

'Ah, well; let that go! . . . Jude, I must say good-bye! But I wanted you to go to the cemetery with me. Let our farewell be there — beside the graves of those who died to bring home to me the error of my views.'

They turned in the direction of the place, and the gate was opened to them on application. Sue had been there often, and she knew the way to the spot in the dark. They reached it, and stood still.

'It is here — I should like to part,' said she.

'So be it!'

'Don't think me hard because I have acted on conviction. Your generous devotion to me is unparalleled, Jude! Your worldly failure, if you have failed, is to your credit rather than to your blame. Remember that the best and greatest among mankind are those who do themselves no worldly good. Every successful man is more or less a selfish man. The devoted fail. . . . "Charity seeketh not her own." '*

'In that chapter we are at one, ever beloved darling, and on it we'll part friends. Its verses will stand fast when all the rest that you call religion has passed away!'

'Well — don't discuss it. Good-bye, Jude; my fellow-sinner, and kindest friend!'

'Good-bye, my mistaken wife. Good-bye!'

THE next afternoon the familiar Christminster fog still hung over all things. Sue's slim shape was only just discernible going towards the station.

Jude had no heart to go to his work that day. Neither could he go anywhere in the direction by which she would be likely to pass. He went in an opposite one, to a dreary, strange, flat scene, where boughs dripped, and coughs and consumption lurked, and where he had never been before.

'Sue's gone from me – gone!' he murmured miserably.

She in the meantime had left by the train, and reached Alfredston Road, where she entered the steam-tram * and was conveyed into the town. It had been her request to Phillotson that he should not meet her. She wished, she said, to come to him voluntarily, to his very house and hearthstone.

It was Friday evening, which had been chosen because the schoolmaster was disengaged at four o'clock that day till the Monday morning following. The little car she hired at The Bear * to drive her to Marygreen set her down at the end of the lane, half-a-mile from the village, by her desire, and preceded her to the schoolhouse with such portion of her luggage as she had brought. On its return she encountered it, and asked the driver if he had found the master's house open. The man informed her that he had, and that her things had been taken in by the schoolmaster himself.

She could now enter Marygreen without exciting much observation. She crossed by the well and under the trees to the pretty new school on the other side, and lifted the latch of the dwelling without knocking. Phillotson stood in the middle of the room, awaiting her, as requested.

'I've come, Richard,' said she, looking pale and shaken, and sinking into a chair. 'I cannot believe – you forgive your – wife!'

'Everything, darling Susanna,' said Phillotson.

She started at the endearment, though it had been spoken

advisedly without fervour. Then she nerved herself again.

'My children — are dead — and it is right that they should be! I am glad — almost. They were sin-begotten. They were sacrificed to teach me how to live! — their death was the first stage of my purification. That's why they have not died in vain! . . . You will take me back?'

He was so stirred by her pitiful words and tone that he did more than he had meant to do. He bent and kissed her cheek.

Sue imperceptibly shrank away, her flesh quivering under the touch of his lips.

Phillotson's heart sank, for desire was renascent in him. 'You still have an aversion to me!'

'O no, dear — I — have been driving through the damp, and I was chilly!' she said, with a hurried smile of apprehension. 'When are we going to have the marriage? Soon?'

'To-morrow morning, early, I thought — if you really wish. I am sending round to the vicar to let him know you are come. I have told him all, and he highly approves — he says it will bring our lives to a triumphant and satisfactory issue. But — are you sure of yourself? It is not too late to refuse now if — you think you can't bring yourself to it, you know?'

'Yes, yes, I can! I want it done quick. Tell him, tell him at once! My strength is tried by the undertaking — I can't wait long!'

'Have something to eat and drink then, and go over to your room at Mrs Edlin's. I'll tell the vicar half-past eight to-morrow, before anybody is about — if that's not too soon for you? My friend Gillingham is here to help us in the ceremony. He's been good enough to come all the way from Shaston at great inconvenience to himself.'

Unlike a woman in ordinary, whose eye is so keen for material things, Sue seemed to see nothing of the room they were in, or any detail of her environment. But on moving across the parlour to put down her muff she uttered a little 'O!' and grew paler than before. Her look was that of the condemned criminal who catches sight of his coffin.

'What?' said Phillotson.

The flap of the bureau chanced to be open, and in placing her muff upon it her eye had caught a document which lay there. 'O — only a — funny surprise!' she said, trying to laugh away her cry as she came back to the table.

'Ah! yes,' said Phillotson. 'The license. . . . It has just come.'

Gillingham now joined them from his room above, and Sue nervously made herself agreeable to him by talking on whatever she thought likely to interest him, except herself, though that interested him most of all. She obediently eat some supper, and prepared to leave for her lodging hard by. Phillotson crossed the green with her, bidding her good-night at Mrs Edlin's door.

The old woman accompanied Sue to her temporary quarters, and helped her to unpack. Among other things she laid out a nightgown tastefully embroidered.

'O – I didn't know *that* was put in!' said Sue quickly. 'I didn't mean it to be. Here is a different one.' She handed a new and absolutely plain garment, of coarse and unbleached calico.

'But this is the prettiest,' said Mrs Edlin. 'That one is no better than very sackcloth o' Scripture!'

'Yes – I meant it to be. Give me the other.'

She took it, and began rending it with all her might, the tears resounding through the house like a screech-owl.

'But my dear, dear! – whatever. . . .'

'It is adulterous! It signifies what I don't feel – I bought it long ago – to please Jude. It must be destroyed!'

Mrs Edlin lifted her hands and Sue excitedly continued to tear the linen into strips, laying the pieces in the fire.

'You med ha' give it to me!' said the widow. 'It do make my heart ache to see such pretty open-work as that a-burned by the flames – not that ornamental night-rails * can be much use to a' ould 'ooman like I. My days for such be all past and gone!'

'It is an accursed thing – it reminds me of what I want to forget!' Sue repeated. 'It is only fit for the fire.'

'Lord, you be too strict! What do ye use such words for, and condemn to hell your dear little innocent children that's lost to 'ee! Upon my life I don't call that religion!'

Sue flung her face upon the bed, sobbing. 'O, don't, don't! That kills me!' She remained shaken with her grief, and slipped down upon her knees.

'I'll tell 'ee what – you ought not to marry this man again!' said Mrs Edlin indignantly. 'You are in love wi' t' other still!'

'Yes I must — I am his already!'

'Pshoo! You be t' other man's. If you didn't like to commit yourselves to the binding vow again, just at first, 'twas all the more credit to your consciences, considering your reasons, and you med ha' lived on, and made it all right at last. After all, it concerned nobody but your own two selves.'

'Richard says he'll have me back, and I'm bound to go! If he had refused, it might not have been so much my duty to — give up Jude. But—' She remained with her face in the bedclothes, and Mrs Edlin left the room.

Phillotson in the interval had gone back to his friend Gillingham, who still sat over the supper-table. They soon rose, and walked out on the green to smoke awhile. A light was burning in Sue's room, a shadow moving now and then across the blind.

Gillingham had evidently been impressed with the indefinable charm of Sue, and after a silence he said, 'Well: you've all but got her again at last. She can't very well go a second time. The pear has dropped into your hand.'

'Yes! . . . I suppose I am right in taking her at her word. I confess there seems a touch of selfishness in it. Apart from her being what she is, of course, a luxury for a fogey like me, it will set me right in the eyes of the clergy and orthodox laity, who have never forgiven me for letting her go. So I may get back in some degree into my old track.'

'Well — if you've got any sound reason for marrying her again, do it now in God's name! I was always against your opening the cage-door and letting the bird go in such an obviously suicidal way. You might have been a school inspector by this time, or a reverend, if you hadn't been so weak about her.'

'I did myself irreparable damage — I know it.'

'Once you've got her housed again, stick to her.'

Phillotson was more evasive to-night. He did not care to admit clearly that his taking Sue to him again had at bottom nothing to do with repentance of letting her go, but was primarily, a human instinct flying in the face of custom and profession. He said, 'Yes — I shall do that. I know woman better now. Whatever justice there was in releasing her, there was little logic, for one holding my views on other subjects.'

Gillingham looked at him, and wondered whether it would ever happen that the reactionary spirit induced by the world's sneers and his own physical wishes would make Phillotson more orthodoxly cruel to her than he had erstwhile been informally and perversely kind.

'I perceive it won't do to give way to impulse,' Phillotson resumed, feeling more and more every minute the necessity of acting up to his position. 'I flew in the face of the Church's teaching; but I did it without malice prepense. Women are so strange in their influence, that they tempt you to misplaced kindness. However, I know myself better now. A little judicious severity, perhaps. . . .'

'Yes; but you must tighten the reins by degrees only. Don't be too strenuous at first. She'll come to any terms in time.'

The caution was unnecessary, though Phillotson did not say so. 'I remember what my vicar at Shaston said, when I left after the row that was made about my agreeing to her elopement. "The only thing you can do to retrieve your position and hers is to admit your error in not restraining her with a wise and strong hand, and to get her back again if she'll come, and be firm in the future." But I was so headstrong at that time that I paid no heed. And that after the divorce she should have thought of doing so I did not dream.'

The gate of Mrs Edlin's cottage clicked, and somebody began crossing in the direction of the school. Phillotson said 'Good-night.'

'O, is that Mr Phillotson,' said Mrs Edlin. 'I was going over to see 'ee. I've been upstairs with her, helping her to unpack her things; and upon my word, sir, I don't think this ought to be!'

'What – the wedding?'

'Yes. She's forcing herself to it, poor dear little thing; and you've no notion what she's suffering. I was never much for religion nor against it, but it can't be right to let her do this, and you ought to persuade her out of it. Of course everybody will say it was very good and forgiving of 'ee to take her to 'ee again. But for my part I don't.'

'It's her wish, and I am willing,' said Phillotson with grave reserve, opposition making him illogically tenacious now. 'A great piece of laxity will be rectified.'

'I don't believe it. She's his wife if anybody's. She's had three children by him, and he loves her dearly; and it's a wicked shame to egg her on to this, poor little quivering thing! She's got nobody on her side. The one man who'd be her friend the obstinate creature won't allow to come near her. What first put her into this mood o' mind, I wonder!'

'I can't tell. Not I certainly. It is all voluntary on her part. Now that's all I have to say.' Phillotson spoke stiffly. 'You've turned round, Mrs Edlin. It is unseemly of you!'

'Well. I knowed you'd be affronted at what I had to say; but I don't mind that. The truth's the truth.'

'I'm not affronted, Mrs Edlin. You've been too kind a neighbour for that. But I must be allowed to know what's best for myself and Susanna. I suppose you won't go to church with us, then?'

'No. Be hanged if I can. . . . I don't know what the times be coming to! Matrimony have growed to be that serious in these days that one really do feel afeard to move in it at all. In my time we took it more careless; and I don't know that we was any the worse for it! When I and my poor man were jined in it we kept up the junketing all the week, and drunk the parish dry, and had to borrow half-a-crown to begin housekeeping!'

When Mrs Edlin had gone back to her cottage Phillotson spoke moodily. 'I don't know whether I ought to do it — at any rate quite so rapidly.'

'Why?'

'If she is really compelling herself to this against her instincts — merely from this new sense of duty or religion — I ought perhaps to let her wait a bit.'

'Now you've got so far you ought not to back out of it. That's my opinion.'

'I can't very well put it off now; that's true. But I had a qualm when she gave that little cry at sight of the license.'

'Now, never you have qualms, old boy. I mean to give her away to-morrow morning, and you mean to take her. It has always been on my conscience that I didn't urge more objections to your letting her go, and now we've got to this stage I shan't be content if I don't help you to set the matter right.'

Phillotson nodded, and seeing how staunch his friend was, became more frank. 'No doubt when it gets known what I've done I shall be thought a soft fool by many. But they don't know Sue as I

do. Though so elusive, hers is such an honest nature at bottom that I
don't think she has ever done anything against her conscience. The
fact of her having lived with Fawley goes for nothing. At the time
she left me for him she thought she was quite within her right. Now
she thinks otherwise.'

The next morning came, and the self-sacrifice of the woman on
the altar of what she was pleased to call her principles was
acquiesced in by these two friends, each from his own point of view.
Phillotson went across to the Widow Edlin's to fetch Sue a few
minutes after eight o'clock. The fog of the previous day or two on
the lowlands had travelled up here by now, and the trees on the
green caught armfuls, and turned them into showers of big drops.
The bride was waiting, ready; bonnet and all on. She had never in
her life looked so much like the lily her name connoted * as she did
in that pallid morning light. Chastened, world-weary, remorseful,
the strain on her nerves had preyed upon her flesh and bones, and
she appeared smaller in outline than she had formerly done, though
Sue had not been a large woman in her days of rudest health.

'Prompt,' said the schoolmaster, magnanimously taking her hand.
But he checked his impulse to kiss her, remembering her start of
yesterday, which unpleasantly lingered in his mind.

Gillingham joined them, and they left the house, Widow Edlin
continuing steadfast in her refusal to assist in the ceremony.

'Where is the church?' said Sue. She had not lived there for any
length of time since the old church was pulled down, and in her
preoccupation forgot the new one.

'Up here,' said Phillotson; and presently the tower loomed large
and solemn in the fog. The vicar had already crossed to the building,
and when they entered he said pleasantly: 'We almost want
candles.'

'You do — wish me to be yours, Richard?' gasped Sue in a
whisper.

'Certainly, dear; above all things in the world.'

Sue said no more; and for the second or third time he felt he was
not quite following out the humane instinct which had induced him
to let her go.

There they stood, five altogether: the parson, the clerk, the couple
and Gillingham; and the holy ordinance was re-solemnized forth-

with. In the nave of the edifice were two or three villagers, and when the clergyman came to the words, 'What God hath joined', a woman's voice from these was heard to utter audibly:

'God hath jined indeed!'

It was like a re-enactment by the ghosts of their former selves of the similar scene which had taken place at Melchester years before. When the books were signed the vicar congratulated the husband and wife on having performed a noble, and righteous, and mutually forgiving act. 'All's well that ends well,' he said smiling. 'May you long be happy together, after thus having been "saved as by fire".' *

They came down the nearly empty building, and crossed to the schoolhouse. Gillingham wanted to get home that night, and left early. He, too, congratulated the couple. 'Now,' he said in parting from Phillotson, who walked out a little way, 'I shall be able to tell the people in your native place a good round tale; and they'll all say "Well done", depend on it.'

When the schoolmaster got back Sue was making a pretence of doing some housewifery as if she lived there. But she seemed timid at his approach, and compunction wrought on him at sight of it.

'Of course, my dear, I shan't expect to intrude upon your personal privacy any more than I did before,' he said gravely. 'It is for our good socially to do this, and that's its justification, if it was not my reason.'

Sue brightened a little.

THE place was the door of Jude's lodging in the outskirts of Christminster — far from the precincts of St Silas' where he had formerly lived, which saddened him to sickness. The rain was coming down. A woman in shabby black stood on the doorstep talking to Jude, who held the door in his hand.

'I am lonely, destitute, and houseless — that's what I am! Father has turned me out of doors after borrowing every penny I'd got, to put it into his business, and then accusing me of laziness when I was only waiting for a situation. I am at the mercy of the world! If you can't take me and help me, Jude, I must go to the workhouse, or to something worse. Only just now two undergraduates winked at me as I came along. 'Tis hard for a woman to keep virtuous where there's so many young men!'

The woman in the rain who spoke thus was Arabella, the evening being that of the day after Sue's re-marriage with Phillotson.

'I am sorry for you, but I am only in lodgings,' said Jude coldly.

'Then you turn me away?'

'I'll give you enough to get food and lodging for a few days.'

'O, but can't you have the kindness to take me in? I cannot endure going to a public-house to lodge; and I am so lonely. Please, Jude, for old times' sake!'

'No, no,' said Jude hastily. 'I don't want to be reminded of those things; and if you talk about them I shall not help you.'

'Then I suppose I must go!' said Arabella. She bent her head against the doorpost and began sobbing.

'The house is full,' said Jude. 'And I have only a little extra room to my own — not much more than a closet — where I keep my tools, and templates,* and the few books I have left!'

'That would be a palace for me!'

'There is no bedstead in it.'

'A bit of a bed could be made on the floor. It would be good enough for me.'

Unable to be harsh with her, and not knowing what to do, Jude called the man who let the lodgings, and said this was an acquaintance of his in great distress for want of temporary shelter.

'You may remember me as barmaid at the Lamb and Flag formerly?' spoke up Arabella. 'My father has insulted me this afternoon, and I've left him, though without a penny!'

The householder said he could not recall her features. 'But still, if you are a friend of Mr Fawley's we'll do what we can for a day or two — if he'll make himself answerable?'

'Yes, yes,' said Jude. 'She has really taken me quite unawares; but I should wish to help her out of her difficulty.' And an arrangement was ultimately come to under which a bed was to be thrown down in Jude's lumber-room, to make it comfortable for Arabella till she could get out of the strait she was in — not by her own fault, as she declared — and return to her father's again.

While they were waiting for this to be done Arabella said: 'You know the news, I suppose?'

'I guess what you mean; but I know nothing.'

'I had a letter from Anny at Alfredston to-day. She had just heard that the wedding was to be yesterday: but she didn't know if it had come off.'

'I don't wish to talk of it.'

'No, no: of course you don't. Only it shows what kind of woman—'

'Don't speak of her I say! She's a fool! — And she's an angel, too, poor dear!'

'If it's done, he'll have a chance of getting back to his old position, by everybody's account, so Anny says. All his well-wishers will be pleased, including the bishop himself.'

'Do spare me, Arabella.'

Arabella was duly installed in the little attic, and at first she did not come near Jude at all. She went to and fro about her own business, which, when they met for a moment on the stairs or in the passage, she informed him was that of obtaining another place in the occupation she understood best. When Jude suggested London as affording the most likely opening in the liquor trade, she shook her head. 'No — the temptations are too many,' she said. 'Any humble tavern in the country before that for me.'

On the Sunday morning following, when he breakfasted later than on other days, she meekly asked him if she might come in to breakfast with him, as she had broken her teapot, and could not replace it immediately, the shops being shut.

'Yes, if you like,' he said indifferently.

While they sat without speaking she suddenly observed: 'You seem all in a brood, old man. I'm sorry for you.'

'I am all in a brood.'

'It is about her, I know. It's no business of mine, but I could find out all about the wedding – if it really did take place – if you wanted to know.'

'How could you?'

'I wanted to go to Alfredston to get a few things I left there. And I could see Anny, who'll be sure to have heard all about it, as she has friends at Marygreen.'

Jude could not bear to acquiesce in this proposal; but his suspense pitted itself against his discretion, and won in the struggle. 'You can ask about it if you like,' he said. 'I've not heard a sound from there. It must have been very private, if – they have married.'

'I am afraid I haven't enough cash to take me there and back, or I should have gone before. I must wait till I have earned some.'

'O – I can pay the journey for you,' he said impatiently. And thus his suspense as to Sue's welfare, and the possible marriage, moved him to despatch for intelligence the last emissary he would have thought of choosing deliberately.

Arabella went, Jude requesting her to be home not later than by the seven o'clock train. When she had gone he said: 'Why should I have charged her to be back by a particular time! She's nothing to me: – nor the other neither!'

But having finished work he could not help going to the station to meet Arabella, dragged thither by feverish haste to get the news she might bring, and know the worst. Arabella had made dimples most successfully all the way home, and when she stepped out of the railway carriage she smiled. He merely said 'Well?' with the very reverse of a smile.

'They are married.'

'Yes – of course they are!' he returned. She observed, however, the hard strain upon his lip as he spoke.

'Anny says she has heard from Belinda, her relation out at Marygreen, that it was very sad, and curious!'

'How do you mean sad? She wanted to marry him again, didn't she? — and he her!'

'Yes — that was it. She wanted to in one sense, but not in the other. Mrs Edlin was much upset by it all, and spoke out her mind at Phillotson. But Sue was that excited about it that she burnt her best embroidery that she'd worn with you, to blot you out entirely. Well — if a woman feels like it, she ought to do it. I commend her for it, though others don't.' Arabella sighed. 'She felt he was her only husband, and that she belonged to nobody else in the sight of God A'mighty while he lived. Perhaps another woman feels the same about herself, too!' Arabella sighed again.

'I don't want any cant!' exclaimed Jude.

'It isn't cant,' said Arabella. 'I feel exactly the same as she!'

He closed that issue by remarking abruptly: 'Well — now I know all I wanted to know. Many thanks for your information. I am not going back to my lodgings just yet.' And he left her straightway.

In his misery and depression Jude walked to well-nigh every spot in the city that he had visited with Sue; thence he did not know whither, and then thought of going home to his usual evening meal. But having all the vices of his virtues, and some to spare, he turned into a public-house, for the first time during many months. Among the possible consequences of her marriage Sue had not dwelt on this.

Arabella, meanwhile, had gone back. The evening passed, and Jude did not return. At half-past nine Arabella herself went out, first proceeding to an outlying district near the river where her father lived, and had opened a small and precarious pork-shop lately.

'Well,' she said to him, 'for all your rowing me that night, I've called in, for I have something to tell you. I think I shall get married and settled again. Only you must help me: and you can do no less, after what I've stood 'ee.'

'I'll do anything to get thee off my hands!'

'Very well. I am now going to look for my young man. He's on the loose I'm afraid, and I must get him home. All I want you to do to-night is not to fasten the door, in case I should want to sleep here, and should be late.'

'I thought you'd soon get tired of giving yourself airs and keeping away!'

'Well – don't do the door. That's all I say.'

She then sallied out again, and first hastening back to Jude's to make sure that he had not returned, began her search for him. A shrewd guess as to his probable course took her straight to the tavern which Jude had formerly frequented, and where she had been barmaid for a brief term. She had no sooner opened the door of the 'Private Bar' than her eyes fell upon him – sitting in the shade at the back of the compartment, with his eyes fixed on the floor in a blank stare. He was drinking nothing stronger than ale just then. He did not observe her, and she entered and sat beside him.

Jude looked up, and said without surprise: 'You've come to have something, Arabella? . . . I'm trying to forget her: that's all! But I can't; and I am going home.' She saw that he was a little way on in liquor, but only a little as yet.

'I've come entirely to look for you, dear boy. You are not well. Now you must have something better than that.' Arabella held up her finger to the barmaid. 'You shall have a liqueur – that's better fit for a man of education than beer. You shall have maraschino, or curaçoa dry or sweet, or cherry brandy. I'll treat you, poor chap!'

'I don't care which! Say cherry brandy. . . . Sue has served me badly, very badly. I didn't expect it of Sue! I stuck to her, and she ought to have stuck to me. I'd have sold my soul for her sake, but she wouldn't risk hers a jot for me. To save her own soul she lets mine go damn! . . . But it isn't her fault, poor little girl – I am sure it isn't!'

How Arabella had obtained money did not appear, but she ordered a liqueur each, and paid for them. When they had drunk these Arabella suggested another; and Jude had the pleasure of being, as it were, personally conducted through the varieties of spirituous delectation by one who knew the landmarks well. Arabella kept very considerably in the rear of Jude; but though she only sipped where he drank, she took as much as she could safely take without losing her head – which was not a little, as the crimson upon her countenance showed.

Her tone towards him to-night was uniformly soothing and cajoling; and whenever he said 'I don't care what happens to me', a thing he did continually, she replied, 'But I do very much!' The closing hour came, and they were compelled to turn out; whereupon Arabella put her arm round his waist, and guided his unsteady footsteps.

When they were in the streets she said: 'I don't know what our landlord will say to my bringing you home in this state. I expect we are fastened out, so that he'll have to come down and let us in.'

'I don't know — I don't know.'

'That's the worst of not having a home of your own. I tell you, Jude, what we had best do. Come round to my father's — I made it up with him a bit to-day. I can let you in, and nobody will see you at all; and by to-morrow morning you'll be all right.'

'Anything — anywhere,' replied Jude. 'What the devil does it matter to me?'

They went along together, like any other fuddling couple, her arm still round his waist, and his, at last, round hers; though with no amatory intent; but merely because he was weary, unstable, and in need of support.

'This — is th' Martyrs' — burning-place,' he stammered as they dragged across a broad street. 'I remember — in old Fuller's *Holy State* * — and I am reminded of it — by our passing by here — old Fuller in his *Holy State* says, that at the burning of Ridley, Doctor Smith — preached sermon, and took as his text *"Though I give my body to be burned, and have not charity, it profiteth me nothing."* * — Often think of it as I pass here. Ridley was a—'

'Yes. Exactly. Very thoughtful of you, deary, even though it hasn't much to do with our present business.'

'Why, yes it has! I'm giving *my* body to be burned! But — ah — you don't understand! — it wants Sue to understand such things! And I was her seducer — poor little girl! And she's gone — and I don't care about myself! Do what you like with me! . . . And yet she did it for conscience' sake, poor little Sue!'

'Hang her! — I mean, I think she was right,' hiccupped Arabella. 'I've my feelings too, like her; and I feel I belong to you in Heaven's eye, and to nobody else, till death us do part! It is — hic — never too late — hic — to mend!'

They had reached her father's house, and she softly unfastened the door, groping about for a light within.

The circumstances were not altogether unlike those of their entry into the cottage at Cresscombe, such a long time before. Nor were perhaps Arabella's motives. But Jude did not think of that, though she did.

'I can't find the matches, dear,' she said when she had fastened up the door. 'But never mind – this way. As quiet as you can, please.'

'It is as dark as pitch,' said Jude.

'Give me your hand, and I'll lead you. That's it. Just sit down here, and I'll pull off your boots. I don't want to wake him.'

'Who?'

'Father. He'd make a row, perhaps.'

She pulled off his boots. 'Now,' she whispered, 'take hold of me – never mind your weight. Now – first stair, second stair—'

'But, – are we out in our old house by Marygreen?' asked the stupefied Jude. 'I haven't been inside it for years till now! Hey? And where are my books? That's what I want to know?'

'We are at my house, dear, where there's nobody to spy out how ill you are. Now – third stair, fourth stair – that's it. Now we shall get on.'

ARABELLA was preparing breakfast in the downstairs back room of this small, recently hired tenement of her father's. She put her head into the little pork-shop in front, and told Mr Donn it was ready. Donn, endeavouring to look like a master pork-butcher, in a greasy blue blouse, and with a strap round his waist from which a steel dangled, came in promptly.

'You must mind the shop this morning,' he said casually. 'I've to go and get some inwards and half a pig from Lumsdon, and to call elsewhere. If you live here you must put your shoulder to the wheel, at least till I get the business started!'

'Well, for to-day I can't say.' She looked deedily into his face. 'I've got a prize upstairs.'

'Oh? — What's that?'

'A husband — almost.'

'No!'

'Yes. It's Jude. He's come back to me.'

'Your old original one? Well, I'm damned!'

'Well, I always did like him, that I will say.'

'But how does he come to be up there?' said Donn, humour-struck, and nodding to the ceiling.

'Don't ask inconvenient questions, father. What we've to do is to keep him here till he and I are — as we were.'

'How was that?'

'Married.'

'Ah. . . . Well it is the rummest thing I ever heard of — marrying an old husband again, and so much new blood in the world! He's no catch, to my thinking. I'd have had a new one while I was about it.'

'It isn't rum for a woman to want her old husband back for respectability, though for a man to want his old wife back — well, perhaps it is funny, rather!' And Arabella was suddenly seized with a fit of loud laughter, in which her father joined more moderately.

'Be civil to him, and I'll do the rest,' she said when she had

recovered seriousness. 'He told me this morning that his head ached
fit to burst, and he hardly seemed to know where he was. And no
wonder, considering how he mixed his drink last night. We must
keep him jolly and cheerful here for a day or two, and not let him go
back to his lodging. Whatever you advance I'll pay back to you
again. But I must go up and see how he is now, poor deary.'

Arabella ascended the stairs, softly opened the door of the first
bedroom, and peeped in. Finding that her shorn Samson was asleep
she entered to the bedside and stood regarding him. The fevered
flush on his face from the debauch of the previous evening lessened
the fragility of his ordinary appearance, and his long lashes, dark
brows, and curly black hair and beard against the white pillow,
completed the physiognomy of one whom Arabella, as a woman of
rank passions, still felt it worth while to recapture, highly important
to recapture as a woman straitened both in means and in reputation.
Her ardent gaze seemed to affect him; his quick breathing became
suspended, and he opened his eyes.

'How are you now, dear?' said she. 'It is I — Arabella.'

'Ah! — where — O yes, I remember! You gave me shelter. . . . I am
stranded — ill — demoralized — damn bad! That's what I am!'

'Then do stay there. There's nobody in the house but father and
me, and you can rest till you are thoroughly well. I'll tell them at the
stone-works that you are knocked up.'

'I wonder what they are thinking at the lodgings!'

'I'll go round and explain. Perhaps you had better let me pay up,
or they'll think we've run away?'

'Yes. You'll find enough money in my pocket there.'

Quite indifferent, and shutting his eyes because he could not bear
the daylight in his throbbing eyeballs, Jude seemed to doze again.
Arabella took his purse, softly left the room, and putting on her
outdoor things went off to the lodgings she and he had quitted the
evening before.

Scarcely half-an-hour had elapsed ere she reappeared round the
corner, walking beside a lad wheeling a truck on which were piled
all Jude's household possessions, and also the few of Arabella's
things which she had taken to the lodging for her short sojourn
there. Jude was in such physical pain from his unfortunate breakdown of the previous night, and in such mental pain from the loss of

Sue and from having yielded in his half-somnolent state to Arabella, that when he saw his few chattels unpacked and standing before his eyes in this strange bedroom, intermixed with woman's apparel, he scarcely considered how they had come there, or what their coming signalized.

'Now,' said Arabella to her father downstairs, 'we must keep plenty of good liquor going in the house these next few days. I know his nature, and if he once gets into that fearfully low state that he does get into sometimes, he'll never do the honourable thing by me in this world, and I shall be left in the lurch. He must be kept cheerful. He has a little money in the savings-bank, and he has given me his purse to pay for anything necessary. Well, that will be the license; for I must have that ready at hand, to catch him the moment he's in the humour. You must pay for the liquor. A few friends, and a quiet convivial party would be the thing, if we could get it up. It would advertise the shop, and help me too.'

'That can be got up easy enough by anybody who'll afford victuals and drink.... Well yes — it would advertise the shop — that's true.'

Three days later, when Jude had recovered somewhat from the fearful throbbing of his eyes and brain, but was still considerably confused in his mind by what had been supplied to him by Arabella during the interval — to keep him jolly, as she expressed it — the quiet convivial gathering suggested by her, to wind Jude up to the striking point, took place.

Donn had only just opened his miserable little pork and sausage shop, which had as yet scarce any customers; nevertheless that party advertised it well, and the Donns acquired a real notoriety among a certain class in Christminster who knew not the colleges, nor their works, nor their ways. Jude was asked if he could suggest any guest in addition to those named by Arabella and her father, and in a saturnine humour of perfect recklessness mentioned Uncle Joe, and Stagg, and the decayed auctioneer, and others whom he remembered as having been frequenters of the well-known tavern during his bout therein years before. He also suggested Freckles and Bower o' Bliss. Arabella took him at his word so far as the men went, but drew the line at the ladies.

Another man they knew, Tinker Taylor, though he lived in the same street, was not invited; but as he went homeward from a late job on the evening of the party, he had occasion to call at the shop for trotters. There were none in, but he was promised some the next morning. While making his inquiry Taylor glanced into the back room, and saw the guests sitting round, card-playing, and drinking, and otherwise enjoying themselves at Donn's expense. He went home to bed, and on his way out next morning wondered how the party went off. He thought it hardly worth while to call at the shop for his provisions at that hour, Donn and his daughter being probably not up, if they caroused late the night before. However, he found in passing that the door was open and he could hear voices within, though the shutters of the meat-stall were not down. He went and tapped at the sitting-room door, and opened it.

'Well — to be sure!' he said, astonished.

Hosts and guests were sitting card-playing, smoking, and talking, precisely as he had left them eleven hours earlier; the gas was burning and the curtains drawn, though it had been broad daylight for two hours out of doors.

'Yes!' cried Arabella, laughing. 'Here we are, just the same. We ought to be ashamed of ourselves, oughtn't we! But it is a sort of housewarming, you see; and our friends are in no hurry. Come in, Mr Taylor, and sit down.'

The tinker, or rather reduced ironmonger, was nothing loth, and entered and took a seat, 'I shall lose a quarter, but never mind,' he said. 'Well, really, I could hardly believe my eyes when I looked in! It seemed as if I was flung back again into last night, all of a sudden.'

'So you are. Pour out for Mr Taylor.'

He now perceived that she was sitting beside Jude, her arm being round his waist. Jude, like the rest of the company, bore on his face the signs of how deeply he had been indulging.

'Well, we've been waiting for certain legal hours to arrive, to tell the truth,' she continued bashfully, and making her spirituous crimson look as much like a maiden blush as possible. 'Jude and I have decided to make up matters between us by tying the knot again, as we find we can't do without one another after all. So, as a bright notion, we agreed to sit on till it was late enough, and go and do it off-hand.'

Jude seemed to pay no great heed to what she was announcing, or indeed to anything whatever. The entrance of Taylor infused fresh spirit into the company, and they remained sitting, till Arabella whispered to her father: 'Now we may as well go.'

'But the parson don't know?'

'Yes, I told him last night that we might come between eight and nine, as there were reasons of decency for doing it as early and quiet as possible; on account of it being our second marriage, which might make people curious to look on if they knew. He highly approved.'

'O very well: I'm ready,' said her father, getting up and shaking himself.

'Now, old darling,' she said to Jude. 'Come along, as you promised.'

'When did I promise anything?' asked he, whom she had made so tipsy by her special knowledge of that line of business as almost to have made him sober again — or to seem so to those who did not know him.

'Why!' said Arabella, affecting dismay. 'You've promised to marry me several times as we've sat here to-night. These gentlemen have heard you.'

'I don't remember it,' said Jude doggedly. 'There's only one woman — but I won't mention her in this Capharnaum!'*

Arabella looked towards her father. 'Now, Mr Fawley, be honourable,' said Donn. 'You and my daughter have been living here together these three or four days, quite on the understanding that you were going to marry her. Of course I shouldn't have had such goings on in my house if I hadn't understood that. As a point of honour you must do it now.'

'Don't say anything against my honour!' enjoined Jude hotly, standing up. 'I'd marry the W— of Babylon* rather than do anything dishonourable! No reflection on you, my dear. It is a mere rhetorical figure — what they call in the books, hyperbole.'

'Keep your figures for your debts to friends who shelter you,' said Donn.

'If I am bound in honour to marry her — as I suppose I am — though how I came to be here with her I know no more than a dead man — marry her I will, so help me God! I have never behaved dishonourably to a woman or to any living thing. I am not a man who wants to save himself at the expense of the weaker among us!'

'There — never mind him, deary,' said she, putting her cheek against Jude's. 'Come up and wash your face, and just put yourself tidy, and off we'll go. Make it up with father.'

They shook hands. Jude went upstairs with her, and soon came down looking tidy and calm. Arabella, too, had hastily arranged herself, and accompanied by Donn away they went.

'Don't go,' she said to the guests at parting. 'I've told the little maid to get the breakfast while we are gone; and when we come back we'll all have some. A good strong cup of tea will set everybody right for going home.'

When Arabella, Jude and Donn had disappeared on their matrimonial errand the assembled guests yawned themselves wider awake, and discussed the situation with great interest. Tinker Taylor, being the most sober, reasoned the most lucidly.

'I don't wish to speak against friends,' he said. 'But it do seem a rare curiosity for a couple to marry over again! If they couldn't get on the first time when their minds were limp, they won't the second, by my reckoning.'

'Do you think he'll do it?'

'He's been put upon his honour by the woman, so he med.'

'He'd hardly do it straight off like this. He's got no license nor anything.'

'She's got that, bless you. Didn't you hear her say so to her father?'

'Well,' said Tinker Taylor, re-lighting his pipe at the gas-jet. 'Take her all together, limb by limb, she's not such a bad-looking piece — particular by candlelight. To be sure, halfpence that have been in circulation can't be expected to look like new ones from the Mint. But for a woman that's been knocking about the four hemispheres for some time, she's passable enough. A little bit thick in the flitch * perhaps: but I like a woman that a puff o' wind won't blow down.'

Their eyes followed the movements of the little girl as she spread the breakfast-cloth on the table they had been using, without wiping up the slops of the liquor. The curtains were undrawn, and the expression of the house made to look like morning. Some of the

guests, however, fell asleep in their chairs. One or two went to the
door, and gazed along the street more than once. Tinker Taylor was
the chief of these, and after a time he came in with a leer on his face.

'By Gad, they are coming! I think the deed's done!'

'No,' said Uncle Joe, following him in. 'Take my word, he turned
rusty at the last minute. They are walking in a very unusual way;
and that's the meaning of it!'

They waited in silence till the wedding party could be heard
entering the house. First into the room came Arabella boisterously;
and her face was enough to show that her strategy had succeeded.

'Mrs Fawley, I presume?' said Tinker Taylor with mock cour-
tesy.

'Certainly. Mrs Fawley again,' replied Arabella blandly, pulling
off her glove and holding out her left hand. 'There's the padlock, see.
. . . Well, he was a very nice, gentlemanly man indeed. I mean the
clergyman. He said to me as gentle as a babe when all was done:
"Mrs Fawley, I congratulate you heartily," he says. "For having
heard your history, and that of your husband, I think you have both
done the right and proper thing. And for your past errors as a wife,
and his as a husband, I think you ought now to be forgiven by the
world, as you have forgiven each other," says he. Yes: he was a very
nice, gentlemanly man. "The Church don't recognize divorce in her
dogma, strictly speaking," he says: "and bear in mind the words of
the Service in your goings out and your comings in: What God hath
joined together let no man put asunder." Yes: he was a very nice,
gentlemanly man. . . . But, Jude, my dear, you were enough to make
a cat laugh! You walked that straight, and held yourself that steady,
that one would have thought you were going 'prentice to a judge;
though I knew you were seeing double all the time, from the way
you fumbled with my finger.'

'I said I'd do anything to — save a woman's honour,' muttered
Jude. 'And I've done it!'

'Well now, old deary, come along and have some breakfast.'

'I want — some — more whisky,' said Jude stolidly.

'Nonsense, dear. Not now! There's no more left. The tea will take
the muddle out of our heads, and we shall be as fresh as larks.'

'All right. I've — married you. She said I ought to marry you
again, and I have straightway. It is true religion! Ha — ha — ha!'

MICHAELMAS came and passed, and Jude and his wife, who had lived but a short time in her father's house after their re-marriage, were in lodgings on the top floor of a dwelling nearer to the centre of the city.

He had done a few days' work during the two or three months since the event, but his health had been indifferent, and it was now precarious. He was sitting in an arm-chair before the fire, and coughed a good deal.

'I've got a bargain for my trouble in marrying thee over again!' Arabella was saying to him. 'I shall have to keep 'ee entirely, — that's what 'twill come to! I shall have to make black-pot and sausages, and hawk 'em about the street, all to support an invalid husband I'd no business to be saddled with at all. Why didn't you keep your health, deceiving one like this? You were well enough when the wedding was!'

'Ah, yes!' said he, laughing acridly. 'I have been thinking of my foolish feeling about the pig you and I killed during our first marriage. I feel now that the greatest mercy that could be vouchsafed to me would be that something should serve me as I served that animal.'

This was the sort of discourse that went on between them every day now. The landlord of the lodging, who had heard that they were a queer couple, had doubted if they were married at all, especially as he had seen Arabella kiss Jude one evening when she had taken a little cordial; and he was about to give them notice to quit, till by chance overhearing her one night haranguing Jude in rattling terms, and ultimately flinging a shoe at his head, he recognized the note of genuine wedlock; and concluding that they must be respectable, said no more.

Jude did not get any better, and one day he requested Arabella with considerable hesitation, to execute a commission for him. She asked him indifferently what it was.

'To write to Sue.'

'What in the name – do you want me to write to her for?'

'To ask how she is, and if she'll come to see me, because I'm ill, and should like to see her – once again.'

'It is like you to insult a lawful wife by asking such a thing!'

'It is just in order not to insult you that I ask you to do it. You know I love Sue. I don't wish to mince the matter – there stands the fact: I love her. I could find a dozen ways of sending a letter to her without your knowledge. But I wish to be quite above-board with you, and with her husband. A message through you asking her to come is at least free from any odour of intrigue. If she retains any of her old nature at all, she'll come.'

'You've no respect for marriage whatever, or its rights and duties!'

'What *does* it matter what my opinions are – a wretch like me! Can it matter to anybody in the world who comes to see me for half-an-hour – here with one foot in the grave! . . . Come, please write, Arabella!' he pleaded. 'Repay my candour by a little generosity!'

'I should think *not*!'

'Not just once? – O do!' He felt that his physical weakness had taken away all his dignity.

'What do you want *her* to know how you are for? She don't want to see 'ee. She's the rat that forsook the sinking ship!'

'Don't, don't!'

'And I stuck to un – the more fool I! Have that strumpet in the house indeed!'

Almost as soon as the words were spoken Jude sprang from the chair, and before Arabella knew where she was he had her on her back upon a little couch which stood there, he kneeling above her.

'Say another word of that sort,' he whispered, 'and I'll kill you – here and now! I've everything to gain by it – my own death not being the least part. So don't think there's no meaning in what I say!'

'What do you want me to do?' gasped Arabella.

'Promise never to speak of her.'

'Very well. I do.'

'I take your word,' he said scornfully as he loosened her. 'But what it is worth I can't say.'

'You couldn't kill the pig, but you could kill me!'

'Ah — there you have me! No — I couldn't kill you — even in a passion. Taunt away!'

He then began coughing very much, and she estimated his life with an appraiser's eye as he sank back ghastly pale. 'I'll send for her,' Arabella murmured, 'if you'll agree to my being in the room with you all the time she's here.'

The softer side of his nature, the desire to see Sue, made him unable to resist the offer even now, provoked as he had been; and he replied breathlessly: 'Yes, I agree. Only send for her!'

In the evening he inquired if she had written.

'Yes,' she said; 'I wrote a note telling her you were ill, and asking her to come to-morrow or the day after. I haven't posted it yet.'

The next day Jude wondered if she really did post it, but would not ask her; and foolish Hope, that lives on a drop and a crumb, made him restless with expectation. He knew the times of the possible trains, and listened on each occasion for sounds of her.

She did not come; but Jude would not address Arabella again thereon. He hoped and expected all the next day; but no Sue appeared; neither was there any note of reply. Then Jude decided in the privacy of his mind that Arabella had never posted hers, although she had written it. There was something in her manner which told it. His physical weakness was such that he shed tears at the disappointment when she was not there to see. His suspicions were, in fact, well founded. Arabella, like some other nurses, thought that your duty towards your invalid was to pacify him by any means short of really acting upon his fancies.

He never said another word to her about his wish or his conjecture. A silent, undiscerned resolve grew up in him, which gave him, if not strength, stability and calm. One midday when, after an absence of two hours, she came into the room, she beheld the chair empty.

Down she flopped on the bed, and sitting, meditated. 'Now where the devil is my man gone to!' she said.

A driving rain from the north-east had been falling with more or less intermission all the morning, and looking from the window at the dripping spouts it seemed impossible to believe that any sick man would have ventured out to almost certain death. Yet a conviction possessed Arabella that he had gone out, and it became a certainty when she had searched the house. 'If he's such a fool, let him be!' she said. 'I can do no more.'

Jude was at that moment in a railway train that was drawing near to Alfredston, oddly swathed, pale as a monumental figure in alabaster, and much stared at by other passengers. An hour later his thin form, in the long great-coat and blanket he had come with, but without an umbrella, could have been seen walking along the five-mile road to Marygreen. On his face showed the determined purpose that alone sustained him, but to which his weakness afforded a sorry foundation. By the uphill walk he was quite blown, but he pressed on; and at half-past three o'clock stood by the familiar well at Marygreen. The rain was keeping everybody indoors; Jude crossed the green to the church without observation, and found the building open. Here he stood, looking forth at the school, whence he could hear the usual sing-song tones of the little voices that had not learnt Creation's groan.

He waited till a small boy came from the school – one evidently allowed out before hours for some reason or other. Jude held up his hand, and the child came.

'Please call at the schoolhouse and ask Mrs Phillotson if she will be kind enough to come to the church for a few minutes.'

The child departed, and Jude heard him knock at the door of the dwelling. He himself went further into the church. Everything was new, except a few pieces of carving preserved from the wrecked old fabric, now fixed against the new walls. He stood by these: they seemed akin to the perished people of that place who were his ancestors and Sue's.

A light footstep, which might have been accounted no more than an added drip to the rainfall, sounded in the porch, and he looked round.

'O – I didn't think it was you! I didn't – O Jude!' A hysterical catch in her breath ended in a succession of them. He advanced, but she quickly recovered and went back.

'Don't go – don't go!' he implored. 'This is my last time! I thought it would be less intrusive than to enter your house. And I shall never come again. Don't then be unmerciful. Sue, Sue! we are acting by the letter; and "the letter killeth"!' *

'I'll stay — I won't be unkind!' she said, her mouth quivering and her tears flowing as she allowed him to come closer. 'But why did you come, and do this wrong thing, after doing such a right thing as you have done?'

'What right thing?'

'Marrying Arabella again. It was in the Alfredston paper. She has never been other than yours, Jude — in a proper sense. And therefore you did so well — O so well! — in recognizing it — and taking her to you again.'

'God above — and is that all I've come to hear? If there is anything more degrading, immoral, unnatural, than another in my life, it is this meretricious contract with Arabella which has been called doing the right thing! And you too — you call yourself Phillotson's wife! *His* wife! You are mine.'

'Don't make me rush away from you — I can't bear much! But on this point I am decided.'

'I cannot understand how you did it — how you think it — I cannot!'

'Never mind that. He is a kind husband to me — And I — I've wrestled and struggled, and fasted, and prayed. I have nearly brought my body into complete subjection. And you mustn't — will you — wake—'

'O you darling little fool; where is your reason? You seem to have suffered the loss of your faculties! I would argue with you if I didn't know that a woman in your state of feeling is quite beyond all appeals to her brains. Or is it that you are humbugging yourself, as so many women do about these things; and don't actually believe what you pretend to, and only are indulging in the luxury of the emotion raised by an affected belief?'

'Luxury! How can you be so cruel!'

'You dear, sad, soft, most melancholy wreck of a promising human intellect that it has ever been my lot to behold! Where is your scorn of convention gone? I *would* have died game!'

'You crush, almost insult me, Jude! Go away from me!' She turned off quickly.

'I will. I would never come to see you again, even if I had the strength to come, which I shall not have any more. Sue, Sue, you are not worth a man's love!'

Her bosom began to go up and down. 'I can't endure you to say that!' she burst out, and her eye resting on him a moment, she turned back impulsively. 'Don't, don't scorn me! Kiss me, O kiss me lots of times, and say I am not a coward and a contemptible humbug – I can't bear it!' She rushed up to him and, with her mouth on his, continued: 'I must tell you – O I must – my darling Love! It has been – only a church marriage – an apparent marriage I mean! He suggested it at the very first!'

'How?'

'I mean it is a nominal marriage only. It hasn't been more than that at all since I came back to him!'

'Sue!' he said. Pressing her to him in his arms he bruised her lips with kisses: 'If misery can know happiness, I have a moment's happiness now! Now, in the name of all you hold holy, tell me the truth, and no lie. You do love me still?'

'I do! You know it too well! . . . But I *mustn't* do this! – I mustn't kiss you back as I would!'

'But do!'

'And yet you are so dear! – and you look so ill—'

'And so do you! There's one more, in memory of our dead little children – yours and mine!'

The words struck her like a blow, and she bent her head. 'I *mustn't* – I *can't* go on with this!' she gasped presently. 'But there, there, darling; I give you back your kisses; I do, I do! . . . And now I'll *hate* myself for ever for my sin!'

'No – let me make my last appeal. Listen to this! We've both re-married out of our senses. I was made drunk to do it. You were the same. I was gin-drunk; you were creed-drunk. Either form of intoxication takes away the nobler vision. . . . Let us then shake off our mistakes, and run away together!'

'No; again no! . . . Why do you tempt me so far, Jude! It is too merciless! . . . But I've got over myself now. Don't follow me – don't look at me. Leave me, for pity's sake!'

She ran up the church to the east end, and Jude did as she requested. He did not turn his head, but took up his blanket, which she had not seen, and went straight out. As he passed the end of the church she heard his coughs mingling with the rain on the windows, and in a last instinct of human affection, even now unsubdued by her fetters, she sprang up as if to go and succour him. But she knelt down again, and stopped her ears with her hands till all possible sound of him had passed away.

He was by this time at the corner of the green, from which the path ran across the fields in which he had scared rooks as a boy. He turned and looked back, once, at the building which still contained Sue; and then went on, knowing that his eyes would light on that scene no more.

There are cold spots up and down Wessex in autumn and winter weather; but the coldest of all when a north or east wind is blowing is the crest of the down by the Brown House, where the road to Alfredston crosses the old Ridgeway. Here the first winter sleets and snows fall and lie, and here the spring frost lingers last unthawed. Here in the teeth of the north-east wind and rain Jude now pursued his way, wet through, the necessary slowness of his walk from lack of his former strength being insufficient to maintain his heat. He came to the milestone, and, raining as it was, spread his blanket and lay down there to rest. Before moving on he went and felt at the back of the stone for his own carving. It was still there; but nearly obliterated by moss. He passed the spot where the gibbet of his ancestor and Sue's had stood, and descended the hill.

It was dark when he reached Alfredston, where he had a cup of tea, the deadly chill that began to creep into his bones being too much for him to endure fasting. To get home he had to travel by a steam tramcar, and two branches of railway, with much waiting at a junction. He did not reach Christminster till ten o'clock.

CHAPTER NINE

On the platform stood Arabella. She looked him up and down.

'You've been to see her?' she asked.

'I have,' said Jude, literally tottering with cold and lassitude.

'Well, now you'd best march along home.'

The water ran out of him as he went, and he was compelled to lean against the wall to support himself while coughing.

'You've done for yourself by this, young man,' said she. 'I don't know whether you know it.'

'Of course I do. I meant to do for myself.'

'What – to commit suicide?'

'Certainly.'

'Well, I'm blest! Kill yourself for a woman.'

'Listen to me, Arabella. You think you are the stronger; and so you are, in a physical sense, now. You could push me over like a ninepin. You did not send that letter the other day, and I could not resent your conduct. But I am not so weak in another way as you think. I made up my mind that a man confined to his room by inflammation of the lungs, a fellow who had only two wishes left in the world, to see a particular woman, and then to die, could neatly accomplish those two wishes at one stroke by taking this journey in the rain. That I've done. I have seen her for the last time, and I've finished myself – put an end to a feverish life which ought never to have been begun!'

'Lord – you do talk lofty! Won't you have something warm to drink?'

'No thank you. Let's get home.'

They went along by the silent colleges, and Jude kept stopping.

'What are you looking at?'

'Stupid fancies. I see, in a way, those spirits of the dead again, on this my last walk, that I saw when I first walked here!'

'What a curious chap you are!'

'I seem to see them, and almost hear them rustling. But I don't revere all of them as I did then. I don't believe in half of them. The theologians, the apologists, and their kin the metaphysicians, the high-handed statesmen, and others, no longer interest me. All that has been spoilt for me by the grind of stern reality!'

The expression of Jude's corpse-like face in the watery lamplight was indeed as if he saw people where there was nobody. At moments he stood still by an archway, like one watching a figure walk out; then he would look at a window like one discerning a familiar face behind it. He seemed to hear voices, whose words he repeated as if to gather their meaning.

'They seem laughing at me!'

'Who?'

'O – I was talking to myself! The phantoms all about here, in the college archways, and windows. They used to look friendly in the old days, particularly Addison, and Gibbon, and Johnson, and Dr Browne, and Bishop Ken—'

'Come along do! Phantoms! There's neither living nor dead hereabouts except a damn policeman! I never saw the streets emptier.'

'Fancy! The Poet of Liberty * used to walk here, and the great Dissector of Melancholy * there!'

'I don't want to hear about 'em! They bore me.'

'Walter Raleigh is beckoning to me from that lane – Wycliffe – Harvey – Hooker – Arnold – and a whole crowd of Tractarian Shades—'

'I *don't want* to know their names, I tell you! What do I care about folk dead and gone? Upon my soul you are more sober when you've been drinking than when you have not!'

'I must rest a moment,' he said; and as he paused, holding to the railings, he measured with his eye the height of a college front. 'This is old Rubric. And that Sarcophagus; and up that lane Crozier and Tudor: and all down there is Cardinal with its long front, and its windows with lifted eyebrows, representing the polite surprise of the University at the efforts of such as I.'

'Come along, and I'll treat you!'

'Very well. It will help me home, for I feel the chilly fog from the meadows of Cardinal as if death-claws were grabbing me through and through. As Antigone said,* I am neither a dweller among men nor ghosts. But, Arabella, when I am dead, you'll see my spirit flitting up and down here among these!'

'Pooh! You mayn't die after all. You are tough enough yet, old man.'

It was night at Marygreen, and the rain of the afternoon showed no sign of abatement. About the time at which Jude and Arabella were walking the streets of Christminster homeward, the Widow Edlin crossed the green, and opened the back door of the schoolmaster's dwelling, which she often did now before bedtime, to assist Sue in putting things away.

Sue was muddling helplessly in the kitchen, for she was not a good housewife, though she tried to be, and grew impatient of domestic details.

'Lord love 'ee, what do ye do that yourself for, when I've come o' purpose! You knew I should come.'

'O – I don't know – I forgot! No, I didn't forget. I did it to discipline myself. I have scrubbed the stairs since eight o'clock. I *must* practise myself in my household duties. I've shamefully neglected them!'

'Why should ye? He'll get a better school, perhaps be a parson, in time, and you'll keep two servants. 'Tis a pity to spoil them pretty hands.'

'Don't talk of my pretty hands, Mrs Edlin. This pretty body of mine has been the ruin of me already!'

'Pshoo – you've got no body to speak of! You put me more in mind of a sperrit. But there seems something wrong to-night, my dear. Husband cross?'

'No. He never is. He's gone to bed early.'

'Then what is it?'

'I cannot tell you. I have done wrong to-day. And I want to eradicate it. . . . Well – I will tell you this – Jude has been here this afternoon, and I find I still love him – O, grossly! I cannot tell you more.'

'Ah!' said the widow. 'I told 'ee how 'twould be!'

'But it shan't be! I have not told my husband of his visit; it is not necessary to trouble him about it, as I never mean to see Jude any more. But I am going to make my conscience right on my duty to

Richard — by doing a penance — the ultimate thing. I must!'

'I wouldn't — since he agrees to it being otherwise, and it has gone on three months very well as it is.'

'Yes — he agrees to my living as I choose; but I feel it is an indulgence I ought not to exact from him. It ought not to have been accepted by me. To reverse it will be terrible — but I must be more just to him. O why was I so unheroic!'

'What is it you don't like in him?' asked Mrs Edlin curiously.

'I cannot tell you. It is something . . . I cannot say. The mournful thing is, that nobody would admit it as a reason for feeling as I do; so that no excuse is left me.'

'Did you ever tell Jude what it was?'

'Never.'

'I've heard strange tales o' husbands in my time,' observed the widow in a lowered voice. 'They say that when the saints were upon the earth devils used to take husbands' forms o' nights, and get poor women into all sorts of trouble. But I don't know why that should come into my head, for it is only a tale. . . . What a wind and rain it is to-night! Well — don't be in a hurry to alter things, my dear. Think it over.'

'No, no! I've screwed my weak soul up to treating him more courteously — and it must be now — at once — before I break down!'

'I don't think you ought to force your nature. No woman ought to be expected to.'

'It is my duty. I will drink my cup to the dregs!'

Half-an-hour later when Mrs Edlin put on her bonnet and shawl to leave, Sue seemed to be seized with vague terror.

'No, no — don't go, Mrs Edlin,' she implored, her eyes enlarged, and with a quick nervous look over her shoulder.

'But it is bed-time, child.'

'Yes, but — there's the little spare room — my room that was. It is quite ready. Please stay, Mrs Edlin! — I shall want you in the morning.'

'O well — I don't mind, if you wish. Nothing will happen to my four old walls, whether I be there or no.'

She then fastened up the doors, and they ascended the stairs together.

'Wait here, Mrs Edlin,' said Sue. 'I'll go into my old room a moment by myself.'

Leaving the widow on the landing Sue turned to the chamber which had been hers exclusively since her arrival at Marygreen, and pushing to the door knelt down by the bed for a minute or two. She then arose, and taking her nightgown from the pillow undressed and came out to Mrs Edlin. A man could be heard snoring in the room opposite. She wished Mrs Edlin good-night, and the widow entered the room that Sue had just vacated.

Sue unlatched the other chamber door, and, as if seized with faintness, sank down outside it. Getting up again she half opened the door, and said 'Richard'. As the word came out of her mouth she visibly shuddered.

The snoring had quite ceased for some time, but he did not reply. Sue seemed relieved, and hurried back to Mrs Edlin's chamber. 'Are you in bed, Mrs Edlin?' she asked.

'No, dear,' said the widow, opening the door. 'I be old and low, and it takes me a long while to un-ray.* I han't unlaced my jumps* yet.'

'I – don't hear him! And perhaps – perhaps—'

'What, child?'

'Perhaps he's dead!' she gasped. 'And then – I should be *free*, and I could go to Jude! . . . Ah – no – I forgot *her* – and God!'

'Let's go and hearken. No – he's snoring again. But the rain and the wind is so loud that you can hardly hear anything but between whiles.'

Sue had dragged herself back. 'Mrs Edlin, good night again! I am sorry I called you out.' The widow retreated a second time.

The strained, resigned look returned to Sue's face when she was alone. 'I must do it – I must! I must drink to the dregs!' she whispered. 'Richard!' she said again.

'Hey – what? Is that you, Susanna?'

'Yes.'

'What do you want? Anything the matter? Wait a moment.' He pulled on some articles of clothing, and came to the door. 'Yes?'

'When we were at Shaston I jumped out of the window rather than that you should come near me. I have never reversed that treatment till now – when I have come to beg your pardon for it, and ask you to let me in.'

'Perhaps you only think you ought to do this? I don't wish you to come against your impulses, as I have said.'

'But I beg to be admitted.' She waited a moment, and repeated, 'I beg to be admitted! I have been in error — even to-day. I have exceeded my rights. I did not mean to tell you, but perhaps I ought. I sinned against you this afternoon.'

'How?'

'I met Jude! I didn't know he was coming. And—'

'Well?'

'I kissed him, and let him kiss me.'

'O — the old story!'

'Richard, I didn't know we were going to kiss each other till we did!'

'How many times?'

'A good many. I don't know. I am horrified to look back on it, and the least I can do after it is to come to you like this.'

'Come — this is pretty bad, after what I've done! Anything else to confess?'

'No.' She had been intending to say: 'I called him my darling Love.' But, as a contrite woman always keeps back a little, that portion of the scene remained untold. She went on: 'I am never going to see him any more. He spoke of some things of the past: and it overcame me. He spoke of — the children. — But, as I have said, I am glad — almost glad I mean — that they are dead, Richard. It blots out all that life of mine!'

'Well — about not seeing him again any more. Come — you really mean this?' There was something in Phillotson's tone now which seemed to show that his three months of re-marriage with Sue had somehow not been so satisfactory as his magnanimity or amative patience had anticipated.

'Yes, yes!'

'Perhaps you'll swear it on the New Testament?'

'I will.'

He went back to the room and brought out a little brown Testament. 'Now then: So help you God!'

She swore.

'Very good!'

'Now I supplicate you, Richard, to whom I belong, and whom I wish to honour and obey, as I vowed, to let me in.'

'Think it over well. You know what it means. Having you back in the house was one thing – this another. So think again.'

'I have thought – I wish this!'

'That's a complaisant spirit – and perhaps you are right. With a lover hanging about, a half-marriage should be completed. But I repeat my reminder this third and last time.'

'It is my wish! ... O God!'

'What did you say O God for?'

'I don't know!'

'Yes you do! But....' He gloomily considered her thin and fragile form a moment longer as she crouched before him in her night-clothes. 'Well, I thought it might end like this,' he said presently. 'I owe you nothing, after these signs; but I'll take you in at your word, and forgive you.'

He put his arm round her to lift her up. Sue started back.

'What's the matter?' he asked, speaking for the first time sternly. 'You shrink from me again? – just as formerly!'

'No, Richard – I – I – was not thinking—'

'You wish to come in here?'

'Yes.'

'You still bear in mind what it means?'

'Yes. It is my duty!'

Placing the candlestick on the chest of drawers he led her through the doorway, and lifting her bodily, kissed her. A quick look of aversion passed over her face, but clenching her teeth she uttered no cry.

Mrs Edlin had by this time undressed, and was about to get into bed when she said to herself: 'Ah – perhaps I'd better go and see if the little thing is all right. How it do blow and rain!'

The widow went out on the landing, and saw that Sue had disappeared. 'Ah! Poor soul! Weddings be funerals 'a b'lieve now-adays. Fifty-five years ago, come Fall, since my man and I married! Time have changed since then!'

DESPITE himself Jude recovered somewhat, and worked at his trade for several weeks. After Christmas, however, he broke down again.

With the money he had earned he shifted his lodgings to a yet more central part of the town. But Arabella saw that he was not likely to do much work for a long while, and was cross enough at the turn affairs had taken since her re-marriage to him. 'I'm hanged if you haven't been clever in this last stroke!' she would say, 'to get a nurse for nothing by marrying me!'

Jude was absolutely indifferent to what she said, and, indeed, often regarded her abuse in a humorous light. Sometimes his mood was more earnest, and as he lay he often rambled on upon the defeat of his early aims.

'Every man has some little power in some one direction,' he would say. 'I was never really stout enough for the stone trade, particularly the fixing. Moving the blocks always used to strain me, and standing the trying draughts in buildings before the windows are in, always gave me colds, and I think that began the mischief inside. But I felt I could do one thing if I had the opportunity. I could accumulate ideas, and impart them to others. I wonder if the Founders had such as I in their minds — a fellow good for nothing else but that particular thing? ... I hear that soon there is going to be a better chance for such helpless students as I was. There are schemes afoot for making the University less exclusive, and extending its influence. I don't know much about it. And it is too late, too late for me! Ah — and for how many worthier ones before me!'

'How you keep a-mumbling!' said Arabella. 'I should have thought you'd have got over all that craze about books by this time. And so you would, if you'd had any sense to begin with. You are as bad now as when we were first married.'

On one occasion while soliloquizing thus he called her 'Sue' unconsciously.

'I wish you'd mind who you are talking to!' said Arabella indig-

nantly. 'Calling a respectable married woman by the name of that—'
She remembered herself and he did not catch the word.

But in the course of time, when she saw how things were going,
and how very little she had to fear from Sue's rivalry, she had a fit of
generosity. 'I suppose you want to see your – Sue?' she said. 'Well, I
don't mind her coming. You can have her here if you like.'

'I don't wish to see her again.'

'O – that's a change!'

'And don't tell her anything about me – that I'm ill, or anything.
She has chosen her course. Let her go!'

One day he received a surprise. Mrs Edlin came to see him, quite
on her own account. Jude's wife, whose feelings as to where his
affections were centred had reached absolute indifference by this
time, went out, leaving the old woman alone with Jude. He impulsively asked how Sue was, and then said bluntly, remembering what
Sue had told him: 'I suppose they are still only husband and wife in
name?'

Mrs Edlin hesitated. 'Well, no – it's different now. She's begun it
quite lately – all of her own free will.'

'When did she begin?' he asked quickly.

'The night after you came. But as a punishment to her poor self.
He didn't wish it, but she insisted.'

'Sue, my Sue – you darling fool – this is almost more than I can
endure! ... Mrs Edlin – don't be frightened at my rambling – I've
got to talk to myself lying here so many hours alone – she was once
a woman whose intellect was to mine like a star to a benzoline lamp:
who saw all *my* superstitions as cobwebs that she could brush away
with a word. Then bitter affliction came to us, and her intellect
broke, and she veered round to darkness. Strange difference of sex,
that time and circumstance, which enlarge the views of most men,
narrow the views of women almost invariably. And now the
ultimate horror has come – her giving herself like this to what she
loathes, in her enslavement to forms! – she, so sensitive, so shrink-
ing, that the very wind seemed to blow on her with a touch of
deference.... As for Sue and me when we were at our own best,
long ago – when our minds were clear, and our love of truth fearless
– the time was not ripe for us! Our ideas were fifty years too soon to
be any good to us. And so the resistance they met with brought

reaction in her, and recklessness and ruin on me! ... There – this, Mrs Edlin, is how I go on to myself continually, as I lie here. I must be boring you awfully.'

'Not at all, my dear boy. I could hearken to 'ee all day.'

As Jude reflected more and more on her news, and grew more restless, he began in his mental agony to use terribly profane language about social conventions, which started a fit of coughing. Presently there came a knock at the door downstairs. As nobody answered it Mrs Edlin herself went down.

The visitor said blandly: 'The doctor.' The lanky form was that of Physician Vilbert, who had been called in by Arabella.

'How is my patient at present?' asked the physician.

'O bad – very bad! Poor chap, he got excited, and do blaspeam terribly, since I let out some gossip by accident – the more to my blame. But there – you must excuse a man in suffering for what he says, and I hope God will forgive him.'

'Ah. I'll go up and see him. Mrs Fawley at home?'

'She's not in at present, but she'll be here soon.'

Vilbert went; but though Jude had hitherto taken the medicines of that skilful practitioner with the greatest indifference whenever poured down his throat by Arabella, he was now so brought to bay by events that he vented his opinion of Vilbert in the physician's face, and so forcibly, and with such striking epithets, that Vilbert soon scurried downstairs again. At the door he met Arabella, Mrs Edlin having left. Arabella inquired how he thought her husband was now, and seeing that the doctor looked ruffled, asked him to take something. He assented.

'I'll bring it to you here in the passage,' she said. 'There's nobody but me about the house to-day.'

She brought him a bottle and a glass, and he drank. Arabella began shaking with suppressed laughter. 'What is this, my dear?' he asked, smacking his lips.

'O – a drop of wine – and something in it.' Laughing again she said: 'I poured your own love-philter into it, that you sold me at the Agricultural Show, don't you remember?'

'I do, I do! Clever woman! But you must be prepared for the consequences.' Putting his arm round her shoulders he kissed her there and then.

'Don't, don't,' she whispered, laughing good-humouredly. 'My man will hear.'

She let him out of the house, and as she went back she said to herself: 'Well! Weak women must provide for a rainy day. And if my poor fellow upstairs do go off – as I suppose he will soon – it's well to keep chances open. And I can't pick and choose now as I could when I was younger. And one must take the old if one can't get the young.'

THE last pages to which the chronicler of these lives would ask the reader's attention are concerned with the scene in and out of Jude's bedroom when leafy summer came round again.

His face was now so thin that his old friends would hardly have known him. It was afternoon, and Arabella was at the looking-glass curling her hair, which operation she performed by heating an umbrella-stay in the flame of a candle she had lighted, and using it upon the flowing lock. When she had finished this, practised a dimple, and put on her things, she cast her eyes round upon Jude. He seemed to be sleeping, though his position was an elevated one, his malady preventing him lying down.

Arabella, hatted, gloved, and ready, sat down and waited, as if expecting some one to come and take her place as nurse.

Certain sounds from without revealed that the town was in festivity, though little of the festival, whatever it might have been, could be seen here. Bells began to ring, and the notes came into the room through the open window, and travelled round Jude's head in a hum. They made her restless, and at last she said to herself: 'Why ever doesn't father come!'

She looked again at Jude, critically gauged his ebbing life, as she had done so many times during the late months, and glancing at his watch, which was hung up by way of timepiece, rose impatiently. Still he slept, and coming to a resolution she slipped from the room, closed the door noiselessly, and descended the stairs. The house was empty. The attraction which moved Arabella to go abroad had evidently drawn away the other inmates long before.

It was a warm, cloudless, enticing day. She shut the front door, and hastened round into Chief Street, and when near the Theatre could hear the notes of the organ, a rehearsal for a coming concert being in progress. She entered under the archway of Oldgate College, where men were putting up awnings round the quadrangle for a ball in the Hall that evening. People who had come up from the country for the day were picnicking on the grass, and Arabella walked along the gravel paths and under the aged limes. But finding this place rather dull she returned to the streets, and watched the carriages drawing up for the concert, numerous Dons and their wives, and undergraduates with gay female companions, crowding up likewise. When the doors were closed, and the concert began, she moved on.

The powerful notes of that concert rolled forth through the swinging yellow blinds of the open windows, over the house-tops, and into the still air of the lanes. They reached so far as to the room in which Jude lay; and it was about this time that his cough began again and awakened him.

As soon as he could speak he murmured, his eyes still closed: 'A little water, please.'

Nothing but the deserted room received his appeal, and he coughed to exhaustion again — saying still more feebly: 'Water — some water — Sue — Arabella!'

The room remained still as before. Presently he gasped again: 'Throat — water — Sue — darling — drop of water — please — O please!'

No water came, and the organ notes, faint as a bee's hum, rolled in as before.

While he remained, his face changing, shouts and hurrahs came from somewhere in the direction of the river.

'Ah — yes! The Remembrance games,' he murmured. 'And I here. And Sue defiled!'

The hurrahs were repeated, drowning the faint organ notes. Jude's face changed more: he whispered slowly, his parched lips scarcely moving:

'*Let the day perish wherein I was born, and the night in which it was said, There is a man child conceived.*'

('Hurrah!')

'*Let that day be darkness; let not God regard it from above, neither let the light shine upon it. Lo, let that night be solitary, let no joyful voice come therein.*'

('Hurrah!')

'*Why died I not from the womb? Why did I not give up the ghost when I came out of the belly? ... For now should I have lain still*

and been quiet. I should have slept: then had I been at rest!'
(Hurrah!')

'There the prisoners rest together; they hear not the voice of the oppressor. . . . The small and the great are there; and the servant is free from his master. Wherefore is light given to him that is in misery, and life unto the bitter in soul?' *

Meanwhile Arabella, in her journey to discover what was going on, took a short cut down a narrow street and through an obscure nook into the quad of Cardinal. It was full of bustle, and brilliant in the sunlight with flowers and other preparations for a ball here also. A carpenter nodded to her, one who had formerly been a fellow-workman of Jude's. A corridor was in course of erection from the entrance to the Hall staircase, of gay red and buff bunting. Waggon-loads of boxes containing bright plants in full bloom were being placed about, and the great staircase was covered with red cloth. She nodded to one workman and another, and ascended to the Hall on the strength of their acquaintance, where they were putting down a new floor and decorating for the dance. The cathedral bell close at hand was sounding for five o'clock service.

'I should not mind having a spin there with a fellow's arm round my waist,' she said to one of the men. 'But Lord, I must be getting home again – there's a lot to do. No dancing for me!'

When she reached home she was met at the door by Stagg, and one or two other of Jude's fellow stone-workers. 'We are just going down to the river,' said the former, 'to see the boat-bumping. But we've called round on our way to ask how your husband is.'

'He's sleeping nicely, thank you,' said Arabella.

'That's right. Well now, can't you give yourself half-an-hour's relaxation, Mrs Fawley, and come along with us? 'Twould do you good.'

'I should like to go,' said she. 'I've never seen the boat-racing, and I hear it is good fun.'

'Come along!'

'How I *wish* I could!' She looked longingly down the street. 'Wait a minute, then. I'll just run up and see how he is now. Father is with him, I believe; so I can most likely come.'

They waited, and she entered. Downstairs the inmates were

absent as before, having, in fact, gone in a body to the river where
the procession of boats was to pass. When she reached the bedroom
she found that her father had not even now come.

'Why couldn't he have been here!' she said impatiently. 'He wants
to see the boats himself – that's what it is!'

However, on looking round to the bed she brightened, for she
saw that Jude was apparently sleeping, though he was not in the
usual half-elevated posture necessitated by his cough. He had
slipped down, and lay flat. A second glance caused her to start, and
she went to the bed. His face was quite white, and gradually becoming rigid. She touched his fingers; they were cold, though his body
was still warm. She listened at his chest. All was still within. The
bumping of near thirty years had ceased.

After her first appalled sense of what had happened the faint
notes of a military or other brass band from the river reached her
ears; and in a provoked tone she exclaimed, 'To think he should die
just now! Why did he die just now!' Then meditating another
moment or two she went to the door, softly closed it as before, and
again descended the stairs.

'Here she is!' said one of the workmen. 'We wondered if you were
coming after all. Come along; we must be quick to get a good place.
... Well, how is he? Sleeping well still? Of course, we don't want to
drag 'ee away if—'

'O yes – sleeping quite sound. He won't wake yet,' she said
hurriedly.

They went with the crowd down Cardinal Street,* where they
presently reached the bridge, and the gay barges burst upon their
view. Thence they passed by a narrow slit down to the riverside path
– now dusty, hot, and thronged. Almost as soon as they had arrived
the grand procession of boats began; the oars smacking with a loud
kiss on the face of the stream, as they were lowered from the
perpendicular.

'O, I say – how jolly ! I'm glad I've come,' said Arabella. 'And –
it can't hurt my husband – my being away.'

On the opposite side of the river, on the crowded barges, were
gorgeous nosegays of feminine beauty, fashionably arrayed in green,
pink, blue, and white. The blue flag of the Boat Club denoted the
centre of interest, beneath which a band in red uniform gave out the

notes she had already heard in the death-chamber. Collegians of all sorts, in canoes with ladies, watching keenly for 'our' boat, darted up and down. While she regarded the lively scene somebody touched Arabella in the ribs, and looking round she saw Vilbert.

'That philter is operating, you know!' he said with a leer. 'Shame on 'ee to wreck a heart so!'

'I shan't talk of love to-day.'

'Why not? It is a general holiday.'

She did not reply. Vilbert's arm stole round her waist, which act could be performed unobserved in the crowd. An arch expression overspread Arabella's face at the feel of the arm, but she kept her eyes on the river as if she did not know of the embrace.

The crowd surged, pushing Arabella and her friends sometimes nearly into the river, and she would have laughed heartily at the horse-play that succeeded, if the imprint on her mind's eye of a pale, statuesque countenance she had lately gazed upon had not sobered her a little.

The fun on the water reached the acme of excitement; there were immersions; there were shouts: the race was lost and won, the pink and blue and yellow ladies retired from the barges, and the people who had watched began to move.

'Well — it's been awfully good,' cried Arabella. 'But I think I must get back to my poor man. Father is there, so far as I know; but I had better get back.'

'What's your hurry?'

'Well, I must go. . . . Dear, dear, this is awkward!'

At the narrow gangway where the people ascended from the riverside path to the bridge the crowd was literally jammed into one hot mass — Arabella and Vilbert with the rest; and here they remained motionless, Arabella exclaiming, 'Dear, dear!' more and more impatiently; for it had just occurred to her mind that if Jude were discovered to have died alone an inquest might be deemed necessary.

'What a fidget you are, my love,' said the physician, who, being pressed close against her by the throng, had no need of personal effort for contact. 'Just as well have patience: there's no getting away yet!'

It was nearly ten minutes before the wedged multitude moved

sufficiently to let them pass through. As soon as she got up into the street Arabella hastened on, forbidding the physician to accompany her further that day. She did not go straight to her house; but to the abode of a woman who performed the last necessary offices for the poorer dead; where she knocked.

'My husband has just gone, poor soul,' she said. 'Can you come and lay him out?'

Arabella waited a few minutes; and the two women went along, elbowing their way through the stream of fashionable people pouring out of Cardinal meadow, and being nearly knocked down by the carriages.

'I must call at the sexton's about the bell, too,' said Arabella. 'It is just round here, isn't it? I'll meet you at my door.'

By ten o'clock that night Jude was lying on the bedstead at his lodging covered with a sheet, and straight as an arrow. Through the partly opened window the joyous throb of a waltz entered from the ball-room at Cardinal.

Two days later, when the sky was equally cloudless, and the air equally still, two persons stood beside Jude's open coffin in the same little bedroom. On one side was Arabella, on the other the Widow Edlin. They were both looking at Jude's face, the worn old eyelids of Mrs Edlin being red.

'How beautiful he is!' said she.

'Yes. He's a 'andsome corpse,' said Arabella.

The window was still open to ventilate the room, and it being about noontide the clear air was motionless and quiet without. From a distance came voices; and an apparent noise of persons stamping.

'What's that?' murmured the old woman.

'Oh, that's the doctors in the Theatre, conferring Honorary degrees on the Duke of Hamptonshire and a lot more illustrious gents of that sort. It's Remembrance Week, you know. The cheers come from the young men.'

'Ay; young and strong-lunged! Not like our poor boy here.'

An occasional word, as from some one making a speech, floated from the open windows of the Theatre across to this quiet corner, at which there seemed to be a smile of some sort upon the marble features of Jude; while the old, superseded, Delphin editions of

Virgil and Horace, and the dog-eared Greek Testament on the
neighbouring shelf, and the few other volumes of the sort that he
had not parted with, roughened with stone-dust where he had been
in the habit of catching them up for a few minutes between his
labours, seemed to pale to a sickly cast at the sounds. The bells
struck out joyously; and their reverberations travelled round the
bedroom.

Arabella's eyes removed from Jude to Mrs Edlin. 'D'ye think she
will come?' she asked.

'I could not say. She swore not to see him again.'

'How is she looking?'

'Tired and miserable, poor heart. Years and years older than
when you saw her last. Quite a staid, worn woman now. 'Tis the
man; – she can't stomach un, even now!'

'If Jude had been alive to see her, he would hardly have cared for
her any more, perhaps.'

'That's what we don't know. . . . Didn't he ever ask you to send
for her, since he came to see her in that strange way?'

'No. Quite the contrary. I offered to send, and he said I was not
to let her know how ill he was.'

'Did he forgive her?'

'Not as I know.'

'Well – poor little thing, 'tis to be believed she's found forgiveness somewhere! She said she had found peace!'

'She may swear that on her knees to the holy cross upon her
necklace till she's hoarse, but it won't be true!' said Arabella. 'She's
never found peace since she left his arms, and never will again till
she's as he is now!'

Notes

Title-page. *'The letter killeth'*. See II Corinthians, III 6: 'the letter killeth, but the spirit giveth life.'

23 *notes made in 1887 and onwards*. He noted in his diary for 28 April 1888: 'A short story of a young man — "who could not go to Oxford" — His struggles and ultimate failure. Suicide. There is something the world ought to be shown, and I am the one to show it to them — though I was not altogether hindered going, at least to Cambridge, and could have gone up easily at five-and-twenty.' (F. E. Hardy, *Life of Thomas Hardy, 1840–1928* (1962) pp. 207–8.)

23 *the death of a woman in the former year*. The woman was possibly his cousin Tryphena Sparks. His poem 'Thoughts of Phena' was written in March 1890.

24 *a fantastic tale*. *The Well-beloved*, which was serialised in the *Illustrated London News* in 1892 and issued in book form in 1897.

24 *burnt by a bishop*. W. W. How, Bishop of Wakefield, announced in the *Yorkshire Post* that he had burnt his copy of *Jude*; at his instigation the novel was withdrawn from Smith's Circulating Library.

25 *the lady who having shuddered at the book. . . .* Jeannette Gilder, in an article in the *New York World*, described it as 'almost the worst book I ever read', continuing: 'When I finished the story I opened the windows and let in the fresh air, and I turned to my bookshelves and I said: "Thank God for Kipling and Stevenson, Barrie and Mrs Humphry Ward."' To Hardy's amazement, on coming to London shortly afterwards, she asked him for an interview. (See *Life*, pp. 279–80.)

25 *Diderot's words*. Diderot argues on these lines in his article on Natural Law in the *Encyclopédie* (1755).

25 *Bludyer*. Name of a 'slashing' book-reviewer in W. M. Thackeray's *Pendennis* (1848).

26 *poor lady in Blackwood*. This was Mrs Oliphant who, in an article 'The Anti-Marriage League' in the January 1896 issue of *Blackwood's*, launched a bitter attack on the novel, bracketing Hardy with Grant Allen as propagandists for free love.

Part-title. *'Yea, many there be . . . do thus?'* I Esdras, IV 26–32.

28 *tilted*. With a canvas 'tilt' or cover.

29 *Miss Fawley's*. Several of Hardy's ancestors lived at a village called Fawley in Berkshire — the 'Marygreen' of the novel. Hardy originally gave Jude the surname 'Head', which was that of his own paternal grandmother, who lived at Fawley as a girl.

30 *harlican*. (Dial.) a term of abuse.

32 *willow-pattern*. Popular pseudo-Chinese decorative design, depicting a river with a bridge and trees, used on blue-and-white transfer-printed pottery and porcelain from 1780 onwards and attributed to Thomas Minton.

32 *med.* (Dial.) might.

34 *tassets.* Pieces of thigh armour.

37 *deedy.* (Dial.) serious.

37 *'Now they that are younger ... my flock.'* Job, XXX 1.

37 *journeyman.* Day-labourer.

37 *or'nary.* (Dial.) insignificant, inferior.

37 *sprawl.* (Dial.) energy.

39 *the Brown House.* Based on the Red Barn, which stood at the junction of the Ridge Way and the main road to Wantage.

41 *Herne the Hunter.* The legendary 'wild huntsman', once a keeper in Windsor Forest. (See Shakespeare's *Merry Wives of Windsor*, Act IV, sc. IV.)

41 *Apollyon.* Demonic monster encountered by Christian in John Bunyan's *Pilgrim's Progress* (1678).

41 *captain with the bleeding hole in his forehead.* He appears in a tale called 'Die Geschichte von dem Gespensterchiff' ('The Story of the Ghost-ship') by the German writer Wilhelm Hauff (1802–27).

42 *Nebuchadnezzar's furnace.* Shadrach, Meshach and Abednego walked unharmed within the flames of the furnace into which they had been thrown by the Babylonian king Nebuchadnezzar. (See Daniel, III.)

44 *Babel.* 'The city and tower, described in Genesis, XI, where the confusion of tongues took place' (*OED*).

44 *night-hawk.* Night-jar.

44 *lirruping.* Or 'larruping'. (Dial.) idle.

45 *Crozier Hotel.* Presumably suggested by the well-known Mitre Hotel in Oxford.

48 *heaven lies about them.* See Wordsworth's ode, *Intimations of Immortality*: 'Heaven lies about us in our infancy!'

50 *Grimm's Law.* The famous law, formulated by Jakob Grimm in 1822, of the invariable pattern of permutation of consonants from their Indo-Germanic form to modern Germanic forms.

51 *cotters.* A cotter is, strictly, a labourer occupying a cottage belonging to a farm; as a sort of outservant.

52 *old Delphin editions.* A series of editions of the classics produced in France in the reign of Louis XIV for the education of the Dauphin – hence the motto on the title-page 'In usum serenissimi Delphini'. They were frequently reprinted in this country.

52 *woes of Dido.* As related in Virgil's *Aeneid*.

52 *the sponge.* 'The soft fermenting dough of which bread is made' (OED).

53 *'Carmen Sæculare'.* Poem by Horace.

53 *'Phoebe silvarumque potens Diana!'* 'O Phoebus, and Diana queen of Forests.' (The first line of the poem.)

54 *Clarke's Homer.* Samuel Clarke's well-known Graeco-Latin edition of the *Iliad* (1729–32).

54 *Griesbach's text.* Famous critical edition of the Greek New Testament by Johann Jackob Griesbach (1745–1812), first published in Halle in 1774–7.

58 *her beloved son, etc.* See Matthew, III 17: 'This is my beloved Son, in whom I am well pleased.'

58 *the characteristic part of a barrow-pig.* The 'pizzle' or penis of a castrated boar.

58 *chitterlings.* Small intestines.

59 *deedily.* Meaningfully, seriously.

59 *in posse.* (Latin) potential.

59 *conjunctive orders.* Hardy presumably means 'orders to get himself joined [to a woman]'.

63 Η ΚΑΙΝΗ ΔΙΑΘΗΚΗ. Greek for 'The New Testament'.

64 *Mizzle.* (Dial.) hurry up.

85 *blackpot.* Black pudding.

86 *glane!'* (Dial.) sneer.

92 *scallops.* 'The stringy part of the fat, which cannot be made into lard' (J. Wright, *English Dialect Dictionary*).

92 *blower.* Device to create an upward draught.

92 *pig-jobbing.* Pig-dealing.

Part-title. *'Save his own soul ... star.'* From 'Prelude', in Swinburne's *Songs before Sunrise*.

Part-title. *'Notitiam primosque ... amor.'* Ovid's *Metamorphoses*, bk IV, ll. 59–60. ('Contiguity caused their first acquaintance; love grew with time.')

97 *Dick Whittington.* Richard Whittington (d. 1423) arrived in London a pauper and remained to become Lord Mayor. He has become celebrated as a hero of pantomime.

97 *'Beersheba'.* Fictitious name for the district in Oxford known as 'Jericho'.

98 *A bell began clanging.* The great bell in Tom Tower rings a 101-stroke curfew at five past nine.

99 *friend and eulogist of Shakespeare.* Ben Jonson (1572–1637).

99 *him who has recently passed into silence.* Robert Browning (1812–89).

99 *that musical one.* A. C. Swinburne (1837–1909).

99 *the well-known three.* J. H. Newman (1801–90), John Keble (1792–1866), Edward Pusey (1800–82).

99 *the form in the full-bottomed wig.* Lord Bolingbroke (1678–1751).

99 *the smoothly shaven historian.* Edward Gibbon (1737–94).

100 *he who apologized for the Church in Latin.* Hardy later said he could not remember whom he had meant.

100 *the saintly author of the Evening Hymn.* Bishop Thomas Ken (1637–1711).

100 *the great itinerant preacher.* John Wesley (1703–91).

100 *One of the spectres.* Matthew Arnold. The quotation is from the preface to his *Essays in Criticism, First Series* (1865).

100 *the Corn Law convert.* Sir Robert Peel (1788–1850). The quotation is from a speech of his to the House of Commons in 1846.

101 *the sly author.* Gibbon. The quotation is from Chapter 15 of his *Decline and Fall* (1776–88).

101 *the last of the optimists.* Robert Browning (1812–89). The quotation is from his 'By the Fireside'.

101 *author of the Apologia.* Newman. The quotation, slightly garbled, is from his *Apologia pro Vita Sua* (1864).

101 *'Why should we faint . . . we die?'* From 'Twenty-fourth Sunday after Trinity' in Keble's collection of devotional poems, *The Christian Year* (1827).

101 *the genial Spectator.* Joseph Addison (1672–1719). The quotation, slightly garbled, is from *The Spectator*, no. 26 (1711).

102 *'Teach me to live . . . to die. . . .'* From the 'Evening Hymn' of Bishop Ken. (See note to p. 100.)

104 *bankers.* Stone benches.

105 *read . . . inwardly digest.* A phrase from a collect in the Book of Common Prayer.

106 *ogee dome.* The ogivally shaped dome of Tom Tower, in Christ Church, which houses the bell called Great Tom. The tower is by Wren.

107 *'For wisdom . . . have it.'* Ecclesiastes, VII 12.

107 *Evangelical.* i.e., an Anglican of the Low Church school in the early Victorian period.

108 *Crozier College, Old-time Street.* Hardy, in a note to Clive Holland, published in the latter's *Thomas Hardy, O.M.* (1933), tentatively identified these as Oriel College and Oriel Lane.

111 *Cardinal College.* Fictitious name for Christ Church.

111 *In quo corriget.* The Latin version of the line quoted in the same sentence.

112 *the dew of Hermon.* The river Jordan was formed by streams from Mount Hermon. See also Psalm, CXXXIII 3.

112 *Cyprus.* Famous for the worship of Venus.

114 *St Silas.* Based on the church of St Barnabas, on the east bank of the canal, near the west end of Cardigan Street.

114 *the Christian Year.* See note to p. 101.

115 *Julian the Apostate.* Roman emperor (331–63) who attempted to restore paganism. His dying words were said to have been: 'Vicisti Galilæe'. ('Thou hast conquered, O Galilean.')

115 *'Thou hast . . . thy breath!'* From Swinburne's 'Hymn to Proserpine'.

116 *Latin cross.* Cross of which the lower limb is larger than the others.

116 *'All hemin . . . di autou!'* From the Greek of I Corinthians: 'But to us there is but one God, the father, of whom are all things, and we in him, and one Lord Jesus Christ, by whom are all things, and we by him.'

118 *erotolepsy.* Seizure by sexual passion.

119 *the cross in the pavement.* There was a cross in the paving of Broad Street marking the spot of the martyrdom of Latimer, Ridley and Cranmer. In 1841 a Martyrs' Memorial was erected in St Giles, nearby.

131 *'Excelsior'.* Poem by Longfellow, much favoured by reciters.

131 *'There was a sound of revelry by night'.* The famous eve-of-Waterloo passage in Byron's *Childe Harold*, canto III, l. 21.

131 *'Ghastly, grim . . . shore!'* From 'The Raven', by Edgar Allan Poe.

132 *well-known writer.* Perhaps Thomas Carlyle, who uses the phrase 'the sleep of a spinning-top' in *Sartor Resartus* (1838), bk I, ch. 3

135 *genius loci.* (Latin) spirit of the place.

135 *the fatuousness of Crusoe.* Robinson Crusoe, having built himself a boat, found it was too big to drag to the water.

135 *'Above the youth's ... rise!'* From 'Götterdämmerung' by Heine.

135 *singularly built theatre.* The Sheldonian, the Senate House of Oxford University, designed by Wren.

136 *great library.* The Bodleian.

137 *Tetuphenay.* A made-up name, apparently based on the Greek τετυφέναι, meaning 'to have beaten'.

137 *The Fourways.* Carfax.

139 *Tinker Taylor.* The name is evidently an echo of the children's counting-out rhyme, 'Tinker, tailor, soldier, sailor', etc.

141 *Nicene.* The creed properly so called was formulated by the Council of Nicæa in 325, though what is commonly referred to as the 'Nicene creed' is somewhat later in origin.

142 *the Ratcatcher's Daughter.* There is a version of this in Charles Chilton's *Victorian Folk Songs* (1965).

144 *the Laocoön.* The famous classical sculpture, now in the Vatican, of Laocoön and his two sons being crushed to death by serpents.

Part-title. *'For there was ... like her!'* Poem no. 106 in H. T. Wharton's *Sappho* (1885).

148 *the days of his vanity.* See Ecclesiastes, IX 9.

151 *murrey-coloured.* Mulberry-coloured.

155 *Paley and Butler.* William Paley's *Evidences of Christianity* (1794) and Joseph Butler's *Analogy of Religion* (1736) were standard works of Christian apologetics.

156 *Wardour Castle.* It was built in 1769–76, the architect being James Paine.

158 *chainey.* (Dial.) china.

158 *chimmer.* (Dial.) chamber.

159 *Ishmaelite.* Outcast; like Ishmael, son of Abraham and Hagar. See Genesis, XVI 12: 'And he will be a wild man; his hand will be against every man, and every man's hand against him.'

163 *Pusey's Library of the Fathers.* English translation from the early Christian fathers, edited by Edward Pusey the Tractarian.

169 *"twitched the robe ... draped".* From Browning's 'Too Late'.

170 *"O ghastly glories ... Gods!"* From Swinburne's 'Hymn to Proserpine'.

172 *brochures.* (French) pamphlets.

172 *the real nature of that rhapsody.* The orthodox justification for the inclusion of the erotic Song of Solomon in the Bible was that it was an allegory of God's relation to the Church.

174 *Ganymedes.* Beautiful boy, whom Zeus carried off to be his cup-bearer.

175 *dew-bit.* Slight refreshment taken before breakfast.

180 *National schoolmaster.* Master at one of the schools set up by the National Society for Promoting the Education of the Poor in the Principles of the Established Church, the largest single provider of elementary schools in early Victorian Britain.

188 *Venus Urania.* Goddess of heavenly, as opposed to earthly, love.

191 *residence of fifteen.* Sue's marriage is to be by special licence, in which case one

434   JUDE THE OBSCURE

party is supposed to have been resident in the parish where the ceremony is performed for fifteen days.

192 *Perpendicular.* In the late English Gothic style so-called.

192 *'...I can find no way ... womanhood!'* From Browning's 'The Worst of It'.

204 *Chief Street.* Fictitious name for High Street.

210 *Sebastiano's Lazarus.* Sebastiano del Piombo's 'Resurrection of Lazarus', in the National Gallery.

213 *'insulted Nature ... rights'.* From Gibbon's *Decline and Fall*, ch. 15.

Part-title. *'Who so prefers ... Pharisee'.* From John Milton's preface to *The Doctrine and Discipline of Divorce* (1643).

220 *'From those foundation ... arise'.* From Michael Drayton's *Polyolbion* (1622).

220 *King Edward 'the Martyr'.* King of England 975–8.

222 *as such ... uplands.* The manuscript reading of this phrase has here been preferred to that of the Wessex and subsequent editions which transposes the words 'only' and 'will'.

223 *Old-Grove Place.* 'Grove Place' is an ancient house in Shaftesbury.

224 *Cowper's Apocryphal Gospels.* B. H. Cowper's *The Apocryphal Gospels* was published in 1874.

224 *Apologetica.* i.e. Christian apologetics.

226 *Joseph the dreamer of dreams.* See Genesis, XXXVII 5: 'And Joseph dreamed a dream', etc.

234 *gin.* Snare or trap.

244 *"who lets the world ... imitation".* From J. S. Mill's *On Liberty* (1859).

244 *argumentum ad verecundiam.* (Latin) appeal to modesty. The phrase is used by Francis Bacon (1561–1626).

245 *"Human development ... diversity".* See ch. 3 of Mill's *On Liberty.*

247 *newel.* Post supporting hand-rail of staircase.

248 *"Where Duncliffe is ... Away...."* From 'Shaftesbury Feair', by the Dorset poet William Barnes (1801–86).

249 *'Where Stour ... fed'.* From Drayton's *Polyolbion.*

250 *toled.* (Dial.) enticed.

251 *good-now.* According to Hardy this phrase is equivalent to the American 'I guess'.

252 *Laon and Cythna.* Heroic lovers in Shelley's *The Revolt of Islam* (1818).

252 *Paul and Virginia.* Lovers in Bernardin de St Pierre's famous novel *Paul et Virginie* (1786).

252 *all abroad.* i.e., all astray.

253 *rummer.* Large glass.

253 *rafted.* (Dial.) troubled, upset.

258 *"The soldier-saints ... bliss".* From Browning's 'The Statue and the Bust'.

260 *"the shadowy third".* From Browning's 'By the Fireside'.

262 *from whom neither length nor breadth ... divide me.* See Romans, VIII 38–9: 'For I am persuaded that neither death, nor life, nor angels, nor principalities, nor powers, nor things present, nor things to come, nor height, nor depth, nor any other creature, shall be able to separate us from the love of God....'

267 *standards.* 'In British Elementary schools: Each of the recognized degrees of proficiency according to which school children are or have been classified' (*OED*).

269 *topper.* According to Wright's *English Dialect Dictionary* a 'topper' is 'a long screed of larch fir'.

Part-title. '*Thy aerial part ... body.*' From *Thoughts of the Emperor Marcus Antoninus Aurelius* translated by George Long (1862).

289 *oneyer.* Perhaps, an individualist.

290 *Via Sacra.* Street in ancient Rome.

290 *Octavia.* Sister of Augustus and wife of Mark Antony.

290 *Livia.* Wife of Augustus.

291 *Aspasia.* Famous Athenian courtesan, mistress to Pericles.

291 *Phryne.* Famous Athenian courtesan, renowned for her beauty.

291 "*Can you keep ... love. ...*" From 'Song' by Thomas Campbell (1777–1844).

294 "*Let the day perish ... conceived!*" Job, III 3.

296 *fly.* Any one-horse covered carriage let out for hire.

299 *Melpomene.* Muse of tragedy.

300 "*For what man is he ... take her.*" Deuteronomy, XX 7.

301 *vitty.* (Dial.) fitting.

302 *house of Atreus.* The royal house of Argos, the tragic destiny of which forms the subject of Aeschylus's *Oresteia.*

302 *house of Jeroboam.* Jeroboam, king of Israel, set up images of other gods, for which he and his house were cursed by the Lord. See I Kings, X.

302 '*Royal-tower'd Thame*'. Last phrase of Milton's 'At a Vacation Exercise'.

305 *Shapes like our own selves hideously multiplied.* From Shelley's *The Revolt of Islam.*

306 *sakes if tidden.* (Dial.) Haven's sake if it isn't.

307 *game o' dibs.* Children's game played with pebbles or the knuckle bones of a sheep.

308 *pleasing anxious beings.* Cf. Thomas Gray's 'Elegy': 'For who, to dumb Forgetfulness a prey, This pleasing anxious being e'er resign'd. ...'

308 *scot-and-lot freeholder.* Till the Reform Act of 1832, one qualification for the vote in borough elections was to be a 'scot-and-lot inhabitant', i.e. such as paid the poor rate.

310 *as a tale that is told.* From Psalm XC, 9.

321 *voot.* (Dial.) foot.

321 *mind.* i.e., remember.

325 *Pugin.* Augustus Welby Northmore Pugin (1813–52) was a pioneer of the Gothic revival in English architecture.

327 "*we have wronged ... no man!*" II Corinthians, VII 2.

327 "*done that which was right in our own eyes*" Judges, XVII 6.

328 *ashlaring.* Giving a stone façade to.

331 *standing.*' Stall.

338 *chaw high.* (Dial.) be genteel, or scornful of the commonplace (chaw = chew.)

338 "*Then shall the man ... iniquity.*" Numbers, V 31.

Part-title. '*...And she humbled ... hair.*' Esther (Apocrypha), XIV 2.

Part-title. *'There are two ... here.'* From Browning's 'Too Late'.

342 *Remembrance Day.* Presumably a fictitious version of the Oxford Commemoration.

343 *church with the Italian porch.* The church of St Mary-the-Virgin in the High Street. It has a porch, erected in 1637, with twisted baroque columns.

344 *Lycaonians.* When St Paul performed a miraculous cure in Lycaonia, the crowd hailed him and Barnabas as Mercury and Jupiter come down to earth. (See Acts, xiv 5–11.)

346 *"For who knoweth ... sun?"* Ecclesiastes, vi 12.

347 *object glass.* Telescope lens.

349 *from Caiaphas to Pilate!* ... From the Jewish High Priest to the Roman Procurator before whom Christ was tried.

352 *Sarcophagus College.* Hardy deliberately left the location of this vague.

352 *Rubric College.* Hardy tentatively identified this as Brasenose.

356 *the coming universal wish not to live.* Schopenhauer regarded the world as, in some sense, kept in being by the will-to-live, and he envisaged its winding-up when humanity should succeed in renouncing the will-to-live.

357 *the eastward position.* The practice of the celebrant of the Eucharist standing on the west side of the altar and facing east (i.e. with his back to the congregation). There was much controversy about this practice, but in 1890 Archbishop E. W. Benson declared the eastward position compatible with the Book of Common Prayer rubric.

359 *chorus of the Agamemnon.* See Aeschylus's *Agamemnon*, ll. 67–8.

360 *swage.* (Dial.) assuage.

362 *"We are made ... to men!"* From I Corinthians, iv 9.

365 *sensitive plant.* Name given to the *mimosa pudica*, which closes its leaves at the slightest touch, and to other plants with similar qualities. Shelley used it as the title of a poem.

366 *chiel is amang them.* See Robert Burns's 'On the Late Captain Grose's Peregrinations Thro' Scotland':

> A chiel's amang you taking notes
> And, faith, he'll prent it.

A 'chiel' means a young man, or a fellow.

374 *Then let the veil ... this hour.* At Christ's death, according to Mark's Gospel, xv 38, 'the veil of the temple was rent in twain from the top to the bottom'.

378 *Rhadamanthine strictness.* In Greek mythology, Rhadamanthus was one of the three judges of hell.

379 *Acherontic shades.* Souls of the departed crossing the River Acheron into Hades.

380 *"the world ... worth".* From Browning's 'The Statue and the Bust'.

381 *"Charity seeketh not her own."* From I Corinthians, v.

382 *steam-tram.* Steam-trams were employed on several tramways in England in the early 1880s.

382 *The Bear.* There was a public house so called in Wantage, the original of Alfredston.

384 *night-rails*. (Dial.) night-gowns, or bed-gowns.

388 *lily her name connoted*. 'Susanna' derives from the Hebrew word for lily.

389 *"saved as by fire"*. See I Corinthians, III 15. 'If any man's work shall be burned, he shall suffer loss: but he himself shall be saved; yet so as by fire.'

390 *templates*. Pieces of wood or metal with shaped edge, used as guides in carving or moulding.

395 *Fuller's Holy State*. Thomas Fuller's *The Holy State and the Profane State* (1642).

395 *"Though I give ... nothing."* From I Corinthians, XIII 3.

401 *in this Capharnaum*. Aramaic spelling of Capernaum, one of the towns in Galilee where Christ did much of his teaching. The reference is to Matthew, IV 13–16, where the people of Capernaum are said to have 'sat in darkness'.

401 *the W— of Babylon*. The Whore of Babylon, referred to in Revelation, XVII–XIX, stands for Rome and the luxury and vice of the world.

402 *flitch*. A 'flitch' means a side of pig.

407 *"the letter killeth"!* See note to title-page.

412 *The Poet of Liberty*. P. B. Shelley (1792–1822).

412 *Dissector of Melancholy*. Robert Burton, author of *The Anatomy of Melancholy* (1621).

412 *As Antigone said*. See the *Antigone* of Sophocles, l. 851: μέτοικος ου ξωσιν, ὸν θανονσιν.

415 *un-ray*. (Dial.) undress.

415 *jumps*. A 'pair of jumps' was a sort of underbodice.

424 *'Let that day ... bitter in soul?'* The quotations are from Job, III.

425 *Cardinal Street*. Fictitious name for St Aldate's Street.

Note on the Text

ACCORDING to Hardy's Preface to *Jude*, 'The scheme was jotted down in 1890, from notes made in 1887 and onwards', and 'the narrative was written in outline in 1892 and the spring of 1893, and at full length ... from August 1893 onwards into the next year; the whole, with the exception of a few chapters, being in the hands of the publisher by the end of 1894'. Some time before the end of 1893 he arranged for serial publication in *Harper's New Monthly Magazine*. By next year, however, he was having qualms and told Harper's that 'the development of the story was carrying him into unexpected fields and he was afraid to predict its future trend'. He asked them to cancel the agreement, but this was not done; so he was forced, as with *Tess*, to go through the novel in detail, altering and bowdlerising it for the magazine public. Judging from the terminal date in the manuscript, the task occupied him till March 1895. The serial version, meanwhile, began to appear in December 1894, running till November of the next year. The first instalment appeared under the title 'The Simpletons', but in the second this was changed to 'Hearts Insurgent' with a note to the effect that 'The author's attention having been drawn to the resemblance between the title "The Simpletons" and that of another English novel [presumably Charles Reade's *A Simpleton*, published in *Harper's* 1872–3], he had decided to revert to the title originally selected.'

The first edition in book form was published in England by Osgood, McIlvaine & Co. on 1 October 1895 (post-dated 1896) in one volume at six shillings and simultaneously by Harper & Brothers in the United States.

Macmillan took over the publishing rights in 1902, and for a new edition produced by them in 1903 Hardy made some revisions, as he did again for the definitive Wessex Edition of 1912.

Examination of the manuscript (now in the Fitzwilliam Museum, Cambridge) shows that Hardy originally conceived the plot rather differently. When the novel opens, Jude has been at Marygreen for only a month, and his arrival follows closely on Sue's departure for Christminster, where – her parents having recently died – she has been taken in charge by the provost of one of the colleges. Jude's motivation for determining to go to Christminster is thus the fact of Sue's presence there. The schoolmaster

Phillotson does not appear in the opening part of the novel — and indeed may not have figured in the novel at all.

The probable implication of the changes [1] is that, as originally conceived, the story was to have centred mainly or entirely on Jude's educational difficulties, but that at some stage in the writing a whole new centre of interest — the marriage question — developed, thus complicating the book's design.

Hardy's revisions in 1903 were described by him as 'slight' and as mainly concerned with 'errors, particularly of repetition'. However, in one scene, that in which Arabella throws the pig's pizzle at Jude as he walks along dreaming of academic fame, Hardy's revisions were, in fact, extensive. It was this scene which had especially outraged reviewers (Mrs Oliphant stigmatised it as 'more brutal in depravity than anything which the darkest slums could bring forth'), and he now bowdlerised it considerably, curtailing references to the indecent 'piece o' the pig'. Among the changes were the following:

[1895] . . . the enterprise of throwing the lump of offal at him, the bladder, from which she had obviously just cut it off, lying close beside her.
[1903] the enterprise of attracting his attention from dreams of the humaner letters to what was simmering in the minds around him.

[1895] Jude held out his stick with the fragment of pig dangling therefrom, looking elsewhere the while, and faintly colouring.
     She, too, looked in another direction, and took the piece as though ignorant of what her hand was doing. She hung it temporarily on the rail of the bridge, and then, by a species of mutual curiosity, they both turned, and regarded it.
[1903] Jude, tossing back her missile, seemed to expect her to explain why she had audaciously stopped him by this novel artillery instead of by hailing him.
     But she, slily looking in another direction, swayed herself backwards and forwards on her hand as it clutched the rail of the bridge; till, moved by amatory curiosity, she turned her eyes critically upon him.

[1895] '. . . on the bridge, wi' that piece o' the pig hanging between ye — haw-haw! What a proper thing to court over!'
[1903] '. . . on the bridge, when he looked at 'ee as if he had never seen a woman before in his born days.'

None of the changes made for the 1912 edition, though numerous, were

---

[1] See J. Paterson, 'The Genesis of *Jude the Obscure*', in *Studies in Philology*, vol. 57 (1960).

as substantial as these. Their most noticeable trend was to give a slightly more sympathetic colour to Sue's character and treatment of Jude.

The text of the present edition is based on that of the Wessex Edition of 1912 and from the fourth impression onwards three additional corrections on pages 24, 66 and 334 have been made. Evidence exists in the Dorset County Museum, Dorchester, that Hardy wished these to be made in reprints of the Wessex Edition, but for some reason this was not done.

General Preface to the Wessex Edition of 1912

IN accepting a proposal for a definite edition of these productions in prose and verse I have found an opportunity of classifying the novels under heads that show approximately the author's aim, if not his achievement, in each book of the series at the date of its composition. Sometimes the aim was lower than at other times; sometimes, where the intention was primarily high, force of circumstances (among which the chief were the necessities of magazine publication) compelled a modification, great or slight, of the original plan. Of a few, however, of the longer novels, and of many of the shorter tales, it may be assumed that they stand today much as they would have stood if no accidents had obstructed the channel between the writer and the public. That many of them, if any, stand as they would stand if written *now* is not to be supposed.

In the classification of these fictitious chronicles — for which the name of 'The Wessex Novels' was adopted, and is still retained — the first group is called 'Novels of Character and Environment', and contains those which approach most nearly to uninfluenced works; also one or two which, whatever their quality in some few of their episodes, may claim a verisimilitude in general treatment and detail.

The second group is distinguished as 'Romances and Fantasies', a sufficiently descriptive definition. The third class — 'Novels of Ingenuity' — show a not infrequent disregard of the probable in the chain of events, and depend for their interest mainly on the incidents themselves. They might also be characterized as 'Experiments', and were written for the nonce simply; though despite the artificiality of their fable some of their scenes are not without fidelity to life.[1]

It will not be supposed that these differences are distinctly perceptible in

[1] Novels of Character and Environment: *Tess of the d'Urbervilles, Far from the Madding Crowd, Jude the Obscure, The Return of the Native, The Mayor of Casterbridge, The Woodlanders, Under the Greenwood Tree, Life's Little Ironies* and *A Few Crusted Characters, Wessex Tales.*

Romances and Fantasies: *A Pair of Blue Eyes, The Trumpet-Major, Two on a Tower, The Well-beloved, A Group of Noble Dames.*

Novels of Ingenuity: *Desperate Remedies, The Hand of Ethelberta, A Laodicean.* [General Editor's note]

442 JUDE THE OBSCURE

every page of every volume. It was inevitable that blendings and alter-
nations should occur in all. Moreover, as it was not thought desirable in
every instance to change the arrangement of the shorter stories to which
readers have grown accustomed, certain of these may be found under
headings to which an acute judgment might deny appropriateness.

It has sometimes been conceived of novels that evolve their action on a
circumscribed scene — as do many (though not all) of these — that they
cannot be so inclusive in their exhibition of human nature as novels wherein
the scenes cover large extents of country, in which events figure amid towns
and cities, even wander over the four quarters of the globe. I am not
concerned to argue this point further than to suggest that the conception is
an untrue one in respect of the elementary passions. But I would state that
the geographical limits of the stage here trodden were not absolutely forced
upon the writer by circumstances; he forced them upon himself from
judgment. I considered that our magnificent heritage from the Greeks in
dramatic literature found sufficient room for a large proportion of its action
in an extent of their country not much larger than the half-dozen counties
here reunited under the old name of Wessex, that the domestic emotions
have throbbed in Wessex nooks with as much intensity as in the palaces of
Europe, and that, anyhow, there was quite enough human nature in Wessex
for one man's literary purpose. So far was I possessed by this idea that I
kept within the frontiers when it would have been easier to overlap them
and give more cosmopolitan features to the narrative.

Thus, though the people in most of the novels (and in much of the shorter
verse) are dwellers in a province bounded on the north by the Thames, on
the south by the English Channel, on the east by a line running from
Hayling Island to Windsor Forest, and on the west by the Cornish coast,
they were meant to be typically and essentially those of any and every place
where

Thought's the slave of life, and life time's fool

— beings in whose hearts and minds that which is apparently local should be
really universal.

But whatever the success of this intention, and the value of these novels
as delineations of humanity, they have at least a humble supplementary
quality of which I may be justified in reminding the reader, though it is one
that was quite unintentional and unforeseen. At the dates represented in the
various narrations things were like that in Wessex: the inhabitants lived in
certain ways, engaged in certain occupations, kept alive certain customs,
just as they are shown doing in these pages. And in particularizing such I
have often been reminded of Boswell's remarks on the trouble to which he
was put and the pilgrimages he was obliged to make to authenticate some

detail, though the labour was one which would bring him no praise. Unlike his achievement, however, on which an error would as he says have brought discredit, if these country customs and vocations, obsolete and obsolescent, had been detailed wrongly, nobody would have discovered such errors to the end of Time. Yet I have instituted inquiries to correct tricks of memory, and striven against temptations to exaggerate, in order to preserve for my own satisfaction a fairly true record of a vanishing life.

It is advisable also to state here, in response to inquiries from readers interested in landscape, prehistoric antiquities, and especially old English architecture, that the description of these backgrounds has been done from the real – that is to say, has something real for its basis, however illusively treated. Many features of the first two kinds have been given under their existing names; for instance, the Vale of Blackmoor or Blakemore, Hambledon Hill, Bulbarrow, Nettlecombe Tout, Dogbury Hill, High-Stoy, Bubb-Down Hill, The Devil's Kitchen, Cross-in-Hand, Long-Ash Lane, Benvill Lane, Giant's Hill, Crimmercrock Lane, and Stonehenge. The rivers Froom, or Frome, and Stour, are, of course, well known as such. And the further idea was that large towns and points tending to mark the outline of Wessex – such as Bath, Plymouth, The Start, Portland Bill, Southampton, etc. – should be named clearly. The scheme was not greatly elaborated, but, whatever its value, the names remain still.

In respect of places described under fictitious or ancient names in the novels – for reasons that seemed good at the time of writing them – and kept up in the poems – discerning people have affirmed in print that they clearly recognize the originals: such as Shaftesbury in 'Shaston', Sturminster Newton in 'Stourcastle', Dorchester in 'Casterbridge', Salisbury Plain in 'The Great Plain', Cranborne Chase in 'The Chase', Beaminster in 'Emminster', Bere Regis in 'Kingsbere', Woodbury Hill in 'Greenhill', Wool Bridge in 'Wellbridge', Harfoot or Harput Lane in 'Stagfoot Lane', Hazlebury in 'Nuttlebury', Bridport in 'Port Bredy', Maiden Newton in 'Chalk Newton', a farm near Nettlecombe Tout in 'Flintcomb Ash', Sherborne in 'Sherton Abbas', Milton Abbey in 'Middleton Abbey', Cerne Abbas in 'Abbot's Cernel', Evershot in 'Evershed', Taunton in 'Toneborough', Bournemouth in 'Sandbourne', Winchester in 'Wintoncester', Oxford in 'Christminster', Reading in 'Aldbrickham', Newbury in 'Kennetbridge', Wantage in 'Alfredston', Basingstoke in 'Stoke Barehills', and so on. Subject to the qualifications above given, that no detail is guaranteed – that the portraiture of fictitiously named towns and villages was only suggested by certain real places, and wantonly wanders from inventorial descriptions of them – I do not contradict these keen hunters for the real; I am satisfied with their statements as

444   JUDE THE OBSCURE

at least an indication of their interest in the scenes.

Thus much for the novels. Turning now to the verse – to myself the more individual part of my literary fruitage – I would say that, unlike some of the fiction, nothing interfered with the writer's freedom in respect of its form or content. Several of the poems – indeed many – were produced before novel-writing had been thought of as a pursuit; but few saw the light till all the novels had been published. The limited stage to which the majority of the latter confine their exhibitions has not been adhered to here in the same proportion, the dramatic part especially having a very broad theatre of action. It may thus relieve the circumscribed areas treated in the prose, if such relief be needed. To be sure, one might argue that by surveying Europe from a celestial point of vision – as in *The Dynasts* – that continent becomes virtually a province – a Wessex, an Attica, even a mere garden – and hence is made to conform to the principle of the novels, however far it outmeasures their region. But that may be as it will.

The few volumes filled by the verse cover a producing period of some eighteen years first and last, while the seventeen or more volumes of novels represent correspondingly about four-and-twenty years. One is reminded by this disproportion in time and result how much more concise and quintessential expression becomes when given in rhythmic form than when shaped in the language of prose.

One word on what has been called the present writer's philosophy of life, as exhibited more particularly in this metrical section of his compositions. Positive views on the Whence and the Wherefore of things have never been advanced by this pen as a consistent philosophy. Nor is it likely, indeed, that imaginative writings extending over more than forty years would exhibit a coherent scientific theory of the universe even if it had been attempted – of that universe concerning which Spencer owns to the 'para-lyzing thought' that possibly there exists no comprehension of it any-where. But such objectless consistency never has been attempted, and the sentiments in the following pages have been stated truly to be mere impres-sions of the moment, and not convictions or arguments.

That these impressions have been condemned as 'pessimistic' – as if that were a very wicked adjective – shows a curious muddle-mindedness. It must be obvious that there is a higher characteristic of philosophy than pessimism, or than meliorism, or even than the optimism of these critics – which is truth. Existence is either ordered in a certain way, or it is not so ordered, and conjectures which harmonize best with experience are removed above all comparison with other conjectures which do not so harmonize. So that to say one view is worse than other views without proving it erroneous implies the possibility of a false view being better or more expedient than a true view; and no pragmatic proppings can make that *idolum specus* stand on its feet, for it postulates a prescience denied to humanity.

And there is another consideration. Differing natures find their tongue in the presence of differing spectacles. Some natures become vocal at tragedy, some are made vocal by comedy, and it seems to me that to whichever of these aspects of life a writer's instinct for expression the more readily responds, to that he should allow it to respond. That before a contrasting side of things he remains undemonstrative need not be assumed to mean that he remains unperceiving.

It was my hope to add to these volumes of verse as many more as would make a fairly comprehensive cycle of the whole. I had wished that those in dramatic, ballad, and narrative form should include most of the cardinal situations which occur in social and public life, and those in lyric form a round of emotional experiences of some completeness. But

> The petty done, the undone vast!

The more written the more seems to remain to be written; and the night cometh. I realize that these hopes and plans, except possibly to the extent of a volume or two, must remain unfulfilled.

October 1911   T.H.

Glossary of Place-names

ALDBRICKHAM. Reading.

ALFREDSTON. Wantage, in Berkshire.

CHRISTMINSTER. Oxford. (For identification of Christminster streets and buildings, see Notes.)

CRESSCOMBE. Letcombe Basset, a village on the northern side of the hills between Fawley and Wantage.

EXONBURY. Exeter.

FENSWORTH. Letcombe Regis, a village between Letcombe Basset and Wantage.

KENNETBRIDGE. Newbury, Berkshire. (It stands on the River Kennet.)

LEDDENTON. Gillingham, a town four miles north-west of Shaftesbury. (The fictitious name was suggested by the River Lodden; and Hardy gives the real name to Phillotson's friend George Gillingham.)

LUMSDON. Cumnor, a village not far from Oxford.

MARYGREEN. Fawley, a village in the hills south of Wantage. (Mary, Hardy's paternal grandmother, lived there as an orphan in childhood.)

MELCHESTER. Salisbury.

MELLSTOCK. Stinsford and Lower and Higher Bockhampton. (Hardy was born in Higher Bockhampton.)

QUARTERSHOT. Aldershot.

SANDBOURNE. Bournemouth.

SHASTON. Shaftesbury. (The name 'Shaston' was an old one for the town and still survives locally.)

STOKE-BAREHILLS. Basingstoke.

WINTONCESTER. Winchester.